P O W !

MO YAN

POW!

TRANSLATED BY HOWARD GOLDBLATT

LONDON NEW YORK CALCUTTA

Seagull Books, 2012

Chinese original © Mo Yan, 2012
English translation © Howard Goldblatt, 2012

ISBN-13   978 0 8574 2 076 3

British Library Cataloguing-in-Publication Data
A catalogue record for this book is available from the British Library

Typeset in Constantia by Seagull Books, India
Printed and bound by Maple Press, USA

Wise Monk, where I come from people call children
who boast and lie a lot 'Powboys', but every word
in what I'm telling you is the unvarnished truth.

Ten years ago, a winter morning; a winter morning ten years ago—what times were those? 'How old are you?' asks Wise Monk Lan, who has roamed the four corners of the earth, his whereabouts always a mystery, but who is, for the moment, living in an abandoned little temple. His eyes are open, his voice seems to emerge from a dark hole in the earth. I shudder on that hot, humid day in the seventh lunar month. 'It was 1990, Wise Monk, and I was ten,' I reply, muttering in a changed tone of voice. We are in a Wutong Temple located between two bustling mid-size cities, built, as the story goes, with funds supplied by an ancestor of the village head, Lao Lan. Although it nestles up to a well-travelled highway, few people come here to burn incense; visitors are a rarity to this building with its musty, outdated aura. A woman in a green over-coat, her hair pinned behind one ear with a red flower, sprawls through a breach in the temple wall that appears to have been opened up for easy access. All I can see of her are a round, pasty face and the fair hand with which she props up her chin. In the bright sunlight, the rings on her fingers nearly blind me. She calls to mind the big house, with its tiled roof, that once belonged to the large landowners of the Lan clan but which was converted into an elementary school during the Republican era. In many legends and the fantasies evolving out of them, women like her were often seen entering and leaving that increasingly dilapidated house in the middle of the night, their skin-crawling screams enough to make a person's heart stop. The Wise Monk sits in the lotus position on a rotting rush mat in front of an ugly, crumbling Wutong Spirit idol, as serene as a sleeping horse. Wearing a cassock that looks like it's made of rain-soaked toilet paper, which will crumble at the slightest touch, he fingers a string of purple prayer beads. Flies have settled on the Wise Monk's earlobes, but none on his shaved head or oily face. Singing birds perch on the branches of a huge gingko tree out in the yard; there are cat yowls in the chorus too—the cries of a pair of feral cats that sleep in a hollow of the tree and snatch the birds off its limbs. A particularly self-satisfied yowl enters the temple, followed a mere second later by the pitiful screech of a bird, and then the flapping of wings as a panicky flock takes to the sky. I don't so much smell the stench of blood as imagine it; I don't so much see the feathers fly and the blood-stained limbs as conjure up the image. The male cat is pressing its claws into its prey and trying to court favour with the tailless female. That missing tail makes her look three parts cat and seven parts fat rabbit. After answering the Wise Monk's questions, I wait for him to ask more; but before I've finished, his eyes are shut and I wonder if his questions have been figments of my imagination, if I've only imagined him snapping his eyes open and emitting that penetrating gaze. Now his eyes are half shut, and the sheaves of nose hair that clear his nostrils by at least an inch twitch like crickets' tails. The sight calls to mind an image from more than ten years before, of our village head, Lao Lan, manicuring his nose hairs with comically small scissors. Lao Lan is the male descendant of the Lan clan, which has produced many prominent individuals: a Provincial Scholar during the Ming, a Hanlin Scholar during the Qing and a General during the Republic. After the Communists seized power, the clan produced a slew of landlord-counterrevolutionaries. By the time the class-struggle campaigns had ended, very few of them remained but those who did rose from the ashes, slowly, and produced Lao Lan, our village head. As a child, I often heard Lao Lan sigh: 'Each generation is worse than the one before!' And I heard Lao Meng, a villager who could read, say: 'One crab's worse than the last. The Lan clan's feng shui has lost its power.' One of the clan's cowherds, Lao Meng had been witness to the family's lavish lifestyle as a child. Pointing to Lao Lan's retreating back, he'd hiss: 'You're not the damned equal of one of your ancestors' cock hairs!' A cold cinder that has risen from the temple roof floats down, like a piece of early spring poplar fluff, to settle lightly on the Wise Monk's shaved head. Then another, its sister, does the same, settling lightly on his head and emanating a subtle, timeless aura that embodies a hidden flirtation. Scars from twelve burning incense sticks adorn his head in a bright pattern, investing it with extraordinary solemnity. Those are signs of honour for true monks, and in the hope that one day I too will possess twelve identical scars, Wise Monk, please let me continue—

My home, a big house with a tiled roof, was so cold and dank that the walls were covered by a layer of frost and my breath left a film, like fine salt, atop the blanket as I slept. They'd finished building the house in time for the first day of winter, and we moved in before the plaster on the walls was dry. After Mother got out of bed, I scrunched down under the covers to escape the cold air knifing into the room. Ever since my father ran off with his slut, Mother was determined to be a strong woman and make a living through her own hard work. Five years passed like a single day and, thanks to that hard work and her native intelligence, she'd put aside enough to build the tallest and sturdiest five-room, tiled house in the village. Any mention of my mother gave voice to the respect in which she was held by all the villagers—they called her a fine example of womanhood. And when they praised her they never forgot to criticize my father. When I was a boy of five, he ran off with a woman known in the village as Wild Mule; where they went no one knew.

'Predestined relationships exist everywhere,' the Wise Monk mutters, as if talking in his sleep, an indication that, even though his eyes are shut, he is paying attention to my story. The woman in the green dress and the red flower behind her ear is still sprawled in the breach in the wall. She fascinates me but I cannot tell if she knows that. The powerful feral cat, a pretty green bird in its mouth, glides up to the temple door like a hunter parading a trophy. It stops in the doorway and, cocking its head, tosses a glance at us, its expression like that of a curious schoolboy—

Five years passed and, while we received no reliable news, rumours about Father and Aunty Wild Mule came every now and then, like the beef cattle that arrived at our tiny station on the local freight train, that were then slowly herded into the village by the yellow-eyed beef merchants and then finally sold to the village butchers (our village was in truth a glorified slaughterhouse). Rumours swirled round the village, like grey birds wheeling in the sky. Some had it that Father had taken Aunty Wild Mule into the great forests of the northeast, where they'd built a cabin out of birch logs, complete with a big oven in which they burnt crackling pine kindling. Snow covered the roof, hot chilli peppers were strung on the walls and sparkling icicles hung from the eaves. They hunted game and gathered ginseng by day and cooked venison at night. In my imagination, the faces of Father and Aunty Wild Mule reflected the burning fire, as if coated with a red glaze. Others claimed that Father and Wild Mule, wrapped in bulky Mongolian robes, roamed the remote stretches of Inner Mongolia. During the day, they rode their horses, sang shepherds' songs and tended herds of cattle and sheep on the vast grass-land; at night, they slipped into their yurt and made a fire with cow chips over which they hung a steel pot. The fatty stewing lamb entered their nos-trils on the wings of its fragrance, and they washed the meat down with thick milky tea. In my imagination, Aunty Wild Mule's eyes sparkled, like black onyx, in the light of the cow-chip fire. Yet another rumour alleged that they'd secretly crossed the border into North Korea and opened a little restaurant in a little border town. During the day they made meat-filled dumplings and rolled noodles to feed the Koreans; at night, after the restaurant closed, they cooked a pot of dog meat and opened a bowl of strong white liquor. Each of them held a dog's leg—two legs out of the pot, and two more inside—with its bewitching aroma, waiting to be eaten. In my imagination, they both hold a fatty dog's leg in one hand and a glass of strong liquor in the other, and alternate between drinking and eating, their cheeks bulging like oily little balls . . . of course, I also think about what happens after the eating and drinking, how they wrap their arms round each other and do you know what—*The Wise Monk's eyes flash and his mouth twitches just before he laughs out loud. He stops abruptly, the lingering echo sounding like the tinny reverberation from a struck gong. I'm momentarily dazed, unable to deter-mine if that bizarre laugh means I should continue speaking honestly or stop. Honesty is always best, I figure, and speaking honestly in front of the Wise Monk seems appropriate. The woman in green is still sprawled in the same place. Nothing has changed—well, hardly anything. She's playing a little game with her spittle, easing bubbles out between her lips until they burst in the sunlight. I try to imagine what those little bubbles taste like—'Go on'—*

They kissed each other's greasy lips, interrupted by frequent belches that saturated the air in the yurt, saturated the air of the little log cabin, saturated the air of the little Korean restaurant, with the smell of meat. Then they undressed each other. I knew what Father's body looked like—he'd often taken me down to the river in the summer to bathe—but I'd only once caught a fleeting glimpse of Aunty Wild Mule's body. But that one time was more than enough. She had a sleek body with an oily green cast that gleamed, almost fluorescent, in the light. My boyish fingers itched to reach out and touch her, and if I had, and if she didn't hit me because of it, I'd have really felt around. How would she have felt? Icy cold or fiery hot? I'd have liked to know, but I never did touch her. So I never knew. But my father did. His hands roamed over her body, her buttocks and her breasts. Father's dark hands and Aunty Wild Mule's pale buttocks and breasts. I imagined his hands as wild and savage, like those of a marauder, squeezing her buttocks and breasts dry. She'd moan, her eyes and her mouth expelling light; Father's too. Wrapped in each other's arms, they'd writhe and roll atop a bearskin coverlet, they'd tumble about on the heated *kang*, they'd 'do it' on the wooden floor. Four hands groping and roaming, four lips pressing and crushing, four legs slithering and entwining, every inch of skin rubbed nearly raw . . . creating heat and setting off sparks, until both bodies gave off a luminescent blue glint, like a pair of enormous, scaly, glittery, deadly serpents coiled in an embrace. Father would close his eyes, the only sound his heavy breathing, but screams would tear from the mouth of Aunty Wild Mule. Now I know why she screamed, but at the time I was innocent where relations between the sexes were concerned and didn't understand the drama playing out between Father and his woman. Her screams banged against my eardrums: 'Oh, my dear . . . I'm dying . . . you're killing me . . .' My head pounded as I waited to see what would happen next. I wasn't scared but I was terribly nervous, afraid that my father and Aunty Wild Mule, and I, the sneaky observer, were involved in something sinful and awful. I watched as Father lowered his head and laid his mouth over hers so he could swallow most of her screams, except for a few fragments that slipped out through the sides of his mouth—*I sneak a look at the Wise Monk to see the effect, if any, of my slightly erotic description. I detect only a slight redness in his impassive face, but perhaps that's always been there. I think I'd be well advised to exercise restraint. Since I've seen through the vanity of life and chosen an ascetic future, relating the episodes from the lives of my parents makes me feel as if I'm talking about the ancients—*

I don't know if it was the smell of meat or Aunty Wild Mule's screams that drew, out of the darkness, hordes of small children—they crowded round the yurt or sprawled up against the doorway of the forest cabin, their little bottoms sticking up in the air as they peeped through the cracks in the logs. Then, in my mind, wolves—a whole pack, not just one—came, drawn by the smell of meat. The children ran off, their clumsy, stumpy bodies leaving marks on the snow as they stumbled away. But the wolves remained, squatting outside the yurt, the teeth grinding in their greedy mouths. I was afraid they'd rip open the yurt or tear down the log cabin, pounce on my father and his woman and have them for dinner. But no, they merely formed a circle round the yurt and then sat on their haunches, waiting, like loyal hunting dogs—

A broad road in front of the dilapidated temple wall connects us to the bustling world beyond. Beyond the weather-beaten bricks of the wall and the breaches caused by casual wall-climbers, beyond the woman in the breach in the wall—she is combing her lush hair, having laid the red flower on the wall beside her. She cocks her head, sending hair cascading over her bosom, and runs a red comb through it, over and over. Each of those jerky movements tugs at my heart. I pity all those strands of hair, I feel sad, I feel an ache in my nose and tears in my eyes. If she'd let me comb her hair, I'm thinking, I'd be gentle, infinitely patient, and not damage a single strand, even if there were tiny insects or spiders between them, even if birds had made their nests to raise fledglings. I think I detect a look of annoyance on her face, an expression common to women who have to deal with a full head of hair. Perhaps smugness is more appropriate. The subdued aroma at the roots of her hair carves its way into my nose and makes me light-headed, as if I am drunk on strong, aged spirits—I see traffic out on the highway. The metal arm of a brick-red truck-mounted crane swings past my field of vision, like a huge oil painting on the move. Twenty-four raised mortars, a ghostly white light glinting off their tubes, their shapes remarkably similar to tortoise-like tanks, pass through my field of vision, like a comic strip. A blue trailer-truck that could be used either for passengers or for freight careens past; a shrill loudspeaker is mounted on the roof, a ring of colourful banners circles the cab, each painted with a woman's fair face that flaps in and out of view, showing off curved brows and bright red lips. A dozen or more people are standing on the trailer bed, dressed in blue T-shirts and baseball caps. They are shouting a slogan in chorus: 'People's Representative Wang Dehou, all work, no play and no show.' But they grow quiet as they pass the temple, the garish trailer now like a glittery coffin on the move. They pass through my line of vision. Off beyond the wall, on one side of the highway, on a lawn directly opposite this crumbling Wutong Temple, an enormous bulldozer chugs along. My gaze passes over the wall; I can see the vehicle's orange canopy, and, every once in a while, its metal arm and hideous scoop.

Wise Monk, I'm telling you everything, holding back nothing. Back then I was a child whose only thought was to eat as much meat as possible. Anyone who gave me a fragrant leg of fatty lamb or a delicious bowl of fatty pork, I didn't care who it was but I'd call him Daddy or go down on my knees and kowtow. Or both. Even today, after all this time, if you visit my hometown and mention my name—it's Luo Xiaotong—you'll see their eyes flash, a strange light, as if you'd mentioned Lao Lan's third uncle Lan Daguan. Why? Because anything associated with me and with meat will scroll through their heads like a comic strip. And that's because of all the tales associated with the third young master of the Lan clan, who was sent overseas after sleeping with more women than you can count, a man of wide experience—those tales will also scroll through their heads like a comic strip. They wouldn't say it but deep down they'd sigh: 'That loveable, pitiful, hateful, respectable, vile . . . but extraordinary meat boy . . . That mysterious, impenetrable Third Young Master . . . that evil son of a bitch . . .'

If I'd been born somewhere else I may not have developed such a strong craving for meat; but fated to be born in Slaughterhouse Village, where everywhere you looked there was meat on the hoof and meat on the slab, bloody hunks of meat and washed-clean chunks of meat, meat that'd been smoked and meat that hadn't, meat that'd been injected with water and meat that hadn't, meat that'd been soaked in formaldehyde and meat that hadn't, pork beef mutton dog donkey horse camel . . . The wild dogs in our village were so fat from eating spoilt meat that grease oozed from their pores, while I was as skinny as a rail because I couldn't have any. For five years I ate no meat, not because we couldn't afford it but because Mother refused to spend. Before Father ran off, there was always a thick layer of grease along the edge of our wok and bones piled up in the corners. Father loved meat, especially pig's head. Every few days he'd bring home a white-cheeked, fatty pig's head with red-tipped ears. He and Mother always argued over it, and eventually the fights turned physical. She was a middle peasant's daughter, brought up to be a hard-working, frugal housewife, to never live beyond her means and to use her money to build a house and own land. After the land-reform period, my obstinate maternal grandfather dug up the family's life savings and bought five acres of land from Sun Gui, a rehabilitated farm labourer. That waste of money unleashed decades of humiliation upon Mother's family. His attempt to swim against the tide of history made my idiot grandfather a village laughing-stock. My father, on the other hand, was born into a lumpen-proletariat family. He spent his youth with my good-for-nothing grandfather and grew up into a lazy glutton. His philosophy of life was: eat well today and don't worry about tomorrow. Take it easy and enjoy life. The lessons of history coupled with my grandfather's teachings made him the kind of man who would never spend only ninety-nine cents if he had a dollar in his pocket. Unspent money always cost him a night's sleep. He often counselled my mother that life was an illusion, everything but the food you put in your belly. 'If you spend your money on clothes,' he'd say, 'people can rip them off your back. If you use it to build a house, decades later you're the target of a struggle.' The Lan clan had plenty of houses but now they're a school. The Lan Clan Shrine was a splendid building that had been taken over by the production team to turn sweet potatoes into noodles. 'Buy gold and silver with your money and you could lose your life. But spend your money on meat and you'll always have a full belly. You can't go wrong.' 'People who live to eat don't enter Heaven' Mother would reply. 'If there's food in your belly,' Father'd say with a laugh, 'even a pigsty is Heaven. If there's no meat in Heaven, I'm not going there even if the Jade Emperor comes down to escort me.' I was too young to care about their words. I'd eat meat while they argued, then sit in the corner and purr, like that tailless cat that lived such a luxurious life out in the yard. After Father left, in order to build our five-room house, Mother turned into a skinflint; food seldom touched her lips. Once the house was built, I'd hoped she'd change her views on eating and let meat return to our table after its long absence. Imagine my shock when her scrimping grew worse. A grand plan was taking shape in her mind—to buy a truck, like the one that belonged to the Lan clan, the richest in the village. A Liberation truck, manufactured at Changchun No. 1 Automobile Plant, green, with six large tyres, a square cab and a bed as solid as a tank. I'd have preferred living in our old, three-room country shack with the thatched roof if that would have put meat back on the table. I'd have preferred travelling down bumpy rural roads on a walking tractor that nearly shook my bones apart if that would have put meat back on the table. To hell with her big house and its tiled roof, to hell with her Liberation truck and to hell with that frugal life which forbade even the smallest spot of grease! The more I grew to resent Mother, the more I longed for the happy days when Father was home. For a boy with a greedy mouth—like me—a happy life was defined by an unending supply of meat. If I had meat, what difference did it make if Mother and Father fought, verbally or physically, day in and day out? No fewer than two hundred rumours concerning Father and Aunty Wild Mule reached my ears over a five-year period. But what instilled a recurring longing in me were those three I mentioned, since meat figured in all of them. And every time the image of them eating meat blossomed in my head, as real as if they were right there with me, my nostrils would flare with its aroma, my stomach would growl, my mouth would fill with drool. And my eyes would fill with tears. The villagers often saw me sitting alone and weeping beneath the stately willow tree at the head of the village. 'The poor boy! they'd sigh. I knew they'd misread the reason for my tears but was I incapable of setting them straight. Even if I'd told them it was the craving for meat that caused the tears, they wouldn't have believed me. The idea that a boy could yearn for the taste of meat until his tears flowed would never have occurred to them—

Thunder rolls in the distance, like cavalry bearing down on us. Some feathers fly into the dark temple, carrying the stink of blood, like frightened children, bobbing in the air and then sticking to the Wutong Spirit. The feathers remind me of the recent slaughter in the tree outside, and announce that the wind is up. It is, and it carries with it the stench of muddy soil and vegetation. The stuffy temple cools down, and more cinders fall out of the air over our heads, gathering on the Wise Monk's shiny pate and on his fly-covered ears. The flies remain unmoved. Studying them closely for a few seconds, I see them rub their shiny eyes with their spindly legs. In spite of their bad name, they're a talented species. I don't think any other creature can rub its eyes with its legs and be so graceful about it. Out in the yard, the immobile gingko tree whistles in the wind which has grown stronger. As have the smells it carries, which now include the fetid stench of decaying animals and the filth at the bottom of a nearby pond. Rain can't be far off. It's the seventh day of the seventh lunar month, the day when the legendary herd-boy and the weaving maid—Altair and Vega—separated for the rest of the year by the Milky Way, get to meet. A loving couple, in the prime of their youth, forced to gaze at each other across a starry river, permitted to meet only once a year for three days—how tortured they must be! The passion of newlyweds cannot compare to that of the long separated, who want only to embrace for three days—as a boy, I often heard the village women say things like that. Lots of tears are shed over those three days, which are fated to be full of rain. Even after three years of drought, the seventh day of the seventh lunar month cannot be forgotten! A streak of lightning illuminates every detail of the temple interior. The lecherous grin on the face of the Horse Spirit, one of the five Wutong Spirit idols, makes my heart shudder. A man's head on a horse's body, a bit like the label of that famous French liquor. A row of sleeping bats hangs upside down from the beam above its head as the dull rumble of thunder rolls towards us from far away, like millstones turning in unison. Then more streaks of lightning, and deafening thunderclaps. A scorched smell pounds into the temple from the yard. Startled, I nearly jump out of my skin. But the Wise Monk sits there, placid as ever. The thunder grows louder, more violent, an unbroken string of crashes, and a downpour begins, the raindrops slanting in on us. What look like oily green fireballs roll about in the yard. Something like a gigantic claw with razor-sharp tips reaches down from the heavens and waits, suspended above the doorway, eager to force its way inside and grab hold of me—me, naturally—and then hang my corpse from the big tree outside, the tadpole characters etched on my back announcing my crimes to all who can read the cryptic words. As if by instinct, I move behind the Wise Monk, who shields me, and I am reminded of the beautiful woman who lay sprawled in the breach in the wall, combing her hair. Now there is no trace of her. The breach has turned into a cascade, and I think I see strands of hair in the cascading water, infusing a subtle osmanthus fragrance into the torrent . . . Then I hear the Wise Monk say: 'Go on—'

My teeth were chattering. So cold! I buried my head under the covers and curled into a ball. Heat from the dead fire under the *kang* had long since disappeared, and the bedding was too thin to protect me from the icy concrete floor. Not daring to move, I wished I could turn into a cocooned bug. Through the bedding I heard the muffled sounds of Mother lighting the fire in the next room, the cracks of splitting firewood (that's how she vented her ire towards Father and Aunty Wild Mule). Why didn't she hurry and get the fire roaring?—that was the only way to drive the damp chill out of the room. At the same time I didn't want her to hurry because as soon as she had the fire going she'd try and get me out of bed. Her first shout would be relatively gentle; her second louder and higher and more annoyed. The third would be a bestial roar. A fourth had never been necessary, for if I hadn't rocketed out from under the covers on the third shout, she'd flick the covers off and whack my bottom with her broom. When it got that far, I knew I was doomed. For if, after the first painful whack, I jumped out of bed and onto the windowsill or scuttled out of range on the far side of the *kang*, she'd jump up without even taking off her muddy shoes, grab me by the hair or the scruff of my neck, press me down against the *kang* and really pound me with that broom. If I didn't try to get away or to resist, which she always took as a sign of contempt, her anger would boil over and she'd beat me even harder. However things progressed, if I was not on my feet by the third shout, my bottom and the poor broom were both bound to suffer. The beatings were accompanied by heavy breathing and guttural sounds—the growls of a wild animal, filled with emotion but devoid of identifiable words. But after the broom had hit me thirty times or so, the strength in her arms began to flag and the edge in her voice grew dull. The shouting would grow softer and softer and then the curses would begin—'little mongrel', 'bastard turtle', 'rabbit runt'—followed by a verbal assault on my father. Actually, she didn't have to waste time on him, since she more or less repeated what she'd said to me, with few inventions. It was never a particularly spirited effort and even I could tell it lacked punch. When you went into the city from our village, you had to pass the little train station. When Mother finished cursing me, she made a quick pass through Father on her way to Aunty Wild Mule, her true destination. Spitting on Father's reputation, she'd move down the narrow tracks to Aunty Wild Mule. Her voice would grow louder once again, and the tears that had come to her eyes while she was cursing Father and me would be seared dry by fury. I would have invited anyone who did not subscribe to the saying 'When enemies come face to face, their eyes blaze with loathing' to look at my mother's eyes while she cursed Aunty Wild Mule. With my father, it was always the same few epithets, over and over, but when it was Aunty Wild Mule's turn the richness of the Chinese language was plumbed as never before. 'My man is a stud horse reduced to fucking a jackass!' 'My man is an elephant humping the life out of a little bitch!' And so on. Mother's classic curses were of her own creation but, even with their many variations, they never strayed far from the central theme. My father, truth be known, had become Mother's principal weapon in exacting revenge. Only by imagining him as a large, powerful beast, and only by depicting Aunty Wild Mule as a little frail animal victimized by his power, was she able to release the loathing that filled her heart. As she described the humiliating effect of Father's genitals on Aunty Wild Mule, the tempo of the broom-beating slowed and the force of each whack lessened until she forgot all about me. At that point, I silently got up, dressed and stood off to one side to listen, fascinated, as she continued to curse brilliantly, and a rash of concerns flooded my mind. First, I was disappointed by the curses hurled at me. If I was a 'mongrel', then which illicit canine affair produced me? If I was a 'bastard turtle', then where did I come from? And if I was a 'rabbit runt', who was the mamma bunny? She thought she was cursing me but she was cursing herself. When she thought she was cursing my father, she was also cursing herself. Even the curses she poured on Aunty Wild Mule, when you think about it, were pointless. My father couldn't turn into an elephant or a stud horse in a million years and, even if he did, how was he supposed to mate with a bitch? A domesticated stud horse might mate with a wild mule, but that would only happen if the mule was willing. Of course I'd have never revealed any of this to Mother—I can't imagine what that would have led to. Nothing to my advantage, that's for sure, and I wasn't stupid enough to go looking for trouble. After she'd tired herself cursing, Mother would cry, buckets of tears. Then, after she'd cried herself out, she'd dry her eyes with her sleeve and walk out into the yard, dragging me along, to begin earning the day's wages. As if to make up for the time wasted beating, cursing and crying, she'd double her speed of activity. At the same time, she'd keep closer watch on me than usual. All this illustrates why a *kang* that was never warm enough held little attraction for me, and all it took to wake me up was the crackling sounds of the stove, whether or not Mother shouted at me. I'd clamber into clothes that were as cold as a suit of armour, roll up the bedding, scurry off to the toilet to pee and then stand in the doorway, hands at my sides, waiting for Mother to tell me what to do. As I've said, she was more than frugal, she was downright mean and not given to casually lighting a fire. But the cold, dank rooms once made us both as sick as dogs: our knees swelled up bright red, our legs grew numb and we had to spend quite a bit on medicines before either of us was back on our feet again. The doctor warned us: If we planned to go on living, we had to warm up the house to burn the chill off the walls. 'Coal is cheaper than medicine,' he said. Mother had no choice but to set up a stove. So she went to the train station and bought a tonne of coal to heat our new house. How I wished the doctor had said: 'Unless you're in a hurry to die, you have to start eating meat.' But he never did; in fact, the quack told us not to eat greasy food, to follow a bland, and if possible vegetarian, diet. It would not only keep us healthy but also help us live longer. Arsehole! He should have known that after Father ran off we were reduced to eating plain food every day, as plain as a funeral procession, as plain as snow on a mountain peak. Five long years and I'll bet the strongest soap in the world couldn't scrape a drop of grease off my intestines.

I've talked so much my mouth is parched. Fortunately, three little hail-stones, no bigger than apricot pits, slant into the temple and land at my feet. If it isn't the Wise Monk, whose powers allow him to see into my heart, who has magically commanded those three hailstones to land at my feet, then it must be a happy coincidence. I sneak a look at him as he sits as straight as a rod, his eyes closed, totally relaxed; but the black hairs poking out amid the gathered flies on his ears quiver and I know he's listening. I was a precocious child of wide experience, who saw many bizarre events and many strange people, but the only person I've ever seen whose ears can boast a clump of black hairs is the Wise Monk. That ear hair alone is enough to inspire reverence for the man; but then there are his extraordinary talents and uncanny tricks. I pick up one of the hailstones and put it in my mouth. As I move it round to keep it from freezing my mucous membranes, it rattles against my teeth. A fox, whose rain-soaked coat gives it a gaunt, scruffy appearance, pauses in the doorway, a sad, pitiful look in its slitted eyes, but before I can react it scurries into the temple and disappears behind the clay idol. It doesn't take long for the rank smell of wet fur to fill the air. I don't find the smell unpleasant, because I've encountered a fox before. I'll talk about that later. Back home, for a while, there was a craze over raising foxes. By then the foxes had lost their legendary mystique, though they still seemed furtive and mysterious; even in cages they were capable of stealth and magical powers. Until, that is, the village butchers began slaughtering them like pigs, like dogs, to be skinned and eaten. Once the foxes could no longer display their reputed supernatural qualities, the legends about them died. Outside, the peals of thunder have turned to crackles, sounds of fury, and wave after wave of scorched air tumbles into the temple, making me tremble with fear and jogging my memory about the legend of the Thunder God smiting sinful beasts and humans. Could this fox have been one of those sinning beasts? If so, then taking refuge here in the temple is like hiding in a strongbox, for the Thunder God will not flatten the temple, no matter how angry he becomes or how violently the Heavenly Dragon writhes, isn't that right? The Wutong Spirit is, in fact, five transcendent beasts. God has permitted them to become divine spirits and has erected a temple to house their iconic representations. They can thus enjoy the worshipful attendance of humans as well as their supply of wonderful food and beautiful women. Why then can't that fox become one of them? Look, another fox has slunk into the temple. I couldn't tell if the first one was male or female but this one is obviously a female, a pregnant one at that. How do I know? Because her sagging belly and swollen teats brush against the wet doorjamb as she slips in. That and her movements, which are less agile than those of her predecessor. Could the first one be her mate? If so, they're safe now, for nothing is fairer than natural law, and heavenly justice will never bring harm to a fox foetus. Little by little the hailstone in my mouth melts, until it's gone, *just as the Wise Monk opens his eyes a crack and looks at me. He seems not to have noticed the foxes, nor is he aware of the sounds of wind, thunder and rain out in the yard, which reminds me of the great divide between us. All right, I'll keep talking—*

The north wind was howling that morning, drawing loud complaints from the fire in the stove. The sheet metal lining the bottom of the flue turned bright red and grey metal filings flew off in bursts. The frost covering the walls was transformed into crystalline beads of water not quite ready to slither to the floor. The chilblains on my hands and feet itched and pus oozed from my ears. The melting of humans is a painful process. Mother, who had prepared corn congee in an undersized metal wok, about half full, selected a turnip from the pickling jar outside the kitchen window, broke it in two and handed me the larger piece. That would be our breakfast. I knew she'd saved at least three thousand RMB in the bank, apart from the two thousand she'd lent Shen Gang, a barbecued-meat vendor, at 20 per cent interest a month (a textbook case of usury, with compound interest). How could I be happy eating that kind of breakfast, given the amount of money we had? But I was a ten-year-old boy whose opinion didn't count. Oh, I complained sometimes, but those complaints were invariably met with looks of distress followed by a tongue-lashing over my youthful ignorance. Mother would tell me she was being frugal for my benefit, so that one day I could buy a house and a car, which in turn would make it easier for her to find me a wife.

'Son,' she'd say, 'that heartless father of yours abandoned us, and I have to show him what I'm made of. I want people in the village to see that we get along better without him.'

She also told me that her father, my grandfather, often told her that a person's mouth is only a conduit, and that after fish and meat or grains and vegetables pass through this conduit there's no longer any difference among them. You can indulge a mule or a horse, but you can't indulge yourself. If you want to live well, you must struggle against your mouth. I saw the logic in what she was saying, that if we'd concentrated on eating well over the five years Father had been gone, then we'd have had no tiled roof over our heads, and what good would a bellyful of fatty food do us if we had to live in a thatched hut? Her and Father's philosophies were poles apart. He'd have said: 'Who wants to live in a mansion if you have to subsist on vegetables and chaff?' I raised both hands in support of Father's view and stomped both feet in rejection of Mother's. I wished he'd come back and take me away with him, even if he sent me right back after a meal of nice, fatty meat. But all he cared about was eating well and enjoying life with Aunty Wild Mule. He'd forgotten I even existed.

We finished our congee, licking the bowls so clean that they didn't need to be washed. Then Mother took me into the yard, where we piled goods onto the bed of the rickety old walking tractor, a Lan clan castaway whose handles still carried the marks of Lao Lan's big hands. The tires were bald, the diesel engine's cylinder and piston were badly worn and the valve stuck, making the engine sound like an old man with a heart condition *and* asthma. When it finally turned over, it belched black smoke. It had both an air and a fuel leak and thus produced a bizarre sound somewhere between a cough and a sneeze. Lao Lan had always been a generous man, and that generosity increased drastically after he made his fortune selling water-injected meat. It was he who invented the scientific method of forcing pressurized water into the pulmonary arteries of slaughtered animals. With this method, you could empty a bucketful of water into a two-hundred-*jin* pig, while with the old method you could barely empty half a bucket of water into the carcass of a dead cow. In the years since, how much of the purchase price for meat the clever townspeople had spent on water from our village will never be known, but I'm sure it would be a shockingly high figure. Lao Lan had a potbelly and rosy cheeks and his voice rang out like a pealing bell. In a word, he was born to be a rich official. That ran in the family. After he became village head, he selflessly taught his water-injection method to the villagers and thus served as the leader of a local riches-through-ruse movement. Some villagers spoke out angrily and some others put up posters accusing him of being a member of the retaliatory landlord class intent on overthrowing the village dictatorship of the proletariat. But talk like that was out of fashion. Lao Lan's response to all of this, announced over the village PA system, was: 'Dragons beget dragons, phoenixes beget phoenixes and a mouse is born only to dig holes.'

Some time later we came to realize that he was like a kung fu master who would never pass on all his skills to his apprentices, someone who would always hold back enough for a safety net. Lao Lan's meat was water-injected, like everyone else's, but it looked fresher and smelt sweeter. You could leave it out in the sun for two days and it wouldn't spoil, while the others' would be maggot-infested if it didn't sell by the first day. So Lao Lan never had to worry about cutting prices if his supply didn't sell right away; meat that looked that good was never in danger of going unsold. My father told me it wasn't water that Lao Lan injected into his meat but formaldehyde. Later, after relations between Lao Lan and our family took a turn for the better, Lao Lan told us that it wasn't enough for the meat to be injected with formaldehyde; in order to keep its freshness and colour, it also needed to be smoked with sulphur for three hours.

A woman who's covered her head with a red coat storms into the temple, interrupting my recitation. Her entrance reminds me of the woman who had been sprawled in the breach in the wall not long before. Where has she gone? Perhaps this woman in red is the incarnation of that one in green. She removes the coat and nods apologetically. Her lips are purple, her skin pasty, her face covered with grey lumps, like a plucked chicken. The light in her eyes is like the cold rain outside. She must have been partly frozen, and completely terrified. She doesn't know how to say what she wants, but it's obvious that her mind is clear. Her coat is made of a cheap fabric from which red water drips to the floor—blood, if I ever saw it. A woman, blood, lightning, thunder, the full range of taboos all at one time. She really needs to be driven out of the temple, but the Wise Monk sits in repose, his eyes shut, steadier even than the human-headed Horse Spirit behind him. As for me, I don't have the heart to force a young full-figured woman out into the storm. Besides, with the temple doors thrown open, anyone is free to enter, so by what authority can I drive her out? With her back to us, she holds her hands out through the door and turns her head away from the rain as she wrings out the coat, sending rivulets of red running across the ground to merge with the rain; the colour remains for a brief moment before flowing out of sight. It hasn't rained like this for a very long time. Water cascades off the eaves, a grey waterfall that imitates the roar of galloping horses. Our little temple shudders in the rain, the bats shriek in fear. Then water seeps in through the roof and bounces, with metallic pings, off the Wise Monk's brass washbasin. After wringing as much water out of her coat as she can, the woman turns and nods once again in a show of embarrassment. Her lips twitch briefly, emitting a thin mosquito-like whine. Those swollen lips look like overripe grapes, a more attractive colour than you see in town on that other type of woman standing beneath a street lamp, moving her legs seductively and puffing away on a cigarette. I notice how her white undergarments stick wetly to her skin, highlighting the curves of her body. Her taut breasts are shaped like frozen pears; they must be icy cold. If I could, I'm thinking, and I truly wish I could, I'd remove her wet clothes, have her lie in a tub of hot water to soak up its warmth and bathe from head to toe. Then she'd wrap a large, dry robe round her, sit on a soft, springy sofa, and I'd make her a cup of hot tea—black tea would be best—with milk, and give her some steamed bread. Finally, after the tea and the bread, she'd get into bed and sleep . . . I hear the Wise Monk heave a sigh, bringing an end to my fantasies, although I can't stop staring at her body. She's looking away now, leaning her left shoulder against the door as she gazes at the falling rain. Her coat, which she holds in her right hand, looks like a newly peeled foxskin. I'll continue, Wise Monk. My voice sounds unnatural because my audience has doubled—

My father and Lao Lan once had a savage fight, during which Lao Lan broke one of my father's little fingers and my father bit off a piece of Lao Lan's ear. Intense hostility broke out between our families, until Father ran off with Aunty Wild Mule; after that a friendship developed between Mother and Lao Lan, and he sold us his old walking tractor for what it would have brought as scrap. He even gave her free, hands-on lessons on how to drive it. Naturally, this was grist for the village gossip mill, which spread unsavoury rumours about Lao Lan and Mother, rumours that I, as the son, referred to as a passing wind, for the benefit of my Father, wherever he was. They were envious of my mother's ability to drive a tractor, and the mouth of an envious woman is little more than a stinking bunghole; words that emerge from it are nothing but a smelly passing wind. Money lined the pockets of Lao Lan, our village head and an impressive specimen of a man who grandly drove a truck into the city to sell his meat, someone who had seen every kind of woman there was. How could someone like that be attracted to my mother, whose hair was seldom combed, whose face was dirty more often than clean and who dressed in little better than rags? I remember him teaching my mother to manoeuvre the tractor on the village threshing ground one winter morning soon after a red sun had emerged over the horizon. A patina of frost covered the nearby haystacks as a red rooster perched on the wall, stretched out its neck and crowed loudly, momentarily drowning out the squeals of pigs waiting to be slaughtered. Puffs of milky white smoke rose from village chimneys; a train pulled out of the station and headed off into the sun. Mother was wearing one of Father's old khaki jackets—it was much too big for her—with a red electric cord round her waist as a belt. She sat on the tractor seat and gripped the handlebars. Lao Lan sat behind her on the edge of the cab, legs spread, hands on top of hers—a true hands-on lesson. Seen from front or back, he clearly had his arms round her. Though she was dressed like a train-station porter, devoid of any trace of femininity, she was still a woman, and that was enough for some of the village women's tongues to wag and for some of the village men's pulses to quicken. Lao Lan was rich, powerful and famously lecherous. Just about every remotely attractive female in the village had flirted with him at one time or another, and he didn't care what people said about him. But Mother was a woman whose husband had left her, and talk about widows is always particularly nasty, so she had to be careful not to give the village gossips anything to talk about. Despite that, she let him teach her his way; it was a sort of 'blinded by greed' decision. The tractor's diesel engine roared into life as wisps of steam rose from the radiator and the smokestack belched clouds of black smoke, all combining to give the lie to husky exhaustion and potent vigour. The machine carried them recklessly in circles, like a tethered ox being whipped to keep moving. Mother's pale cheeks began to flush and her ears turned as red as a rooster's cockscomb. It was bitterly cold that morning, a dry, windless cold that nearly froze the blood in my veins and nipped painfully, like a cat, at my skin. And yet sweat dotted Mother's face and steam rose from her hair. It was her first time with a machine, her maiden attempt to steer a vehicle of any kind, even one as simple as a walking tractor. She was in obvious high spirits, unbelievably excited. What other explanation could there be for breaking out into a sweat on one of the coldest days of the year? The light in her eyes stunned me by its beauty, the first time I'd seen anything like it since Father had run off. After a dozen revolutions on the threshing floor, Lao Lan jumped off with an agility that belied his obesity. As Mother tensed and looked round to see where he was, the tractor lurched towards a ditch. 'Turn the handlebars!' Lao Lan screamed. 'Turn the handlebars!' Mother clenched her teeth, tightened the muscles in her cheeks and managed to steer the tractor away only seconds before ploughing into the ditch. Lao Lan had been turning in place, following her progress, never taking his eyes off her, as if a rope were tied round her waist and the other end clenched in his hand, and shouting instructions: 'Look straight, not at the wheels, they won't fall off. Don't look at your hands. They're too coarse, not worth looking at. That's it, ride it like a bicycle. I told you that you could strap a sow into that seat and it could drive it in circles. But you're no sow, you're a grown woman! Give it some gas, what are you afraid of? All dick-head machines are alike. You don't want to spoil it, just treat it like a pile of junk. The more you baby it, the more trouble it'll cause. That's it, now you've got it, you've stopped being an apprentice. You can drive it home. Mechanization is the future of agriculture. Know who said that? Do you, you little bastard?' Lao Lan asked, looking at me. I didn't feel like answering—it was too cold and my lips were nearly frozen stiff. 'Okay, drive it away. Since you're a widow and you have a little boy, you don't have to pay me for three months.' Mother jumped off the tractor, her legs so rubbery she could hardly stand. But Lao Lan reached out to support her. 'Be careful,' he said. Mother blushed and looked like she wanted to say something but all she could manage was a brief stammer. The joy she felt had nearly robbed her of speech. A few weeks earlier we'd told Master Gao, the local clerk, that we wanted to buy Lao Lan's old tractor but hadn't heard back from him. I was only a child, yet even I knew we had no chance. My father had bitten a chunk off the man's ear and ruined his looks—there was no way he was going to sell us anything. If it'd been me, I'd have said: 'So, Luo Tong's family wants to buy my tractor, do they? Ha! I'll drive it into the bay and let it turn to rust before I'll sell it to them.' But then, just when we'd lost hope, we heard from Master Gao: 'The village head is willing to sell it to you at scrap cost. He said you can pick it up tomorrow morning at the threshing ground. He said that he is, after all, the head of the village and that it's his job to see the villagers prosper. He said he'll even teach you to drive it.' Mother and I were so excited we couldn't sleep that night. She kept saying what a good man Lao Lan was and what a bad man she'd married. And then she rounded it off with a stream of abuse for Aunty Wild Mule. That was when I learnt that Aunty Wild Mule had been the cause of the fight between Lao Lan and Father. I'll never forget that morning. That time it was early summer.

This woman's eyes are really big. There's a tadpole-shaped mole at the corner of her mouth, from which one dark red hair curls out. I'm captivated by the strange look in her eyes, a look of madness. She still has the coat in her hand, holding it up and shaking it out every now and then, making popping sounds. Rain slants in through the door and water continues to drip from her body, forming a muddy pool at her feet. Which, I suddenly realize, are bare. A pair of very large feet, probably a size forty, looking out of place on her body. Leaves have stuck to the tops of her feet, and her water-soaked toes have turned white. As I talk on, I think about her background. In such weather, on a day like this, why would a woman with high arching breasts show up in a little temple in the middle of nowhere? Especially one that enshrines five spirits with superhuman sexual prowess, one that generations of intellectuals have called an 'obscenity'? Though I have many doubts, my mind begins to fill with warm images. I'm dying to walk up and throw my arms round her, but I don't dare, given the presence of the Wise Monk, especially since I've come with the hope of signing on as a novice and am spewing out my life story for his benefit. The woman seems to understand what I'm feeling, for she keeps looking at me, and her lips, which were clamped shut when she entered, are parted enough for me to see her glinting teeth. They're slightly yellow and not particularly straight, but they seem to be hard and healthy. She has bushy brows that nearly meet above her eyes, which gives her a lively appearance, sort of foreign. I can't tell if the way she tugs at her pants, which tend to stick to her buttocks, is intentional, but every time she lets go they cling to her skin again. I'm sympathetic but have no idea how to help. If I were in charge of this little temple, I'd forget about religious taboos and commandments and ask her into the back room, where she could get out of those wet clothes. Let her put on one of the Wise Monk's cassocks and lay her clothes out at the head of his bed to dry. But would he approve? Without warning, she scrunches up her nose and lets fly a loud sneeze. 'My lady, you do as you please,' the Wise Monk says, his eyes still shut. She bows and flashes a smile in my direction, then walks past me, clothes in hand, over behind the Horse Spirit.

Early summer mornings found the people exhausted, since the nights were so short. They'd barely closed their eyes, it seemed, and the sun was up. Father and I ran out into the dust-blown street but could not escape Mother's shouts from the yard. We were still living in the three-room shack inherited from Grandfather, passing the days in chaotic exuberance. Our shack looked particularly shabby, tucked in among a bunch of newly built red-tiled houses, like a beggar kneeling in front of a clutch of landlords and rich merchants, in silks and satins, asking for alms. The wall round our yard came up barely to an adult's waist and was topped by weeds. It couldn't keep out a pregnant bitch, let alone a thief. In fact, the pregnant bitch from the home of Guo Six often jumped into our yard to feast on our discarded bones. I used to watch, fascinated, as she scaled the wall, her black teats scraping the top and then swaying as she landed. Father carried me on his shoulders so I could look down on Mother as she scraped and sliced and chopped with her cleaver, cursing us as we walked by. She had to scavenge sweet potato scraps from the garbage heap in front of the train station. Thanks to my lazy, gluttonous Father, we lived a life of extremes, with potfuls of meat on the stove during the good times and empty pots during the bad. In response to Mother's curses, he'd say: 'Any day now, very soon, the second land-reform campaign will begin, and you'll thank me when it does. Don't for a minute envy Lao Lan, since he'll wind up like that landlord father of his, dragged off to the bridgehead by a mob of poor peasants to be shot.' He'd aim an imaginary rifle at Mother's head and fire: Bang! She'd grab her head with both hands and pale with fright. But the second land-reform campaign didn't come and didn't come, and poor Mother was forced to bring home rotten sweet potatoes for the pigs, two little animals that never got enough to eat and that squealed hungrily most of the time. It was so annoying. 'What the hell are you squealing for?' Father shouted at them once, 'Keep it up and I'll toss you two little bastards in a pot and have you for dinner!' Cleaver in hand, Mother glared at him. 'Don't even think about it. Those are my pigs. I raised them, and no one's to harm a hair on them. Either the fish dies or the net breaks.' 'Take it easy,' Father said, laughing gleefully. 'I wouldn't touch those skin-and-bones animals for anything.' I took a long look at the pigs—there really wasn't much meat on either of them, although those four fleshy ears would have made for good snacking. To me, the ears were the best part of a pig's head—no fat, not much grease and tiny little bones that crunch nicely. Best eaten with cucumbers, the thorny ones with flowers, some mashed garlic and sesame oil. 'We can eat their ears!' I said. Mother glared at me. 'I'll cut off your ears and eat them first, you little bastard!' Steaming, she came at me with her cleaver and I ran fearfully into Father's arms. She grabbed hold of my ear and jerked it hard while Father tried to pull me free—by the neck—and I screamed for all I was worth, afraid my ear would be ripped off. My screams sounded like the squeals of the pigs being slaughtered in the village. Finally, Father managed to yank me free. After examining my bruised ear, he looked up and said: 'How can you be so mean? People say that even a tiger won't eat its young, so I guess that makes you worse than a tiger!' Rage turned Mother's face waxen and her lips purple; she stood at the stove, shaking from head to toe. Emboldened by my father's protection, I cursed, spitting out her full name: 'Yang Yuzhen, you stinking old lady, you're making my life a living hell!' Stunned by my outburst, she just gaped at me, while Father chuckled as he picked me up and took off at a run. We were already out in the yard by the time we heard Mother's shrill wail: 'I'm so mad I could die, you little bastard . . .' Her two pigs wagged their curly tails and began rooting in the mud at the base of the wall, like convicts trying to burrow under a prison wall to freedom. Father rapped me on the head and said softly: 'You little imp, how did you know your mother's name?' I looked into his swarthy, sombre face: 'I heard you say it!' 'When did I ever tell you her name was Yang Yuzhen?' 'You told it to Aunty Wild Mule. You said: "Yang Yuzhen, that stinking old lady, is making my life a living hell!"' Father clamped his hand over my mouth. 'Shut up, damn you,' he said under his breath. 'I've been a pretty good father so far, so don't go and ruin things for me now.' His supple hand gave off a peppery tobacco smell; it was not the sort of man's hand you usually saw in a farming village. But he'd been a lazy good-for-nothing most of his life and never done any sort of work with his hands. I snorted in dissatisfaction. Mother came out of the house, the cleaver still in her hand, and her hair standing up round her head like the magpie's nest in the village willow tree. 'Luo Tong,' she shouted, 'Luo Xiaotong, you two sons of bitches, you scruffy bastards, I wouldn't care if I died today if I could take the two of you with me. Today will see the end of this family!' The terrible look on her face was proof that this was no joke, that this time she meant it, that she was ready to kill us both. Ten men are no match for a woman on the warpath, they say. In a situation like this, meeting the charge meant certain death. The best option? Run for your life! My father may have led a dissipated life but he was no fool. The smart man avoids dangers ahead. He swept me up, tucked me under his arm, turned and ran towards the wall, not the gate, which would have been a mistake, since, though we owned nothing of value, Mother had inherited from her family the bad habit of securing the gate with a brass lock at night. Actually, if there was one thing we owned that could bring in enough to buy a pig's head, it was that lock. I'm sure that whenever my father's hunger for meat came upon him, he must have thought of selling it. But Mother loved that lock as much as she loved her own ears, since it was part of her dowry, the one gift that symbolized her parents' feelings for her. If Father had carried me over to the gate, even if he'd broken it down, the time wasted would have allowed Mother to reach us with her cleaver and open up our heads like blossoming flowers. So he carried me to the wall instead, and all but somersaulted over it, putting my enraged Mother and a whole lot of trouble behind us. I harboured no doubts about her ability to scamper over the wall, like we'd done, but she chose not to. Once she'd driven us out of the yard, she stopped chasing us. She jumped about for a while at the foot of the wall, then went back inside to finish chopping the rotting sweet potatoes and fill the air with loud curses. It was a brilliant way to let off steam: no blood-letting and no mess, no falling foul with the law, yet I knew that those rotten potatoes were substitutes for the heads of her bitter enemies. But now, as I think back, the true bitter enemy in her mind was neither Father nor me—it was Aunty Wild Mule. She was convinced that the slut had seduced my father, and I simply can't say if that was or was not a fair assessment of the situation. Where Father and Aunty Wild Mule's relationship was concerned, the only ones who knew who seduced whom, who cast the first flirtatious glance, were the two of them.

When I reach this point in my tale, an unusual warm current floods my heart. The woman who has just hidden behind the statue of the Horse Spirit looks a lot like Aunty Wild Mule. Though she seems familiar I won't let my thoughts turn in that direction, because Aunty Wild Mule died ten years ago. Or perhaps she didn't. Or perhaps she did and has been reborn. Or perhaps someone else's soul came back to use her body. Waves of confusion ripple through my mind as the scene before me seems to float in the air.

My father was much smarter than Lao Lan. He'd never studied physics but he knew all about positive and negative electricity; he'd never studied biology but he was an expert in sperm and eggs; and he'd never studied chemistry but he was well aware that formaldehyde can kill bacteria, keep meat from spoiling and stabilize proteins, which is how he guessed that Lao Lan had injected formaldehyde into his meat. If getting rich had been on his agenda he'd have had no trouble becoming the wealthiest man in the village, of that I'm sure. He was a dragon among men, but dragons have no interest in accumulating property. People have seen critters like squirrels and rats dig holes to store up food, but who's seen a tiger, the king of the animals, do something like that? They spend most of their time sleeping in their lairs, coming out only when hunger sends them hunting for prey. Most of the time my father cared only about eating, drinking and having a good time, coming out only when hunger pangs sent him looking for money. Never for a moment was he like Lao Lan and people of that ilk, who accumulated blood money, putting a knife in white and taking it out red. Nor was he interested in going down to the train station to earn porter's wages by the sweat of his brow, like some of the coarser village men. Father made his living by his wits. In ancient times, there was a famous chef named Pao Ding who was an expert at carving up cows. In modern times, there was a man who was an expert at sizing them up—my father. In Pao Ding's eyes, cows were nothing but bones and edible flesh. That's what they were in my father's eyes too. Pao Ding's vision was as sharp as a knife, my father's was as sharp as a knife *and* as accurate as a scale. What I mean to say is: if you were to lead a live cow to my father, he'd take two turns round it, three at the most, occasionally sticking his hand under the animal's foreleg—just for show—and confidently report its gross weight and the quantity of meat on its bones, always within a kilo of the digital scale used in England's largest slaughterhouse. At first, people thought he was a windbag but after testing him several times they turned into believers. In dealings between cattlemen and slaughterhouses, his presence took blind luck out of the equation and established a basis of fairness. Once his authority and status were in place, both the cattlemen and the butchers courted his favour, hoping to gain an edge. But as a man of vision, he'd never jeopardize his reputation for petty profits, since by doing so he'd smash his rice bowl. If a cattleman came to our house with wine and cigarettes, my father tossed them into the street, then climbed onto our garden wall and cursed loudly. If a butcher came with the gift of a pig's head, my father flung it into the street, then climbed onto our garden wall and cursed loudly. Both the cattlemen and the butchers said that Luo Tong was an idiot but also the fairest man they knew. Once his reputation for being upright and incorruptible was established, people trusted him implicitly. If a transaction reached a stalemate, the parties would look at him to acknowledge that they wanted things settled. 'Let's quit arguing and hear what Luo Tong has to say!' 'All right. Luo Tong, you be the judge!' With a cocky air, my father would walk round the animal twice, looking neither at the buyer nor at the seller, then glance up at the sky and announce the gross weight and amount of meat on the bone, followed by a price. He'd then walk off to smoke a cigarette. Buyer and seller would reach out and smack hands. 'It's a deal!' Once the transaction was completed, buyer and seller would come up to my father, each hand him a ten-yuan note and thank him for his labours. The old-style brokers were dark, gaunt, wretched old men, some with queues hanging down their backs. They were proficient in the art of haggling via finger-signs made from deep within their wide overlapping sleeves, thus lending the profession an air of mystery. My father's appearance took the confusion out of buying and selling cattle and brought an end to the darker aspects of the process. He effectively drove the shifty-eyed brokers off the stage of history. This remarkable advance in the buying and selling of cattle on the hoof could, with only a bit of exaggeration, be called revolutionary. Displays of my father's keen eye were not limited to cattle but worked with pigs and sheep as well. Like a master carpenter who can build a table but can also build a chair, and, if he's especially talented, a coffin, my father had no trouble sizing up even camels.

When I reach this point, I seem to hear the barely audible sound of sobbing from behind the Wutong Spirit. Can it really be Aunty Wild Mule? If it is, why hasn't her face changed in more than a decade? No, that's impossible, it can't be. But if she isn't, why can't I tear myself away from her? Perhaps she's Aunty Wild Mule's ghost. Legend has it that ghosts don't cast a shadow. Too bad I didn't think to see if she cast a shadow when she came in. But it's a rainy day, dark and gloomy, and no one casts a shadow when there's no sun. So it wouldn't have done me any good if I'd thought to look. What's she doing there behind the idol? Rubbing the rump of the human-headed Horse Spirit? A decade ago I heard someone say that there are women who will kneel before this idol and burn incense to plead for the restoration of their impotent husbands' manhood, then go round to the rear and pat the rump of the handsome, powerful, magnificent young stallion. I know there's a wall behind the statue, and a little door that opens onto a tiny windowless room that's so dark you have to light a lantern to see, even in the middle of the day. The room is furnished with a wobbly bed covered by a blue quilt made of coarse cotton. The bundle of rolled wheat straw that serves as a pillow and the quilt are greasy. Hordes of fleas lie in wait, ready to jump excitedly and noisily onto anyone who enters with exposed skin, as do the bedbugs resting on the walls: 'Meat, here comes meat!' they seem to squeak in excitement. People eat the flesh of pigs, dogs, cows and sheep; fleas and bedbugs eat the flesh of humans. This is known as the subjugation of one species by another or, simply, tit for tat. The woman, whether or not she's Aunty Wild Mule, I want to tell her: 'Come out here! Don't let those evil creatures spoil your sumptuous skin and flesh. And you surely don't want to pat the horse's rump. My heart aches for you and I wish you'd come out and pat me on the rump.' I say that, even though I'm aware that, if she is my Aunty Wild Mule, then my thoughts are sinful. But I can't control my desires. If this woman will take me away with her, I'll give up my plan to join your order, Wise Monk. I can't tell any more of my story right now. I'm confused. The Wise Monk seems to be able to read my mind, since I didn't say any of this but merely thought it. But he knows. His sardonic laugh brings an end to my lustful thoughts. All right, I'll go on—

Father carried me on his shoulder over to the threshing ground early one summer day. After our village was turned into a huge slaughterhouse, the fields, for all intents and purposes, were left fallow, since only a fool would till a field and not take up butchering, thanks to the advent of injecting water into the meat. Then, once the fields lay fallow, the threshing ground was converted into the place where cattle were bought and sold. The township officials had wanted to use the government square, so they could collect a management fee, but the people would have none of it. When they came to the cattle exchange with soldiers, to force the people to stop doing business there, they ran up against men armed with butcher knives. Fights broke out and people nearly died. Four butchers were arrested. Their wives organized a protest and went to the county seat to stage a sit-in demonstration, some with cowhides over their shoulders, some with pigskins, some with sheepskins. They raved and ranted, vowing that if their demands were not met then they'd take them to the provincial capital, and if that didn't work then they'd board a train to Beijing. The very prospect—women draped in the hides of slaughtered animals showing up on Changan Avenue in the capital—was too frightening to contemplate. No one knew what to do with them, but the county chief was sure to lose his job if the protest continued. So in the end the women won. Their husbands were freed, the township officials' dream of great wealth was shattered and the village threshing ground once again teemed with animals, everything from cattle to dogs. There was even talk that the township chief received an earful from the county chief.

Seven or eight cattle merchants were sitting on their haunches at the edge of the threshing ground, smoking cigarettes as they waited for the butchers to show up. Their cattle stood off to the side, absent-mindedly chewing their cud, oblivious to their impending doom. The merchants, most of them from West County, spoke with funny accents, like actors on the radio.

They showed up every ten days or so, each bringing two heads of cattle, maybe three. For the most part, they came on a slow, mixed freight-and-passenger train, man and beast in one car, arriving around sunset. They didn't reach our village till after midnight, even though the little station where they got off was no more than ten *li* away. A stroll that should have taken no more than a couple of hours took these merchants and their cattle a good eight. First, the cattle, made dizzy by the swaying of the train, had to be forced up to the exit, where the ticket-collectors, in blue uniforms and billed caps, checked to see that every passenger had a ticket, animals included, before being allowed to get on the road. Passing through the turnstile was the signal for the cows to leave a foul, watery mess on the ground and on the ticket-collectors' trouser legs, as if teasing or mocking them, perhaps getting even. In the spring came the chicken and duck merchants, also from West County, carrying their loads in baskets woven out of bamboo or reed strips, balanced on each end of a wide, sleek, springy shoulder pole that weighed them down as they left the station and then flew down the road, leaving the cattle merchants in their dust. They wore wide straw hats and draped blue capes over their shoulders as they sprinted along, an impressively carefree sight in contrast to the sloppy, manure-covered and dejected cattle merchants who shaved their heads, left their shirts unbuttoned and wore faddish mirrored sunglasses. Their feet splayed in a V as they headed into the red setting sun, rocking from side to side, like sailors when they step ashore, walking to our village on the dirt road. When they reached the historic Grand Canal, they led their cattle up to the water to let them drink their fill. Weather permitting—that is, if it wasn't unbearably cold—they washed their cattle, thus improving the animals' spirits as well as their appearances until they gleamed like new brides. Once the cows were clean, it was the merchants' turn and they lay on the fine sand of the riverbank and let the cold water wash over them. If young women happened to pass by, the men would howl like dogs baying at females in heat. Then, once they'd spent enough time horsing round, they'd climb up onto the bank and turn the cattle loose to feed on night grass while they sat in a circle to fill their stomachs with meat and baked flat bread, washing it all down with liquor. They'd carry on until the stars lit up the sky; then they'd retrieve the animals and stumble drunkenly down the road to our village. Why did they prefer to reach our village in the middle of the night? That was their secret. When I was young, I asked my parents and some of the village greybeards that very question. But they just gave me stony looks, as if I'd asked them the meaning of life or a question whose answer everyone knew. Leading the cattle into the village was a signal for the village dogs to set up a chorus of barks, which woke up everyone—man, woman, young and old—and informed them that the cattle merchants had arrived. In my youthful memories, they were a mysterious lot, and this sense of mystery was surely heightened by their late-night arrival in our village. I couldn't stop thinking that there had to be some profound significance to their timing but the grown-ups apparently never thought so. I recall how, on some moonlit nights, when the silence was broken by a chorus of dog barks, Mother would sit up, wrapped in the comforter, stick her face close to the window and gaze at the scene out on the street. That was before Father left us but already there were nights when he didn't come home. Without a sound, I'd sit up too and look past Mother out the window, watching the cattle merchants drive the animals ahead of them, slipping silently past our house, the newly bathed cattle glinting in the moonlight like giant pieces of glazed pottery. If not for the chorus of dog barks, I'd have thought I was observing a beautiful dreamscape. Even their barking couldn't take away all the mysery of that sight. Our village boasted several inns but the merchants never bedded down in any of them; instead, they led their cattle straight to the threshing floor and waited there till dawn, even if a wind was howling or it was raining, even if the air was bitter cold or steamy hot. There were stormy nights when innkeepers went out to drum up business, but the merchants and their cattle remained in the inhospitable elements like stone statues, unmoved, no matter how flowery the invitation. Was it because they didn't want to part with that little bit of money? No. People said that, after they sold their cattle, they went into town to get drunk and whore round, on a spending spree that stopped only when they had barely enough to buy a ticket for the slow train home. Their lifestyle could not have been more different from that of the peasants, with which we were so familiar. Their thinking too. As a youngster, on more than one occasion, I heard some of our more eminent villagers sigh: 'Hai, what kind of people are they? What in the world is going on in those heads?' That's right, what in the world could they be thinking? When they came to market they brought brown cows and black ones, males and females, fully grown cows and young calves; once they even brought a nursing heifer whose teats looked like water jugs. Father had trouble estimating a price for her since he didn't know if the udder was edible.

The cattle merchants scrambled to their feet when they saw my father. They'd be wearing mirrored sunglasses even early in the morning, an eerie sight, though they smiled as a show of respect. He'd take me down off his shoulders, get down on his haunches ten feet or so from the merchants, take out a crumpled pack from which he'd remove a crooked, damp cigarette. The cattle merchants would take out their packets, and ten or more cigarettes would land on the ground by Father's feet. He'd gather them up and lay them back down neatly. 'Lao Luo, you old fuckhead,' one of the merchants would say, 'smoke 'em. You don't think we're trying to buy your favours with a few paltry cigarettes, do you?' Father would just smile and light his cheap smoke as the village butchers started showing up, in twos and threes, looking like they were fresh from a bath, though I could smell the scent of blood on their bodies (which goes to prove that blood—whether from cows or pigs—never washes off). The cattle, smelling the blood on the butchers, would huddle together, their eyes flashing with fear. Excrement would spurt from the bung-holes of the young cows; the older ones looked composed, though I knew they were pretending—I could see the tails draw up under their rumps to keep from emptying their bowels and the tremble in their legs, like the ripples on a pond from a passing breeze. Peasants care deeply for their cows; to kill one, especially one advanced in years, has long been considered a crime against nature. A leprous woman in our village often ran over to the head of the village and wailed at the graveyard in the late-night stillness. Only one phrase, over and over: 'Who among our ancestors killed a cow and left his sons and grandsons to suffer for it?' Cows cry. Before that old milk cow that so troubled my father was slaughtered, it fell to its knees in front of the butcher and a torrent of tears spilt from its watery blue eyes. The hand holding the knife trembled as tales about cows flooded the butcher's mind. The knife slipped from his hand and clattered to the ground. Weak at the knees, he knelt in front of the cow, loud wails bursting from his lungs. That was the end of his butcher days; he became a specialist in raising dogs instead. When he was asked why he'd knelt in front of the cow and wailed, he'd answered: 'I saw my dead mother in its eyes, and I thought it was her reincarnated soul.'

This one-time butcher's name was Huang Biao; and after he began raising dogs, he tended that cow the way a son would care for his ageing mother. When the fields were lush with edible grass, we'd see him leading the old cow over to the edge of the river to graze. Huang Biao walked along, followed by the cow, no tether needed. People heard him say: 'Let's go down to the river, Mother, where there's lots of nice, fresh grass.' And people heard him say: 'Let's go home, Mother, it's getting dark. You don't see too well and I don't want you to eat anything poisonous.' Huang Biao was a man of vision. People laughed when he began raising dogs. But after only a few years there were no more laughs. He bred local dogs with German wolfhounds who produced litters that were both fearless and smart, fine animals that made wonderful watchdogs, excellent at alerting their masters to trouble. They could smell from half a mile away the officials and journalists on their way to the village, coming to investigate trafficking in illegal meat. They'd bark up a din, warning the butchers in time to clean up the area and hide the incriminating evidence. A couple of newspaper reporters once came to the village posing as meat merchants, hoping to expose the illegal meat trade for which the place had become notorious. They went so far as to smear pig and cow blood on their coats to get past the butchers' sharp eyes, but they could not fool the noses of Huang Biao's mixed-breed dogs, a dozen of which chased them from one end of the village to the other, nipping and biting at their heels until the men's IDs fell out of the crotches of their pants. The complicity of corrupt local officials was just the beginning—Huang Biao also played a major role in keeping the inspectors from finding evidence of illegal meat production in the village. He also bred food dogs, stupid animals that wagged their tails for anyone— owner or thief, it made no difference. With their simple minds and gentle dispositions, the food dogs spent most of their time eating and sleeping, which put plenty of meat on their bones. The supply of those dogs always fell short of the demand—customers lined up to buy them as soon as they were born. Blossom Hamlet, about five or six *li* from our village, was home to families of Korean descent for whom dog meat was the number-one delicacy. This meant they were skilled dog-meat chefs who opened restaurants in the county seat, in the big cities, even in the provincial capital. Blossom Hamlet dog meat gained its fame thanks mainly to the supply of animals from Huang Biao. His meat smelt like dog when it was cooked but gave off a beefy aroma.

Why? Because he weaned the pups days after they were born in order to speed up the bitches' reproductive cycle and fed them milk that came, unsurprisingly, from his old cow. When they saw how rich the sale of dogs made Huang Biao, some mean-spirited people in the village attacked him cruelly: 'Huang Biao, you think you're a dutiful son by treating an old milk cow like your mother, but you're really a shameless hypocrite. If that old cow is your mother, then you shouldn't squeeze her teats to feed a bunch of puppies. If you do, you've turned your mother into a bitch. And if she's a bitch, then you're a son of a bitch. And if you're a son of a bitch, that makes you a dog, doesn't it?' Incensed by this hounding, he showed the whites of his eyes. Instead of trying to figure out why they kept taunting him, he picked up his trusty butcher's knife and went after them and the murder in his eyes made them run for their lives. But one day Huang Biao's lovely new wife set the dogs loose, the stupid ones following the smarter mongrels, on her husband's tormentors, and in a matter of moments human shrieks and canine growls filled the village's twisting streets and byways. As she laughed gloriously, her skin as white as ivory, he stood there with a silly smile, scratching the coal-black skin of his neck. Before taking a wife, Huang Biao had been a frequent visitor to a spot beneath Wild Mule's window, where he sang to her in the middle of the night. 'Go home, little brother,' she'd say to him. 'I've got my man. But don't worry, I'll find you a wife.' And she did—a girl who worked in a roadside shop.

Negotiations began as soon as the butchers arrived. As they circled the animals, a casual observer may have thought they were having trouble deciding which ones to buy. But if one of them reached out and grabbed a halter, within three seconds the others would do the same, and, lightning quick, all the cows would be chosen. No one could recall seeing two butchers fight over the same animal, but if that had happened, the dispute would have been quickly resolved. Competitors are rivals in most occupations but the butchers in our village, thanks to the prestige and organizational skills of Lao Lan, were united in friendship, prepared to confront any and all militant opponents as a brotherhood. Once they adopted Lao Lan's water-injection method, they were bound together by their windfall profits and their illegal activity. When each of them had a halter in his hand, the peddlers approached languidly and the bargaining began. Now that my father had cemented his authority, these negotiations took on little importance, became pro forma, a mere custom, for it was left to him—he had the last word. The men would jockey back and forth for a while, then walk up to my father, cow in tow, like applicants for a marriage licence at the town office. But something special occurred on this particular day: instead of heading straight for the cows, the butchers chose instead to pace at the edge of the square, their meaningful smiles making the observers uncomfortable. And when they passed in front of my father, something unpleasant seemed to lurk behind those fake smiles, as if a conspiracy were afoot, one that could erupt at any moment. I cast a timid glance at Father—he sat there woodenly smoking one of his cheap cigarettes, just like every other day. The better cigarettes tossed his way by the peddlers lay on the ground, untouched. That was his custom: once the deals were struck, the butchers would come over, gather up the cigarettes and smoke them. And as they smoked, they would praise my father for his incorruptibility. 'Lao Luo,' one would say, half in jest, 'if all Chinese were like you, Communism would have been realized decades ago.' He'd smile but say nothing. And that would be the moment when my heart would swell with pride and I'd vow that this was how I'd do things, that this was the kind of man I wanted to be. It was obvious to the peddlers as well that something was in the air that day, and they turned to look at my father, except for a few who coolly observed the butchers as they paced. A tacit agreement had been reached: they would all wait to see what happened, like an audience patiently waiting for the play to begin.

Outside, the rain has let up a little, the thunder and lightning have moved away. In the yard, the stone path is submerged under a layer of water on which float leaves—some green, some brown. There is also a plastic blow-up toy, its legs pointing skyward. It appears to be a toy horse. Before long the rain stops altogether, and a breeze arrives from the fields, rustling the leaves of the gingko tree and sending down a fine silver spray, as if through a sieve, poking holes in the water below. The two cats stick their heads out of the hole in the tree trunk, screech briefly and pull their heads back in. I hear the pitiful mewling of kittens somewhere in that hole and I know that, while the sky was opening up, sending torrents of water earthward, the tailless female has had her litter. Animals prefer to give birth during downpours, so my father says. I see a black snake with a white pattern slithering through the water. Then there's a silvery fish that leaps into the air, twisting its flat body like a plough blade, beautiful yet powerful, graceful and smooth, making a moist, crisp noise as it re-enters the water, like the slap Butcher Zhang gave me, his hand slippery from pig grease, when he caught me sneaking a piece of meat. Where has that fish come from? It alone knows the answer. It can barely swim in the shallow water, its green dorsal fin exposed to the air. A bat emerges from the temple and flies past, followed by a swarm of bats, all from the same place. The other two hailstones that landed at my feet have melted before I could suck on them. Wise Monk, I say, it'll be dark soon. No response.

A bright red sun rose above the fields in the east, looking like a blacksmith's glowing face. The leading actor of the play finally appeared in the square: our village head, Lao Lan, a tall, husky man with well-developed muscles (that was before he got fat, before his belly bulged, before his jowls sagged). He had a bushy brown beard, the same colour as his eyes, which made you wonder if he was of pure Han stock. All eyes were on him the minute he strode into the square, his face glowing in the sun. He walked up to my father but his gaze was fixed on the fields beyond the squat earthen wall, where rays of morning sun dazzled the eye. The crops were jade green, the flowers were in bloom, their scent heavy on the air, the skylarks sang in the rosy red sky. My father, who was nothing in the eyes of Lao Lan, might as well not have been sitting by the wall at all. And if my father meant nothing to him, naturally, it was even worse for me. But perhaps he was blinded by the sun. That was the first thought that entered my juvenile mind, but I quickly grasped that Lao Lan was trying to provoke my father. As he cocked his head to speak to the butchers and the peddlers, he unzipped his uniform pants, took out his dark tool and let loose a stream of burnt-yellow piss right in front of my father and me. Its heated stench assailed my nostrils. It was a mighty stream, I'd say a good fifteen metres; he'd probably been saving up all night, going without relieving himself so he could humiliate my father. The cigarettes on the ground tumbled and rolled in his urine, swelling up until they lost their shape. A strange laugh had arisen from the clusters of butchers and peddlers when Lao Lan took out his tool, but they broke that off as abruptly as if a gigantic hand had reached out and grabbed them by the throats. They stared at us, slack-jawed and tongue-tied, their faces frozen in stunned surprise. Not even the butchers, who knew that Lao Lan wanted to pick a fight with my father, imagined that he'd do something like this. His piss splashed on our feet and on our legs, some even spraying into our faces and our mouths. I jumped up, enraged, but Father didn't move a muscle. He sat there like a stone. 'Fuck your old lady, Lao Lan!' I cursed. My father didn't make a sound. Lao Lan wore a superior smile. My father's eyes were hooded, like a farmer taking pleasure from the sight of water dripping from the eaves. When Lao Lan finished pissing, he zipped up his pants and walked over to the cattle. I heard long sighs from the butchers and peddlers, but couldn't tell if they were sorry nothing more had happened or happy that it hadn't. The butchers then walked in among the cattle and in no time made their selections. Then the peddlers walked up and the bargaining commenced. I could tell their hearts weren't in it, that something other than the best bargain was on their minds. Though they weren't looking at my father, I was sure they were thinking about him. And what was he doing? He'd brought his knees up and hidden his face behind them, like a hawk sleeping in the crotch of a tree. Since I couldn't see his face, I had no way of knowing what he looked like at that moment. But I was unhappy with what I saw as weakness. I may have only been a boy but I knew how badly Lao Lan had humiliated my father, and I also knew that any man worth his salt would not take that without a fight; I'd proved that by my curses. But Father remained silent, as if he were stone dead. That day's negotiations were brought to a close without his intervention. Yet when they were over, all the parties walked up as usual and tossed some notes at his feet. The first to do this was none other than Lao Lan himself. That mongrel bastard, apparently not content to piss in my father's face, took out two brand-new ten-yuan notes and snapped them between his fingers to get my father's attention. It didn't work—Father kept his face hidden behind his knees. This seemed to disappoint Lao Lan, who took a quick glance round him, then flung the two notes at my father's feet, one of them landing in the middle of the still-steaming puddle of piss and lying nestled against the soggy, disintegrating cigarettes. At that moment my father might as well have been dead. He'd lost face for himself and his ancestors. He was less than a man, no better than the bloated cigarettes swimming in his adversary's piss. After Lao Lan tossed down his money, the peddlers and butchers followed his lead, sympathetic looks on their faces, as if we were father-and-son beggars who deserved their pity. They tossed down double the usual amount, which might have been a reward for not resisting or an attempt to copy Lao Lan's generosity. As I stared at those notes, fallen at our feet like so many dead leaves, I began to cry, and at long last Father looked up. There was no sign of anger on his face, nor of sadness, nothing but the lustre of a dried-out piece of wood. As he gazed at me coldly, a look of perplexity began to show in his eyes, as if he had no idea why I was crying. I reached out and clawed at his neck. 'Dieh,' I said, 'you're no longer my father. I'll call Lao Lan Dieh before I ever call you that again!' Momentarily stunned by my shouts, the men burst out laughing. Lao Lan gave me a thumbs-up. 'Xiaotong,' he said, 'you're really something, just what I need, a son. From now on, you're welcome at my house any time. If it's pork you want, that's what you'll get, and if it's beef, you'll have that too. And if you bring your mamma along, I'll welcome you both with open arms.' That was too great an insult to ignore and I rushed at him angrily. He swiftly sidestepped my charge and I wound up face down on the ground with a cut and bleeding lip. 'You little prick,' he said, guffawing loudly, 'attacking me after calling me Dieh!

Who in his right mind would want a son like you?' Since no one offered to help me up, I had to get to my feet on my own. I walked over to my father and kicked him in the shin to vent my disappointment. Not only did that not make him angry, he wasn't even aware of what I'd done. He just rubbed his face with his large, soft hands, stretched his arms, yawned like a lazy tomcat, looked down at the ground and then, slowly, conscientiously, carefully picked up the notes steeping in Lao Lan's piss, holding each one up to the light, as if to make sure it wasn't counterfeit. Finally, he picked up the new note from Lao Lan that had been splashed with piss and dried it on his pants. Now that the money was stacked neatly on his knees, he picked it up with the middle two fingers of his left hand, spat on the thumb and forefinger of his right and began to count it. I ran up to grab it, wanting to tear the notes to shreds and fling the pieces into the air (of course I'd fling them in Lao Lan's face), to avenge our humiliation. But he was too fast for me. Jumping to his feet, he held his hand high in the air. 'You foolish boy,' he muttered, 'what do you think you're doing? Money's money—it's not to blame, people are. Don't take your anger out on money.' Grabbing his elbow, I tried to claw my way up his body and rip that shameful money out of his hand. But I didn't stand a chance, not with a full-grown man. I was so angry then that I rammed my head into his hip, over and over, but he just patted me kindly on the head and said: 'That's enough now, son, don't get carried away. Look, over there, Lao Lan's bull. It's getting angry.'

It was a big, fat, tawny Luxi bull with straight horns and a hide like satin stretched over its rippling muscles, the kind I'd see later on athletes on TV. It was a golden yellow, all but its face, which, surprisingly, was white. I'd never seen a white-faced bull. Castrated, the way it looked at you out of the corner of one of its red eyes was enough to make your hair stand on end. Now that I think back, that's probably the look people describe when they talk about eunuchs. Castration changes a man's nature; it does the same with bulls. By pointing to the bull, Father made me forget about the money, at least for the moment. I turned in time to see Lao Lan swagger out of the square, leading his bull. Why not swagger, after the way he'd humiliated my non-resisting father? His prestige in the village and among the cattle-peddlers had just undergone a dramatic increase. He'd gone up against the only person who dismissed him as irrelevant, and won; no one in the village would defy him again. That only makes what happened next so startling that I'm not sure I believe it even now, years later. The Luxi bull stopped in its tracks. Lao Lan tugged its halter. To no avail. Without the slightest effort, the bull made a mockery out of Lao Lan's show of strength. A cattle butcher by trade, he exuded an odour that could make a timid calf shake like a leaf and cause even the most stubborn animal to meekly await its death when he stood in front of it, butcher knife in hand. Unable to get the bull moving again, he went round, smacked it on the rump and gave an ear-piercing yell. Now, most animals would have lost control of their bowels in the wake of this smack and that yell, but the Luxi bull didn't so much as blink. Still enjoying the glow of victory over my father, and acting like a cocky soldier, Lao Lan kicked the bull's underbelly with no thought to its nature. The bull shifted its rump, split the air with a loud roar, lowered its head and flung Lao Lan into the air on its horns, as if he weighed no more than a straw mat. The peddlers and butchers were shocked, shocked and speechless. None of them dared to go to Lao Lan's aid. The bull lowered its head again and charged. Now, Lao Lan was no ordinary man, and when he saw those horns coming at him he had enough presence of mind and strength of body to roll out of the way. Eyes blazing red with anger, the bull turned to charge again, and Lao Lan rolled out of the way a second time and then a third . . . When he was finally able to scramble to his feet, we saw that he was injured, though only slightly. He stood there, facing down the bull, hips shifted to the side and his eyes not leaving the the animal for a second. The bull lowered its head, slobber gathering at the corners of its mouth, and snorted loudly as it prepared for the next charge. Lao Lan raised his hand to distract the bull but he was only putting up a brave front, like a frightened bullfighter who'll do anything to save face. He took a cautious step forward; the bull didn't move. Rather, it dropped its head even lower, a sign that the next charge was imminent. Lao Lan finally abandoned his macho posturing, gave one last blustery yell, turned and ran for his life. The bull took off after him, its tail sticking out stiff and straight, like an iron rod, its hooves spraying mud in every direction like a machine gun. Meanwhile, Lao Lan, who was hell-bent on escaping, headed instinctively towards the onlookers, hoping to find salvation in a crowd. But rescuing him was the last thing on their minds. The men ran for their lives, shrieking loudly and cursing their parents for not giving them more than two legs. Luckily, the bull had enough human intelligence to single out Lao Lan and not vent its anger on anyone else. Sand flew into the air as the peddlers and the butchers scrambled over walls and up trees. Lao Lan, stupefied by his predicament, ran straight towards Father and me. In desperation, Father grabbed me by the nape of my neck with one hand and the seat of my pants with the other and flung me up onto the wall only seconds before Lao Lan ran up and took refuge behind him, grabbing his clothes to keep him in front of him and thus screen him from the charging bull. My father retreated and so, of course, did Lao Lan, until they both were backed up against the wall. Father waved his money in front of the bull and began to mutter: 'Bull, ah, bull, there's no bad blood between you and me, not now, not ever, so let's work this out . . .' It all happened faster than words can describe. Father threw the money at the bull's face and leapt onto its back before the animal knew what was happening. Then he stuck his fingers in the bull's nose, grabbed its nose ring and jerked its head up high. The cows from West County were farm animals, so they all had nose rings. Now, the nose is a bull's weak spot, and no one, not the best farmer alive, knew more about bulls than my father, though he wasn't much of a farming man. Tears sprang to my eyes as I sat there, on top of the wall. I'm so proud of you, Dieh, and of how you've washed away our humiliation and reclaimed our lost face through your wise and courageous action. The butchers and peddlers ran up to help him and wrestle the white-faced, yellow bull to the ground. So that it wouldn't get up again and hurt anyone, one of the butchers ran home rabbit-fast to fetch a butcher knife, which he then offered to the now waxen-faced Lao Lan, who took a step backward and waved away the man, turning the task over to someone else. The butcher turned from side to side, knife in hand. 'Who'll do it? No one? Well, then, I guess it's up to me.' He rolled up his sleeves, wiped the blade against the sole of his shoe, then hunkered down and closed one eye, like a carpenter with a plumb line. Taking aim at the slight indentation in the bull's chest, he plunged the knife in. When he pulled it out, blood spurted into the air and painted my father red.

Now that the bull was dead, everyone felt it safe enough to climb down. Blackish red blood continued to flow from the wound, bubbling like a fountain, releasing a heated odour into the crisp morning air. The men stood about like deflated balloons, shrivelled and diminished somehow. There was so much they wanted to say but no one said a word. Except my father, who tucked his head down low between his shoulders, opened his mouth to reveal a set of strong but yellow teeth, and said: 'Old man in the sky, I was so scared!' Everyone turned to look at Lao Lan, who wished he could crawl into a hole. He tried to cover his embarrassment by looking down at the bull, whose legs were stretched out straight, its fleshy thighs still twitching. One of its blue eyes remained open, as if to release the hatred still inside. 'Damn you!' Lao Lan said as he kicked the dead animal. 'You spend your whole life hunting wild geese only to have your eye pecked out by a gosling.' He then looked up at my father. 'I owe you one, Luo Tong, but you and I aren't finished.' 'Finished with what?' Father asked. 'There's nothing between you and me.' 'Don't you touch her!' hissed Lao Lan. 'I never wanted to touch her—she asked me to,' replied Father with a proud little laugh. 'She called you a dog, and she'll never let you touch her again.' I had no idea what that was all about, but later, of course, I realized out they were talking about Aunty Wild Mule, who owned a little wine shop. But when I asked him, 'Dieh, what were you talking about?' 'Nothing a child needs to know,' is what he answered. 'Son,' Lao Lan said, 'didn't you say you wanted to be a member of the Lan clan? Then why did you call him Dieh just now?' 'You're nothing but a pile of stinking dog shit!' I said. 'Boy,' he said, 'you go home and tell your mother that your father's found his way into Wild Mule's cave and can't get out.' That made my father as angry as the bull, and he lowered his head and charged at Lao Lan. They were at each other's throat for no more than a moment before the others rushed over and separated them. But in that brief moment Lao Lan managed to break my father's little finger and my father to bite off half of Lao Lan's ear. Spitting it out angrily, Father said: 'How dare you say things like that in front of my son, you dog bastard!'

Without a sound, the woman slips through the narrow space separating me from the Wise Monk, the wide hem of her jacket lightly brushing the tip of my nose, her chilled calf rubbing against my knee. Flustered, I can't go on with my tale for a moment. She carries the Wise Monk's ancient brass washbasin into the water-soaked courtyard, showing me the profile of her gaunt face, the hint of a smile hidden in her eyes. The mass of clouds above us parts to reveal patches of rosy sky, tinged by gold in the west as the fire clouds of sunset burn their way past. The bats that make their home in the temple wheel in the out-side air and sparkle like gold beans. The woman's face lights up gloriously. Her oversized jacket, made of homespun cotton, has a row of brass buttons down the front. She bends over to lay down the laundry-filled basin; it wobbles in the shallow water. She then wades leisurely round the yard, the water cov-ering her calves. The hem of her robe held up in her hands reveals tanned thighs and white buttocks. Imagine my surprise to note that she is wearing nothing underneath! That is to say, if she takes off her robe she'll be standing there naked. The large robe must be the Wise Monk's. I know the details of his personal belongings like the back of my hand but I've never seen that partic-ular robe. Where did she find it? I think back to a moment before, when she passed by me, and recall a musty smell, one that now permeates the air in the courtyard. She strolls aimlessly for a moment before heading to a corner of the wall, urgently, where she makes loud splashing noises; that fish leaps out of the water again behind her, then falls back. She is holding the hem of her robe higher than ever, in order to keep it dry, exposing her buttocks. When she reaches the wall, she grips the hem of her robe even higher with her left hand, bends over and, with her right hand, digs out the twigs and grass that clog up the drain and flings them over the wall. Her buttocks, like brass cym-bals, proudly greet the fire clouds in the western sky. Now that the drain is unclogged, she stands up and moves to the side to watch the water flow towards her, carrying twigs and the little plastic horse. The laundry-filled brass basin moves a few feet before settling on the ground. The body of the fish slowly comes into view; for a moment it is able to keep swimming, but it is quickly laid out flat and all it can do is flap about in desperation, splashing water everywhere. I think I hear its shrill screams. The cobblestone path emerges first from the water, followed by the dirt round it. A toad jumps out of the mud, the loose skin under its mouth popping in and out. Frogs set up a din of croaks in the ditch beyond the wall. The woman opens the hand holding the hem of her robe, then smoothes the wrinkles with the other hand, the wet one. The fish flaps up next to her. Though she watches it for a moment and then looks over to where we sit, it is, of course, beyond my ability to decide what she should do about that unfortunate creature. She runs a few steps, muddying her feet and nearly falling in the process but presses that recalcitrant fish to the ground with both hands, then straightens up and looks our way again. She sighs and, in the redness of the sunset, reluctantly picks up the fish and flings it away, its tail snapping back and forth as it sails over the wall and out of sight. But the glittery golden arc it traces in the air imprints itself on my mind, where it will remain for a very long time. She walks over to where the brass basin lies, picks out a shirt and smoothes the collar, then shakes it hard, sending out waves of sound. The red shirt looks like a ball of fire in the sunset. The woman's resemblance to Aunty Wild Mule has led me to sense that there is a special and extraordinarily close relationship between us. Even though I am nearing the age of twenty, when I look at that woman I feel like a boy of seven or eight; and yet, the pounding of my heart and the stirrings of that thing between my legs declare to me that I am that child no longer. She lays the shirt on top of the cast-iron incense burner directly opposite the temple entrance, and spreads the remaining clothes on top of the still-wet wall. With rapt attention I watch how nimbly, how energetically, she jumps up to smooth out each item, over and over. Finished with her work, she walks to the temple entrance, as if it were the door to her home, throws her arms out to stretch her upper torso, then puts her hands on her hips to limber her midsection. Her buttocks shift as if rubbing against an invisible object. I don't know how I'll ever be able to take my eyes off that body, but the possibility of becoming a disciple to the Wise Monk is important enough to make me sacrifice such visual pleasures. For an instant I wonder: if she were to take my hand and lead me to some faraway place, the way Aunty Wild Mule did with my father, would I be able to refuse?

Mother told me to secure the rear hatch of the walking tractor while she went to the wall to drag over a couple of baskets of cow and goat bones. Bending down, she picked up each basket and dumped its bones into the tractor bed. These were discarded bones we'd bought, not the remains of our meals. If we'd eaten the meat off this many bones, even 1 per cent of that many, I'd have had no complaints and no need to miss my father, I'd have stood firmly beside my mother as she denounced him and Aunty Wild Mule for their crimes and their sins. There had been times when I'd felt like cracking open a couple of fresh-looking bovine leg bones just to get at the marrow, but the hawkers always cleaned them out before selling. Once they were loaded, Mother told me to help her dump in some scrap metal. This so-called scrap metal actually included intact machine parts: diesel-engine flywheels, connecting joints for construction scaffolds, even some manhole covers from the city's sewer system; a little of everything. Once we found a Japanese mortar, brought to us on the back of a mule by an old man in his eighties and an old woman in her seventies. Back when we were just starting out, we bought everything as scrap and then sold it back as scrap—at a minuscule profit. We figured things out, though, and began sorting the scrap and selling it to appropriate companies in town. We sold construction materials to builders, manhole covers to sewer industries and machine parts to hardware stores. But since we couldn't find the right buyer for the mortar, we kept it at home as a collectible. I'd made up my mind not to sell it even if we did find a buyer. A typical boy—warlike—I was fascinated by weapons. Since my father had run off with another woman, I'd not been able to raise my head round other children, but now that I owned a mortar I could walk with my back straight, cockier than those who had fathers at home. I once overheard a couple of young village bullies quietly agree to stay clear of Luo Xiaotong because his family had a mortar and he'd use it against anyone who offended him, taking lethal aim at the offender's house. *POW!* the place would go up in smoke, burn to the ground! You can imagine how proud *that* made me. I was so happy I could burst. Selling scrap metal to speciality buyers did not bring in as much as the items were worth new but it did sell for more than ordinary scrap and that was how we were able to build a house with a tiled roof in five years.

After we'd loaded the scrap metal, Mother dragged over some cardboard boxes and laid them on the ground. Then she told me to draw water from the pump. This was one of my regular chores, and I knew that the handle was cold enough to peel the skin off my hands. So I put on stiff pigskin safety gloves we'd picked up on our rounds. Almost everything we owned, in fact, from foam pillows to a spatula, had come the same way. Some of our pickings had never even been used—my wool cap, for instance, which was brand-new army ration. It smelt like mothballs and had the date of manufacture— November 1968—stamped in red on the inside. My father was still a bed-wetting little boy back then, my mother a bed-wetting little girl, and me, well, I wasn't. With the gloves on, my hands were next to useless, but it was a bitterly cold day and the base of the pump was frozen solid. A leak at the edge puffed out air each time I pressed down on the handle but no water came out. 'Hurry up!' Mother shouted irritably. 'Stop dawdling. "A poor child grows up fast" but you're ten years old and can't even draw water from a well. Raising you has been a waste of time and effort. All you're good at is eating— eat eat eat. If you devoted half your eating talent to getting your chores done, you'd be a model worker with a red sash.' Mother grumbled, I seethed. Ever since you left us, Dieh, I've been eating pig and dog food and dressing like a beggar and working like a beast of burden. But nothing makes her happy. Dieh, when you left you were looking forward to a second land reform. Well, I'm looking forward to it more than you ever did. But it won't ever come. It's easier for people to get rich illegally. They're afraid of nothing. After Father left, Mother came to be known as the Queen of Trash. That should have made me the Queen of Trash's son, but in fact I was the Queen of Trash's slave. Her grumbling grew to cursing, and my self-pity shrank to despair. I took off the gloves and grabbed the pump handle with my bare hands. With a sucking sound they immediately stuck to the cold metal. Go ahead, pig iron handle, be cold, be frozen, peel the skin off my hands if you want to. It's hopeless anyway. Smash a broken jar—what difference does it make? I'll freeze to death, so what! She'll wind up with no son, and her big house with a tiled roof and her big truck will be meaningless. She's actually dreaming about my child marriage. Marriage to whom, you ask? To Lao Lan's stupid daughter, that's who. A year older, and a head taller, she doesn't even have a real name—only a nickname, Tiangua, Sweet Melon. A nose infection all year round means she always has two lines of snot above her mouth. Mother would love to improve her social standing by linking up with the Lan clan, and all I think about is setting up my mortar and flattening the Lan house. Dream on, Mother! So what if my hands stick to the pump handle! They belonged to 'her son' before they belonged to me. I pushed down, there was a gurgle and water gushed into the bucket. I immediately buried my face in it and began to drink. Stop that, she shouted. She didn't want me drinking cold water. But I ignored her. Best to drink till my belly ached and I was rolling on the ground like a donkey that's stopped turning a millstone. After I carried the bucket over to her, she told me to fetch the ladle. I did. Then she told me to splash water on the paper—not too much and not too little, just enough to give it a coat of ice. That done, she spread another layer of paper over the ice and I splashed on more water. We'd done this so many times it had become routine; there was no need for words. What I spread over the paper was water; what we received in return was money. What the butchers in town injected into the meat was water; what they received in return was also money. After Father ran off, Mother would not allow herself to wallow in self-pity. So, deciding to become a butcher, she apprenticed herself to Sun Zhangsheng. I went along. Mother and Sun's wife were distant cousins. But the 'white knife in, red knife out' profession is not suited to women; and even though Mother had an abundance of patience and endurance, she never matched the ferocity of Madame Sun. She and I did all right when it came to slaughtering young pigs and sheep but adult cows were a different matter altogether. They made things almost impossible as we stood there clutching a glinting butcher knife. 'This is no job for you, Aunty,' Sun Zhangsheng said to Mother. 'They're telling people in town to sell undoctored meat, so sooner or later what we're doing will be illegal. We butchers earn our living by injecting the meat with water. The day they put a stop to that is the day our profits dry up.' He's the one who urged Mother to take up the scavenging business—it required no capital and was a guaranteed livelihood. He was right. In three years, everyone within thirty *li* knew us as the Queen and Prince of Trash.

We carried the frozen paper over to the tractor, then tied it down with rope. Our destination was the county seat, which we visited every few days and which always left me very sad. So many delicacies were sold there, I could smell them from twenty *li* away, especially the meat, but also the fish. Yet for me meat and fish might as well not have existed. Mother had our provisions all ready—two cold corncakes and a lump of salted greens. If, by hook or by crook, we got a good price for our scrap, slipped a thing or two past a buyer— local businesses had become increasingly clever over the years, after being cheated by scrap-peddlers from all over—she'd be in a good mood and I'd be rewarded with a pig's tail. We'd sit on our haunches in a sheltered area by the front gate of the local-products business—in the summer we'd sit under a shady tree—and treat ourselves to all the aromas wafting over from a street that slanted off from where we sat while we chewed on corncakes and salted greens. Stewed meat was sold from a dozen open-air cooking pots—the heads of pigs, sheep, cows, mules and dogs; the feet of pigs, sheep, cows, mules and camels; the livers of pigs, sheep, cows, mules and dogs; the hearts of pigs, sheep, cows, mules and dogs; the stomachs of pigs, sheep, cows, mules and dogs; the entrails of pigs, sheep, cows, mules and dogs; the lungs of pigs, sheep, cows, mules and dogs; and the tails of pigs, sheep, cows, mules and camels. There was also roasted chicken, roasted goose, braised duck, steamed rabbit, barbecued pigeon and fried sparrow . . . the cutting boards groaned under every possible kind of steaming, and colourful meat. The sellers held gleaming knives; some cut the fine meat into strips, some into chunks. Their red, oily faces looked hale and hearty. Some had thick fingers, some thin; some had long fingers, some short. They were all lucky fingers, free to caress the meat at will, covered in grease and overlain with redolence. How happy I'd have been to turn into one of those fingers. But it was not to be. More than once I was tempted to snatch a piece of meat and stuff it into my mouth, but the knives in their hands were powerful deterrents. So I chewed on my half-frozen corncake as the cold winds swirled round me, and wept tears of sadness. My mood improved if Mother rewarded me with a pig's tail, but how much meat did one of those have? A few mouthfuls at best. I even crunched up the little bones and swallowed them. But the pig's tails merely made the meat-starved worms in my stomach hungrier, and as I stared at the multi- hued meats in front of me my tears flowed unchecked. 'Why are you crying, son?' Mother asked. 'I miss Dieh.' Her face darkened. But after pondering my answer, she smiled sadly and said: 'It's not him you miss, son, it's the taste of meat. Don't think you can put something over on me. I can't satisfy that craving of yours, at least not now. The mouth is first to fall prey to pampering, which is inevitably accompanied by trouble. Throughout history, many heroic individuals have lost sight of their ambition and come to grief by surrendering to their mouths. So don't cry, son. I promise you, the day will come when you'll eat your fill of meat. Once we've got a nice house and a truck, once we've got you married, to show that bastard of a father what I can do, I'll cook you a whole cow, then let you climb inside it and eat your way out!' 'Niang,' I said, 'I don't want a nice house or a truck, and I don't want to get married. All I want is a big plate of meat.' 'Son,' she said solemnly, 'do you think I have no cravings? I'm human too, I'd love to eat a whole pig too! But life demands that you keep your dignity, and I want your father to see that we're better off without him.' 'Better off?' I said. 'Like hell we are! I'd rather be a starving beggar with Dieh than live like this with you.' 'That hurts, boy,' she said. 'I skimp and I save, storing up my anger to pay him back. And for what? For you, you little bastard!' Then she turned her anger on my father: 'Luo Tong, I say, Luo Tong, you son of a black-dick donkey, you've ruined my life . . . If I feasted on fine, spicy food, if I ate and drank what I wanted, my eyes would shine and I'd be as enticing as that whore!' Mother's mournful outburst moved me to the depths of my soul. 'You're right, Mother,' I said. 'If you ate big meaty meals, I guarantee that within a month you'd turn into a goddess, more beautiful than Aunty Wild Mule. Then Dieh would abandon her and fly back to you.' 'Tell me the truth, Xiaotong,' she asked, her tears flowing, 'am I really more beautiful than her?' 'Sure you are, Niang,' I said confidently. 'Then why did he go after a slut who'd been screwed by every man in town? Not just go *after* her but run off *with* her?' I rushed to Father's defence: 'I heard him say he didn't go looking for Aunty Wild Mule, that she went looking for him.' 'What's the difference?' Mother growled. 'If the bitch doesn't wiggle her arse, the mutt's wasting his time. If the mutt isn't interested, the bitch wiggles her arse for nothing.' 'Mother,' I said, 'you wiggle so much you've got me all confused.' 'You little snot,' she snapped, 'don't pretend you're confused. You knew what was going on between your father and Wild Mule but you helped him keep it a secret. If you'd told me, I'd have stopped him from running off.' 'How?' I asked timidly. 'I'd have chopped off his legs', she snapped, glaring at me. Wow! Lucky Dieh, I thought. 'You haven't answered my question,' she said. 'If I'm more beautiful than Wild Mule, why did he run off for her?' 'Because her family eats meat at every meal,' I said. 'It was the smell of meat that drew him to her.' 'Then if I cook meat every day from now on,' Mother sneered, 'will your father's sense of smell bring him home?' 'You bet it will!' I said gleefully. 'If you cook meat every day, he'll be home in no time. He can smell something eight hundred *li* away upwind and three thousand downwind.' I used fine-sounding words to encourage Mother, hoping that her anger would wilt in the face of my reason and that she'd lead me over to the meat street, take out some of the money she'd hidden in her clothes and then buy a pile of fragrant, tender meat for me to eat my fill. Even if I ate myself into the grave, I'd at least be a ghost with a full belly. She wasn't convinced. Brimming over with resentment, she walked up to the wall, hunkered down and ate her cold corncake. But my words had not been entirely in vain. Soon, with great reluctance, she went over to a little cafe near the meat street and chatted with the owners for the longest time, trotting out a litany of lies: my father was dead and wouldn't they take pity on his widow and orphaned child . . . They finally knocked ten fen off the price of a skinny-as-a-string-bean pig's tail; she held it tight it in her hand, as if afraid of it sprouting wings and flying away. Then she dragged me to an out-of-the-way spot and shoved it into my hands: 'Here, you greedy little thing. Eat! But when you're finished I expect you to work hard.'

The woman straddles the threshold, one foot in and one foot out, leans against the doorframe, purses her lips and stares at me, as if listening to my tale. Her eyebrows, which nearly touch in the middle, arch up and down, as if she were recalling a distant memory. I find it hard to continue my tale under the scrutiny of her dark eyes, whose pull I reluctantly force myself to resist. The penetrating power of her gaze is so intimidating that my mouth seems frozen shut. I badly want to talk to her, to ask her name or where she's from. But I lack the courage. And yet I want desperately to be friends. I gaze hungrily at her legs, at her knees. There are bruises on her legs and a bright scar on one of her knees. We're so close that I can smell the roasted-meat fragrance that warms the air round her; it goes straight to my heart and invigorates my soul. What strong yearnings! The palms of my hands itch, my mouth drools and it's all I can do to keep from rushing into her arms to fondle her and let her caress my powerful desire. I want to suck her breasts, want her to suckle me; I want to be a man but am far more willing to become a child, to be that five- or six-year-old little boy again. Images of the past float into my mind, begin-ning with the time I went with Father to Aunty Wild Mule's house for a meaty meal. I think about how he nibbled her neck while I was busy feasting on all that meat, and how she stopped chopping and bumped her arse against him as she said in a soft, hoarse voice: 'Don't let the boy see you, you horny mutt.' 'So what if he sees?' I heard Father reply, 'My son and I are best friends.' I recall how steam rose from the pot and filled the air with a captivating aroma . . . the sky darkens during all that, the red shirt draped across the cast-iron incense burner is now deep purple. The bats fly low, the gingko tree casts broad shadows on the ground and two stars twinkle in the black canopy of the heav-ens. Mosquitoes buzz round the temple as the Wise Monk places his hands on the floor, rises to his feet and walks over behind the idol. I see that the woman is now inside and is following the Wise Monk, so I fall in behind her.

The Wise Monk touches the flame of a cigarette lighter to the wick of a thick white candle, which he then sticks into a wax-filled candleholder. One look at the shiny lighter tells me it's an expensive one. The woman is calm and composed, perfectly at ease with her surroundings, as if this were her home. She picks up the candleholder and carries it into the room where the Wise Monk and I sleep. A black pot rests on the briquette stove on which we cook; water is boiling. She sets down the candleholder on a purple stool and looks over at the Wise Monk without saying anything. He points to the rafters with his chin. I look up to see two grain stalks, waving like weasel tails in the flickering candlelight. She climbs onto the stool, takes down three spikes, then jumps to the floor and rubs them between her hands to break up the chaff. Finally, she blows on her open hands and tosses several dozen golden kernels of grain into the pot, then puts back the lid and sits down without a sound. The Wise Monk sits on the edge of the kang, wooden, wordless. The flies no longer swarm in and round his ears, which are now fully exposed—thin, virtually transparent and eerily insubstantial. Perhaps the flies have sucked out all the blood. Or so I think. The mosquitoes, on the other hand, continue to buzz overhead, and fleas spring onto my face. When I open my mouth, a couple of them wind up in my throat. I sweep my hand through the air and manage to catch a handful of both insects. Grown up in a village of butchers, I'm used to killing, even at the cost of goodwill. But if I am to become the Wise Monk's disciple, I must respect the elemental taboo against the taking of animal life. So I open my hand and let the winged insects fly off and the leapers jump away.

Squeals of pigs in their death throes spread throughout the village—the slaughter had begun. The air was redolent with the aroma of barbecued meat. Now that we were loaded and ready to go, Mother reached under the seat and took out the crank handle, which she fitted into the cross-hair opening; then she took a deep breath, bent down, spread her legs and turned with all her might. The first couple of turns were sluggish, but then it got smoother. Mother's movements were bold and explosive, like a man's. The flywheel whirred, the exhaust pipe sputtered. Her first wave of energy spent, Mother straightened up; she was breathing hard, open-mouthed, like a swimmer coming up for air. The engine died. She'd have to do it all over again. Once was never enough, I knew that. When the end of the year rolled round, the tractor's starter was always our biggest headache. Mother looked at me, imploring me to help. So I grabbed the crank handle, yanked it with all my might and sent the flywheel spinning. A few more yanks like that and my strength was exhausted. Where was someone who went all year long without a shred of meat supposed to get his strength from? When I loosened my grip, the crank handle spun backward and knocked me to the ground, throwing a scare into Mother, who rushed over to see if I was hurt. I lay there pretending I was dead, and feeling pretty good about it too. If that crank handle had really knocked the life out of me, first to die would have been her son; next to die would have been me, the person. Life without meat isn't worth clinging to. A smack from a crank handle was nothing compared to the pain of going without meat. Mother pulled me to my feet and checked her son over from head to toe. When she saw I wasn't hurt, she pushed me to the side. 'You're useless, go stand over there,' she said, disappointment creeping into her voice.

'I haven't got the strength.'

'What happened to it?'

'Dieh says that only meat makes a man strong.'

'Nonsense!'

Mother continued turning the crank, her body heaving up and down, hair flying behind her like a tail. Usually, after three or four tries, the ancient engine reluctantly turned over and coughed once or twice like a sickly billy goat. But not that day. On that day it said no—n-o, no. It was the coldest day of the year, with clouds blotting out the sky, dampness in the air and the northern wind cutting our faces like a knife. It felt like snow. On days like that even our tractor balked at going outside. Mother's face was red, her breathing laboured, her forehead beaded with sweat. She cast an accusing look at me, as if it was my fault. I tried to look pained and pathetic, which was difficult, given the joy that filled my heart. On a bitterly cold winter day like that, I was in no mood to sit on a seat colder than ice and bump round for three hours on our way to the county seat some sixty *li* away, just so I could gnaw on cold corncakes and salted greens, not even if she rewarded me with a pig's tail. What would I have done if she'd rewarded me with a pair of pickled pig's feet? Who cares, since that'd never happen!

Though she was deeply disappointed, Mother refused to give up. The coldest days were not only ideally suited to slaughterhouse work but also to the sale of scrap. On frigid days, the injected water would not seep out of the slaughtered animals and the meat would not spoil; on frigid days, buyers of scrap, preferring to stay warm, were content to cast a cursory glance at the material, which meant that our water-soaked paper would pass inspection with ease. Mother untied the electric cord that served as a belt, then took off her brown men's jacket and tucked her new cast-off sweater into her trousers; she was small but full of energy and quite impressive. Words were embroidered on the front of her sweater round the image of a girl performing a flying kick. Mother treasured that sweater; green flecks flew off it when she took it off at night, making her moan softly. When I'd ask if she was in pain, she'd say no but that taking it off gave her a nice tingly feeling. Now that I've accumulated a bit of knowledge I know all about static electricity, but at the time I thought she'd laid her hands on something magical. Once I considered sneaking the sweater out of the house to sell it for the price of half a pig's head, but in the end I couldn't go through with it. There were plenty of things I didn't appreciate about my mother, but I couldn't help thinking about some of her virtues. My greatest complaint about her was that she wouldn't let me eat the meat I craved. But she didn't eat any either. If she'd gone off and feasted behind my back, forget about the sweater—I'd have sold her to a slave trader without batting an eye. But she suffered along with me, struggling to make ends meet, and wouldn't allow herself even a pig's tail, so what could I say? With Mother taking the lead, her son could only follow, sustained by the hope that one day Father would return and bring these hard times to an end. Determined to spare no effort, she resumed her stance, took two deep breaths, then one more, held it, bit down on her lip and turned the crank as hard as she could. The flywheel spun at the rate of a couple of hundred RPMs, about the equivalent of five horsepower; if that wasn't sufficient to fire it up, then that was one sorry fucking tractor, a true bastard—not your ordinary bastard but one for the ages, that's right, a bastard for the ages. Mother flung the crank handle to the ground, her strength sapped. The tractor just smiled indifferently, not making a sound. Mother's face was sallow, her stare blank; she was defeated, disheartened, she'd lost the battle. All in all, she looked better this way. What disgusted and frightened me was how she could be so full of fight, so proud and confident, for that was when she was the most miserly, when what she really wanted was for us to eat dirt and drink the wind. The way she was now opened up the possibility that she'd part with enough to make some noodles, fry up some cabbage, add a little vegetable oil, maybe even put in some smelly shrimp paste that was so salty it nearly made you jump in the air. In a village where electric lights had lit up houses for more than a decade, our large, tile-roofed home went without. When we lived in the hut my grandfather had left us, we had electric lights, but now we'd gone back to the dark ages and used kerosene lamps. She wasn't being miserly, Mother said. This was her way of protesting against the corrupt village officials who kept hiking the price of electricity. When we ate dinner by lamplight, her face glowed proud in the dim room. 'Go ahead, raise the price,' she'd say, 'raise it until it costs eight thousand a unit. I couldn't care less because I don't use any of your damned electricity!' When she was in a good mood, we'd eat in the dark—no lamps or anything—and if I complained, she'd simply say: 'You're eating dinner, not doing needlework. Don't tell me you need light to avoid shovelling food up your nose!' She was right, I never did get food up my nose. Stuck with a mother who advocated hard struggles and plain living, I had to resign myself to my bad luck and simply forget about putting up a fight.

Unable to get our tractor started, Mother walked out into the street, perhaps to seek some advice. Would she go to Lao Lan? Perhaps, since the tractor was his castoff and he knew the thing better than anyone. She hurried back in a little while. 'Son,' she said, excitedly. 'Light a fire. We're going to burn this son of a bitch!'

'Did Lao Lan tell you to do that?'

She hadn't expected that. 'What's wrong with you?' She stared into my eyes. 'Why are you looking at me like that?'

'Nothing,' I said. 'Let's burn it.'

She went over to the wall and came back with an armload of discarded rubber, which she laid on the ground under the tractor. Then she went into the kitchen and returned with a piece of burning kindling with which she touched off the rubber, sending black, noxious smoke into the air. Over the years we'd accumulated lots of discarded rubber, which we could sell only by melting it down and making cubes out of it. Our house was in the heart of the village, and our unhappy neighbours had been quite vocal about the

noxious fumes, since the black, oily residue rained down on them. Granny
Zhang, who lived to the east, even showed Mother a ladleful of water as proof.
Mother ignored her, but I took a look: black tadpole-like things floated on
the surface, obviously bits of our ash and dust. 'Doesn't it bother you that we
have to drink water like this?' said Granny Zhang angrily. 'It'll make us sick!'
'No, it doesn't bother me, not at all!' replied Mother, no less angrily. 'I won't
be happy until all you people who sell doctored meat are dead and buried.'
Granny Zhang thought twice about saying anything in return when she saw
the red glare of fury in Mother's eyes. This was followed by a visit from some
men who complained to Mother; but she rushed out into the street, bawling
and protesting that she and her son were being harassed, and quickly drew
a crowd. Lao Lan, whose house was directly behind ours, had the authority
to approve building sites. Before my father left home, Mother had nagged
him into asking Lao Lan for permission to build a house, for which he waited
to have his palm greased. Father let that palm go ungreased, since he wasn't
interested in building a house in the first place. 'Son,' he said to me when
Mother wasn't around, 'if we had meat in the house, we'd eat it ourselves.
Why give it to him?' After Father left home, Mother went over to get his permission, taking a packet of biscuits as tribute. She'd barely walked out of his
door when those biscuits came flying out and landed on the street. Then,
less than six months after we'd started burning rubber, we ran into him on
the road to the county seat. He was riding a green, three-wheeled motorbike
with the word Police on the windshield. He was wearing a white helmet and
a black leather jacket. A big, well-fed hunting dog sat in the sidecar, a pair of
sunglasses perched on its snout, giving it a scholarly air, until it snarled at us
and my hair stood on end. Our tractor wasn't working at the time, and poor
Mother was frantic, flagging down vehicles and pedestrians, asking for help
but being rebuffed each time. This time she grabbed hold of the man's handlebars, without knowing who he was—until he took off his helmet. He
climbed off his motorbike and kicked the tractor's rusty bumper. 'You should
get rid of it,' he snorted, 'and get another one.' 'I will,' said Mother, 'after I
build a house.' Lao Lan nodded. 'I see you've got your pride.' He got down on
his haunches and helped us with the repairs, for which we—Mother dragged
me over—thanked him profusely. 'Keep your shitty thanks,' he said as he
wiped his hands on a rag. Then he patted me on the head: 'Has your father

come back home?' I shoved his hand away and glared at him. 'Temper, tem-per!' he laughed. 'Your father's a bastard, if you ask me!' 'You're a bastard!' I replied. Mother smacked me. 'How dare you talk to the nice uncle like that!' she scolded. 'That's all right,' he said, 'not to worry. Write to your father and tell him he can come back. Tell him I've forgiven them both.' He climbed back on his motorbike and started it up. It coughed and black smoke belched out of the exhaust pipe. The dog barked. 'Yang Yuzhen,' he shouted to my mother, 'stop burning rubber. I'll let you build your house. Come over tonight and pick up the permit!'

The captivating smell of millet gruel fills the room. The woman takes the lid off the pot, and I'm amazed to see how much gruel there is, easily enough for three people. She fetches three black bowls from the corner and fills them with a wooden spoon that's discoloured from searing. One spoonful, a second and a third; one spoonful, a second and a third; one spoonful, a second and a third. All three bowls are filled to the brim, and there's plenty more in the pot. I'm puzzled, surprised, flabbergasted. Has all that gruel really come from those few dozen kernels of grain? That woman, just who, or what, is she? A demon? A genie? The two foxes that have taken refuge in the temple during the downpour saunter into the room, lured by the smell of the gruel, female in front, male at the back and the three furry little kits stumbling in between. They're as cute as can be, especially the silly way they walk. They say that animals tend to have their offspring when there's thunder and lightning and the sky opens up. There's truth in that saying. The adult foxes sit in front of the pot, looking up at the woman, their eyes pleading one moment and staring greedily at the pot the next. Their stomachs growl, the sound of hunger. The kits scurry under their mother's belly in search of her teats. The male's eyes are moist, its lively expression seems to indicate that it's about to say something. I know exactly what it will say if it opens its mouth and speech emerges. The woman glances at the Wise Monk, who sighs and pushes his bowl of gruel over to the female fox. Following his lead, she pushes her bowl over to the male. Both animals nod to the Wise Monk and the woman to show their appreciation, then begin to eat, carefully, since the gruel is hot, their eyes filling with tears. Imagine my embarrassment as I look down at my bowl, not knowing if I should eat. 'Go ahead, eat,' the Wise Monk says. I know I'd never have a chance to eat gruel this good again, so I join the foxes and we each polish off three bowls. When they finish, they belch in satisfaction and, trailed by the kits, amble out of the room. At that moment I realize that the pot is empty, that not a kernel remains. I am contrite, but the Wise Monk is already seated on the kang fingering his beads, seeming half asleep. And the woman? She is sitting in front of the briquette stove playing with an iron poker. A dying fire casts its weak light onto her face, which is as lively and expressive as ever. A smile hints at the recollection of fond memories, but perhaps also at the absence of thought altogether. I rub my slightly bulging belly as the sound of newborn foxes sucking their mother's teats drifts in from outside. The sound of kittens nursing in the tree trunk is beyond my range of hearing, but I think I actually see them suckle. Which gives rise to a powerful urge to suckle. But where is there a tit for me? I'm not sleepy, but I need to overcome the urge to suckle, so I say, 'Wise Monk, I'll go on with my story—'

Mother was overcome with excitement, chattering like a sparrow, once she had the building permit in hand. 'Xiaotong,' she said, 'Lao Lan isn't so bad after all. I thought he had something else in mind but he handed me the permit without a word.' For the second time, she unrolled the document, with its red seal, for me to see. Then she sat me down to talk about the difficult road that we—mother and son—had walked since Father ran off. Her narration was tinged with sadness but not enough to diminish her sense of joy and pride. I was so sleepy I could barely keep my eyes open; my head drooped and I fell asleep. When I woke up, she was sitting on the floor in the dark, leaning against the wall, a jacket thrown over her shoulders, still talking. If I hadn't been endowed with steel nerves from the day I was born, I tell you, she'd have scared the life out of me. Her long-winded narration was only a dress rehearsal; the real performance began six months later, on the night our big house, with its tiled roof, was completed. It was our last night in the tent we'd set up in the yard, and light from an early winter moon lit up our new house beautifully, the mosaic tiles embedded in the walls absolutely radiant. We nearly froze from the wind blowing into the tent from all four sides; Mother's narration raced out into the night, reminding me of the pig's guts flung round by the butchers. 'Luo Tong,' Mother said, 'Luo Tong, you heartless bastard, you thought your son and I couldn't survive without you, didn't you? Well, we not only survived, we even built a big house! Lao Lan's house is fifteen feet high, ours is a foot higher! Lao Lan's walls are made of concrete, ours are decorated with mosaic tiles!' Her incorrigible vanity repelled me. Lao Lan's walls may have been made of concrete but the house had suspended ceilings decorated with fancy ceramic tiles, and a marble floor. Our outer walls had mosaic tiles but they were whitewashed on the inside, the posts exposed, and a layer of stove cinders covered the pitted floor. Here is what you can say about Lao Lan's house: 'The meat in buns doesn't show in the creases' while ours was more a case of 'Donkey droppings are shiny on the outside.' A moonbeam lit up Mother's mouth, much like a film close-up. Her lips never stopped moving; saliva bubbled at the corners. I pulled the damp blanket up over my head and fell asleep to the drone of her voice.

'Don't say any more, child.' It's the first time the woman has spoken. The cadence of her voice brings to mind filigrees of honey and gives the impression that there is little in life that she hasn't experienced. She smiles, hinting at deep mysteries, then takes a few steps back and sits on a rosewood chair that magically appeared when I wasn't looking (but perhaps it's been there all along). She waves to me and speaks for the second time: 'Don't say anything, child. I know what you're thinking.' I can't take my eyes off her. I watch as she slowly, dramatically, undoes the brass buttons of her robe, then snaps her arms out to the sides like an ostrich spreading its wings, giving an unobstructed view of the gorgeous flesh hidden by that plain, threadbare robe. My heart is intoxicated, my soul possessed; I've taken leave of my senses. A buzzing erupts in my ears; my body is chilled; my heart is pounding; my teeth are chattering; I feel like I'm standing naked on ice. Beams of light emerge from her eyes and her teeth as she sits illuminated by flames from the stove and the candle. Her breasts, like ripe mangoes, sag slightly in the centre to form fluid arcs, the nipples rising gracefully, like the captivating mouths of hedgehogs. They summon me intimately but my feet feel as if they have taken root. I sneak a glance at the Wise Monk, who is sitting with his hands pressed together, looking more dead than alive. 'Wise Monk,' I say softly, painfully, as if wanting to take strength from him to save myself but also seeking his approval to act upon my desire. But he doesn't stir; he might as well be carved from ice. 'Child.' The woman speaks again, but the words do not appear to have come from her mouth; they seem to have emerged from somewhere above her head or low in her belly. Sure, I've heard stories about ventriloquists who can speak without opening their mouths but those people are either martial-arts masters, buxom women or circus clowns, not ordinary people. They're strange, mysterious individuals one associates with black magic and infanticide. 'Come here, child.' There's that voice again. 'Don't deny what you feel in your heart. Do what it

tells you to do. You're a slave to your heart, not its master.' But I keep up the struggle, knowing that if I take a step forward I won't be able to go back, not ever. 'What's the matter? Haven't I been on your mind all along? When the meat touches your lips, why won't you eat it?' I'd sworn off meat after my little sister died, and remained true to that vow. Now, just looking at meat turns my stomach, makes me feel guilty somehow and reminds me of all the trouble it's caused in my life. Thoughts of meat restore my self-control—some of it, at least. She snickers, and the sound is like a blast of cold air from deep down in a cave. Then she says—this time I'm sure the words come from her mouth, which opens and closes contemptuously, 'Do you really think you can lessen your sins by not eating meat? Do you really think that not sucking on my breasts will be proof of your virtue? You may not have eaten meat for years but it has never been far from your mind. Even though you pass up the opportunity to suck on my breasts today, they will not be far from your mind for the rest of your life. I know exactly what you're like. Don't forget, I've watched you grow up and I know you as well as I know myself.' Tears gush from my eyes. 'Are you Aunty Wild Mule? You're still alive? You didn't die, after all?' It feels as if an affectionate wind were trying to blow me over to her; but her mocking grin stops me. 'What business is it of yours if I am or am not Wild Mule?' she sneers. 'And what business is it of yours if I'm alive or dead? If you want to suck on my breasts, come here. If you don't, then stop thinking about it. If sucking on my breasts is a sin, then not sucking on them, though you want to, is a greater one.' Her piercing mockery makes me want to crawl into a hole, makes me want to cover my head with a dog pelt. 'Even if you could cover your head with a dog pelt,' she says, 'what good would that do you? Sooner or later you'd have to take it off. And even if you vowed to never take it off, it would slowly rot away and fall apart to expose that ugly potato head of yours.' 'So what should I do?' I stammer, beseechingly. She covers herself with her robe, crosses her left leg over her right and says (commands): 'Tell your tale—'

The tractor's frozen engine crackled and popped from the blaze of burning rubber. Mother turned the crank. The engine sputtered and black smoke rolled out of the exhaust. Excitedly, I jumped to my feet, even though I really didn't want her to start up the engine; it died as quickly as it had come to life. She replaced the spark plug and turned the crank again. Finally, the engine caught and set up a mad howl. Mother squeezed the gas lever and the flywheel whirred. Though it hardly seemed possible, the shuddering of the engine and the black smoke from the exhaust told me that this time she'd succeeded. On that morning, as water turned to ice, we were going to have to go to the county seat, travel down icy roads into a bone-chilling wind. Mother went into the house and came out wearing a sheepskin coat, a leather belt, a black dogskin cap and carrying a grey cotton blanket. The blanket, of course, was something we'd picked up, as were the coat, the belt and the cap. She tossed the blanket on top of the tractor, my protection against the wind, then took her seat up front and told me to open the gate, the fanciest gate in the village. No gate like it had ever been seen in our century-long history. It was double-panelled, made of thick angle iron, impenetrable even by a machine gun. Painted black, it sported a pair of brass animal-head knockers. The villagers held our gate in awe and reverence; beggars stayed away. After removing Mother's brass lock, I strained to push the panels open as the icy wind streamed into the yard from the street. I was freezing. But I quickly realized I couldn't let that bother me, for I spotted a tall man slowly walking our way from the direction in which the cattle merchants entered the village; he was holding the hand of a four- or five-year-old little girl. My heart nearly stopped. Then it began to pound. Even before I could make out his face I knew it was Father, that he had come home.

Morning, noon and night for the five years that he'd been gone, I'd imagined Father's homecoming as a spectacular occasion. The actual event was remarkably commonplace. He wasn't wearing a cap, and pieces of straw stuck to his greasy, uncombed hair; more straw was stuck in the little girl's hair, as if they'd just climbed out of a haystack. Father's face was puffy, there were chilblains on his ears and salt-and-pepper whiskers covered his chin. A bulging, khaki-coloured canvas knapsack, with a ceramic mug tied to the strap, was slung over his right shoulder. He was wearing a greasy, old-fashioned army greatcoat; two buttons were missing—their threads hung loose and their outlines were still visible. His pants were of an indistinguishable colour and his almost-new knee-high cowhide boots were mud-spattered although their tops shone like patent leather. The sight of those boots reminded me of Father's long-lost days of glory; if not for those boots, he'd have presented a truly dismal sight that morning. The girl wore a red wool cap with a little pompom that bounced as she struggled to keep pace with Father. She was wearing an oversized red down parka that went down nearly to her feet and made her look like an inflated rubber ball rolling down the road. She had dark skin, big eyes, long lashes and thick brows that nearly met to form a black line over her nose and that seemed out of place on a girl so young. Her eyes reminded me immediately of Father's lover, Mother's bitter enemy—Aunty Wild Mule. I didn't hate the woman, in truth I sort of liked her, and before she and Father ran off I used to love going over to her little wine shop, where I could feast on meat. That was one of the reasons I liked her, but not the only one. She was good to me; and once I discovered that she and Father were having an affair, I felt closer to her than ever.

I didn't call out nor did I do what I'd imagined I'd do, which was to rush madly into his arms and tell him about all the terrible things that had happened to me since he left. I also didn't report his arrival to Mother. All I did was scamper out of the way and stand absolutely still, like a bemused sentry. When she saw that the gate was open, Mother grabbed the handlebars and began to move the massive beast. She reached the gate at the same moment as Father with the little girl in tow.

'Xiaotong?' he said, in a voice filled with uncertainty.

I didn't say a word but stared at Mother's face, which had turned ashen, and at her eyes, which had frozen in their sockets. The tractor lurched like a blind horse towards the gate and Mother slid out of the cab as if she'd been shot.

Father froze, agape. Then he closed his mouth. Then opened it, then he closed it again. He looked at me guiltily, as if hoping I'd come to his rescue. Out of the corner of my eye I saw him lay his knapsack on the ground and let go of the little girl's hand before taking a few hesitant steps towards Mother. He turned back to look at me one more time, and I looked away. When he reached her—finally—he picked her up in his arms. Her eyes remained frozen in their sockets as she stared blankly at his face, as if sizing up a stranger. He opened his mouth—the yellow teeth again—then closed it— and the teeth disappeared. Only a few guttural sounds emerged. Without warning, Mother reached out and scratched his face. Then she fought her way out of his arms and ran to the house on legs that wobbled so much they looked as limp as noodles. She zigged and she zagged, a slipshod trajectory, but somehow managed to get inside our big house with its tiled roof. She slammed the door shut behind her, so hard that a pane of glass came loose, crashed to the ground and shattered into a million pieces. Deathly silence. Then an unswerving howl, followed by wails that swerved and spun.

Father stood in the yard like a rotting tree, embarrassment writ large across his face; as before, his mouth opened and closed, closed and opened. I saw three gashes on his cheek. Ghostly white at first, they soon filled with blood. The little girl looked up at him and began to bawl. 'Daddy, you're bleeding,' she cried out shrilly, in a lilting out-of-town accent. 'Daddy, you're bleeding . . .'

Father picked her up. She wrapped her arms round his neck and said through her sobs: 'Let's go away, Daddy.'

The tractor was still roaring, like a wounded animal. I went over and turned it off.

With the engine stilled, the crying sounds from Mother and the little girl thudded against my eardrums. Some early risers on their way to fetch water walked over to see what was wrong. Furious, I slammed the gate shut.

Father stood up with the girl in his arms and walked over to me. 'Don't you know who I am, Xiaotong?' he asked, his voice heavy with apology. 'I'm your dieh . . .'

My nose ached, my throat closed up.

He ruffled my hair with his big hand. 'Look how much you've grown since I last saw you,' he said.

Tears spilt from my eyes.

He wiped them dry. 'Be a good boy,' he said. 'Don't cry. You and your mother have done well. It does my heart good to see how well you're getting along.'

Finally I managed to squeeze the word Dieh out of my throat.

He set the girl on the ground and said: 'Jiaojiao, say hello to your brother.'

The girl tried to hide behind his legs while she eyed me timidly.

'Xiaotong,' he said, 'this is your sister.'

The girl had beautiful eyes that reminded me of the woman who always cooked meat for me. I liked her at once. I nodded.

With a sigh of relief, Father picked up his knapsack, then took me by one hand and the little girl by the other, and walked up to the house. Mother's wails came in waves, each swell greater than the last; by the sound of it, she wasn't going to stop anytime soon. Father lowered his head to think for a minute and then he rapped on the door. 'Yuzhen, I've been a terrible husband . . . I've come back to apologize and make it up to you . . .'

Tears gathered in his eyes, and in mine.

'I've come back to help make a good life for us all. The facts prove that the Yang family knows how life is supposed to be lived, and that the Luo family doesn't. If you can forgive me . . . I hope you can find it in your heart to forgive me . . .'

Father's profound self-criticism both moved and disappointed me. If he was serious about doing what he said, then if he stayed, he'd quit eating pig's head, wouldn't he? Mother yanked the door open and stood there, hands on her hips, her face ashen, her eyes red, her gaze searing. Father stumbled backward and the little girl scooted behind him, shaking from head to toe.

Mother spewed words like lava from a volcano: 'So this is what you've become, Luo Tong, you heartless bastard! Five years ago, you abandoned your wife and son to run off with that fox demon and live the good life. How dare you come back?'

'I'm scared, Daddy,' the little girl sobbed.

'How nice for you, a bastard child thrown into the bargain!' said Mother as she glared at the girl. 'The spitting image!' she snarled. 'A little fox demon! Why haven't you brought the big fox demon back with you? If she showed her face round here, I'd rip her cunt right out of her!'

Father smiled in embarrassment, his body language clearly saying 'You have to lower your head when you're under someone else's eaves.'

Mother slammed the door shut again. 'You take that bastard child and get the hell out of here,' she shouted from the other side. 'I don't want to see either one of you again! You didn't give us a thought until the fox demon tired of you and threw you out. Go away! You're already dead in the hearts of your wife and son.'

She stormed into her room and began to cry once more.

His eyes closed, Father was breathing like an asthmatic on his last legs. 'Xiaotong,' he said, once his breathing returned to normal, 'I hope you and your mother have a good life. I'll be going now . . .'

He rubbed my head a second time, then squatted to let the girl climb onto his back. But she was too small, and her coat too bulky; she made it halfway before sliding back to the ground. So he reached behind him, grabbed her by the legs and boosted her onto his back. Then he stood up and leaned forward, sticking his neck out as far as it would go, like an ox in a slaughterhouse. His bulging knapsack swayed under his arm, like a cow's stomach hanging from a butcher block.

'Don't go, Dieh,' I cried, grabbing his overcoat. 'I won't let you go!'

I banged on the door. 'Niang!' I shouted to Mother. 'Niang, please let Dieh stay . . .'

'Tell him to get the hell out of here,' she screamed, 'the farther the better.'

I stuck my hand in through the gap where the glass pane had been, unlatched the door and flung it open.

'Go in, Dieh,' I said. 'You're staying for me.'

He shook his head and began to walk away with the girl on his back. But I grabbed his coat and began to cry again at the same time as I tried to pull him back through the door. As soon as we were inside, the heat from the stove wrapped itself round us. Mother was still cursing but not as loudly as before. And each outburst was followed by sobs.

Father set down the girl while I arranged a pair of stools round the stove for them. Perhaps no longer as frightened by Mother's crying, the girl seemed to gain a bit of courage. 'Daddy,' she said, 'I'm hungry.'

Father reached into his knapsack and took out a cold bun, which he broke into pieces and set on top of the stove. The smell of toasted buns quickly filled the room. He untied his ceramic mug and cautiously asked: 'Is there any hot water, Xiaotong?'

I fetched the vacuum bottle from the corner and filled his cup with warm, murky water. After making sure it wasn't too hot, he said: 'Here, Jiao-jiao, have some water.'

The girl looked at me, as if seeking my permission. I nodded, trying to be friendly. So she took the cup and began to drink, gurgling like a thirsty calf. Mother burst out of her room, snatched the mug out of the girl's hand and flung it into the yard, where it clattered noisily. Then she turned and slapped her. 'There's no water here for you, you little fox demon!'

The girl's cap was knocked off her head, exposing a pair of braids that had been curled up and pressed down under it, little white ties on the ends. '*Wah!*' she burst out crying, turned and ran into Father's arms, who jumped to his feet, trembling violently, his fists clenched. I knew it was wrong but I was hoping he'd slug Mother; but he slowly unclenched his fists and held the girl close. 'Yang Yuzhen,' he said softly, 'I know how you must loathe me, and I wouldn't blame you if you flayed me with a knife or shot me dead. But you have no right to hit a motherless child . . .'

Mother stumbled backwards, the icy look in her eyes beginning to thaw. She fixed her gaze on the little girl's head, and kept it there for a long moment. Finally, she looked up. 'What happened to her?'

'It didn't seem like much,' he said softly, 'just a touch of diarrhoea. But that went on for three days, and then she died . . .'

The hate on Mother's face was replaced by one of goodwill. But the anger in her voice remained: 'Retribution, that's what it was, divine retribution!'

Then she went into the other room, opened a cupboard and brought out a packet of stale biscuits. She tore open the oilpaper wrapping, took some out and handed them to Father. 'Give them to her,' she said.

Father shook his head, refusing to take them.

Now awkward, Mother laid them on the stove and said: 'No matter what kind of woman winds up in your arms, a bad life and a cruel death await her. The only reason I'm still alive is that my karma is stronger than yours!'

'I wronged her, and I wronged you.'

'Keep your fine words to yourself, they mean nothing to me. You can talk till the heavens open up, and I still won't share my life with you. A good horse doesn't graze the grass behind it. If you had any backbone, I couldn't keep you here even if I wanted to.'

'Niang,' I said, 'let Dieh stay.'

'Aren't you afraid he'll sell the house to feed his face?' she asked with a snide grin.

'You're right,' Father said, smiling bitterly, 'a good horse doesn't graze the grass behind it.'

'Xiaotong,' Mother turned to me. 'Let's you and me order some meat and wine at a restaurant. After suffering for five years, we deserve to enjoy ourselves for a change.'

'I won't go,' I said.

'You little shit! Don't do anything you'll regret.' Mother turned and walked outside. She'd taken off her sheepskin jacket and her black dogskin cap. Now she was wearing a blue corduroy jacket, and the collar of her red sweater that gave off sparks showed above her jacket. Back straight, head thrown back, she had a spring in her step, like a newly shod mare.

My anxiety lifted once she passed through the front gate. I picked up one of the baked buns and handed it to the girl, who looked up at Father; he nodded his approval. She took it from me and began eating, big bites followed by little ones.

Father took out a couple of cigarette butts from his jacket, rolled them both into a torn piece of newsprint and lit it at the stove. Through the blue smoke that emerged from his nostrils, I took note of his grey hair and the oozing chilblains on his ears. I thought back to the times he and I had gone to the threshing ground, where he'd priced the cattle, and to the times he'd taken me to Aunty Wild Mule's house, where I'd been fed plenty of meat, and I was filled with mixed emotions. I turned my back to him to keep from crying.

Then, out of the blue, I was reminded of our mortar. 'Dieh,' I said, 'we have nothing to fear, no one will ever pick on us again, because we've got a big gun.'

I ran to the side room, ripped away the carton paper, picked up the heavy base, and, straining mightily, stumbled out into the yard with it in my arms. I set it down carefully in front of the door.

Father walked out, followed by his daughter.

'Xiaotong, what's this?'

Without stopping to answer, I ran back into the side room, picked up the heavy tripod, carried it into the yard and laid it beside the base. On my third trip, I carried out the sleek tube, then assembled the whole thing, quickly and expertly, like a trained artilleryman. Then I stepped back and proudly declared: 'Dieh, you're looking at a powerful Japanese 82 mm mortar!'

He walked up cautiously to the mortar, bent down and examined it carefully.

When we'd first accepted the heavy weapon, it had been so rusted it had looked like three hunks of scrap metal. I'd attacked the rust with bricks, knocking off the biggest chunks, then switched to sandpaper and removed it from every inch of the metal, even inside the tube. Finally, I rubbed on several coats of grease, until it recaptured its youth, regained its metallic sheen; now it squatted open-mouthed on the ground, like a lion, ready to roar.

'Dieh,' I said, 'look inside the tube.'

Father turned his attention to the tube as a glare lit up his face. When he looked up, there was a sparkle in his eyes. I could see how excited he was. 'This is something,' he said, rubbing his hands together. 'Really something. Where'd you get it?'

I shoved my hands into my pockets and pawed the ground as nonchalantly as possible.

'From an old guy and his wife, who brought it on the back of an old mule.'

'Have you fired it?' he asked as he turned his attention back to the tube. 'I'm sure it'll fire, this is the real thing!'

'I was planning on going to South Mountain Village in the spring to look up that old man and his wife. They must have shells. I'll buy every one they've got, and the next person who picks on me will see what this thing can do to his house!' I looked up at Father and, with an ingratiating look, said, 'We can begin by blasting Lao Lan's house!'

With a bitter smile, Father shook his head but said nothing.

The girl had finished her baked bun. 'Daddy,' she said, 'I'm still hungry.'

Father went back inside and came out with the charred buns.

The girl was shaking. 'No,' she said. 'I want a biscuit.'

Father looked at me, obviously embarrassed. I ran inside, picked up the packet of biscuits Mother had tossed down by the stove and held them out to her. 'Here,' I said, 'eat.'

She reached out to take them but Father swept her up in his arms like a hawk taking a chicken.

She burst out crying.

'Be a good girl, Jiaojiao,' he said, wanting her to stop crying. 'We don't eat other people's food.'

That unexpected comment chilled my heart.

He shifted the girl, who would not stop crying, onto his back and patted me on the head with his free hand. 'Xiaotong,' he said, 'you're a big boy now, and you'll do better than your dieh ever did. Now you've got this mortar, and I know I won't have to worry about you.'

With his daughter settled on his back, he turned and walked to the gate. I struggled to hold back my tears as I ran after him.

'Do you have to go, Dieh?'

He cocked his head to look at me. 'Be careful with that mortar. Use it only when you have to, and don't use it on Lao Lan's house.'

The hem of his overcoat slipped through my fingers. After bending forward to make it easier for his daughter to hold on, he walked down the frozen road in the direction of the train station. He'd taken only a dozen steps or so when I shouted. 'Dieh—'

Though he didn't turn back to look, she did. A radiant smile spread across her tear-streaked face, like an orchid in spring or a chrysanthemum in autumn. She waved, sending sharp pains through that ten-year-old heart of mine. I sat down on my haunches and watched as, in about the time it takes to smoke a pipeful, the figures of my father and the little girl disappeared round a bend in the road. Then, after about twice as long, but from the opposite direction, Mother came rushing down the road with the head of a pig, white with red showing through. 'Where's your dieh?' she asked, alarmed, when she reached me.

Full of revulsion over the pig's head, I pointed towards the station.

Somewhere far off a rooster crows, weak but clear, and I know we've reached that moment when total darkness precedes the dawn. The sun will be up soon, and the Wise Monk still hasn't moved. Somewhere in the room a mosquito drones wearily. The candle has burnt down, the cool wax in the

*candleholder is shaped like a chrysanthemum. The woman lights a cigarette
and squints as the smoke drifts into her eyes. Then, with a burst of energy,
she stands and shrugs her shoulders, sending her robe sliding to the floor, like
dry tofu crust, gathering pathetically round her ankles. She steps on it with
both feet before sitting back in her chair, where she spreads her legs and first
rubs, then pinches, her nipples, spewing white streams of milk. I am both
aroused and mesmerized. As I sit, I watch as the slough of my body maintains
its shape, like a cicada, on the stool, while another me, this one stripped naked,
walks towards the streams of milk. They spray onto his forehead and into his
eyes, leaving drops on his face, like pearly tears. The milk spews into his
mouth; the strong taste of human milk fills mine. He kneels in front of the
woman and rests his head, with its chaotic mop of hair, on her belly, keeping
it there for a long time. Finally, he looks up and asks, as if talking in his sleep:
'Are you Aunty Wild Mule?' She shakes her head, then nods, then sighs and
says: 'You foolish little boy.' She cups her right breast and stuffs the nipple into
his mouth . . .*

A loud noise overhead sends down a mixture of broken tiles, rotting grass and mud from the sky; it smashes a bowl and drives a bamboo chopstick into the mildewed wall like an arrow. The woman who has sated me with her full breasts, the woman who is as warm as a sweet potato fresh from the oven, shoves me away. As she extracts her nipple from my mouth, stabbing pains attack my heart, I feel light-headed and fall to the floor on all fours. I try to scream but hardly any sound emerges, as if hands are choking me. Her eyes are glassy as her gaze sweeps the area as if seeking something. She wipes the wet nipples with her fingers and glowers at me. I jump to my feet, rush over and throw my arms round her. Bending, I begin to kiss her neck. She reaches down and pinches my belly, hard, then pushes me away and spits in my face. Then she turns and walks out of the room, buttocks swaying. I follow her, driven to distraction, and watch as she walks up to the Horse Spirit and mounts it from behind. The human-headed statue, with her on its back, flies out of the temple, filling the air with the sound of clattering hooves. I hear birds welcome the dawn with their chirps and, farther away, bovine mothers calling to their calves. I know that this is the hour they feed their young, and in my mind's eye I can see the calves hungrily bumping the teats with their heads as the happy yet agonizing mothers hunker down; but the breast that had been suckling me has vanished, so I sit on the cold, damp ground and cry shamelessly. After I have run out of tears, I look up and spot a hole the size of a basket in the roof, through which early morning sunlight enters like a tide. I smack my lips, as if I'd just awakened from a dream. But if this has been a dream, why does the taste of milk linger in my mouth? The injection of this mysterious liquid into my body carries me back to my youth, and even my adult body begins to shrink. If it hasn't been a dream, then where did the Aunty Wild Mule who isn't my Aunty Wild Mule go? I sit there staring woodenly at the Wise Monk, whom I'd forgotten, as he slowly returns to wakefulness, like

a python emerging from hibernation. Folding up his body in that room, suffused with the golden glow of dawn, he begins his qigong breathing exercises.
The Wise Monk is dressed in ordinary clothing—yes, it is the threadbare robe
the woman who suckled me had worn. He has a unique way of exercising.
Folding up his body, he takes his penis in his mouth and rolls round on his
wide bed like a wind-up toy with a taut spring. Steam rises from his shaved
head in seven distinct colours. At first, I didn't think much of his trifling
exercise regimen, but when I tried it I realized that rolling round on the bed is
no big deal, nor is folding up my body that way, but taking my penis in my
mouth—now that's a challenge.

Once he's finished, the Wise Monk stands on his bed to limber up, like a
horse that's been rolling in soft sand. A horse will shake its body to send loose
sand flying; the Wise Monk shakes his body to create a rainfall of sweat. Some
of the drops hit me in the face, and one flies into my mouth. I am astounded
to discover that his sweat has the fragrance of osmanthus, which now spreads
throughout the room. He is a big man with large, whirlpool-shaped scars on
his left breast and belly. Though I've never seen bullet wounds, I know that is
what they are. Most people shot in those vital areas go straight down to the
underworld, and to be not just alive but hale and hearty can only mean that
he enjoys great good fortune and an enviable karma, a man born under a lucky
star. As he stands on the bed, his head nearly brushes against the rafters, and
it seems to me that if he stretched himself as tall as he could, then he might
be able to stick his head out through the hole in the roof. Wouldn't that be a
fright—his head, with its incense scars, sticking up through the roof tiles at
the rear of the temple? Just think how stunningly strange that would look to
the hawks wheeling low in the sky. As the Wise Monk limbers up, his body is
exposed. It's a young man's body, in contrast to his old man's head. If not for
a slight paunch, it could be mistaken for the body of a thirty-year-old man;
but once he puts on his threadbare robe and sits cross-legged in front of the
Wutong Spirit, no one who saw only his face and bearing would doubt that he
was a man just shy of a hundred. Now that he's shaken the sweat off his body,
and is good and limber, he climbs off the bed. What I observed has vanished
under a robe that seems about to disintegrate. This has all the qualities of a
hallucination. I rub my eyes and, like the heroes in wildwood tales who ponder
their reactions to strange encounters, I bite my finger to see if I am dreaming.

A pain shoots through my finger, proof that I am in the flesh and that what I observed was real. The Wise Monk—at this moment he is a faltering Wise Monk—seems to have at that moment discovered me as I crawl up to him; he reaches out, pulls me to my feet, and, in a voice dripping with compassion, says: 'Young patron, is there something this aged monk can do for you?' 'Wise Monk,' I say, a myriad feelings welling up inside me, 'Wise Monk, I haven't finished my story from yesterday.' The Wise Monk sighs, as if recalling events of the day before. 'Do you want to continue?' he asks compassionately. 'If I keep it inside, Wise Monk, and don't let it all out, it will become an open sore, a toxic boil.' He shakes his head ambiguously. 'Come with me, young patron,' he says. I follow him into the temple's main hall, where we stop in front of the Horse Spirit, one of the five. In this just and honourable place, we kneel on the rush mat, which looks so much more tattered than it did yesterday, dotted, as it is, with grey rain-produced mushrooms. The flies that seemed to have crawled round in his ears the day before now swarm back and cover them completely; two hang in the air for a moment before landing on his exceptionally long, twisting eyebrows which shake like branches supporting squawking birds. I kneel beside the Wise Monk, my buttocks resting on the heels of my feet, to continue my story. But I am beginning to wonder if I am still firm in my goal to become a monk. It seems to me that, in the space of one night, my relationship with the Wise Monk has undergone a significant change. The image of his young, robust body, which radiates sexual passion, keeps appearing in front of my eyes and his threadbare monk's robe turns transparent, throwing my heart into turmoil. But I still feel like talking. As my father taught me: anything with a beginning deserves to have an ending. I continue—

Regaining her composure, Mother grabbed me by the arm and led me in the direction of the station, taking long strides.

My right arm grasped in her left hand and the white, pink-tinged pig's head in her right, we walked faster and faster and then finally broke into a run.

I tried to twist free of her iron grip but she held on. I was angry at her. Father came home this morning, Yang Yuzhen, and your attitude stinks! He's a good man who's down on his luck. The fact that he swallowed his pride and bowed to you may not qualify as earth-shattering but it was enough to draw tears. What more do you want, Yang Yuzhen? Why provoke him with such vile language? He gave you a way out, but instead of climbing off your high horse you cried and wailed and bawled and spewed a stream of ugly curses at a man who made a small mistake. How do you expect a respectable man to take that? Then, to make things worse, you dragged my little sister into it. Your slap sent her cap flying and exposed a white cotton knot, and then you made her cry, breaking the heart of someone who has the same father but a different mother—me. Yang Yuzhen, why can't you understand Father's feelings? Yang Yuzhen, a bystander—me—saw things more clearly than the actor—you—and you should know that you ruined everything with that slap. It destroyed any conjugal feelings he might have retained, it froze his heart. And mine. You're such a heartless mother that you've made me, Luo Xiaotong, wary of you. I was hoping he'd come back to live with us but now I think that leaving was the best thing he did. If it'd been me, I'd have left, and so would anyone with a shred of dignity. In fact, I should have gone with him, Yang Yuzhen, and left you to enjoy the good life in a five-room, tiled-roof house all by yourself!

My mind was racing, my thoughts all over the place, as I stumbled along behind Yang Yuzhen, my mother. My struggling to get away and the weight of the pig's head slowed us down. People stared at us—some curious, others obviously puzzled. On that extraordinary morning, the sight of my mother dragging me down the road leading from the village to the train station must have struck passers-by as a scene from a strange yet lively little drama. And it wasn't just people: even the dogs first looked, then barked, at us; one even nipped at our heels.

Though she was reeling from an emotional blow, she refused to let go of the pig's head. Instead of dropping it, the way a film actress might do, she held it tightly, like a beaten soldier who refuses to let go of his weapon. Holding on to me with one hand and clutching the unheard of purchase of a pig's head, meant to patch up things with my dieh, with the other, she ran as fast as she could, though it was difficult. Water glistened on her gaunt cheeks. Sweat or tears? I couldn't tell. She was breathing hard, yet she continued to gasp out a stream of curses. *Should she have been sent down to the Hell of Severed Tongues for that, Wise Monk?*

A motorbike passed us, a line of white geese hanging from the rear cross-bar, necks twisting as they writhed like snakes. Dirty water dripped from their beaks, like a bull urinating as it walks; the hard, dry road was lined with water stains. The geese honked pitifully and their little black eyes were forlorn. I knew their stomachs had been filled with dirty water, for anything that emerged from Slaughterhouse Village, dead or alive, did so full of water: cows, goats, pigs, sometimes even hen's eggs. A Slaughterhouse Village riddle runs: In the village of butchers, what is the only thing you can't inject with water? After two years, no one but I knew the answer. *How about you, Wise Monk, do you know the answer?* It's water! In a village of butchers, the only thing you can't inject with water is water itself!

The man on the motorbike turned to look at us. What's so damned interesting about us? I may have hated Mother, but not as much as I hated people who stared. She'd told me that people who laugh at widows and orphans suffer the wrath of Heaven. Which is what happened: he was so busy staring at us that he ran into a poplar tree. As he flew backward, his heels struck the goose-covered rear crossbar and all those soft, pliable necks got tangled up in his legs and he tumbled into a ditch. He was wearing a leather overcoat that shone like a suit of armour and a fashionable knit cap. Large-framed sunglasses perched on his nose. In a word, he was dressed like a film tough. There'd been rumours of bandits on the road for a while, so even Mother had begun to dress that way in an effort to keep up her courage; she even learnt how to smoke, though she refused to spend money on decent cigarettes. *Wise Monk, if you could have seen Mother in her black leather over-coat and cap and sunglasses, a cigarette dangling from her lips, sitting proudly on our tractor, you wouldn't have believed she was a woman.* I didn't get a good look at the man's face when he passed us, nor when he turned back to look. But when he somersaulted into the ice-covered ditch, his cap and sunglasses flying through the air, I had a perfect view—he was the township government's head cook and purchasing agent, a frequent visitor to our village. For years, he'd bought everything that contained animal fat or protein and then served it up on the tables of the Party and government officials. A man with political credentials impeccable enough to guarantee the safety, the very lives, of our township leaders, he'd been one of Father's drinking buddies. His name was Han, Han *shifu*. Father told me to call him Uncle Han.

Back when Father used to go to town to share a meaty meal with Uncle Han, he'd usually let me tag along. Once, when he left me home, I ran the ten *li* into town and found them at a restaurant called Wenxiang Lai, where they appeared to be having a serious discussion. A steaming pot of dog meat on the table saturated the area round them with its fragrance. I burst out crying the minute I saw them—no, better to say I burst out crying the minute I smelt the dog meat. I was terribly upset with Father. Unconditionally loyal, firmly in his camp in all his disputes with Mother, I even went so far as to keep secret his relationship with Aunty Wild Mule. And he went off for a meal of good meat leaving me at home! No wonder I burst out crying. 'What are you doing here?' he asked coldly when he saw me. 'Why didn't you bring me along if you knew there was going to be meat? Am I your son or aren't I?' Embarrassed, he turned to Uncle Han: 'Lao Han, have you ever seen anyone with a greedier mouth than this son of mine?' 'You came here to enjoy some meat and left me home with Yang Yuzhen to eat turnips and salted greens, and you call *me* greedy? What kind of dieh are you?' Just talking like that upset me even more. With the fragrance of the dog meat filling my nostrils, tears gushed from my eyes and ran down my cheeks until my face was wet. Uncle Han laughed. 'That son of yours, Lao Luo, he's quite a boy. He sure knows how to talk. Come here, young man,' he said. 'Sit down and eat to your heart's content. I hear you're a boy who lives to eat meat. Youngsters like you are the smart ones. Come see me anytime. I guarantee you won't go hungry. Boss lady, bring this boy a bowl and chopsticks.'

That was a wonderful meal. I ate and I ate, keeping the 'boss lady' busy adding dog meat and soup to the pot. I ate with single-minded concentration, not even stopping to answer Uncle Han's questions. 'He can eat half a dog at one sitting,' Father said to the owner. 'What's wrong with you, Lao Luo?' Uncle Han asked, 'How could you neglect your son like this? You have to let him eat. Meat makes the man. Know why we Chinese are no good at sports? It's because we don't eat enough meat. Why not give Xiaotong to me, let me raise him as my son? He'd have meat at every meal.'

I swallowed the piece of dog meat I was chewing and, moved to tears, stared at Uncle Han with an unprecedented depth of emotion. 'What do you say, Xiaotong, want to be my son?' He patted me on the head. 'You have my word you'll never go hungry.' I nodded enthusiastically . . .

Poor Uncle Han now lay in the roadside ditch, anxiously watching as we ran past his motorbike, which lay at the foot of the poplar tree, engine running, wheels twisted out of shape by the tree trunk yet still turning—barely—the rims rubbing against the fenders.

'Are you going into town, Yang Yuzhen?' he called out from behind us. 'Tell them to come to my rescue . . .'

I doubt Mother understood what he was shouting, for she was full of annoyance and anger, perhaps even of remorse and hope. I could only guess. Even she may not have known for certain. I recalled with gratitude the meal that Uncle Han had treated me to, and I wouldn't have minded helping him out of the ditch, if only I could have pulled my arm free of Mother's grip. But no luck.

A fellow on a bicycle shot past, like he was afraid of us. It was Shen Gang, who owed us two thousand yuan. Actually, it was a lot more than that, since he'd borrowed the money two years earlier, at 20 per cent interest per month. Interest upon interest, which meant—I heard Mother say—it was now over three thousand. We'd gone more than once to collect. At first he acknowledged the debt and said he'd pay us back soon. Later, he tried the dead-dog trick. Staring at Mother, he'd say: 'Yang Yuzhen, I'm like a butchered pig that has no fear of boiling water. I've got no money and my life's not worth a thing to you. My business failed, and if you see anything worth taking then please do so. Either that or turn me over to the police—I don't mind a place that provides food and lodging.' We looked round in his house, and all we could see were a pot loaded with pig bristles and a rickety old bicycle. His wife lay on the sleeping platform, moaning like she was desperately ill. He'd come to us two years before, on the eve of the lunar New Year, wanting to borrow money to import a batch of cheap Cantonese sausage and then sell it over the holidays at a profit. Won over by his alluring scheme, Mother agreed to lend him the money. She pulled out the greasy notes from an inside pocket, then wet her fingers and counted them, again and again.

Before handing them over, she said: 'Shen Gang, don't forget how hard it's been for a single mother, with her poor child, to save up this money.'

'If you don't think you can trust me, Big Sister,' Shen Gang replied, 'then don't lend it to me. There are people out there, lots of them, who can't wait to lend me the money. I just feel sorry for the two of you, and want you to have the opportunity to make a packet . . .'

Well, he did bring in a truckload of sausage, which he unloaded, crate after crate, and stacked it in his yard in piles that rose higher than his fence. Everyone in the village said: 'Shen Gang, this time you've really struck it rich!' With a piece of sausage dangling from his lips, like a big cigar, he announced smugly: 'The money will roll in so fast I won't be able to stop it.' But Lao Lan dampened the mood when he walked by: 'Don't let it go to your head, young man, unless you've arranged for some cold storage. Otherwise, one breath of warm air will have you lying in the yard and crying your eyes out.' Those were particularly cold days, so cold that the dogs tucked their tails between their legs when they walked. Shen Gang bit down on the frozen sausage and said indifferently: 'Lao Lan, you prick of a village head, you should be happy to see one of your villagers get rich. Don't worry, you'll get your tribute.' 'Shen Gang,' replied Lao Lan, 'don't take a good man's heart for a donkey's guts, and don't be in too big a hurry to congratulate yourself. The day will come when you'll beg me to help. The man who runs the township's cold storage is my sworn brother.' 'Thanks,' said Shen Gang, still cocky, 'many thanks. But I'll let my sausage turn to dog shit before I come begging at your door.' Lao Lan's eyes narrowed into a smile. 'All right,' he said, 'you've got spine, and if there's one thing we Lans admire, it's that. Back during our wealthier days, we always placed a pair of vats outside our gate over lunar New Year's. One was filled with white flour, the other with millet, and any family too poor to celebrate the holiday was encouraged to take what they needed. There was only one man, a beggar, Luo Tong's grandfather, who stood in the gateway and cursed my grandfather: "Lan Rong, can you hear me, Lan Rong? I'll die of hunger before I take a kernel of your rice!" My grandfather summoned all my uncles and said: "Hear that? The man out there shouting insults at us has balls! You can offend other people but not him. If you meet up with him, bow your heads and bend low!"' 'That's enough,' Shen Gang interrupted. 'You can stop boasting about your glorious past.' 'Sorry about that,' Lao Lan said. 'Worthless descendants simply can't forget their predecessors' glories. Good luck with your get-rich scheme.'

Unfortunately for Shen, what happened next proved the wisdom of Lao Lan's words. During the holidays, a freak warm southeast wind rose up and turned the willow trees green. The cold-storage building in town was full, and there was no room for Shen Gang's meat. Moving his sausage crates out onto the street, he bellowed through a battery-powered bullhorn: 'Village elders, fellow citizens, help me, please. Take a crate of sausage home to your tables. Pay me only if can. If you can't, consider it a respectful gift.' But no one came to claim any of the gloomy, rapidly spoiling sausages. Except for the dogs, for whom spoilt meat was still meat. They tore open the crates and ran off with lengths of sausage, turning the village into a big banquet table and adding a new unpleasant odour to air already heavy with the fetid smell of slaughter. It was a year to remember for the wild dogs. The day the meat began to spoil, Mother paid him her first visit. But the loan remained unpaid until . . .

Father's second departure was perhaps more important to Mother than Shen Gang's delinquent loan, because all she did was greet him with a wordless glower. A grease-covered tin on the rear rack of Shen's bicycle gave off a mouth-watering smell. I knew what it was—red steamed pig's head and cooked entrails. My mind was flooded with the captivating image of braised pig's feet and twisted lengths of braised pig's guts, and I swallowed hungrily. The momentous family occurrence of that morning had not eradicated—in fact, it had increased—my yearning for meat. The sky is high, the earth is vast, but neither is the equal of Lao Lan's mouth; Father is close, Mother is dear, but neither matches the appeal of meat! Meat, ah, meat, the loveliest thing on earth, that which makes my soul take flight. Today was supposed to be a day when I could satisfy my yearning for meat but Father's second departure shattered that fanciful dream, or at least put it off for a while. I hoped it was only a slight delay.

The pig's head hung from Mother's hand; I could eat some of it if Father came home with us. But if he remained unshakeable in his refusal to return, whether Mother, in a fit of anger, would cook it and let me at it or sell it and make me go hungry was anyone's guess. Wise Monk, I was a truly unworthy child. Only moments before I'd been in agony over my Father's second departure, but then the smell of meat drove out every other thought from my mind. I knew I'd never amount to much. If I'd been born during a time of revolution and was unfortunate enough to be an officer in the enemy camp, all the revolutionary forces would have had to do was offer me a plateful of meat and I'd have surrendered my troops unconditionally. But then, if the tables were turned, and the enemy had offered me two bowls, I'd have brought my forces back and surrendered to them. Those were the kinds of despicable thoughts that filled my head. Later on, great changes occurred in my family, and once I could satisfy my desire whenever I felt like it, I finally realized that there were many things in this world more precious than meat.

Another bicycle went past.

'Hey, Yang Yuzhen, where are you off to? Going to sell that pig's head?'

I knew this one too. He was someone else who cooked braised pork; he too carried a tin on his bicycle and it too gave off a meaty aroma. He was Lao Lan's brother-in-law. He'd been called Su Zhou as a child; I forget his formal name. Perhaps that was because his nickname was so special—the name of that city down south. Su Zhou, Suzhou, what were his parents thinking when they gave him a name like that? He was one of the few men in our village who was not a butcher. Some people said he was a Buddhist, that he was opposed to killing, but he braised and sold the entrails of slaughtered animals. Grease on his lips and cheeks all day long, he reeked of meat from head to toe—you'd be hard pressed to consider him a Buddhist. I also knew that he added food colouring and formaldehyde to the meat, so his products were just like Shen Gang's—bright colour, strange smell. Doctored meat was supposed to be bad for your health, but I'd rather eat unhealthy meat than healthy turnips or cabbages. I still thought of him as a good man. As Lao Lan's brother-in-law, as his virtual lackey, he should have got on well with the older man. Surprisingly, he did not. Most people tried to get on the good side of our local despot but usually came away disappointed; this made Su Zhou an odd man in their eyes. Su Zhou said, 'There are consequences to everything, good and evil.' He said it to adults, he said it to children and when he was alone he probably said it to himself.

Su Zhou looked back as he rode past. 'Yang Yuzhen,' he shouted, 'if you're selling that pig's head, you don't need to go to town. Take it over to my place and I'll give you the same price. "There are consequences to everything, good and evil."'

Mother ignored him and ran on, dragging me behind her. Su Zhou was pedalling hard, trying to move against a headwind that had suddenly begun to blow. It bent the bare branches of the roadside poplars and set up a loud rustle, and the sky turned dark; the sun, at a height double that of the trees, trickled down thin red rays. Every once in a while we saw dried-up cow patties on the whitened, windswept road. The farming life of our village was dead and buried; the fields lay fallow and no one raised cows any longer. So those droppings had been left by the furtive cattle merchants from West County. The sight of those patties took me back to the glorious days when I'd accompanied Father as he priced cattle and reminded me of the enchanting fragrance of cooked meat. I swallowed a mouthful of saliva and looked up at Mother's face. Rivulets of sweat—possibly mixed with tears—dampened the collar of her sweater. Yang Yuzhen, I hate you and I pity you! My thoughts then turned inescapably to the pink oval face of Aunty Wild Mule. Dark eyebrows that met in the middle, above a pair of eyes with a little white showing, atop a long and lovely pointed nose that rose above a wide mouth. The look on her face always reminded me of an animal although I didn't know which one. Later, a man came to our village selling a fine breed of foxes. When I looked into their rabbit-hutch cages and saw the secretive looks on their faces, then I knew.

Every time I went with Father to Aunty Wild Mule's house, she greeted me with a smile and handed me a steaming piece of beef or pork. 'Eat,' she'd say, 'eat as much as you want. There's more where that came from.' Her smile seemed to me tinged with something slightly devious, slightly evil, as if she were trying to lure me into doing something wrong simply because it would amuse her. I liked her anyway. She never actually got me to do anything wrong. Even if she had, I'd have gone along with it. Then I saw her and Father in each other's arms—*and I tell you the truth, Wise Monk*—I was moved to tears by the sight. I didn't know then about what went on between men and women, and I couldn't understand why Father pressed his lips against hers, or why they made all those slurping sounds, like they were trying to suck something out of each other's mouth (and they actually did suck out something sweet and delicious). Now I know that's called smooching, or, more refined, kissing. I, of course, had no idea what it felt like but the expressions on their faces and the way they moved struck me as something quite passionate; it may have also been agonizing because I saw tears in Aunty Wild Mule's eyes.

Mother was almost worn out; by the time Su Zhou rode past, her pace had slowed considerably, as had mine. It was not because she was having second thoughts, no, not that. She still wanted to get to the train station and bring Father home. Take my word for it. She was my mother, and I understood her; I could tell what she was thinking just by looking at her face and listening to her breathe. The main reason she was slowing down was exhaustion. She'd risen before dawn, lit a fire, cooked breakfast, loaded the tractor; then, taking advantage of the freezing temperature, poured water on the paper to make it heavier. Then had followed the dramatic reunion with Father, and she'd run off to buy a pig's head, and, I suspect, a bath at the sulphur springs that had just opened in our village (I could smell the sulphur when I saw her at the door). Her face glowed, her spirits soared and her hair was wet, all evidence of a bath. She'd come home filled with hope and happiness only to have Father's second departure hit her like a bolt of lightning or a bucket of icy water, chilling her from head to toe. Any other woman suffering a blow like that would have gone mad or cried her eyes out; my mother stood there glass-eyed and slack-jawed, but only for a moment. She knew that falling to the ground and pretending to die was not in her best interest, nor, especially, was another round of tears. What she needed to do was get to the train station as fast as possible and, before the train left, stop that homeless man—who had somehow retained his integrity—from leaving. For a while after Father left the first time, Mother had been fond of a saying she'd picked up somewhere: 'Moscow doesn't believe in tears!' It became her mantra. That and Comrade Su Zhou's 'There are consequences to everything, good and evil' were a pair of couplets that spread through the village. Mother's fondness for this saying revealed her grasp of reality. Crying does not help in a crisis. Moscow didn't believe in tears, nor did Slaughterhouse Village. The only way to deal with a crisis was to take action.

We stood at the door of the station's waiting room, trying to catch our breath. Ours was a tiny station on a feeder line, and only a few local freight trains that also carried passengers stopped there. A wall with posters, fragments of slogans still stuck to them, stood in the windswept plaza. Underground enemies had scrawled counterrevolutionary slogans in chalk, mostly insults hurled at leaders of the local Party and government organizations. A woman selling roasted peanuts had set up shop in front of the wall—she wore a dark red scarf and a white surgical mask that showed only her eyes and their furtive look. A man stood beside her, arms crossed, a cigarette dangling from his lips, bored stiff. An iron basin sat on the rear rack of the bicycle in front of him, and the smell of cooked meat wafted across from beneath a strip of gauze. It wasn't Shen Gang, and it wasn't Su Zhou. Where had they gone? Had all their beautiful, ambrosia-scented meat already wound up in someone else's stomach? How would I know? One sniff told me that the meat in that man's basin was beef and cow entrails, and that it had been injected with a large amount of food colouring and formaldehyde, which made it look fresh from the slaughterhouse and smell quite wonderful. My gaze sidled over to it, like a fishhook, aiming to snatch a piece. But my body was in the grip of my mother and being reluctantly dragged to the waiting-room door.

It was one of those spring doors that had been out of fashion for more than a decade. You had to fight to get it open, which it did at last and with a loud clang. When you let go, it sprang shut and then bounced right back— if you hadn't moved away, it would slam into your backside and make you stumble if you were lucky and knock you to the floor if you weren't. I pulled the door open for Mother, then leapt in behind her; by the time the door slammed shut I was safely inside, ruining the crafty door's plan to send me flying.

I immediately spotted Father and the pretty girl he and Aunty Wild Mule had created—my little sister. Thank God they hadn't left yet.

Someone—I don't know who—flings a bloody, foul-smelling army uniform through the door, and it lands between the Wise Monk and me. I stare at the ominous object, startled, and wonder what's going on. There's a coin-sized hole in the uniform, right where the rank smell is the strongest. I also detect the faint odour of gunpowder and cosmetics. Something white is tucked into one of the pockets. A silk scarf? Filled with curiosity, I reach out to touch it but just then a pile of mud and rotting reeds, loosened by shards of roof tile, falls from the sky and covers the bloody clothes, and there, between the Wise Monk and me, a tiny grave is created. I look into the rafters, where a sun-drenched skylight has broken through the blackness. I'm terrified that this temple, forgotten by the world, is about to come crashing down, and I begin to fidget. But the Wise Monk doesn't budge, having regulated his breathing so as to appear absolutely still. The haze outside has cleared and bright sunlight covers the ground, turning the dampness in the yard into steam. The leaves on the gingko tree have an oily sheen, radiating life. A tall man in an orange leather jacket, drab olive wool pants and bright red calfskin knee-length boots, his hair parted in the middle, wearing a pair of small, round sunglasses and gripping a cigar between his teeth, materializes in the courtyard.

The man stands straight and stiff; his dark skin, with its reddish glow, reminds me of one of those arrogant yet brave US army officers you see in war films. But he's not one of those—he's Chinese through and through. And the second he opens his mouth to speak I can tell he's a local. Despite his familiar accent, his clothes and the way he moves tell me there's something mysterious about his origins, that he's no ordinary man. He's been around. Compared to him, our resident VIP, Lao Lan, looks like a country bumpkin. (As I think this I can almost hear Lao Lan say: 'I know those urban petty bourgeois look down on us, think we're a bunch of country bumpkins. Crap! Just who are they calling country bumpkins? My third uncle was a pilot in the Chinese Air Force, a drinking buddy of Chennault, the Flying Tigers leader. Back when most Chinese hadn't even heard about the US, my third uncle was making love to an American woman. How dare they call us bumpkins?') The man walks up to the temple and smiles, a mischievous, childlike gleam in his eyes. I feel as if I know him, that we're close. He unzips his pants and aims a stream of piss at the temple door, and some of the drops splash onto my bare feet. The man's tool does not suffer in comparison with that of the Horse Spirit behind the Wise Monk. He must be trying to humiliate us, but the Wise Monk doesn't so much as twitch; in fact, a barely perceptible smile appears on his face. There's a direct line between his face and the man's tool, while I can only see it out of the corner of my eye. If he can look straight at it and not be upset, why should I let a sideways glance upset me? The man's bladder holds enough to drown a small tree. The urine bubbles, like the foam on a glass of beer, as it pools round the Wise Monk's tattered prayer mat. Finally finished, he shakes his tool contemptuously. Realizing that we're ignoring him, he turns his back, stretches his arms and throws out his chest and a muted roar emerges from his mouth. Sunlight shines through his right ear, turning it as pink as a peony. I catch sight of a crowd of women who look like 1930s dance-hall socialites, in form-

fitting qipaos *that show off their curvaceous, slim bodies, their hair permed in loose or tight curls, their bodies glittering with jewellery. The way they carry themselves, the way they frown and the way they smile—modern women would have trouble keeping up. Their bodies give off a stale but regal odour, and I find it deeply moving. I have a feeling that we are somehow related. The women are like brightly feathered birds, warbling orioles and trilling swallows—chirp-chirp, tweet-tweet—as they rush to surround the man in the leather jacket. Some of them tug at his sleeves, others grab his belt; some sneak a pinch on his thigh, others stuff slips of paper in his pockets; some even feed him sweets. One of them, of an indeterminate age, seems more daring than the others. She wears silver lipstick and a white silk* qipao *with a red rose embroidered on the breast that, at first glance, makes her look as if she's been struck by bullets but has survived. High breasts, like doves. She looks like a siren. She walks up to the man, jumps into the air, her stiletto heels leaving the muddy ground, and grabs hold of his large ear. 'Xiao Lan, you're an ungrateful dog!' she curses in a sweetly husky voice. The man called Xiao Lan responds with an exaggerated scream: 'Ouch, Mamma, I might be ungrateful to others but not to you.' 'How dare you argue with me!' she says, squeezing harder. The man cocks his head and pleads: 'Mamma, dear Mamma, not so hard. I'll be good from now on. Why don't I make it up by taking you out for a late-night snack?' The woman lets go: 'I know your every move like the back of my hand,' she says spitefully, 'and if you think you can get frisky with me, I'll get someone to cut off your balls, you dog bastard!' Cupping his crotch with his hands, the man shouts: 'Spare me, Mamma, I need these little treasures to carry on my line.' 'You can carry on your old lady's thighs,' she curses. 'But I'll give you a chance to redeem yourself for the sake of my sisters out there. Where will you take us?' 'How about Heaven on Earth?' he asks. 'No. They've hired a new bouncer, a foreign devil with terrible BO. Just a whiff's enough to make me ill,' says a woman with big eyes, a pointy chin and a shrill voice. She's in a purple* qipao *with tiny flowers and has tied her hair with a purple silk band. Lightly made-up, she has a refined, cultured look, a sort of cornflower elegance. 'Then let Miss Wang decide,' says a woman so fat she's nearly bursting through the seams of her yellow silk* qipao. *'She's shared meals with Xiao Lan in every eatery in town, so she must know where to go.' Miss Wang manages to keep smiling, though there is the trace of a sneer. 'You can't*

*beat the shark's fin soup at Imperial Garden. What do you think, Mrs Shen?'
she says, seeking the opinion of the woman who'd pinched Xiao Lan's ear a
moment earlier. 'If Miss Wang likes Imperial Garden, that's good enough for
me,' replies Mrs Shen with aristocratic nonchalance. 'Then let's go!' cries the
man says with a wave of his arm as he sets off in the company of the women,
his arms circling the nicely rounded buttocks of the two closest to him. They're
gone before I know it but their fragrances remain, saturating the air in the
compound and merging with the smell of the man's urine to produce a strange,
irritating, ammonia-tainted odour. The sound of a car engine and they're off.
As tranquillity returns to the temple and its compound, I cast a glance at the
Wise Monk and know what's expected of me: to continue my story. 'Since
there's a beginning, there has to be an ending.' So I say—*

There were only a few people waiting for trains, which made the waiting
room seem bigger than it was. Father and his daughter were curled up on a
slatted wooden bench near the central heater. Another dozen passengers sat
here and there. Warm sunlight filtering in through the dirty windows lent a
silvery sheen to Father's hair. He was smoking a cigarette; white wisps of
smoke rose from both sides of his face and seemed to hang in the air round
his head, as if they hadn't emerged from his mouth or nose but had oozed
from his brain. His cigarette smelt terrible, like burnt rags or rotting leather.
By then he'd fallen on such hard times that he was reduced to scrounging
cigarette butts off the street, no better than a beggar. Worse, in fact. I knew
of beggars who lived extravagant lives, who ate good food and drank good
wine, who passed their days in the lap of luxury, smoking high-class cigarettes and drinking imported whisky. During the day they dressed in rags
and walked the streets and used a number of tricks to get alms. At night they
changed into Western suits and leather shoes and headed off to karaoke par-
lours to sing their hearts out, and then set off to find a girl. Yuan Seven in
our village was one of those high-flying beggars. Traces of him could be found
in every big city in the country. A man of the world, he'd seen it all and done
it all; he could imitate a dozen or more domestic dialects, even a few phrases
in Russian. The minute he opened his mouth you knew he was someone special, and even Lao Lan, the supreme authority in our village, treated him with
a measure of respect and never dared to show him up. He had a good-looking
wife at home and a son in middle school who always received good grades.

He proudly admitted that he had families in ten or more big cities, putting him in the enviable position of having a happy home to return to no matter where he was. Yuan Seven dined on sea cucumbers and abalone, drank Mao-tai and Wuliangye and smoked Yuxi and Da Zhonghua cigarettes from Yunnan. A beggar like that could turn down an offer to be county magistrate. If my father had been that kind of beggar, the Luo family would have been the envy of all. Unfortunately, he was in a sort of limbo between life and death, reduced to smoking cigarette butts off the street.

The waiting room was warm and toasty and seemed to possess a dreamy atmosphere. Most of the travellers dozed as they waited, making the place look a bit like a henhouse. Their belongings, in bundles big and small, lay at their feet, alongside fake snakeskin bags that threatened to burst at the seams. The only 'hens' who looked out of place were two men with no luggage except for well-worn faux-leather satchels resting against their legs. They were lying on a bench, face to face, the space between them covered by a sheet of newspaper on which lay a pile of sliced, red-speckled pigs' ears. Not what you'd call fresh but still good enough to eat. I knew they were from animals that had died—not slaughtered but sick pigs treated to look palatable. Where I come from, it doesn't matter what kills an animal—swine fever, erysipelas or hoof-and-mouth disease. We have ways to make any kind of meat look appetizing. There's no crime in being greedy but there is in being wasteful—that particular reactionary comment was enunciated by our very own Village Head Lan, and the old son of a bitch could have been shot for it. The men were feasting and getting drunk on what people call white lightning, local stuff but sort of famous, produced by Master Liu's family. Who was Master Liu? you ask. I couldn't say. Though no Liu family I knew ever made spirits, unscrupulous individuals distilled them under that family name. The smell alone was enough to kill you. Perhaps it was distilled methanol? Methanol, formaldehyde—China's become a nation of chemical wizards. Formaldehyde and methanol are like money in the bank. I swallowed a mouthful of saliva and watched them hand the green bottle back and forth, sipping and smacking their lips, stopping only to pick up a pig's ear—no chopsticks required, hands only—and stuff it into their mouths. The one with the long, skinny face even tipped back his head and dropped one into his mouth just to make my mouth water, the no-good arsehole, the cunning prick. By the look of him, he could have been a cigarette-peddler, even a cattle thief. He was no good, whatever line of work he was in, but he thought he was something special. So you're eating and drinking—big deal! If we wanted to eat at home, we'd do better than you. Our butchers can tell the difference between meat from a sick animal and meat from a slaughtered one, and they'd never be caught smacking their lips over meat from a sick pig. Sure, if there was no slaughtered pork they might eat a little from a sick pig. I once heard Lao Lan say that we Chinese are blessed with iron stomachs that can turn rotten stuff into nutrients. My mouth watered as I gaped at the pig's head in Mother's hand.

Father seemed to sense that someone was standing in front of him. He looked up, and his face turned purple from embarrassment. His lips parted to expose the yellow teeth. His daughter, my little half-sister Jiaojiao, who had been sleeping beside him, woke up. The sleepy eyed girl's pink face could not have been cuter. She snuck up close to Father and sneaked a look at us from under his arm.

Mother made a sound in her throat—a fake cough.

Father made a sound in his throat—a fake cough.

Jiaojiao had a coughing fit and her face turned red.

I could tell she'd caught a cold.

Father gently thumped her back to stop the coughing.

Jiaojiao coughed up a wad of phlegm, and began to cry.

Mother handed me the pig's head, reached down and tried to pick up the girl. Jiaojiao began to cry harder and burrowed into Father's protective arms, as if Mother had the thorny hands of a child-snatcher. People who bought and sold children or who bought and sold women often stopped here, because it was a rich village. The peddlers of human cargo did not arrive with stolen children or bound women in tow. They were too clever for that. They'd walk up and down the village streets pretending to sell wooden hairbrushes or bamboo head-shavers. The fellow who sold combs could talk with the best of them and had a terrific routine—a string of witty remarks and plenty of humour. To prove the quality of his head-shavers he'd even saw a shoe in half with one of them.

Mother straightened up, stepped back and wrung her hands, then took a quick look round as if hoping someone would come to her aid. Three seconds after she turned to look at me, her eyes clouded over and my heart ached to see her so helpless. She was, after all, my mother. As she let her hands drop, she looked down at the floor, possibly to take in Father's boots, which, despite the mud, looked to be of pretty good leather. They were the only evidence of the respectable stature he'd once enjoyed.

'This morning,' she said so softly you'd have thought she was talking to herself, 'my words were too strong . . . it was cold, I was tired, in a bad mood . . . I've come to apologize . . .'

Father fidgeted in his seat, as if being bitten by fleas. 'Don't talk like that, please,' he waved his hands and stammered. 'You were right, I deserve everything you said. I should be apologizing to you . . .'

Mother took the pig's head from me and rolled her eyes at me. 'Why are you standing there like a moron? Help your dieh with his things so we can go home.'

Then she glared at me once more and headed for the door, which creaked on rusty hinges. The pig's head flashed white for an instant before vanishing. 'Damn door,' I heard her grumble.

I hopped over, sparrow-like, to the bench where Father sat to take the bulging canvas satchel from him but he grabbed the strap, looked me in the eye and said: 'Xiaotong, go home and take care of your mother. I'd be a burden to you both . . .'

'No,' I insisted, refusing to let go. 'I want you to come with me, Dieh.'

'Let go,' he began sternly but then grew forlorn. 'Son,' he said, 'A man needs dignity the way a tree needs bark. Your dieh has fallen on hard times but he's still a man, and what your mother said is true—a good horse doesn't graze the land behind it.'

'But she apologized!'

'Son!' I could see his mood darkening. 'A man's heart is easily bruised, like the roots of a tree.' He yanked the satchel out of my hand and waved his hand towards the exit. 'Go now, and do as your mother says.'

'Dieh,' I sobbed, tears gushing from my eyes, 'don't you want us any more?'

His eyes were moist as he looked at me. 'That's not it, my boy, that's not what this is about. You've got a good head on your shoulders, I don't have to explain things to you.'

'Yes, you do!'

'Go, now,' he said decisively. 'Go, and stop bothering me!' He picked up his satchel, pulled Jiaojiao to her feet and took a quick look round, as if to find a better place to sit. Everyone was looking at us, agog with curiosity, but he didn't care. He picked up Jiaojiao and moved her to a rickety slat bench by the window. Before he sat down, he fixed his bulging eyes on me. 'What are you hanging round for?' he bellowed.

I backed up fearfully. He'd never spoken to me like that, at least not that I could recall. I turned and looked at the door behind me, wishing Mother could tell me what to do. But it was shut tight and not in the least welcoming. Only a few snowflakes blew in through the cracks.

A middle-aged woman in a blue uniform and a stiff hat walked into the waiting room with a red battery-powered bullhorn. 'Tickets! Tickets! All passengers for Train 384 to the Northeast Provinces line up with your tickets.'

The passengers scrambled to their feet, tossed their bundles over their shoulders and lined up to have their tickets punched. The two men gulped down what remained in their bottles, gobbled up the last of the pigs' ears, wiped their greasy mouths, then belched and staggered up to the gate. Father fell in behind them, carrying Jiaojiao.

I stood there staring at their backs, wishing he'd turn to see me one more time. I refused to believe that he could walk away from me so easily. But he didn't turn, and I stood there, unable to take my eyes off his overcoat, so dirty and greasy it shone, like a wall in a butcher's house. But Jiaojiao, whose little face poked up over his shoulder, sneaked a look at me. The ticket-collector was waiting, her arms crossed, next to the gate at the platform.

As the train rumbled up it sent a shudder through the floor. The next thing I heard was a long, shrill whistle, and an old steam engine suddenly loomed up behind the gate, belching thick black smoke as it clanked its way into the station.

As soon as the woman opened the gate to punch the tickets, the line surged forward, like under-chewed meat hurrying down your throat. Before I knew it, it was Father's turn—this was it. Once he went through the gate, he'd disappear from my life forever.

I was standing no more than fifteen feet from him. As he handed the crumpled ticket to the woman, I shouted at the top of my lungs: 'Dieh—'

Father's shoulders jerked, as if he'd been shot. But still he refused to turn. Snowflakes blown in through the gate by a northern breeze stuck to him as if he were a dead tree.

The ticket-collector eyed Father suspiciously, then turned to me with a strange look. Then she squinted at the ticket he'd handed her, examining it front and back as if it were counterfeit.

Much later, no matter how hard I try, I can never recall exactly how Mother materialized in front of me. She still held the pig's head, white with a tinge of red, in her left hand, while she pointed assertively at Father's shiny back with her right. Somewhere along the line she'd undone the buttons of her blue corduroy overcoat; the red polyester turtleneck sweater peeked out from underneath. That image has stuck with me all these years and always gives way to mixed feelings. 'Luo Tong,' she began, pointing at his back, 'you son of a bitch, what kind of a man walks out on his family like that?'

If a moment before my shout hit Father like a bullet in the back, then Mother's angry outburst was like the spray from a machine gun. I saw his shoulders begin to quake and Jiaojiao, who had been secretly watching me with her dark little eyes, tucked her head deeper in his arms.

With a dramatic gesture, the ticket-collector punched Father's ticket and then stuffed it into his hand. Out on the platform, passengers were disembarking from the train, like beetles rolling their precious dung, threading their way past lines of people impatient to board. With a barely concealed smirk, the ticket-collector looked at Mother, then at me and then finally at Father. Only she could see his face. The canvas bag, to which his enamel mug was attached, slipped off his shoulder, forcing him to reach out and grab the strap. Mother chose that moment to fire a lethal salvo: 'Go, then, just go! What kind of man are you? If you had an ounce of pride, you'd walk off holding your head high and not slink away like a dog to that bitch of yours! You obviously don't have an ounce of pride, or you wouldn't have come back this time. And not just come back, but laden with excuses and apologies. A few unkind words and you crumple, is that it? Did you give a single thought over the past few years to how your wife and child were getting along? Do you even care that they've suffered things no human being should be put through? Luo Tong, you are a heartless bastard, and any woman who falls into your hands is fated to wind up just like me—'

'That's enough!' Father spun round. His face was the colour of clay tiles that never see the sun; his scraggly beard like frost on those tiles. But he'd no sooner spun round than his body, displaying some momentary vigour, shrank back in on itself, and he said again—'That's enough'—but this time in a shaky voice that seemed to come from somewhere deep in his throat.

Out on the platform, a whistle jogged the ticket-collector back to life.

'The train's departing,' she shouted, 'it's about to leave the station. Are you going or aren't you? What's your problem?'

Father turned back, again with difficulty, and stumbled forward. The bag slipped off his shoulder but this time he didn't care if it dragged along the floor like a cow's stomach stuffed with rotting grass.

'Hurry!' the ticket-collector urged.

'Wait!' Mother shouted. 'Just wait until the divorce papers are signed. I'm not going to be a straw widow any longer.' Then, to emphasize her contempt, she said: 'I'll pay for the ticket.'

Mother grabbed me by the hand and bravely headed towards the exit. I could hear her crying, though she tried to stifle the sobs. When she let go of my hand to open the door, I looked back, and there was Father, sliding to the floor, his back up against the gate, which the ticket-collector, anger and disappointment writ large on her face, was trying to shut. Through the gaps in the gate I watched the train make its way out of the station and, amid the rumble of the iron wheels and the low swirling smoke from the engine, my eyes filled with tears.

I dry my eyes with the back of my hand. A couple of teardrops stick to the skin. I'm moved by my own tale of woe, but the monk reacts with what seems to be a sardonic smile. 'What do I have to do to get a little sympathy from you?' I grumble. I don't know, but I'll find a way to touch your heart. Whether I become a monk or not makes no difference at this point. All I care about is using the sharp point of my story to break through the crust of ice that shrouds your heart. Outside, the sun is strong, and I can tell its location by the tree's shadow: it's off in the southeast, about two pole-lengths from the horizon, by the measuring standard we use back home. A big chunk of the water-soaked compound wall, which has blocked our field of vision, even with its cracks and holes, crumbles after being pounded by a night of rain. All it will take to topple what remains is a strong gust of wind. The two cats that hardly ever leave the comfort and protection of the tree are taking a leisurely stroll atop the teetering portion of the wall. When they head east, the female is in front; when they head west, the male takes the lead. There's also a young roan stallion, a fine animal with a satiny coat rubbing against what's left of the wall. Wanting to lie down, but unable to find a reason for doing so, this is the excuse the wall needs. Its remains are strewn across the ground, dead. Most of it has collapsed into a ditch, sending stagnant water flying ten feet in the air, only to fall back in a bright cascade. The female cat crawls out of the ditch, covered with mud; no sign of the male. Caterwauling grief spills from her mouth as she paces beside the ditch. The young colt, on the other hand, gallops away, feeling its oats. Despite the male cat's bad luck, a collapsing wall is an exciting event. And the bigger and more intimidating the occurrence, the greater the sense of excitement. Now the highway beyond the compound lies spread out before us, as does a rammed-earth stage that has been thrown up on the broad grassy field on the other side, surrounded by colourful banners stuck in the ground and a large horizontal, slogan-bearing banner in front. A generator is up and running on a yellow truck; a blue-and-white TV van is parked off to the side. A dozen little men in yellow shirts run about dragging black cables behind them. Ten motorcycles in an impressive triangular forma-tion, the sun shining behind them, come our way at thirty miles an hour. 'There's nothing more impressive than a motorcycle gang!' I heard that line in a film once, and it's stayed with me ever since. When something makes me really happy or miserably sad, that's what I shout: 'There's nothing more impressive than a motorcycle gang!' 'What does that mean?' my sister once asked me. 'It means exactly what it says,' I replied. If that darling little girl were with me now, I'd point to the motorcycles across the way and say, 'Jiao-jiao, that's what "There's nothing more impressive than a motorcycle gang!" means.' But she's dead, so she'll never know. Ah, that makes me so sad. No one knows my sorrow!

The motorcycles stay in tight formation, as if welded together with an invisible steel pipe. The bikers wear identical white helmets and uniforms, their waists cinched by wide belts from which hang black holsters. Two black sedans with red and blue flashing lights and blaring sirens are thirty yards or so behind the motorcycles, leading the way for three even blacker cars. Wise Monk, those are Audis, so the men inside them must be high-ranking cadre. The Wise Monk's eyes open a crack and send purple rays of light to the cars but just as quickly draw them back. Another pair of police cars brings up the rear; no sirens. I follow the passage of this overweening caravan with my eyes, so excited I feel like shouting. But the Wise Monk's statue-like calmness cools my ardour in a heartbeat. 'It has to be a big shot,' I say softly, 'a very big shot.' Wise Monk ignores my comment. What's a big shot like that doing on a day like this? I think to myself. Not a holiday, not a special day, just another day. Oh, of course! How could I forget? It's the first day of the Carnivore Festival, Wise Monk. It's a holiday created by the butchers in my village. Ten years ago, we—I, mainly—came up with this holiday, but it was quickly taken over by people in the township. One celebration later, it was quickly taken over by people in the city. Wise Monk, I got as far away from the village as possible after my mortar attack on Lao Lan, but I still get the news and hear all kinds of talk about me. If you take a trip to my hometown, Wise Monk, and ask the first person you meet on the street: 'Does the name Luo Xiaotong mean anything to you?', you'll get an earful of gossip and rumours. I'll be the first to admit that a lot of what you'll hear has been blown out of proportion, and things other people did have somehow got stuck to my name. But there's no denying that Luo Xiaotong—the Luo Xiaotong of ten years ago, not now—was special. There was, of course, someone else who had a similar reputation, and I don't mean Lao Lan. No, it was Lao Lan's third uncle, a man who had relations with forty-one different women in the space of a single day, a remarkable feat that

made it into the Guinness Book of Records. *Or so that bastard Lao Lan said, for what it's worth, and that's what I heard too. Wise Monk, there's nothing about my hometown I don't know. The Carnivore Festival goes on for three days with a virtually endless array of events dealing with meat. Producers of every imaginable butchering and meat-processing machine erect display booths in the city square; discussion groups meet in the hotels to talk about raising livestock, meat processing and the nutritional value of various meats. At the same time, restaurants, big and small, host lavish spreads to display their culinary genius. The phrase 'mountains and forests of meat' goes a long way towards describing these three days, a time for stuffing yourself as much and as often as you can. One of the highlights is the meat-eating competition in July Square, which attracts gourmands from all across the land. The winner receives three hundred and sixty meat coupons, each of which allows him to eat his fill at any of the city's restaurants. Or, if he prefers, he can trade them in for three thousand and six hundred jin of meat. I said the competition was one of the highlights of the Festival, but its true showstopper is the Meat Appreciation Parade. All festivals build up to a climax, and the Carnivore Fes-*
tival is no exception. The twin cities linked by the highway form a metropolis, like a weightlifting dumb bell. The participants in the grand parade traverse this street. Those from East City walk to the west, those from West City head east, and at a point along the way they meet, passing shoulder to shoulder in opposite directions. I tell you, Wise Monk, I've had a premonition that today those two factions will meet at a spot right in front of this temple of ours, in the broad field across the highway, and I'm certain that our wall collapsed just so we could have an uninhibited view of that encounter. I know you have great powers, Wise Monk, so it must have been you who made this happen . . . I'm babbling on and on when I spot a silver-grey Cadillac speeding in our direction from West City under the protection of a pair of Volvos. No motor-cycles or police cars leading the way, but the vehicles exhibit a casual noncha-lance and indifferent dignity. When the cars reach a spot opposite the temple, they swerve onto the field and slam on the brakes with a bold self-assurance, especially the Cadillac, which sports a pair of golden cattle horns welded to the hood, creating the image of a charging animal coming to an abrupt stop. The car and its screeching halt affect me profoundly. 'Take a look at that, Wise Monk,' I say softly, barely above a whisper. 'We've got a big shot in our midst,

the real thing.' Well, the Wise Monk just sits there, in a repose greater than the Horse Spirit behind him, and now I begin to worry that he might die in that position. If he does, who will listen to my story? But I can't bear to waste my viewing time on him—what's happening across the way is too good to miss. First to emerge—all from the silver-grey Volvos—are four husky men in black windbreakers and sunglasses. Their crewcuts stand up like a hedgehog's bristles, and to me they look like four lumps of charcoal in human form. Then the Cadillac passenger opens his door and steps out; he too is in a black windbreaker—a fifth lump of charcoal. He hustles to the rear door; he opens it with one hand while he holds the other protectively over the door to allow a dark passenger to step out, his movements quick yet dignified. A head taller than his bodyguards, he has extraordinarily large ears that look as if they've been carved out of red crystal. He is all in black, except for the white silk scarf round his neck, and he is chewing on a cigar as thick as a link of Guangwei sausage. The scarf is as light as a feather. The merest of puffs—and I truly believe this— would send it floating into the air. I'm pretty sure the cigar is Cuban, though it could be a Philippine import. Bluish smoke emerges from his mouth and nose to form beautiful patterns in the sunlight. After a few minutes, three American Jeeps drive up from East City, covered with green camouflage netting, replete with leaves and branches. Four men in white suits jump out of the Jeeps and form a protective cordon round a woman in a white miniskirt. Actually, it's so short that the word skirt hardly applies. Every movement reveals the lacy edge of her underwear. Her long legs are like ivory columns, the skin slightly pink. White, high-heeled lambskin boots stop just above her knees; a small red silk scarf makes her neck seem ringed with dancing flames. Her small, lovely face is partially hidden behind a pair of oversized sunglasses. She has a slightly pointed chin, a tiny mole just to the left of her mouth and loose almost brunette hair that falls to her shoulders. She walks up confidently to within three feet of the big man. He is shielded from the back by the four men in white who stand at a distance of about five feet. She removes her sunglasses to reveal a pair of mournful eyes and with a sad smile begins to speak. 'Lan Laoda, I am Shen Gongdao's daughter, Shen Yaoyao. I know that if my father came here today he would not return alive, so I laced his drink with a sleeping potion and came to die in his place. You can kill me, Elder Brother Lan, but I beg you to spare my father.' The man stands there like a statue, and

I can't tell what effect her words have on him because his eyes are hidden behind his sunglasses. But I guess she's put him in an awkward position. Shen Yaoyao stands calmly in front of him, chest thrown out to receive a bullet. Elder Brother Lan carelessly flings his cigar in the direction of the Jeeps, turns and heads back to his Cadillac. His driver steps up to open the door for him. The car backs up, the driver turns the wheel and the car skids back onto the road. Then the four men in black open their windbreakers, draw their weapons and shoot holes in the three Jeeps before climbing back into their Volvos and racing to catch up with the Cadillac, leaving a cloud of dust in their wake. In the temple, a choking miasma of gunpowder terrifies me and makes me cough. As if a scene from a film has played out in front of me. This is no dream. Three Jeeps leaking oil and sitting on flat tyres prove that. So do the four men in white who stand there dumbstruck. And finally, so does the self-possessed woman in white. I see two threads of tears running down her face but she puts on her sunglasses again and her eyes vanish from view. What happens next is the most exciting part—she begins to walk up to the temple entrance. It's a joy to watch her. Some beautiful women lose their appeal when they walk. Others walk elegantly but aren't particularly attractive. This one has a gorgeous figure, a lovely face and a graceful walk; she is, in other words, a woman of rare beauty. And that is why even Lan Laodu, as cold and brutal a man as there ever was, did not have the heart to shoot her. The way she's walking now gives no indication of the frightening scene that has played out across the way only moments before. Now that she's drawn closer, I can see she's wearing nylon stockings, and those nylon-encased thighs arouse me more than bare thighs ever could. Her knee-high lambskin boots are adorned with lambskin tassels. I can only see her from the waist down, because I don't have the nerve to gaze at the top half of her body. As she steps over the threshold, the subtle fragrance of her perfume lets loose a flood of sentiments in me. Never before has such an exalted feeling visited my humble mind. But it does now. My mouth hungers at the sight of her delectable knees. If I had the courage, I'd fall to my knees to lick hers. Me, Luo Xiaotong, once a local tough who feared neither Heaven nor earth. If the Emperor's wife's tits had been within reach, I'd have fondled them. But today? I'm as timid as a mouse. The woman lightly brushes the Wise Monk's head with her hand. My God! How strange, how bizarre, how lucky, the Wise Monk's head. She doesn't touch mine. And by the time I find the courage to lift my tear-streaked face in the hope that she will, all I see is her splendiferous back. Are you up to hearing more, Wise Monk?

At noon, when Father showed up for the second time in our yard with my sister in his arms, Mother appeared perfectly calm, as if he was only returning from visiting the neighbours with his daughter. His behaviour surprised me too. Calm, his movements natural, nothing like a down-and-out man coming home after having endured the storms of inner struggle. He was just an ordinary home-loving husband who'd taken his daughter to the market.

Mother shrugged off her overcoat and put on a pair of canvas over-sleeves she'd picked out of the trash so she could scrub the pot, fill it with water and gather fuel for the stove. To my surprise, instead of the usual scrap rubber, she fed it with the finest pine, wood left over after building the house. She'd squirrelled that away after chopping it up for kindling, waiting, I supposed, to burn it on some special occasion. As the room filled with the scent of burning pine, the firelight filled my heart with warmth. Mother sat in front of the stove, looking a bit like a woman who's sold a wagonload of fake scrap without getting caught by the inspectors from the local-products office.

'Xiaotong, go to Old Zhou's and buy three *jin* of sausage.' She stiffened her leg, took three ten-yuan notes from her purse and handed them to me. 'Make sure it's freshly steamed,' she said cheerfully. 'And on the way home, buy three *jin* of dried noodles at the corner store.'

By the time I made it back, red, oily sausage and dried noodles in hand, Father had changed out of his overcoat and Jiaojiao had taken off her down coat. The lined jacket he now wore was shiny with grime and missing a few buttons but he looked more respectable than in his overcoat. Jiaojiao too was wearing a lined jacket—white with a red floral pattern, with sleeves not long enough to cover her rail-thin arms—over lined red-checked pants. She was a lovely, docile creature, like a little white-fleeced lamb, and I couldn't help but feel a sense of affection towards her. Both she and Father were sitting at a red, stumpy-legged catalpa-wood table we brought out only over New Year's; the rest of the year, Mother lovingly wrapped it in plastic and hung it from the rafters, out of the way. Now she placed on it two bowls of steaming hot water and then brought out a jar enclosed in plastic. As soon as she opened the wrapping and unscrewed the cap to reveal its sparkling white contents, my eyes and sensitive nose told me that it contained sugar crystals. Now, there couldn't have been many children with a greedier mouth than mine and, no matter how cleverly Mother hid them, I always managed to ferret out my favourite foods. All but this jar of sugar. I had no idea when she'd bought it or found it. Obviously, she was craftier than I thought, certainly craftier than me, which got me thinking: How much more good food has she hidden away?

Far from being guilty about hiding the sugar from me, she seemed proud of it. She scooped out a spoonful and dumped it into Jiaojiao's bowl, a display of generosity I never thought I'd see till the sun rose in the west or a chicken laid a duck's egg or a pig gave birth to an elephant.

Jiaojiao looked up at Mother, her bright eyes full of apprehension, and then at Father, whose eyes shone. He reached over and plucked the knit cap off her head. Next, Mother held a spoonful of sugar over Father's bowl but stopped before pouring it in, and I noticed a little-girl pout form on her lips as a pink blush spread across her cheeks. I simply couldn't figure that woman out! She placed the jar on the table in front of him—hard—and said, softly: 'Put it in yourself. That way you won't have anything to say about me!'

Father gazed into her face with obvious puzzlement but she quickly turned away so she wouldn't have to endure the look in his eyes. He took the spoon out of the jar and put it into Jiaojiao's bowl, then screwed the cap back on. 'What right does someone like me have to eat sugar?' Stirring the mixture in his daughter's bowl, he said: 'Jiaojiao, thank your aunty.'

She obeyed, timidly, but failed to please Mother. 'Drink it,' she said. 'There's no need to thank anyone.'

Father dipped the spoon into the sugar water, blew on it, then carried it up to her mouth. But then he abruptly poured it back into her bowl and, flustered, picked up his bowl and drank its contents in one gulp. The water was so hot his lips pulled back to expose clenched teeth and perspiration dotted his forehead. Then he picked up Jiaojiao's and poured half the sugar water into his now-empty bowl. When he laid the two bowls together, I guess to see if the contents were even, I wondered what he had in mind. It soon became clear. He pushed his bowl across the table to me and said, apologetically: 'Xiaotong, this bowl's for you.'

That really touched me. The gluttonous desire gnawing at my belly had been swept away by a noble spirit. 'I'm too big for that stuff, Dieh,' I said. 'Let her drink it.'

Another wheeze rumbled in Mother's throat. Turned away from us, she dried her eyes with that black towel. 'It's for all of you!' she said angrily. 'I may not have much but I've always got water!' She kicked a stool up to the table and, without looking at me, said: 'Why are you still standing there? If Dieh tells you to drink, then drink!'

Father set the stool straight for me and I sat down.

Mother untied the braided grass string round the cuts of sausage and placed them on the table in front of us. I think she gave Jiaojiao the thickest piece. 'Eat it while it's hot,' she said. 'The noodles will be ready in a minute.'

The sound of music out on the street, from both the east and the west, is deaf-
ening. The Carnivore Festival parade is drawing near. Thirty or more panicky
jackrabbits dash out of the planted fields on both sides of the highway and
come together in front of the temple entrance, where they engage in whispered
conversations. One of them, with a droopy left ear that looks like a wilted
vegetable leaf, and white whiskers, appears to be the leader and lets out a
shockingly shrill cry. Now I know rabbits, and I can assure you that that is
not the sort of noise commonly made by them. But all animals produce dis-
tinctive sounds in an emergency, to alert members of their species to danger.
As I expected, the rest of the rabbits react to the command by shouting all at
once and then bounding into the temple. The beauty of their leaps across the
threshold is indescribable. They run straight to a spot behind the Wutong
Spirit, where a breathless discussion breaks out. All of a sudden it occurs to
me that there's a fox family back there—the entry of the rabbits is the equiva-
lent of a meal delivered to their door. But there's nothing anyone can do about
that, not now. It's best left to nature, since the foxes will be angry if I alert the
rabbits. Ear-splitting musical notes erupt from a pair of loudspeakers on the
stage across the way. It is jubilant music with a foot-tapping beat and a great
melody, an open invitation to start dancing. During the decade that I roamed
the country, Wise Monk, I worked for a while at a dance hall called Garden of
Eden. They had me dress in a white uniform and told me to keep smiling as I
attended to well-fed and liquored-up or just plain horny, red-faced customers
who visited the men's room. I turned on the taps for them and, when they were
finished washing their paws, handed them folded hot towels. Some accepted the
towels and then, when their hands were dry, thanked me as they handed them
back, often tossing a coin into the dish placed there for tips. Every once in a
while, a particularly generous customer would leave a ten-yuan note, and, on
more than one occasion, a hundred-yuan one. Anyone that free with his money
must have been well heeled and lucky in love. For people like that, life was

good. Then there were those who ignored my ministrations and used the electric hand-dryer on the wall. One glance at their impassive expressions told me
that life was not so good to them. Chances are that they were expected to
cough up the money for a bunch of drunken sots, most likely corrupt individuals who held some sort of power over them. No matter how much they hated
them, they had to grin and bear it. Losers like that get no sympathy from me.
Good people don't spend their money in degenerate places like that and, as
far as I'm concerned, I wouldn't have minded getting Lao Lan's third uncle to
mow them all down with his machine gun. But the cheapskates who didn't
even drop a coin into my dish were the worst; just a look at their glum faces
made me angry; even Lao Lan's third uncle's machine gun would not have
erased the loathing I held for them. I think back to when I, Luo Xiaotong, was
a real operator and lament that I'm now a phoenix that has fallen to the earth,
no better than a chicken. No man of substance tries to relive past glories. You
have to lower your head if you stand beneath an eave. Wise Monk, whoever
made up the saying 'Success at a young age brings bad luck to a family' must
have had me in mind. Smiling on the outside and seething on the inside, I
waited on those bastards who came in to relieve themselves, all the while
recalling my glorious past and my sad memories. Every time I saw one of them
out the door, I cursed inwardly: You lousy bastard, I hope you slip and break
your neck while walking, drown while drinking, choke to death while eating
or croak while sleeping. I listened to the goings-on outside when the stalls and
urinals were empty—hot, passionate music one minute and slow, romantic
melodies the next. Sometimes I felt driven to do something worthwhile with
my life, but there were other times when I fantasized being out in the muted
dance-hall light, holding close a girl with bare shoulders and perfumed hair,
dancing dreamily. If the fantasy played on, my legs began to move to the beat.
But those dreamy moments were shattered by the next stream of arseholes
with their dicks in their hands. Do you have any idea how much humiliation
I've suffered, Wise Monk? One day I actually set a fire in the men's room. I
quickly put it out with a fire extinguisher, but the dance-hall boss, Fatty Hong,
dragged me over to the police station and accused me of arson. I convinced
the interrogating officer that one of the drunken patrons had set the fire. Since
I'd saved the day by putting it out, the owner ought to reward me. In fact, he'd
agreed to that, but then had second thoughts. He was a cruel, bloodsucking

slave driver, happy to chew up his employees and swallow them whole. By taking me to the authorities, he figured he could save the reward money and withhold the three months' pay he owed me. 'Mr Policeman,' I said, 'you're a wise arbiter who won't be fooled by the likes of Fatty Hong. You may not know it, but he likes to hide in the men's room and call you all sorts of names. He'll be taking a leak and saying terrible things about the police . . .' Well, it worked. The police let me go. They said I'd committed no crime. Of course I hadn't. That damned Lao Lan, on the other hand, definitely had. But he was a member of the Municipal Standing Committee and no stranger to TV shows, where he made high-sounding pronouncements and never missed an opportunity to mention his third uncle. Third Uncle, he claimed, was a patriotic overseas Chinese who had brought glory to the descendants of the Yellow Emperor with his thick, powerful penis. Third uncle was returning to China to fund the building of a Wutong Temple in order to enhance the virility of local men. Lao Lan, the creep, managed to win over his audience with a line of bullshit. Ah, yes, I forgot, that man with the enormous ears we saw a short while ago—I wouldn't be surprised if Lao Lan's third uncle looked just like that as a young man—often showed up at the Garden of Eden dance hall, and once even flipped a green note into my dish. I later learnt that it was a US hundred-dollar note! It was brand new; the edges so sharp I got a paper cut while I examined it. That bled for a long time. When he wore a white suit with a red tie, he was tall and imposing, like a mighty poplar. When he wore a dark green suit with a yellow tie, he was tall and imposing, like a mighty black pine. When he wore a burgundy suit with a white tie, he was tall and imposing, like a mighty red fir. I never did see what he looked like when he was out there dancing, but I could envision him holding the prettiest girl in the dance hall, she in a white or dark green or purple strapless gown, shoulders and arms looking as if they'd been carved out of white jade, draped in fine jewellery, with big limpid eyes and a beauty spot near her mouth, the two of them gliding across the dance floor under the gaze of the other patrons. Applause, fresh flowers, fine liquor, women, all his for the taking. I dreamt of becoming someone like that one day—a lavish tipper and a big spender, surrounded by beautiful women as I swaggered down the street like a spotted leopard, secretive yet extravagant, giving bystanders the impression that a mysterious, unfathomable spectre had just passed by. Are you still listening, Wise Monk?

Round nightfall, the snowfall intensified, and before long our compound lay beneath a blanket of white. Mother picked up her broom and had barely begun to sweep the snow away when Father took it from her. His movements were strong and firm, and I was reminded of what people in the village said about him: Luo Tong is good at what he does. Too bad 'you can't make a thoroughbred till a field'. As darkness fell, he seemed to grow larger, especially in the light reflected off the snow. A clear path opened up behind him in hardly any time. Mother walked down path and shut the gate, the metal latch making a resounding clang that shook the snowy dusk. Darkness took over, the only light a misty reflection of the snow on the ground and in the air. Mother and Father stomped their shoes beneath the eaves and shook their clothes free of snow; I think they even dusted it off each other with a towel. I was sitting in the corner no more than half a step from the pig's head, and I could smell its cold, raw aroma, but I was more interested in trying to penetrate the darkness and see their expressions. Unfortunately, I wasn't very successful, and all I could make out were their swaying shadows. I heard my sister's laboured breathing in front of me, like a little wild beast hiding in the dark. I'd gorged myself at noon; by nightfall, undigested pieces of sausage and noodles rose up my throat, only to be chewed once more and sent back down. I've heard people say that's a disgusting thing to do, but I wasn't about to throw out any food. Now that Father was home, my diet was likely to change, but exactly how and to what extent remained a puzzle. He looked so dejected, so docile and submissive, that I had an uncomfortable feeling that my hopes—of his return resulting in more meat on the table—were doomed to be dashed. But be that as it may, the event had created an opportunity to stuff myself with the sausage, which, admittedly, was long on starch filler and short on meat, although the thin casing did come from an animal. And I mustn't forget that, when the sausage was gone, I'd enjoyed two bowls of noodles. Then there was the pig's head, which rested on the chopping board, so close I could reach out and touch it. When would it find its way into my digestive system? Mother wasn't planning on selling it, I hoped.

I'd shocked Father by how much and how fast I'd eaten at lunch. Afterwards, I heard Mother say the same thing about my little sister. I hadn't noticed—I was too busy eating. But it was easy to imagine the sorrowful looks on the adults' faces as they watched us, brother and sister, gobble our food like starving, other-worldly beasts, even stretching our necks and rolling our eyes as we tried to swallow partially chewed pieces of sausage. Our rapacious style didn't so much disgust them as cause them deep distress and self-recrimination. It's my guess that that was when they decided not to divorce after all. Time for the family to live a decent life, for them to supply their children with the food and clothing they deserved. I belched in the darkness and, as I chewed my cud, I heard a belch from my sister, something she did with practised familiarity. If I hadn't known it was her sitting across from me, I swear, on pain of death, I'd have never guessed that a four-year-old girl could have made that sound.

Without doubt, a stomach full of sausage and noodles placed a heavy burden on my intestines and diminished my desire for meat on that snowy night, but it did nothing to erase thoughts of that pig's head, whose muted light gleamed in the darkness. In my mind's eye I watched it chopped in half and dumped into a pot of boiling water, the scene so vivid I could even smell the unique aroma. And my thoughts didn't stop there—I saw a family of four sitting round a big platter from which meat-flavoured steam billowed into the air. It smelt so good that I was nearly transported to that intoxicating moment between sleep and wakefulness. I watched Mother, looking solemn and dignified, stick a red chopstick into the head and twist and turn it a few times to neatly separate the meat from the bones. 'Eat up, children,' she announced proudly, picking the bones out of the pot. 'Eat until you're full. Today you can have as much as you want!'

That night, Mother did something totally out of character—she lit the room's glass-shaded oil lamp, flooding our house with light for the first time and casting enlarged shadows onto a white wall from which hung strings of leeks and peppers. Jiaojiao, who had perked up after a difficult day, brought her hands together in the beam of light to form a dog's head on the wall.

'A dog, Daddy,' she said excitedly, 'it's a dog!'

Father shot a quick glance at Mother before he said somewhat forlornly: 'Yes, it's Jiaojiao's little black puppy.'

Jiaojiao then moved her hands and fingers to form the silhouette of a rabbit, not perfect but definitely recognizable. 'No, it's not a dog,' she said, 'it's a bunny, a little bunny.'

'You're right, it's a bunny. Our Jiaojiao's a clever little girl.' But having praised his daughter, he turned to Mother apologetically, 'She's still a child, hasn't figured out the world yet.'

'Do you really expect her to, at her young age?' Mother said tolerantly and then surprised us all by putting her hands together to decorate the wall with the silhouette of a rooster, complete with cockscomb and tail, and then finished it off with a crisp *cock-a-doodle-doo*! What a shock! I'd become so used to her constant complaints and scolding over the years, plus the ever-present scowl and sour demeanour, that the possibility of her knowing how to do hand shadows, not to mention how to crow like a rooster, never occurred to me. I have to admit that once again I had mixed emotions. From the moment Father appeared at our gate that morning with his daughter on his shoulders, I'd experienced nothing but mixed emotions. I don't know any other way to describe what I was feeling.

Joyful laughter burst from Jiaojiao's throat, and what passed for a smile appeared on Father's face.

Mother looked tenderly at Jiaojiao, heaved a sigh, and said: 'It's always the adults who cause these messes, never the children.'

'That's right,' said Father without looking up. 'One mistake after another, and always by me.'

'We've all made mistakes, so no more of that talk.' Mother stood up and deftly slipped on her over-sleeves. 'Xiaotong,' she said, raising her voice, 'you little rascal, I know you hate me, a stingy old bag who hasn't let you so much as taste meat over the last five years. Am I right? Well, today is going to be different. I've cooked this pig's head as a reward to the troops. You can eat till you burst!'

She placed the chopping board alongside the stove, laid the pig's head on it, then picked up her little hatchet, took the target's measure and swung.

'We just had sausage . . .' Father stood up. 'Earning enough to get by has been hard on you two,' he said to stop her. 'Why not sell this pig's head? A person's stomach is like a sack you fill up no matter what you put in it, chaff and vegetables or meat and fish . . .'

'Is that really you talking?' Mother's dripped sarcasm but then quickly changed her tune: 'I'm as human as the next person,' she said, deadly serious, 'with a red mouth, white teeth, flesh and blood. I know how good meat tastes. I never ate it, but back then I was foolish and ignorant. When it comes down to it, the mouth is the most important thing in life.'

Wringing his hands, Father began to say something, but stopped. Instead, he took a few steps back, then strode forward, reached out and said to Mother: 'Here, let me.'

She hesitated briefly before laying down the hatchet and stepping away.

Father rolled up his sleeves, pushed up the tattered cuffs of his vest beneath his shirtsleeves, picked up the hatchet and raised it over his head. Without, it seemed, taking aim, he took an easy swing, then another, and the pig's head split right down the middle.

Mother was studying Father, who had stepped away from the chopping board, with a look so ambiguous that even I, a son who thought he could read her mind and anticipate her every move, had no idea what she was thinking. But here's what it boiled down to: the moment Father split that pig's head in two, Mother's mood underwent a change. She pursed her lips slightly and poured half a bucket of water into the pot on the stove, a little too forcefully, I thought, since some of it splashed over the sides onto a box of matches on the stove rack. She then tossed the bucket into the corner, where it rattled noisily and gave us a bit of a fright. Father stayed where he was, looking awkward and unsure and not a pretty sight. We all watched as Mother picked up half the head by the ear and tossed it into the pot, followed by the other half. I wished I could have reminded her that the best way to bring out the flavour of a pig's head was to season it with fennel, ginger, green onions, garlic, Chinese cinnamon and cardamom and, finally, a spoonful of Korean vinegar, but that was Aunty Wild Mule's secret recipe. In days past, I'd often sneaked over to her restaurant with Father to feast on meat dishes she'd prepared, and more than once I'd watched her cook a pig's head. I'd even seen Father split one for her—one chop, maybe two, but never more than three, and it was done. She'd gaze at him with admiring eyes. Once I heard her say: 'Luo Tong, I say, Luo Tong, you're the best at anything you put your hand to, with no help from any teacher!'

There was something special about Aunty Wild Mule's pig's head, which had earned her a fine reputation, not only in our village but also, thanks to her greedy customers, all the way to the market town fifteen or twenty *li* away. Even Lao Han, who had the onerous responsibility of overseeing township officials' dietary concerns, made the trip every three or four days. He arrived with a shout of 'Old Wild!' and she came out running. 'Elder Brother Han,' she said (that's what she called him, a term of endearment). 'Got one in the pot? I'll take half.' 'I sure do. It'll be ready in a minute. Have some tea while you wait.' She poured the tea and lit his cigarette, smiling broadly. 'Did you say that officials from the city are here?' 'They're fans of your cooking. Mayor Hua says he wants to meet you. Old Wild, your future looks bright. Have you heard that his wife's on her deathbed? She won't last more than a couple of days. Once she's gone, he might just take you home. But when you're the mayor's wife, living in the lap of luxury, don't turn your back on your friends!' Father coughed then to attract Uncle Han's attention. He turned and spotted Father, stared at him with buggy yellow eyes. 'Luo Tong, you old son of a bitch, is that you? What the fuck are you doing here?' 'Why the fuck shouldn't I be here?' Father replied, neither servile nor overbearing. Uncle Han's taut face relaxed as he absorbed the language of Father's reply, and then smiled, revealing a set of teeth as white as limestone. 'Be careful,' he said, 'you're nothing but a bum, while Wild Mule, well, she's a piece of fruit just ripe for the picking. There are plenty of potential pickers, and if you try to keep this juicy titbit to yourself those others might gang up and relieve you of your cock.' 'You can both shut your traps,' snapped Aunty Wild Mule, 'and you can stop treating me like a toy for your entertainment, a little something for you to snack on. Get me mad, and I'll take the knife to both of you.' 'My, my, what a feisty thing we've got here,' Han said. 'After all the sweet talk, how can you turn on me like that? Aren't you afraid of offending one of your most loyal customers?' Aunty Wild Mule pulled half a cooked pig's head out of the pot with her steel hook; it was coated with a fragrant red sauce. I couldn't take my eyes off it and was drooling before I knew it. She laid it on a chopping board, picked up a gleaming cleaver, twirled it, and—*whack*—chopped off a fist-sized piece. Sticking a skewer through it, she held it up to me. 'Take it, Xiaotong, you greedy little cat, before your chin drops off!' 'I thought you were saving that for me, Old Wild,' grumbled Uncle Han, clearly annoyed. 'Mayor Hua says he wants to sample your meat!' 'You mean Mayor Dickhead, that piss-ant of a Party secretary? He may have power over you but do you honestly believe he can handle me?' 'Aren't you the fierce one! And I mean fierce! I give up, I'm no match for you. Does that let me off the hook? Now, hurry up and wrap the meat in lotus leaves so I can be on my way. But I'm not lying. Mayor Hua plans to come here.' 'Put your Mayor up against my boy, and there's no comparison. Mayor Hua smells like piss, doesn't he, son?' Aunty Wild Mule asked me genially. I wasn't about to waste my time respond-ing to such an idiotic question. 'OK, then, like shit, how's that?' asked Uncle Han. 'Our Mr Mayor Hua smells like shit, and we won't dick around with him, OK? As for you, dear Aunty, won't you please give me the meat I came for?' Han took out his pocket watch and looked at it with increasing annoyance: 'How long have we known each other, Old Wild? I beg you, don't smash my rice bowl. My wife and children depend on me to put food on the table.' Aunty Wild Mule expertly picked out the bones of what was left of the pig's head, singeing her hands in the process and sucking in her breath as her fingers nimbly opened up the head yet somehow retained its shape. She wrapped it in lotus leaves, tied it with braided grass and pushed it over to him. 'Now, get out of here. Go pay your respects to your patrons!' If Mother had thoughts of preparing a pig's head that came close to Aunty Wild Mule's, she'd have had to add a spoonful of finely ground alum, Aunty Wild Mule's secret ingredient. She never hid her secrets from me. But Mother clapped on the lid without adding anything, content to let it cook in plain water. How could anything good come of that? But it was, after all, pig's head. And me? I was, after all, a boy who loved to eat meat but who hadn't enjoyed the experience in years.

The fire in the belly of the stove was as hot as blazes. The flames lit up Mother's face. Thanks to the pine oil, the firewood burnt hot and long, making it unnecessary to add any more. Mother could have walked off to do something else but she chose not to. She sat in front of the stove with quiet serenity, hugging her knees and resting her chin in her hands as she stared at the kaleidoscopic crackling of the fire, which never strayed from its purpose. Her eyes? They radiated a luminous sparkle.

The water began to boil, making a rumbling sound, as if from far away. I was sitting in the doorway with Jiaojiao, who yawned loudly, her open mouth a scene of perfect little white teeth.

'Put her to bed,' Mother said to Father without turning.

Father picked Jiaojiao up and stepped out into the yard. When he returned, she was in his arms, head on his shoulder, snoring softly. He stood behind Mother, waiting for something.

'A comforter and pillows are stacked at the head of the *kang*. Cover her with the one with orchids for now. I'll make you another one tomorrow.'

'That's putting you to an lot of trouble,' Father said.

'Stop talking nonsense,' Mother replied. 'Even if she was a child you picked up off the street, I couldn't make her sleep on a pile of hay, could I?' As Father carried Jiaojiao into the bedroom, Mother blew up at me: 'What are you hanging round here for? Go outside and pee and then off to bed! A slow boil like this won't be ready till morning.'

My eyelids were getting heavy, my thoughts growing fuzzy. I felt as if the special aroma of one of Aunty Wild Mule's cooked heads was floating in the air, coming at me in waves. All I had to do was close my eyes for it to settle in front of me. I stood up. 'Where am I supposed to sleep?' I asked.

'Where do you think?' said Mother. 'Where you always sleep.'

My eyelids drooped as I walked out into the yard; snowflakes fell on my face and drove away some of the sleepiness. The fire sent its light into the yard as a backdrop for the falling snow, clear and beautiful, like a dream. In the midst of this wonderful sight I saw our tractor tipped over in the yard, its load of rubbish blanketed by snow, looking like a monstrous beast. The snow had also partially covered my mortar but it had retained its shape and its metallic colour; the tube pointed into the dusky sky. I just knew it was a healthy, happy mortar and that all it needed was ammunition to move into action.

I went back inside and flopped down on the bed, hesitating a moment before stripping naked and slipping under the covers. Jiaojiao jerked away when my cold feet touched her warm skin, so I quickly pulled them back.

'Go to sleep,' I heard Mother say. 'There'll be meat on the table when you wake up in the morning.'

I could tell by the tone of voice that she was in a good mood again. The lamplight was fading, leaving only the flickering light from the fire in the stove to see by. The door was open a crack to let the firelight filter in and land on the dresser. A question swirled dimly through the fog in my brain: Where are Mother and Father sleeping? They aren't going to stay up all night watching the pig's head cook, are they? The question kept me awake, and I couldn't help but hear them talk. I even covered my head with the comforter to keep out the conversation but every word made its way into my ears.

'A heavy snowfall will guarantee a good harvest next year,' said Father.

'You ought to let some new thoughts into your head,' Mother said coolly. 'Farmers are different these days. They used to live off what they planted in the ground. It all depended on how the old master in the sky felt about things. Good winds and plenty of rain meant a bumper crop—buns in the pot and meat in their bowls. Bad winds and no rain meant soup in the pot and husks in their bowls. But things have changed. No one's fool enough to work the fields. Drenching ten acres of land with your sweat can't bring in as much as selling one pigskin . . . but why am I telling you this?'

'Someone has to work the farms . . .' Father mumbled under his breath. 'That's what a farmer does.'

'I do believe the sun is rising in the west,' Mother said, mocking him. 'You hardly ever went out into the field when you were home. Are you planning to become a farmer now that you're back?'

'Farming's all I know,' said Father, clearly embarrassed. 'There's no more need for someone to rate cattle. Or I can go out collecting rubbish with you.'

'I won't let you do that,' she said. 'You're not cut out for that kind of work. Rubbish collecting is for people with no sense of shame, no face at all. It's halfway between robbing and stealing.'

'After the life I've led, how much face can I have left? If you can do it, so can I.'

'I'm not a brainless woman,' she said. 'You're back and we've got a house, so Xiaotong and I won't go out any more. If you want to leave I won't stop you. It doesn't make sense to keep someone around who doesn't want to be there. It's better for someone like that to just leave . . .'

'I said what I wanted to say earlier today, in front of the children,' Father said. 'I didn't do well. A poor man is short on ambition. A skinny horse has long hair. I came looking for you with a dogskin round my head, and I'm grateful you took me back. We are, after all, husband and wife. Like a bone and a tendon—if you break the bone, it's still connected to the tendon.'

'You've accomplished something. If nothing else,' said Mother, 'since you've been away you've learnt how to sweet-talk a person . . .'

'Yuzhen.' Father's voice softened. 'I owe you. From now on, I'll pay you back if I have to be your slave.'

'We'll see who's the slave,' Mother said. 'How do I know you won't run off with another Wild Mule one of these days?'

'Why must you hit me where it hurts?'

'You think you know pain?' Mother's anger boiled over. 'I don't mean as much to you as one of her toes . . .' She was crying now. 'Do you know how many times I threw a rope over the rafters? If it hadn't been for Xiaotong—even if there'd been ten Yuzhens, they'd all be dead now.'

'I know . . .' The words were spoken with difficulty. 'There's nothing worse than what I did to you. I don't deserve to live.'

He probably reached out and touched her then, because I heard her growl: 'Don't you lay a hand on me . . .' But from what she said next, I knew he didn't move his hand: 'Go grope her. What good does it do you to grope an old hag like me?'

The strong odour of cooking meat flooded into my room through the slightly open door.

A large truck converted into a float is at the head of a line of marchers from East City. The front is decorated with an enormous cream-coloured laughing cow's head. Of course I know how absurd that is. All the animal images at the Carnivore Festival are emblematic of the bloody business of butchering. In my life I've seen more than my share of grievous looks on the faces of animals just before they're slaughtered, and have heard more than my share of plaintive cries. I know that people these days promote humane slaughter methods, bathing the animals with warm water, playing soft music, even giving them full-body massages to hypnotize them, all by way of a prelude to the knife. I once saw a TV show that promoted these humane methods, hailing them as a major advance for humanity. Human beings have extended the concept of benevolence to the animal world but continue to invent and manufacture powerful, cruel weapons for the excruciating death of humans. The more powerful, the more lethal the weapon, the greater the profits. I may not yet have taken my Buddhist vows but I'm aware that so much of what human beings say and do runs counter to the spirit of Buddhism. Isn't that right, Wise Monk? I note a smile on his face but can't tell if that's a sign that he's affirmed my enlightenment or that he's mocking my shallowness. A few dozen young people in baggy red pants, white jackets with buttons down the front, white cotton towels over their heads and red silk sashes round their waists stand in a circle on the bed of the cow-headed float. Their faces painted red, they passionately pound a drum with drumsticks as thick as laundry paddles. The beats of this very big drum go right to the hearts of all within hearing. Attached to the sides of the float are banners proclaiming in big, decorative, Song Dynasty–style characters: Kenta Hu Meat Group. They are followed by a chorus of 'rice-sprout' singers, all girls in the bloom of youth. Dressed in white pants and red jackets, cinched with green silk sashes, they dance to the beat of the drum, hips and buttocks moving in choreographed rhythm. Next in line is a rooster-

headed float, sporting a rooster and a hen. Every few minutes the rooster thrusts out its neck and releases a bizarre crowing noise. And every few minutes the hen lays a larger-than-life egg, accompanied by a burst of clucks. A truly imaginative float, so true to life it should get the most votes and win first place in the float category at the Festival climax. Of course I know that the crowing and clucking come from humans inside the bellies of the birds. The truck is identified as belonging to Aunty Yang Poultry Corporation. Eighty men and women in four columns come next, all in cockscomb hats and feathered arms; they flap their 'wings' as they walk. 'To keep sickness away,' they intone, 'eat an egg every day' and 'Keep a healthy supply of Aunty Yang's eggs.' The parade from West City approaches behind a formation of camels. I don't realize they're real animals until they pass in front of me. A rough count reveals more than forty of them, all draped in colourful garb reminiscent of prize-winning model workers. A short acrobatic man in front performs a nifty tumbling manoeuvre every few steps. He carries a showy baton loaded with oversized copper coins that make a whirring sound when he thrusts it up and down. Under his direction, the camels begin to prance, making the brass bells round their necks ring out shrilly. A well-trained honour guard indeed. A pole rising above the hump of a white-faced camel in the formation bears a flag embroidered with large characters; I don't even have to read it to know that Lao Lan's contingent is approaching. On the basis of the United Meatpacking Plant, where I was employed ten years before, Lao Lan founded the Rare Animals Slaughterhouse Corporation. The camel joints and ostrich steaks they produced earned a reputation for supplying high nutritional value to the people's diet and generating considerable wealth for the company. Word has it that the son of a bitch sleeps on a waterbed, that his toilet is trimmed in gold, that his cigarettes are ginseng flavoured and that he dines daily on a whole camel hoof, a pair of ostrich feet and an ostrich egg. A two-column contingent of twenty-four ostriches follows the camels. Each is ridden by a youngster, boys on the left, girls on the right. The boys are wearing white sneakers, white knee-high socks topped by two red stripes, blue shorts, white shirts and red streamers round their necks. The girls are in white leather shoes over ankle-length white socks to which are tied red knitted pompoms; they are wearing sky-blue dresses with short skirts and golden bows on the tops. The boys' closely cropped hair makes their heads look like little rubber balls. The girls' braids are tied at the ends by strips of red silk, making their heads resemble little embroidered balls. All the riders are sitting up, backs straight, chests thrown out proudly. The ostriches hold their triangular heads high—spirited, proud, arrogant marchers, despite the lacklustre grey of their feathers. Bright red silk bands round their necks offset their lack of colour. Seemingly incapable of slow movements, the ostriches take long, running strides that cover at least three feet; annoyingly hindered by the slow-moving camels ahead of them, all they can do is twist and turn their long, curved necks. The two contingents—East City and West City—have stopped, and a chorus of turbulent and chaotic drumbeats, gong clangs, music strains and marchers' shouts fill the air. A dozen TV journalists jockey for position to film the scene. One of them, wanting to get a special shot, has come too close to a camel; it angrily bares its teeth, then roars and spits a gooey missile at the man, temporarily blinding both him and his camera. He screams as he jumps out of the way, drops his camera, bends over and wipes his eyes with his sleeve, as a man responsible for the arrangement of the parade participants raises his flag and shouts at everyone to take their places on the Festival grounds. The cow-headed and chicken-headed floats make slow turns onto the grassy field, followed by a seemingly unending body of parade contingents. The acrobat, with his martial bearing, steps nimbly and smiles broadly as he leads the East City camel unit onto the grass. The abused journalist standing by the side of the road assails his tormentor with loud curses but is totally ignored. The camels are more or less orderly as they move forward, but the twenty-four ostriches seem angry about something, and their formation breaks down as they run helter-skelter towards the temple grounds, drawing terrified shrieks from their riders, some of whom slide quickly out of the saddle, while others cling to the necks of their mounts, their young faces drenched with sweat. Once the ostriches reach our yard they huddle together, shuffling back and forth. That's when I discover that the birds' feathers, which looked so dull from a distance, are actually quite beautiful in the sunlight. It's a simple beauty, like priceless Qin Dynasty brocade. Some employees of the Rare Animals Slaughterhouse Corporation frantically try to herd the ostriches back, but all they manage to do is scare them further. I look into the ostriches' hate-filled little eyes, listen to their hoarse screeches and watch as one of them kicks a worker in the knee. Knocked to the ground, he grabs his injured knee and utters a cry of pain, his face waxen and his forehead beaded with sweat. The ostriches take off running, the hard knuckles of their feet pounding loudly on the ground. I know that those feet can kick as hard as a horse, and I've been told that a mature bird isn't afraid to take on a lion. An ostrich's toes are hardened from a lifetime of running across the savanna, so it's a foregone conclusion that the man sitting on the ground yelping in pain has a badly injured knee. When a couple of his friends lift him up by the arms, he immediately sits back down. By now, most of the children have slid off their mounts, all but one girl and one boy who hold on tenaciously. Rivulets of sweat smear the paint on their taut faces until they look like artists' palettes. The boy is clutching the joint connecting the ostrich's wings to its body as he bounces up and down with every step the bird takes. He holds on to the wings even when his rear end is up in the air; but then the ostrich makes a mad dash and he slips side-ways under the mouth-gaping, eye-popping stares of the people round him, none of whom makes a move to come to his rescue. A moment later, he's lying on the ground clutching two fists full of feathers, until someone walks over and picks him up. He bites his lip as the tear dam bursts. Meanwhile, the riderless ostrich has rejoined the herd and is breathing heavily and noisily through its open mouth. The girl still has her arms wrapped round the neck of her bird, though it is trying its best to dislodge her. But she's too much for it, thanks to a panic attack and, in the end, she gets it to slump to the ground, neck and head lying in the dirt, tail end pointing skyward, flinging mud behind it as it paws the ground in vain.

All that pork lay heavily in my stomach, churning and grinding like a lit-ter of soon-to-be-born piglets. But of course I was no sow, so I couldn't possibly know what that felt like. The belly of the pregnant sow at Yao Qi's nearly scraped the ground when she grunted her way over to the snow-covered garbage heap in front of the newly opened Beauty Hair Salon, to root out edible titbits. Lazy, fat and carefree, she was, as anyone could see, a happy sow, in a different class from the two skinny-as-jackals, moody, human-hating little pigs we'd once raised. Yao Qi made sausage out of meat so fatty that even the dogs turned their noses up at it, filled with sweet potato starch and red-dyed bean-curd skin, to which he added chemical ingredients no one knew about. The end result was a product that looked good, smelt nice and sold well; the money rolled in. He raised pigs as a hobby, not as an investment, and definitely not for the fertilizer produced, the way people once did. So his pregnant sow came out early in the morning, every morning, not to scavenge food but to play in the snow, take leisurely strolls and get a little exercise. I sometimes saw Yao Qi on the steps of his house (which didn't look as good as ours but was actually as sturdy as a fortress), left arm tucked under his right armpit, a cigarette in his right hand, squinting dreamily at the meanderings of his pig. Rays of light from the red sun turned his angular face into a slice of barbecued pork.

I'd eaten so much pork that the mere memory of Yao Qi's pig made me ill. The hideous outline of the pregnant sow undulated in front of my eyes, the stench of garbage churned in my stomach. All you sordid representatives of humanity, how can you think of filling your bellies with pork? Pigs feast on garbage and shit. Therefore, so do you! The day I become supreme ruler, I'll cast all the world's pork eaters into sties and turn them into muck-swilling pigs. I'm tormented by regret, shamed by ignorance. How could I have coveted that pig's head that Mother cooked without condiments, the one covered by a layer of white fat? The filthiest, most shameful thing the world has ever seen, good only for feeding the wild cats that live out their lives in the sewers . . . Ah—ugh—I actually picked up chunks of that foul, wiggly stuff with my filthy claws and stuffed them into my mouth, transforming my stomach into a garbage sack . . . Ah—ugh—I'm going to stop being a ruminate . . . Ah—ugh—I vigorously deposited what I'd brought up on the ground. Disgusting, so disgusting! My stomach lurched spasmodically at the repugnant sight of my vomit, and sent whatever was left down there erupting into my throat and mouth. A dog waited patiently and quietly close by. Father walked up behind me, holding Jiaojiao's hand in one of his and thumping me on the back with the other to relieve my anguish.

My stomach had collapsed into itself, my throat was on fire and my guts were tied up in knots, but I felt better, less burdened, like the sow after she's delivered her litter. I repeat: I was no sow, so I couldn't possibly know what that felt like. I looked at Father with tears in my eyes. He dried my face with his hand.

'It's good to get that out of your system,' he said.

'Dieh, I swear I'm never going to eat meat again!'

'Don't make promises you can't keep,' he said, with a look of fatherly concern. 'Always remember, son, you mustn't make vows, no matter what. That's like kicking the ladder away after you've climbed the wall.'

It would not take long for his words to prove prophetic. A new desire to eat meat materialized only three days after throwing up all that pork, and it would not go away. I began to wonder if the boy who had expressed revulsion towards meat and had called it every rotten thing he could think of was actually someone else, someone without a heart.

We stood in the doorway of the Beauty Hair Salon, next to the spinning barber pole, studying the price list in the window. After polishing off one of the richest breakfasts in memory, we were carrying out Mother's instructions to have our hair cut.

By all appearances—her face glowed, her spirits were high—Mother was in a good mood. Tossing the greasy dishes into the sink, she said to Father, who stepped up to help: 'Stay where you are and leave this to me. New Year's is just round the corner. What day is it today, Xiaotong, the twenty-seventh or twenty-eighth?'

Did she really expect me to answer that? The meat I'd just eaten had already made its way up into my throat and was waiting for me to open my mouth to make its escape. Besides, I had no idea what day it was. During the dark days before Father's return, dates were the farthest thing from my mind. I hadn't enjoyed a minute's rest, not even during the major holidays. I'd been, for lack of a better term, a slave.

'Take them out to get haircuts,' Mother said, sounding like she was making a fuss, though the emotions written on her face when she looked at Father put the lie to that. 'Go to the mirror and tell me if it's human beings that look back at you! You all look like you've crawled out of a doghouse. Maybe you don't care what people think but I do.'

I almost croaked when I heard the word haircut.

Father scratched his head. 'Why waste the money? I'll buy some clippers and gnaw at their heads instead.'

'Clippers? We've got those.' Mother took some money out of her pocket and handed it to Father. 'No, this time they need a real haircut. Fan Zhaoxia knows what she's doing, and she doesn't charge much.'

'There are three heads here,' said Father with a sweep of his arm. 'How much do you think that will cost?'

'For those three hard heads of yours, give her ten yuan.'

'What?' Father reacted with predictable alarm. 'For ten yuan you can buy half a sack of rice.'

'Three shaved heads are not going to make the difference between rich and poor,' Mother said charitably. 'Go on, take them over.'

'Um . . .' Father didn't know what to say. 'Peasants' heads aren't worth that kind of money.'

'Ask Xiaotong what he thinks about letting me cut his hair,' Mother said cleverly.

Holding my belly with my hands, I wobbled my way outside. 'Dieh!' I said in utter dejection, 'I'd rather die than let her cut my hair!'

Portly Yao Qi walked up, stuck his head in and took a good look at Father, who was agonizing over the cost of professional haircuts. 'Lao Luo!' he bellowed as he smacked Father on the back of the neck.

'What?' Father turned and remarked calmly.

'Is it really you?'

'Who else would it be?'

'Aren't you something—the prodigal son returns! What about Wild Mule?'

Father shook his head. 'Don't ask.' Then he opened the door and took us inside the salon.

'I say, you really are something,' Yao Qi's voice followed us in. 'A wife, a mistress, a son and a daughter. Of all the men in Slaughterhouse Village, you're the best!'

Father shut the door in Yao Qi's face. Yao Qi pushed it back open and, one foot in, carried on: 'I've missed seeing you about all these years.'

Father ignored him and, with a wry smile, pulled my sister and me over to a dusty bench strewn with dog-eared magazines that had been flipped through and pawed over more times than I could imagine. The bench was a replica of the one in the station's waiting room, so it was either made by the same carpenter or stolen by the salon owner. A swivelling barber-chair with a footrest and a leather seat—so cracked it looked like it had been slashed—awaited us. The mirror on the wall in front of the chair had rippled and faded, creating only blurred reflections. A narrow shelf under the mirror was crowded with shampoos, hair gels and mousse (that's right, it's called mousse). A pair of electric clippers hung from a rusty nail on the wall alongside a dozen coloured illustrations of fashionable hairstyles worn by young models—men and women; some still stuck fast to the wall while others had begun to peel away. The red brick floor had undergone a change in colour thanks to all the black, white and grey hair that had lain atop it, that and the mud tracked in by customers. A strange and pungent smell—not quite fragrant but far from offensive—in the air inside made me sneeze—three times in a row. It must have been contagious because Jiaojiao did the same thing, three times in a row. She looked funny yet adorable with her face scrunched up with every sneeze.

'Who's thinking of me, Daddy?' She blinked. 'Is it my mother?'

'Yes,' Father said, 'it must be.'

A sombre expression creased Yao Qi's face as he remained standing at the door, one foot in, one foot out, neither this nor that, a sort of androgynous stance.

'Lao Luo,' he said heavily, 'I'm glad you're back. I'll come by to see you in a couple of days. There's something important I want to talk to you about.'

With that he was gone; the door slid shut, keeping the clean, snow-injected air outside and thickening the foul air inside. Our sneezing contest over, Jiaojiao and I were more or less acclimated to the smell of the shop. The barber wasn't there at the moment but I knew she'd just left, because the minute I walked in the door I spotted something in the corner that looked like one of those public telephone booths I'd seen in town. A woman in a purple coat was sitting under a semi-circular canopy, her neck stiff and her head covered with brightly coloured curlers. She looked a bit like an astronaut, a bit like a rice-sprout girl at a New Year's celebration and a bit like Pidou's niang. Actually, that's who she was. Pidou's dieh was the butcher Big Ear, which made Pidou's niang Big Ear's wife. There was just one thing that kept her from looking exactly like Pidou's niang: I hadn't seen her for a long time and now she was sort of puffy, as if she had a meatball tucked in each cheek. I remembered her as having full eyebrows that swept across her forehead, the Goddess of Bad Luck. But she'd plucked them bare and replaced them with thin pencilled lines of green and red like caterpillars that dine on sesame leaves. She sat there holding a picture book in her hands, held as far out as her arms could reach—she was obviously farsighted. She hadn't looked up once since we entered, in the affected manner of a noblewoman who ignores a beggar. Shit! What are you but a self-satisfied, stinking old hag! No matter what you do—you could pull out every hair on your head, you could peel the skin from your face and you could colour your lips redder than pig's blood— you'd still be Pidou's niang and a butcher's old lady! Go ahead, ignore us— we can do the same to you! I sneaked a look at Father, who sat there remote and indifferent, quite aloof, actually, as distant as the sky on a cloudless day, as unapproachable as the head monk in a Shaolin Temple, as detached as a red-capped crane in a flock of chickens, as standoffish as a camel in a herd of sheep . . . The barber-chair was unoccupied, a soiled white smock covered with fine hairs draped over its back. The sight of all that hair made the back of my neck itch; and, when it occurred to me that it might be from Pidou's niang, the itch grew downright painful.

I'd been obsessively protective of my head since childhood, something my father knew all too well. That was because every time I had a haircut I had hairs all over my body that itched worse than lice. I can count the hair-cuts I've submitted to in my life so far. After Father left, we had not only a pair of clippers in the house but also a pair of barber's shears and a Double Arrow straight razor. Admittedly, every item in this nearly complete set came from our scavenger days and, after Father left, Mother put these rusty instru-ments to use in the battle of the scalp—my scalp—to save money without having to rely upon favours from anyone. Fourth Brother Kui, a neighbour of ours, gave professional-quality haircuts but Mother was unwilling to seek his help. My screams usually proved which of us was losing the battle.

Wise Monk, let me tell you about my worst haircut experience—and I'm only slightly exaggerating. When no amount of threats or inducements had any effect on me, Mother tied me to a chair to give me a New Year's haircut.

She'd added plenty of muscle since Father left, and acquired a powerful grip. I tried anchoring myself to the floor, I tried rolling round like a donkey and I tried burying my head between my legs, like a dog, but nothing worked, and in the end I was strapped to the chair. I think I probably bit her on the wrist during our struggle, since my mouth was filled with the taste of burnt rubber. I was right, as I found out once I was strapped in and she examined her left wrist—it bled from two punctures and a dozen little purple tooth marks. A look of weary sadness spread across her face. I began to feel a bit of regret plus a bit of apprehension, but most of all a sense of satisfaction about what I'd done to her. Little guttural moans were followed by two lines of discoloured tears running down her cheeks. I was screaming at the top of my lungs and pretending I knew nothing about her injured hand or the look of sadness on her face; I wasn't sure what would happen next, but deep down I knew there was no escape. Sure enough, the tears stopped and the sad look went away. 'You bastard,' she smirked, 'now you've done it, you little bastard. How dare you bite your mother! Merciful heavens,' she said as she looked skyward, 'open your eyes and look at the sorry excuse for a son I've raised! Not a son—a wolf, a contemptuous wolf! I've slaved to raise him, putting up with every shitty mess he made, and for what? So he can sink his teeth into me? I've endured back-breaking work, sweat by the bucketful and every imaginable indignity. They say the goldthread plant is bitter. Well, it's not as bitter as my life. They say vinegar is sour. Well, it's downright sweet compared to my life. After all that, this is what I ended up with! You haven't got all your teeth yet and your wings aren't hard enough to fly away, and still you sink your fangs into me? In a few years, when your teeth are grown and your wings are strong, you'll be ready to chew me up and spit me out! Well, you little bastard, I'll kill you with my own hands before I let that happen!' Mother was still cursing when she picked up a turnip as long as my arm, one she'd brought up from the cellar that morning, and broke it over my head. I felt as if my head had exploded and I saw half a turnip fly off somewhere just as the other half pounded my head, over and over and over. It hurt, but not unbearably. For a worthless child like me, that sort of pain is like the powerful Zhang Fei snacking on bean sprouts, easy as one, two, three. But I made it look like she'd knocked me senseless and let my head sag to the side. She grabbed my ear and pulled my head up straight. 'If you think you can fool me into thinking I've killed you, you're very much mistaken. You can roll your eyes, you can foam at the mouth, you can have a fainting spell. You're very much alive, but even if you're not I'm going to shave that scabby head of yours! If I, Yang Yuzhen, can't do that, then I've got no business being your mother!' She put a basin on top of the stool in front of me and pushed my head down into the hot water. It was really hot—hot enough to debristle a hog—and I could no longer hold back. Glug glug glug . . . 'Yang Yuzhen, you stinking old woman, Yang Yuzhen, I'm going to have my dieh finish you off with that don-key dick of his!' That filthy, disgusting curse really hit home, for I heard her screech just before a hailstorm of fists descended on my head. I screamed for all I was worth—it was my only chance for a miracle. Hoping some demon or ghost or the gods of heaven and earth would hurry up and put an end to the torture, I'd have gladly banged my head in three—no, make that six, or nine—loud kowtows to anyone who came to my rescue. Hell, I'd have called him Daddy, Dear Daddy. But it was Mother—no, not Mother, Yang Yuzhen, that bloodthirsty old woman, the hag my dieh had abandoned, who walked up, a yellow plastic apron round her waist, sleeves rolled up, a straight razor in her hand, creases in her forehead. Shave my head? She was going to cut it off! 'Help!' I shouted. 'Help . . . murder . . . Yang Yuzhen is going to murder me . . .' I guess my shouts weren't as effective as I thought, because her rage was abruptly replaced by snorts of laughter. 'You little swine, is that the best you can come up with?' I turned to see a bunch of more fortunate children— those lucky fellows—at our gate craning their necks to see what was going on inside—Yao Qi's son Fengshou, Chen Gan's son Pingdu, Big Ears' son Pidou, and Song Gujia's daughter Feng'e . . . I'd stopped hanging out with that crowd since my dieh ran off, not willingly, Dieh, but because I didn't have the time. Yang Yuzhen yanked me out of school and, at my young age, turned me into a coolie labourer, working me ten times harder than a poor cowherd in the old society. She got me wondering if she was really my mother. Tell me, Dieh, was I some cast-off baby born out of wedlock that you brought home from that run-down kiln where they made earthen crockpots? No real mother could bear to treat her child as mercilessly as she treats me. I guess I've lived long enough, so go ahead, Yang Yuzhen, kill me in front of those children. I felt the cold steel of her razor on my scalp. The moment of danger had arrived! I scrunched down my neck, like a threatened turtle. Emboldened by the sight, the children, like rats that had licked the cat's arse, moved in, through the gate and into our yard, drawing closer and closer to the house until they were standing just beyond the door, giggling and watching the comedy play out in front of them. 'Aren't you ashamed to be crying like that? Especially in front of your friends. Fengshou, Pingdu, Pidou, do you cry when you're getting your heads shaved?' 'No,' chorused Pingdu and Pidou. 'Why should we? It feels good.' 'You hear that?' She waved the clippers in front of me. 'A tiger doesn't eat her young. What makes you think your mother would do anything to hurt you?' While I was dredging up all those bad memories of the shaved-head incident, Fan Zhaoxia, owner of Beauty Hair Salon, walked in from one of the inner rooms, wearing a white smock, her hands in her pockets and looking like a woman's doctor. Tall and slim, she had a full head of black hair and fair skin but her face was marred by purple lumps and her breath carried the heated odour of horse feed. I knew that she and Lao Lan had a special relationship and that she was the one who kept his head neatly shaved. According to what I heard, she also trimmed his beard, a process that took upwards of an hour, while he slept. There was even talk that she shaved him while sitting in his lap. I wanted to tell Dieh all about Lao Lan and Fan Zhaoxia, but he kept his head down and refused to look at me.

'About time, Zhaoxia?' Pidou's niang put down her book and shot a gaze at the other woman's mottled face. Fan Zhaoxia tossed an indifferent glance at the golden-yellow watch on her wrist.

'Another twenty minutes,' she said.

Fan Zhaoxia painted the nails of her long, slender fingers a seductive red. As far as Mother was concerned, any woman who used lipstick or painted her nails was a flirt, and whenever she saw one she muttered curses through clenched teeth, as if venting pent-up loathing. My one-time disapproval of women who did things like that came from my mother, but then all that changed. I'm ashamed to admit it, but now when I see a woman with red lips and painted nails my heart races and I can't take my eyes off her. Fan Zhaoxia picked up the smock from the back of the chair, shook it open and snapped it in the air a couple of times.

'Who's first?' she asked, still in that indifferent tone.

'You first, Xiaotong,' Father said.

'No,' I said, 'you first.'

'Hurry up,' fussed Fan Zhaoxia.

With a look my way, Father stood up, crossed his arms, walked up to the chair and cautiously sat down; the springs creaked beneath his weight.

Fan Zhaoxia first tucked in Father's collar and then tied the smock round his neck. I saw her face in the mirror. She was frowning, a mean look. His face was next to hers, twisted and ugly in the rippled mercury.

'How do you want it?' she asked, still frowning.

'Shaved,' he said in a muted voice.

'Aiya!' Pidou's niang blurted out in astonishment, apparently recognizing Father at that very moment. 'Aren't you—'

Father grunted a response, neither answering her unfinished question nor turning his head.

Fan Zhaoxia took a pair of electric clippers from a peg on the wall and turned it on, producing a low hum. Pressing down Father's head, she pressed the clippers into his tangle of hair. A pale swath of skin opened up down the middle as clots of hair, dense as felt, rained down on the floor.

As I recall the scene of Father's cascading hair, what plays out in front of my eyes is actually something different: the handsome fellow named Lan— we'll call him Lao Lan's third uncle (that's because the image that follows matches exactly what Lao Lan said)—is marrying that lovely woman with the beauty spot at the corner of her mouth—that's right, Shen Yaoyao—in a Western-style ceremony in a towering church room that glitters like gold. He is wearing a dark Western suit, a white shirt and a black bow tie, with a purple boutonnière tucked into his breast pocket. His bride is in white, with a long train held off the floor by a pair of angelic little boys. She has a face like a peach blossom, eyes like twinkling stars; the milk of happiness flows down her face. Candles, music, fresh flowers and fine wine create a romantic aura. But no more than ten minutes have passed since a white-haired old man on his way to the church was shot in the chest in his sedan, and the smell of gun-powder has already invaded the church's vestibule. Is this another of your tricks, Wise Monk? Then I see the girl sprawled across her father's body, shat-tering the silence with her wails, mascara-laden tears coursing down her face, as the handsome young man stands silently and impassively to one side. The next image—in a fancy room—is of the young woman, cutting off her beautiful hair. I can see her bloodless face in the mirror on the wall, her wrinkled mouth turned down at the corners. I see her recollections as she shears through the strands of hair. At some hazy place that beautiful young woman and the handsome young man are making love in strange positions. Her passion-filled face rushes towards me, then crashes into the mirror and shatters into a million pieces. Then I see her in dark blue clothes, her head covered by a blue and white scarf as she kneels before an old Buddhist nun. Wise Monk, just the way I kneel in front of you. The old nun takes her in, Wise Monk, but you still haven't taken me in. I'd like to ask if that handsome young man hired someone to kill the beautiful young woman's father. I also want to ask what they wanted. I know you'll never answer my question, but now that I've shared my suspicions with you I can put them out of my mind. If I don't, they'll overload my brain and drive me crazy. There's something I want to tell you, Wise Monk. One summer day around noon, more than a decade ago, when everyone in Slaughterhouse Village was asleep, I walked the streets aimlessly like a bored dog, sniffing here and there. When I reached the Beauty Hair Salon entrance, I put my face up against the glass to see what was going on inside. What I saw was an electric fan hanging on the wall, turning from side to side, and the barber, Fan Zhaoxia, in her white smock, seated in Lao Lan's lap with a straight razor in her hand. For a moment I thought she was going to cut his throat, but then I could tell that they were doing you-know-what. She held the razor high over her head in order to keep it away from his face. Her legs were spread and hooked over the arms of the barber-chair. A look of rapture twisted her face out of shape. But she held on to that razor, as if to prove to anyone sneaking a look inside that they were working, not having sex. I wanted to tell someone about these strange goings-on but there was no one to tell, only a black dog sprawled beneath a plane tree, panting away, its tongue lolling to the side. I backed up several paces, picked up a brick and flung it with all my might, then turned to run as fast as I could. I heard the sound of shattering glass behind me. Wise Monk, I'm ashamed to reveal that I was capable of something so despicable, but I think that if I don't tell you it will be an act of disloyalty. I know people call me a Powboy, but that was then. Now, every word I tell you is the unvarnished truth.

The East City and West City processions continue to make their way to the grassy field. The pig float, the sheep float, the donkey float, the rabbit float . . . all the floats—dedicated to a host of animals whose bodies are offered for the consumption of humans—head to their assigned spots, surrounded by people of every imaginable shape and size who arrange them in square formations to await the arrival of the reviewing VIPs. All but Lao Lan's ostriches, which are running about in our yard. Two of them are fighting over a muddy article of clothing—orange in colour—as if it were a tasty titbit. I recall the woman who'd showed up the day before in a torrential rainstorm, and that scene saddens me. Every few minutes an ostrich sticks its head through the temple door, curiosity flashing in its tiny round eyes. The aura of lassitude emanating from the boys and girls sitting on the rubble of the collapsed wall is in stark contrast to the ostriches' frenetic action. Employees of Lao Lan's company jabber nonstop into mobile phones. Another ostrich pokes its head inside, but this time it opens it big mouth and pecks the top of the Wise Monk's head. Instinctively, I throw one of my shoes at it but the Wise Monk casually raises his hand and deflects the flying missile. He opens his eyes and presents a smiling countenance—the look of a kindly grandfather watching his grandson take his first steps—to the bird. A black Buick, horn blaring, screams down the road from the west, speeds past the floats and comes to a screeching halt in front of the temple. A man with an expansive belly steps out of the car. He is wearing a grey double-breasted suit with a wide red-checked tie; the label still on his sleeve is that of a famous and expensive brand. But no matter what fancy names he wraps himself in, those big yellow eyes tell me he's my mortal enemy Lao Lan. Several years ago, Wise Monk, I fired off forty-one mortar shells, and the last of them sliced Lao Lan in two. As a result, I took off for destinations unknown to lie low. I later heard that he hadn't died after all; in fact, his business ventures thrived and he was in better health than ever. Out of the car also emerges a fat woman in a purple dress and dark red high heels. She's dyed a section of her permed hair a bright red, like a cockscomb. She has on six rings, three gold and three platinum, a gold necklace and a string of pearls. She's fleshed out quite a bit, but I see at first glance that it's Fan Zhaoxia, the woman who screwed Lao Lan with a razor in her hand. While I was on the run, rumour had it that she and Lao Lan had got married, and the scene in front of me proves that the rumour was true. As soon as her feet are on the ground, she spreads her arms and runs to the children sitting on the pile of rubble. The girl who'd fought with her ostrich until she pinned it to the ground runs to Fan Zhaoxia. She enfolds the girl in her arms, covering her face with kisses like chickens pecking at rice and fills her ears with 'my dear this' and 'my little darling that'. I look at the pretty little girl's face with mixed feelings. What a surprise that Lao Lan, that bastard, could sire such a nice offspring, a girl who reminds me of my deceased stepsister Jiaojiao, who would have now been a girl of fourteen. Lao Lan lets fly with a string of curses at his staff, who are lined up in front of him, arms at their sides. One tries to explain matters and is rewarded with a faceful of spit. Lan's ostrich team was to put on a dance performance at the Carnivore Festival opening ceremony—a true spectacle that would leave a lasting impression on visiting businessmen and, more importantly, on all the leading officials. Words of praise and order forms would follow in large numbers. But before the show has begun it has fallen apart, thanks to these idiots. The hour for the opening ceremony is nearly upon them and Lao Lan's forehead is bathed in sweat. 'Get those ostriches in here this minute or I'll turn every one of you into ostrich feed!' They need no more prodding to take after the birds. And the uncooperative birds that they are, they miss no opportunity to race away on powerful feet like the shod hooves of crazed horses. Lao Lan rolls up his sleeves to join the fray but his first step lands in a pile of loose ostrich shit and he winds up flat on his back. His employees, who rush to help him to his feet, have to scrunch up their faces to keep from laughing. 'Think that's funny, do you?' Lao Lan is caustic in his comments. 'Go ahead, laugh, why don't you?' The youngest-looking among them cannot hold back—he bursts out laughing, immediately affecting the others, who join in, and that includes Lao Lan himself. But only for a moment. 'You think it's so goddamn funny?' he roars. 'I'll fire the next one of you who so much as giggles!' Somehow, they manage to stop. 'Go get my rifle. I'm going to put a bullet into every one of those damned birds!'

Three nights after New Year's, my family of four sat round a fold-up table waiting for Lao Lan. The man who had a third uncle whose prodigious member had gained for him considerable fame; the man who was my father's mortal enemy; the man who had broken one of my father's fingers only to have my father bite off half his ear; the man who had invented the high-pressure injection method, the sulphur-smoke treatment, the hydrogen-peroxide bleach method and the formaldehyde-immersion system; the man who had earned the nickname of 'Hanlin butcher' and who, as our village head, had led the villagers onto the path of prosperity; the man whose word was law and who enjoyed unrivalled authority—Lao Lan. Lao Lan, who had taught my mother how to drive a tractor; Lao Lan, who had screwed the barber Fan Zhaoxia in her barber-chair; Lao Lan, who'd sworn he'd put a bullet into every last ostrich; Lao Lan, the mention of whose name upsets the hell out of me!

The table groaned under platters of chicken, duck, fish and red meat but we couldn't eat it, even though the heat and the aroma were quickly dissipating. That must be the most painful, most annoying, most disgusting, most aggravating thing in the world. I tell you, I once vowed that if I had the power I'd rid the world of every last eater of pork. But that was an angry outburst after I'd stuffed myself with so much pork that I nearly died of an intestinal disorder. Man is quick to adapt to changing circumstances and to bend his words to the situation—no one disputes that. It's the way we are. On that occasion, the mere thought of pork made me nauseous and gave me a belly-ache, so why shouldn't I have shot off my mouth? I was, after all, a boy of ten. You can't expect a boy of that age to sound like the Emperor, whose golden mouth and jade teeth utter words that cannot be changed, can you? When I got home from Beauty Hair Salon that day, Mother brought out some leftover pork from that morning.

Enduring the pain in my gut as best as I could, I said, 'No more for me. If I ever eat another bite of the stuff, I'll turn into a pig.'

'Really?' she said sarcastically. 'My son's had his head shaved and has sworn off eating pork. Is he leaving home to become a monk?'

'Just you wait and see,' I said. 'The next time I eat pork will definitely be the day I become a monk.'

A week later, my vow to Mother still rang in my ears but I was hungry for pork once more. And not just pork—I was hungry for beef too. And chicken and donkey and the flesh of any edible animal that walked the earth. Mother and Father got busy as soon as lunch was over. She sliced the stewed beef, braised pork liver and ham sausage she'd bought and laid them out on fine Jingde platters borrowed from Sun Changsheng, while Father scrubbed the table, also borrowed from Sun Changsheng, with a wet rag.

Everything we needed for this spur-of-the-moment meal for our guest we were able to borrow from Sun Changsheng, whose wife was my mother's cousin. The look on his face let us know us how he felt about the loan but he said nothing. Mother's cousin, on the other hand, frowned as she watched my parents walk out with their possessions, not at all happy with her relatives. Not quite forty, this woman already had thinning hair, which, with no sense of embarrassment, she wove into short braids that stuck up on the sides of her head like dried beans. The sight put my teeth on edge.

As she took things out of her cupboard, following my mother's list, she muttered, her voice growing louder and louder: 'Yuzhen, no one lives like you two, getting by with nothing. I'm not talking about a houseful of furniture. You don't even own a spare set of chopsticks!'

'You know our situation,' Mother replied with a smile, 'how we had to put all our money into building the house.'

Her cousin looked at Father disapprovingly: 'Part of running a household is furnishing the basics. Always borrowing what you need is not the answer.'

'It's important for us to get on his good side,' Mother explained. 'He is, after all, the village head, someone who oversees . . .'

'I don't know how Lao Lan thinks, but after putting in a hard day's work at this, you might well wind up eating all the food yourself,' her cousin carried on. 'If I were him, I wouldn't go. Not in times like these. And certainly not for a paltry meal. If you want to get on his good side, take him a red envelope filled with money.'

'I sent Xiaotong three times before he agreed to come.'

'That might give Xiaotong some standing, but if you're going to have him over, do it right. He'll laugh if you give him common fare. Don't invite some-one if you're afraid of spending money. Since you're set on hosting him, then go ahead and spend. I know you too well. Even small change sticks to your ribs.'

'People aren't mountains, they can change . . .' Mother's face grew red as she struggled to hold on to her temper.

'Except it's easier to change the course of a river than a person's nature.' Mother's cousin was intent on making things hard for her.

Sun Changsheng was the one who snapped first. 'That's enough!' he growled at his wife. 'If your mouth itches, rub it against the wall. You fart three times for every time you kowtow. Your good deeds don't make up for your bad behaviour. Why must you offend your cousin who only wants to borrow a few things?'

'I'm just looking out for them,' Mother's cousin defended herself.

'She hasn't offended me,' Mother hurried to appease him. 'I know what to expect from her. I wouldn't have come if we weren't kin. It gives her the right to talk to me like that.'

Sun Changsheng took out a packet of cigarettes and handed one to Father: 'Yes, who doesn't have to lower their head when they're beneath an eave?'

Father nodded, with no indication of whether or not he agreed.

I revisited the furniture-borrowing episode in my mind, from beginning to end, as a means of passing an excruciatingly long time. An inch or more of kerosene had burnt off in the lamp, and a long ash had formed on the wick of the candle left over from New Year's, but there was still no sign of Lao Lan. Father turned to look at Mother.

'Maybe we should snuff out the candle?' he said cautiously.

'Let it burn,' she said as she flicked the wick with her finger and sent the ash flying. The candle flared, brightening the room and adding to the sheen of the meat on the table, especially the captivating red skin of the barbecued chicken.

Jiaojiao and I ran to the cutting board, our eyes glued to Mother's hands as she sliced up the chicken; we were fascinated by how deftly she separated the meat from the bones. One drumstick was placed on the platter, and then the second.

'Mother,' I asked, 'is there such a thing as a three-legged chicken?'

'There might be,' she smiled, 'but what I'd really like to see is a four-legged one. That way, you could each have one to satisfy those hungry worms in your bellies.'

It was a bird from the Dong Family shop. They prepared only local, free-range chickens—not those stupid caged birds raised on chemical feed, with meat like cotton filling and bones like rotten wood. No, their chickens are smart—they live on weeds and seeds and insects, and grow up with nice. Firm meat and solid bones. First-rate nutrition and a wonderful taste.

'But I heard Ping Shanchuan's son, Ping Du, say that even though the Dongs raise wild chickens, they fill them with hormones when they're alive and add formaldehyde when they're dead.'

'So?' asked Mother as she picked off a pinch of loose meat and put it into Jiaojiao's mouth. 'Farmers have iron stomachs.'

Jiaojiao was her lively self again, and her relationship with Mother was improving all the time. As she opened her mouth for the meat, she kept her eyes on Mother's hand. Next, Mother picked a larger piece off the back and stuffed it into my mouth, skin and all. I swallowed it without chewing, so fast it seemed to slide down my throat of its own accord. Jiaojiao licked her lips with her bright red tongue just as Mother picked off another piece of chicken and put it into her mouth.

'Be good, patient children for just a little longer,' she said. 'After our guest has finished, you can have what's left.'

Jiaojiao was still staring at Mother's hand.

'That's enough,' Father said. 'Don't spoil her. Children need their manners, it's no good to spoil them.'

He went out and paced the yard for a moment.

'It doesn't look like he's coming,' he said when he returned. 'I must have offended him terribly.'

'I don't think so,' Mother said. 'He said he'll be here, and he will. Lao Lan means what he says.' She turned to me. 'What did he say to you, Xiaotong?'

'How many times do I have to tell you?' I complained. ' "All right," he said. "I'll be there, for your sake. You can count on it." '

'Should we send Xiaotong to remind him?' Father asked. 'Perhaps he's forgotten.'

'No,' Mother insisted. 'He won't forget.'

'But everything's getting cold,' I said, growing more and more annoyed. 'He's only the head of a little village.'

Father and Mother looked at me at the same time and smiled.

The son of a bitch is more than the head of a little village. I hear that the municipal government has designated Slaughterhouse Village as a new economic development zone in order to attract foreign investment. Factories and high-rise buildings are popping up out of the ground; a vast man-made lake has appeared out of nowhere and quickly become home to tourist skiffs shaped like swans and ducks. All round the lake fancy new villas are springing up, creating a sort of fairyland. The men who live in them drive fancy cars— Mercedes, BMW, Buick, Lexus or, at the very least, Red Flag. The women parade their purebreds—Pekingese, poodles, shar peis, papillons, some that look like sheep but aren't, even one that looks more like a tiger than a dog. A pair of mastiffs once dragged a fair-skinned woman with soft, white hands and a charmingly delicate appearance down to the lakeshore. The lovely 'vacation wife' was on her back, like she was doing the backstroke or ploughing a field. In today's society, Wise Monk, the best that labouring people can hope for is to make enough to live a decent life. Most never even manage that, satisfied if they have enough to eat and a means of keeping warm. Only the bold, the heartless and the shameless find ways to strike it rich. Take that bastard Lao Lan. If he wants money he gets it; if he wants fame he gets it; and if he wants status he gets it—what does that say about social equality? The monk just smiles. I know my anger isn't worth anything, sort of like a beggar venting his anger by grinding his teeth, but perhaps that's where I am now, and perhaps I'll take such things more calmly after shaving my head, becoming a monk and undergoing three years of Buddhist cultivation. But for now I'm just someone who says what's on his mind, and that, Wise Monk, is reason enough to take me on as a novice. If enlightenment eludes me, you can drive me out with your staff. Look, Wise Monk, that marauding Lao Lan has had a rifle sent over. I wonder if he really has the guts to turn the Wutong Temple that his ancestors built into a slaughterhouse. I'll bet he does. I know what he's capable of. He's taken the big-bore rifle from the hands of his sweaty, panting assistant. To be precise, it ought to be called a musket. It doesn't look like much but it's a powerful weapon. My dieh had one of those in the past. Lao Lan is spewing filth, and those yellow eyes of his look like gold-plated balls. Don't be fooled by his suit and his polished shoes—he's still a thug, through and through. He looks at the ostriches; they cock their heads and look back at him. He pulls the trigger just as a gob of bird shit lands on his nose. He tucks his neck down into his shoulders, jerks the barrel into the air and sends a musket ball in a blast of flames across a broad swath of temple eaves. Amid the dying roar of the explosion rain down shards of broken tiles just beyond the temple door, no more than a couple of paces from where we're sitting. A cry of alarm escapes my lips but the Wise Monk remains seated peacefully, as if nothing has happened. Enraged, Lao Lan flings the musket to the ground and wipes the filth off his face with tissues handed to him by his assistant. Then he looks up into the sky, which is deep blue, nearly black, except where dark clouds gather. A scattered flock of white-bellied magpies loudly announces its passage from north to south. The fouler of Lao Lan's nose is a member of that flock. 'That's magpie shit, Boss Lan,' his assistant says, 'and that's a good sign.' 'Enough of your arse-kissing!' snaps Lao Lan. 'Magpie shit is still shit. Reload the musket. I'm going to blow every fucking one of those birds out of the sky.' An underling rushes up, kneels on one knee—his right— and lays the musket across his upturned knee—his left. He opens the sleek powder horn and pours in a measure of powder. 'More powder,' Lao Lan commands. 'Fill it up, damn it. I've had nothing but bad luck today. A couple of good shots should blast that away.' As he bites down on his lip, the underling stuffs the powder into the barrel with a ramrod as Fan Zhaoxia walks up with the girl in her arms: 'What sort of shitty birdbrain antics are you up to? Look what you did to our poor Jiaojiao!' My heart lurches when I hear that name. A mixture of rage and sorrow twists and turns its way into my head. They actually named their daughter Jiaojiao, the same as my little sister? Was it deliberate? And was it kindness or malice? Images of Jiaojiao's adorable face when she was healthy and her face twisted in pain just before she died flash through my mind. One of Lao Lan's underlings, a youthful boy with a girlish face, walks up and says with respectful earnestness: 'Boss Lan, Madam, we shouldn't be wasting time here, we should be at the ceremony site getting the camels ready. If they perform well, the reviews will be positive. As far as the ostriches are concerned, we can try again next year.' Fan Zhaoxia gives the young man an approving look. 'He's got the mind of a thug,' she says of Lao Lan. 'So what?' Lao Lan fires back with an angry glare. 'Where do you think we'd be today if I didn't? A rebellion by the effete will fail, even after a decade. A rebellion by thugs succeeds with a single shot. What are you waiting for? Give me that when you're finished!' he barks at the fellow loading the musket. The man hands it to him carefully with both hands. 'Take Jiaojiao out of the way,' Lao Lan says to Fan Zhaoxia, 'and cover her ears. I don't want to damage her eardrums.' 'You're like a dog that can't stop eating shit,' she grumbles as she backs away with the girl. The girl stretches out an arm and cries out shrilly: 'Papa, I want to shoot too!' Lao Lan takes aim at the ostriches. 'You flat-feathered fiends, you ingrates,' he mutters, 'all I asked of you was to dance. Well, you can go report to the King of Hell!' A fiery yellow ball explodes in front of him, followed by a deafening roar and a cloud of black smoke. As pieces of musket fly in all directions, the figure of Lao Lan stands transfixed for an instant before falling to the ground. Fan Zhaoxia shrieks and drops the child in her arms. Lan's men are stunned for a moment. Then they snap out of their stupor and rush to him, filling the air with shouts of 'Boss Lan! Boss Lan!'

Lao Lan's aides pick him up—his hands are a bloody mess, his face black with soot. 'My eyes! Damn it, my eyes!' he screams through his pain, 'I can't see! I can't see you now, Third Uncle!' Third Uncle means a great deal to the lousy bastard, but why shouldn't he? Most members of the previous generation of Lans were shot, and the few who survived died during the difficult years that followed. Only this unworldly third uncle occupies an iconic spot in his mind. His aides place Lao Lan in the back seat of the Buick; Fan Zhaoxia squeezes into the front with the girl in her arms, and the car makes its unsteady way up to the highway, where, with a blast of its horn, it speeds off to the west and runs smack into a contingent of stilt-walkers who scatter in confusion. One of them barely makes it out of the way, only to have a stilt sink into the mud and topple him to the ground. Several of his fellow walkers hop across the asphalt to extricate him from his troubles. All this reminds me of a Mid-Autumn Festival a decade ago, when my little sister and I scooped up locusts that were sticking their tails into the road's hard surface to lay eggs. My mother was dead by then and my father had been arrested, which effectively orphaned my sister and me. We were on our way to South Mountain to look for mortar shells, with the white moon rising in the east and the red sun setting in the west—in other words, dusk. We were hungry and miserable. A breeze rustled the leaves of nearby crops and autumn insects chirped in the grass— all sounds of desolation. We pulled locusts off the road stretching their abdomens as far as they'd go, then scrounged together some dry kindling, built a fire and flung the misshapen locusts into the flames, where they curled up and gave off a special fragrance. Wise Monk, this was an evil deed, I know that. Eating an egg-laying female locust is the same as eating hundreds of them. But if we hadn't eaten them we'd have starved. This is a problem I've never been able to resolve. Wise Monk gives me a pointed look whose meaning escapes me. The West City stilt-walkers, all employees of a restaurant called

Xiang Man Lou, wear white uniforms and chef's hats bearing the restaurant's name. Wise Monk, it's an establishment capable of offering a complete formal banquet, featuring both Chinese and Manchu delicacies. The executive chef, a disciple of Manchu palace chefs, is as skilful as you'd imagine him to be. But he's hot-tempered. A Hong Kong restaurant once tried to lure him away with a monthly salary of twenty thousand Hong Kong dollars, but failed. Japanese and Taiwanese tourists flock to the restaurant to sample its delicacies. These are the only occasions when he deigns to appear in the kitchen; the rest of the time he occupies a seat in the restaurant and drinks oolong tea from a small dark red teapot (all that tea has turned his teeth black). Well, the stilt-walkers are ill fated, for as soon as they leave the asphalt road their stilts stick in the grassy soil, and soon their formation is thrown into disarray. Their corresponding unit from East Town is a contingent of thirty or so marchers from the Lekoufu Sausage Factory, each of whom holds a red string attached to a big, red, sausage-shaped balloon. The pull of the balloons is strong enough to send the men up onto the balls of their feet, looking as if they could float into the blue sky at any minute.

The first time I followed Mother's instructions to go to Lao Lan's house was a bright, sunny afternoon. Melting snow on the road, paved only that autumn, was turning into a dirty sludge; a pair of tyre tracks in the middle, left moments before by an automobile, exposed a bit of the black asphalt underneath. No villager was taxed for the road to be asphalted—Lao Lan had paid for it all, and it was a boon to the villagers who needed to reach the highway into town. That boosted Lao Lan's prestige to an all-time high, or, as they say, when the river floods, all boats rise.

As I walked down the road, which Lao Lan had named Hanlin Avenue, after the famous academy of scholars, I watched water drip, like translucent pearls, from roof tiles facing the sun. The tattoo of dripping water, the cool, earthy aroma of the soil and the melting snow—each left an impression on my mind and seemed to sharpen my senses. The ground near the roadside houses, out of the sun, was still covered by snow; some obscured by piles of garbage and much of it stippled by the jumbled prints of wandering dogs and chickens unsure of their footing. People were entering and leaving Beauty Hair Salon. Thick black smoke billowed from the chimney sticking out from under the eaves; black tar oozed from its base and stained the snow beneath. Yao Qi was standing in his usual pose, smoking his pipe on the steps of his house, a man frozen in deep thought. He waved when he saw me and, though I'd have preferred to ignore him, on second thought I walked up and looked him in the eye, instantly reminded of the indignity I'd suffered at his hands. After Father ran off, he'd once said to me in front of a group of good-for-nothings: 'Xiaotong, go home and tell your mom to leave her door unlocked for me tonight!' They'd had a big laugh but I'd retorted angrily: 'Yao Qi, fuck you and all your ancestors!' This time I was ready to cut him down to size with every dirty saying I could think of but he took me by surprise: 'Good Nephew Xiaotong,' he began amiably. 'What's your dieh up to these days?'

'Do you really expect me to tell you?' I replied icily.

'You've got quite a temper, young man,' he said. 'Go home and tell him to come see me. I need to talk to him about something.'

'Sorry,' I said, 'I'm not your message boy, and he wouldn't come to see you anyway.'

'Yes, quite a temper,' he said, 'and obstinate to boot.'

Putting Yao Qi behind me, I turned into Lan Clan Lane, which connected to Hanlin Bridge over Five Dragons River behind the village and became the highway to the county seat. A VW Santana was parked in front of the Lan house. The driver was inside, listening to music, while the neighbourhood children ran round touching the bright exterior with their fingers. The lower half of the car was covered with mud. Obviously, someone of authority was visiting Lao Lan and, since it was mealtime—and drinking time—I could smell the aromatic clouds emanating from inside. Distinguishing the various meaty smells was easy—it was as if I could see them. Then I recalled Mother's admonition: 'Never call on someone at mealtime. Your arrival will be awkward for them and embarrassing for you.' But I wasn't there looking for a free snack; on the contrary, I was there to invite Lao Lan to our house for a meal. So I decided to interrupt the party and do what Mother had sent me to do.

It would be my first time inside the Lan compound. And it was just as I'd said earlier. From the outside, the Lan house looked less impressive than ours. But once I was in their front yard I discovered the fundamental difference between the two: ours was like a bun made from white flour wrapped round a filling of rotten cabbage leaves; theirs was a bun made of whole-grain flour wrapped round three delicacies. Theirs had a multi-grain, highly nutritious skin, dark grain with no impurities. And though ours was nice and white, it was made of trashy, chemically whitened flour that's bad for your health. Stored for years in a war-preparedness warehouse, it was wheat powder denuded of all nutritive value. Using edible buns as a metaphor for homes is a stretch, I know that, Wise Monk, so forgive me. But with my poor educational background, that's the best I can come up with. Well, I'd no sooner stepped into the yard than his two fierce wolfhounds erupted in loud, threatening barks. They were chained to splendid doghouses by nickel-plated chain collars that rattled with every move. Instinctively, I backed up against the wall to prepare to ward off an attack. Unnecessarily, as it turned out, because they thought I was beneath them, and their half-hearted barks were mere formalities. Their bowls were filled with fine food, which included bones with plenty of bright red meat on them. Wild beasts survive on raw meat— it's what keeps them mean and fearless. 'If you feed a ferocious tiger nothing but sweet potatoes, in time it'll turn into a pig.' Lao Lan said that, and it made the rounds in the village. He also said, 'Dogs walk the earth eating shit, wolves travel the world eating meat.' 'Character qualities stubbornly resist change.' That's something else he said, and it too made the rounds in the village.

A man in a white cap emerging from the eastern room with a food hamper nearly bumped into me. It was Lao Bai, chef at the Huaxi Dog Meat Restaurant, a talented specialist in preparing dog meat and a distant cousin of dog-breeder Huang Biao's wife. Since Bai had come out of that particular room, it was clear that a banquet was in progress and that Lao Lan would not be anywhere else. So I clenched my jaw, walked up and opened the door. The captivating smell of dog meat hung heavy in the air. A steaming copper hot pot sat in the centre of a large revolving dining table surrounded by several diners, including Lao Lan, all busily devouring the food and drink. Their faces shone—half sweat and half oil—as they plucked dripping chunks of dog meat from the hot pot and crammed them into open mouths that complained of the heat but were immediately cooled by slugs of chilled beer. Tsingtao Beer, the best, of course, served in tall glasses, bubbles rising amid the amber liquid. The first to spot me was a fat woman with a face the colour of garnet, but she said nothing— she simply stopped eating, puffed up her cheeks and stared at me.

Lao Lan turned and froze for a moment before his face creased into a broad smile. 'What do you want, Luo Xiaotong?' He turned to the fat woman before I could answer and said, 'The world's most gluttonous boy is in our midst.' Then he turned back to me. 'Luo Xiaotong, people say you'll call anyone Dieh who offers you a good meaty meal. Is that right?'

'Yes.'

'Well, then, son, sit down and dig in. I want you to know that this is a Huaxi dog-meat hot pot, enhanced with more than thirty herbs and spices, the likes of which I'm sure you've never sampled.'

'Come here, youngster,' said the fat woman, whose accent revealed her as a foreigner. The person next to her, obviously a subordinate, echoed her comment: 'Come here, youngster.'

I swallowed to stop myself from drooling.

'But that was before,' I said. 'Now that my own dieh is back, there's no need to call anyone else Dieh.'

'Why did that arsehole come back anyway?' asked Lao Lan.

'This is where he was born and where my grandparents are buried. Why shouldn't he come back?' It was up to me to make a case for his return.

'Now that's a good boy, sticking up for your dieh even at your young age,' Lao Lan said. 'Just what a son ought to do. Luo Tong may be a coward but his son isn't.' He nodded and sipped his beer. 'So, what do you want?'

'This wasn't my idea,' I said. 'My mother sent me to invite you to dinner tonight.'

'Will miracles never cease? Your mother is the world's meanest person. She'll pick up a bone a dog's gnawed clean and take it home to make soup. Why the invitation?'

'You know why,' I said.

'What's the boy's name?' the fat lady mumbled as she chewed on a piece of dog meat. 'Oh, yes, it's Luo Xiaotong. How old are you, Luo Xiaotong?'

'I don't know.'

'Do you really not know how old you are?' she asked, 'Or do you not want to tell us? How dare you talk that way in front of the village head! What grade are you in? Primary school or high school?'

'I don't go to school.' I snarled. 'I hate school.'

The woman laughed for some strange reason, even squeezed out a few tiny tears. I decided to ignore her, for she had terrible table manners. I didn't care if she was a mayor's mother or the wife of the provincial governor or if she herself was a mayor or something even higher.

I turned to Lao Lan and said sombrely: 'Tonight. Our place for dinner and drinks. Please don't forget.'

'All right, I'll be there, for your sake. You can count on it.'

The final two contingents of marchers meet on the highway. The one from West City represents the Madonna Fur Coat Factory, famous for all sorts of leather goods. Owning a Madonna fur or leather coat is the dream of young men and women with empty purses. The contingent comprises twenty male and twenty female models. It's now midsummer, but they are all wearing the company's fur and leather products; they approach the reviewing stand from west to east and, at a signal from the group leader, begin to strut as if on a catwalk. The male models have closely cropped hair and wear stern expressions. Their female counterparts, who have dyed their hair in a rainbow of colours, have that special model look as they sashay along in colourful furs and leathers but display no emotion, more wild animals than human. Even on such a blistering summer day, their unseasonal attire produces not a drop of sweat. Wise Monk, I've heard rumours of a fire dragon elixir that allows a person to bathe in a frozen river in the heart of winter. From the looks of it, there is perhaps also an ice-and-snow elixir that allows a person to stroll under the sun wearing a fur coat on one of the hottest days of summer.

From East City comes a float shaped like a medicinal tablet with the words Di-a-Tab in the Song Dynasty calligraphic style, sponsored by Ankang Pharmaceutical Group. What surprises me is the absence of marchers for a company as famous as Ankang. Just a float, rolling down the street like a gigantic medicinal tablet. I know all about that so-called anti-indigestion remedy, which I'd encountered five years before, when I was wandering the streets of a well-known city and saw little flags with Di-a-Tab ads flapping in the wind from utility poles on both sides of the street. I also saw a Di-a-Tab ad on a huge LCD TV screen above the city square: a single Di-a-Tab is released into an enormous stomach stuffed to bursting with meat; it dissolves into a white mist that then emerges from the mouth. The accompanying text, bland beyond belief, read: 'After eating a side of beef, with Di-a-Tab you get relief.' The idiot who wrote that obviously knows nothing about meat. The relationship of meat to humans is very complex, and there are only a few people on this earth who understand it as well as I do. The way I see it, the creators of Di-a-Tab ought to be dragged over to the grassy knoll by the Wutong River Bridge—East City's old execution ground—and shot. After eating your fill of meat, you sit back quietly to enjoy the digestive process, a post-gustatory delight. But these idiots come along with Di-a-Tab, which just shows how low the human race has fallen. Am I right or am I not, Wise Monk?

Finally, all the contingents of marchers are in their assigned spots on the grassy field and, for the moment, the highway in front of the temple looks deserted. A white utility van speeds in our direction from West City, turns off the highway when it reaches the temple and stops under a gingko tree. Three brawny men jump out. One is middle-aged and dressed in an old army uniform faded nearly white from too many launderings. Lively and spry despite his age, he is clearly a man of unusual abilities. I recognize him right away—Lao Lan's follower Huang Bao, a man who's had considerable dealings with our family and who yet remains a mystery, at least to me. The men take a large net out of the van and then spread it open. Then two of them, one on each end, begin walking towards the ostriches, and I know that the end is nigh. Huang Bao has obviously been sent on a mission for Lao Lan, and as such is playing the role of commander. The ignorant ostriches run straight towards the net, and the necks of three of them are immediately snagged by its holes. All the rest, flustered by the trap the others have stumbled into, turn and run, leaving the unfortunate three to struggle and complain hoarsely. After fetching a pair of garden shears from the van, Huang Bao goes up to the net, and—snip, snip, snip—separates the birds' heads from their bodies at the thinnest part of the necks. The now-headless torsos perform a brief macabre dance before toppling over, spurts of dark blood gushing like a runaway hose from their truncated, python-like necks. The stink of blood seeps into the temple just as Huang Bao and his crew's mortal enemy arrives on the scene, a manifestation of the saying 'Every evil man fears someone worse.' Five stony-faced men in black emerge from somewhere behind the temple. The tallest among them, wearing sunglasses, a cigar dangling from his lips, is the mysterious Lan Daguan. As his four henchmen charge Huang Bao and his men, they draw rubber truncheons from their belts and, without a 'by your leave', begin cracking open heads. The sickening crunches and spurts of blood chill my heart. No matter what, Huang

Bao has been counted as one of us, a fellow villager. I see him holding his head in pain. 'Who are you?' he shouts. 'Who gave you orders to attack us?' Blood oozes from between his fingers. His attackers remain silent and simply raise their truncheons once more. Huanb Bao has lost this battle; stumbling over to the highway, he runs away, shouting: 'Just wait, you guys. . .' Now you may think none of this makes any sense but it's all happening before my eyes. Lan Daguan crouches in front of one of the ostrich heads, reaches out and touches hairs that are still quivering. Then he stands up, takes out a white silk hand-kerchief, cleans his blood-stained finger with it and then throws it away. It is swept up by a gust of wind before it hits the ground and, like an oversized white butterfly, flaps its way over the temple roof and disappears from view. He now walks up to the temple and stands there a moment before removing his sun-glasses, as if to show his face. I see the ravages of time on that face and the depths of melancholy in those eyes. A piercing crackle fills the air, a burst of loudspeaker static, followed by a man's husky announcement: 'Stand by for the Tenth Annual Twin Cities Carnivore Festival and Foundation-Stone-Laying Ceremony for the Meat God Temple!'

At last, Lao Lan, a brown wool overcoat over a military uniform, appeared in the circle of light cast by the lantern and candles in our house, preceded by a hearty 'Ha-ha!' His uniform was the real thing: the collar and shoulders still bore traces of insignias and epaulettes. His overcoat, with its bright shiny buttons, was that of a field officer. A dozen or so years earlier, woollen uniforms like that were worn only by local Party cadres, a sign of their status, in much the same way as the legendary grey Dacron Mao tunics symbolized a commune cadre. Lao Lan had the nerve to go out in a woollen uniform despite the fact that he was only a village cadre, which proved that he did not consider himself a minor official. It was rumoured in the village that he and the town mayor were sworn brothers; as a result, in his estimation, all the county and township heads were beneath him. And with justification, since they found it necessary to get in his good graces for their promotions and personal wealth.

Lao Lan stepped into our brightly lit living room and, with a shrug, let his overcoat slip into the hands of the seemingly simple-minded but actually brilliant Huang Bao, who had entered right on his heels and now stood there respectfully holding the coat and looking like a flagpole. He was the cousin of Huang Biao, who had put down his butcher's knife and begun raising dogs, and of course, the brother-in-law of Huang Biao's pretty wife. A martial-arts master, he was a wizard with spears and clubs and able to fly over eaves and walk up walls; nominally, he was the leader of the village militia while in fact he was Lao Lan's personal bodyguard.

'Wait outside,' Lao Lan said to him.

'Why?' Mother said generously. 'He can sit with us.'

But Huang Biao stepped nimbly out of the living room and disappeared into our yard.

Lao Lan rubbed his hands and apologized: 'Sorry to have kept you waiting. I returned late from an appointment in the city. With all the snow and ice on the ground, I told my driver to go slow.'

'You honour us by taking time out of your busy schedule, with so many village matters to attend to . . .' Father spoke with obsequious formality from where he stood behind the round table, trying to make himself as unobtrusive as possible. 'We are extremely grateful.'

'Ha-ha, Luo Tong,' Lao Lan said with a dry laugh. 'You've changed since I last saw you.'

'Getting old,' Father said as he took off his cap and rubbed his shaved scalp. 'Nothing but grey hair.'

'That's not what I'm talking about. Everyone grows old. What I meant was you've got better at expressing yourself since I last saw you. And you've lost that old fight you used to have. These days you talk like an intellectual.'

'Now you're making fun of me,' Father said. 'I've done lots of strange things in the past but the troubles I've had since then have shown how wrong I was. All I can do is beg your forgiveness . . .'

'What kind of talk is that?' Lan subconsciously reached up and touched his damaged ear as he carried on magnanimously, 'Who doesn't do weird things at some point in their life? And that includes sages and emperors.'

'All right, you two, enough of that talk,' Mother said warmly. 'Village Head, please sit.'

Lan deferred to Father a time or two before taking the chair Mother had borrowed from her cousin.

'Come sit, all of you, don't stand about. Yang Yuzhen, you've worked hard enough.'

'The food's getting cold,' Mother said. 'I'll go fry some eggs.'

'I'd rather you sit,' Lao Lan said. 'You can fry the eggs when I say so.'

Lao Lan sat in the seat of honour, surrounded by Mother, Jiaojiao, Father and me.

Mother opened a bottle and filled glasses. Then holding up hers, she said: 'Thank you, Village Head, for the honour of visiting this humble abode.'

'How could I refuse an invitation from someone so renowned as the man of the hour, Luo Xiaotong?' He emptied his glass. 'Have I got that right, Mr Luo Xiaotong?'

'No one's ever been a guest in our house,' I said. 'No one's ever deserved it before today.'

'What kind of talk is that?' Father said with a censorious look in my direction. Then he apologized. 'Youngsters will say anything. Just ignore him.'

'I see nothing wrong in what he said,' said Lao Lan. 'I like boys with a bit of spunk. Xiaotong's future as a man looks bright from what I see of him as a boy.'

Mother placed a drumstick on Lao Lan's plate. 'Talk like that gives him a big head, Village Head. Best to avoid it.'

Lao Lan picked up the drumstick and laid it on my plate, then picked up the second one and laid it on the plate in front of Jiaojiao. She was timidly pressed up against Father, and I saw sadness mixed with affection in his eyes.

'Say thank you.'

'Thank you!'

'What's her name?' Lao Lan asked Father.

'Jiaojiao,' Mother answered. 'She's a good girl, and smart too.'

Lao Lan kept placing morsels of meat and fish onto Jiaojiao's and my plates.

'Eat up, children,' he said. 'Go ahead, eat whatever you like.'

'What about you?' Mother said. 'Not to your taste?'

He picked up a peanut with his chopsticks and popped it into his mouth.

'Do you think I came here for the food?' he asked as he chewed the peanut.

'We know,' Mother said. 'You're the village head, with many honours and awards, someone who's well known at the city and provincial levels. I can't imagine there's any food you haven't tasted. We invited you here to express our regard for you.'

'Pour me another,' Lao Lan said as he held out his glass.

'Oh, I'm sorry . . .'

'Him, too,' he said, pointing to Father's empty glass.

'I *am* sorry,' she said as she obeyed his instructions. 'You're the first guest we've ever had, and I have a lot to learn . . .'

Lao Lan held his glass out to Father and said: 'Lao Luo, there's no need to talk about the past in front of the children. For the future, if you will do me the honour, bottoms up!'

Father held out his glass with a shaky hand: 'Like a plucked rooster and a scaled fish, I have nothing to show.'

'Nonsense,' Lao Lan said as he banged his now-empty glass on the table and looked hard into Father's face. 'I know who you are—you're Luo Tong!'

Thousands of fat pigeons flap noisily into the July sky amid strains of rousing music, followed promptly by thousands of colourful balloons. As the pigeons fly over the temple, a dozen or more grey feathers flutter to the ground and merge with the blood-spattered ostrich feathers. The surviving ostriches are huddled under a big tree, which they must assume is a protective umbrella. The carcasses of the three birds that had come to grief at Huang Bao's hands lie in front of the temple and are a disturbing sight. From his spot in front of the temple, as he looks up at the balloons and follows their southern, wind-blown journey across the sky, Lan Laoda heaves a tortured sigh. An ancient white-haired nun with ruddy cheeks slowly walks out from behind the temple, aided by a pair of much younger nuns, and stops in front of Lan Laoda. In a voice that betrays neither humility nor pride, she asks: 'For what purpose has the esteemed patron summoned this ancient nun?' Hands clasped before him, Lan Laoda bows humbly: 'Reverend Mother, my wife, Shen Yaoyao, has taken up temporary residence in your esteemed nunnery, and I ask the Reverend Mother to watch over her.' 'Esteemed patron,' the ancient nun replies, 'the woman Yaoyao has already shaved off her hair and taken her vows. Her name in Buddha is Huiming, and I must ask the patron to not disturb her medita-tions, as per her wish. This ancient nun is but her messenger. In three months she will present the esteemed patron with an important item. Please return in time to receive it.' Before the nun can say goodbye, Lan Laoda takes out a cheque from his pocket. 'Reverend Mother, I see that your honourable nunnery is in need of repair, and I humbly ask that you accept this contribution to that end.' The nun clasps her hands in front of her. 'Boundless virtues will accrue to the esteemed patron for his generous gift. May the Buddha protect and bestow upon him a long, happy and healthy life!' Lan Laoda hands the cheque to one of the younger nuns, who accepts it with a smile and then her brows shoot up in amazement at the figure written on it. I have a clear view of this young nun, with her almond eyes and cheeks like peaches, her red lips and white teeth; her scalp glistens with a green tint and exudes an aura of youth. The other young nun, who also stands behind their ancient superior, has full lips, pitch-black eyebrows and skin with the sheen of fine jade. What a shame that such lovely young women have chosen a cloistered life. I know, Wise Monk, that such thoughts are vulgar, but I mustn't hide what is in my heart, for that would be an even greater sin. Is that not right? The Wise Monk nods ambiguously. The fifth stage of the celebration is now underway and the ear-throbbing loudspeaker announces a display of mass calisthenics: 'Exercise Number One: The Phoenix descends, a hundred wild beasts dance.' A roar from the edge of the field gradually dies out and is replaced by primitive music from the loudspeaker, the sort that evokes pleasant feelings of the remote past. Meanwhile, Lan Laoda seems almost obsessed by the backs of the ancient nun and her two attendants. The grey habits, white collars and green-tinged shaved scalps look so unsullied, so clean and refreshing. A pair of bright-coloured phoenixes dancing in the air creates an atmosphere of elegant mystery on the Festival grounds below. This is the Tenth Annual Carnivore Festival, as I well know, and thus grander than those before it. Just witness the splendid performances at the opening ceremony. The long-tailed phoenixes, crafted by the finest kite artisans, put on one of those splendid performances. As for the dancing beasts, I would not be surprised to see a performance with real and man-made beasts together. The twin cities are home to every animal imaginable, all but unicorns, just as it is home to all birds imaginable, except phoenixes. I know that Lao Lan's Huachang Camel Dancing Troupe will distinguish itself during this stage of the Festival. What a shame that his Ostrich Dancing Troupe has been put out of commission.

Lao Lan's words of praise filled me with pride and I was, quite literally, bursting with joy. In that brief moment I had been given the rare privilege of sitting at a table with adults. So when they raised their glasses in a toast, I picked up the bowl in front of me, poured out the water in it. 'May I have some of that, please?' I asked as I held it out to Mother.

'What?' she blurted out in surprise. 'You want what they're drinking?'

'It's not good for children,' Father said.

'Why not? It's been such a long time since I've been happy, and I can see you're happy too. It's worth celebrating—with a drink!'

'You're right, Xiaotong,' said Lao Lan, his eyes flashing, 'a drink is exactly what's called for! Anyone who can reason like that—adult or child—deserves a drink. Here, I'll pour.'

'No, no, Elder Brother Lan,' Mother objected. 'He'll get a big head.'

'Hand me the bottle,' Lao Lan said. 'I know from experience that there are two types of people in this world you mustn't offend. One is punks and hoodlums, the so-called lumpenproletariat. They're straight when they're standing and flat when they're lying down: if one eats, none goes hungry, so folks with a family and a job, with progeny to carry on the line, anyone who enjoys prestige and authority will stay clear of this type. Ugly, snot-nosed, grime-covered children, who are kicked about like mangy dogs, comprise the other. The likelihood that they will grow up to be thugs, armed robbers, high officials or senior military officers is greater than for well-behaved, nicely dressed, clean-scrubbed good boys.' He filled my bowl. 'Come on, Luo Xiao-tong, Mr Luo, have a drink with Lao Lan!'

Boldly I held out my bowl and clinked it against his glass, which, when it produced the unusual sound of porcelain on glass, filled me with joy. He drained his glass at one go. 'That's how I show my respect!' he said as he banged his glass upside down on the table to show it was empty. 'I drained mine,' he said. 'You can sip yours.'

The moment my lips touched the rim of the bowl I could smell the pungent aroma of strong liquor and I didn't much like it. Still, in the grip of excitement, I swallowed a big mouthful. First, my mouth was on fire, then the flames burnt their way down my throat, singeing everything they touched and then into my stomach.

'That's enough!' said Mother, snatching the bowl out of my hands. 'A taste is all you need. You can have more when you grow up.'

'No, I want more now.' I reached out to get back my bowl.

Father gave me a worried look but offered no opinion.

Lao Lan took the bowl and poured most of the contents into his glass: 'Esteemed nephew, any man worthy of his name knows when to give and when to take. We'll share this glass—you finish what I leave.'

For the second time, porcelain on glass rang out, and, only seconds later, bowl and glass were empty.

'I feel great,' I said. I really did, greater than ever. Like I was floating, and not lightly like a feather on the wind but like a melon on the water, carried along by river currents . . . All of a sudden my eyes were drawn to the greasy little paws of Jiaojiao—busy drinking, we'd forgotten all about my bewitching little sister. But she was a smart one, just like her brother, like me, Luo Xiaotong. While we were otherwise engaged, and loudly so, she took the ancient adage 'Help yourself and you'll never be cold or hungry' to heart, but without resorting to those odd instruments, chopsticks. Who needs them when you have hands? Jiaojiao had been launching sneak raids on the meat and the fish and the other delicacies in front of her, until not only her hands but her cheeks too were coated with grease. She smiled when I looked her way—so adorable, so innocent—and it nearly melted my heart. Even my feet, which suffered chilblains every winter, tingled as if they were soaking in hot water. I picked out the best-looking anchovy from the can, leaned across the circular table and dangled it in front of Jiaojiao. 'Open wide!' I said. She looked up, opened her mouth and swallowed the little fish, just like a kitten. 'Eat till you burst, little sister,' I said. 'The world belongs to us. We've pulled ourselves out of the quagmire of misery.'

'I'm afraid the boy's drunk,' Mother said to Lao Lan, clearly embarrassed.

'I'm not,' I insisted, 'I'm *not* drunk!'

'Do you have any vinegar?' Lao Lan asked in a slightly muffled voice. 'Get some into him. Some carp soup would be better.'

'Where am I supposed to get my hands on carp soup?' replied Mother, frustrated. 'And I've got no vinegar either. I'll just give him some cold water and send him off to bed.'

'That's no good,' Lao Lan said with a loud clap of his hands. Huang Bao, whom we'd forgotten, materialized in our midst, his catlike footsteps making no sound. If not for the cold bursts of wind he let in through the open door, we'd have assumed he'd dropped out of the sky or shot up from the ground. His eyes were fixed on Lao Lan's mouth as he awaited his command. 'Go,' Lan said, not loudly yet with authority. 'Get us some carp soup, and quickly. While you're at it, have them prepare two *jin* of shark's fin dumplings. But the soup first. The dumplings can wait.'

A guttural sound of acknowledgement, and Huang Bao vanished much the same way he'd appeared; the icy chill of that third of January 1991, evening, suffused with the smell of snowbound earth and the cold rays of starlight, flooded the room in the brief moment between the door swinging open and shut. And for the first time I glimpsed the mystery, the solemnity and the authority permeating the life of an important person.

'We can't let you do that!' Mother was apologetic. 'We invited you to dinner—we can't let you spend your money!'

Lao Lan laughed magnanimously: 'Yang Yuzhen, you still don't get it, do you? I accepted your invitation to strike up a friendship with your son and your daughter. We're nearly in our forties—who knows how much longer we'll be bouncing about? No, the world is theirs, and in another ten years or so they'll have to put their abilities to good use.'

Father poured more drink from the bottle. 'Lao Lan,' he said sombrely, 'Not until this moment have I been convinced that you are better than me. Now I know it to be true. I will work for you willingly from this day forward.'

'We two, you and me,' Lao Lan said, pointing first to Father and then to himself, 'are made of the same stuff.'

My parents and Lao Lan drank a great deal on that unforgettable evening. Their faces changed colour: Lao Lan's turned yellow, Father's white and Mother's red.

*Contingents from both East City and West City gradually disperse as night
begins to fall, leaving the grassy field and the road littered with empty drink
cans and torn flags, with paper flowers and used manure bags. A small army of
sanitation workers in yellow vests hurriedly cleans up as foremen with bullhorns
shout instructions. At the same time, walking tractors, three-wheeled flatbeds,
horse-drawn carts with rubber wheels and a host of other vehicles are transporting barbeque braziers, electric grills, deep fryers and other cooking
equipment onto the grounds. A Carnivore Festival night market where meats of
all varieties will be available is being set up on the grounds in order to lessen the
environmental impact on urban centres. The enormous generator truck remains
in place to supply power. The night promises to be one for the record books.
After talking up a storm during the day and witnessing all sorts of enthralling
sights, I'm running out of steam. Although the several bowls of mystery porridge
I'd finished off the night before have moved more slowly through my digestive
system than most foods, it was, after all, soupy porridge, and as the sun begins
to set, my stomach growls and the first pangs of hunger rise up inside me. I steal
a look at the Wise Monk, hoping he'll notice the passage of time and lead me
over to the little room in the rear to get some rest and something to eat. I might
even run into that mysterious woman I met last night. Once again she may
magnanimously undo her blouse and nurture my body and enrich my soul with
her sweet milk. But the Wise Monk's eyes remain shut and the hairs in his ears
twitch, a sure sign that he's concentrating on my tale—*

After I finished my carp soup and polished off the shark's fin dumplings
on that memorable evening, Jiaojiao whined that she was sleepy. Time for
Lao Lan to get up from the table and say his goodbyes. Father and Mother
jumped to their feet—Father was cradling Jiaojiao in his arms and patting
her bottom with practised clumsiness—to see the village's most eminent
individual to the door.

Huang Bao—his timing perfect, as always—came into the room to drape Lao Lan's overcoat over his shoulders, and then glided over to open the door for his superior's exit. But Lao Lan was in no hurry to leave. There was apparently something more that he had to say to my parents. He turned first to Father and then looked down into the face of my sister, tucked into the crook of Father's arm.

'She looks like she came out of the same mould,' he said emotionally.

These words of praise, whose deeper meaning was unclear, immediately dampened the mood. Mother coughed drily, a sign of how ill at ease Lao Lan's comment had made her, while Father twisted his head into an awkward angle to look at his daughter's face.

'Jiaojiao,' he said, 'thank the good man.'

Lao Lan took a red envelope out of his overcoat pocket and tucked it between Father and Jiaojiao: 'That's a good luck gift on our first meeting.'

Flustered, Father reached down for it: 'We can't accept this.'

'Why not? It's for her, not you.'

'That doesn't matter . . .' Poor Father was reduced to mumbling.

Then Lao Lan took out a second red envelope and handed it to me: 'You'll give a little face to an old friend, won't you?' he said with a sly wink.

I took it without a second's hesitation.

'Xiaotong . . .' Mother's voice was full of anguish.

'I know what you're thinking,' Lao Lan said as he stuck his arms into the sleeves of his overcoat. 'I'm telling you, money's no damned good. You aren't born with it and you can't take it with you when you die.'

His words were as heavy as lead weights thudding to the floor. Mother and Father were dumbstruck and incomprehension filled their eyes as they struggled in vain with the mystery Lao Lan had just revealed to them.

'Yang Yuzhen, there's more to life than the pursuit of money,' Lao Lan said from the doorway. 'The children need an education.'

I was clutching my red envelope; Father had tucked Jiaojiao's down between them. Having accepted them we could not, under any circumstance, refuse to keep them. Complex emotions clouded our minds as we saw him to the door. Light from both the lantern and the candles burst through the opening and spread across the yard and shone on Mother's tractor and the little mortar I hadn't yet moved into the house. A yellow canvas tarp covered the tube, making it look like a doughty warrior in disguise, lying in the grass and waiting for the call from its commander to attack. I thought back to a few days earlier, when I'd vowed to fire at Lao Lan's house, an unsettling thought at this moment. What was I thinking? There's nothing wrong with Lao Lan. Hell, he's a good man, a role model, and I wondered about the source of my loathing for him. Since my thoughts were beginning to confuse me, I cast them out. Perhaps it was all just a strange dream—dream dream dream—the opposite of the opposite—that's what Mother used to say to break the spell of her bad dreams, and did the same for mine. Tomorrow, no, as soon as Lao Lan leaves, I'll move it into the storeroom. 'Put weapons into a storeroom, turn horses loose on South Mountain,' that is how peace will reign on earth.

Lao Lan walked briskly but with a bit of a wobble. Who knows, perhaps it wasn't Lao Lan who was wobbling but me. This was my first time with alcohol, also my first time keeping company with adults, and not just any adults but the eminent Mr Lao Lan—a distinct honour. I felt like I'd made my entry into the world of grown-ups, and left behind Fengshou, Pingdu and Pidou, ignorant children who'd looked down on me, still stuck in childhood.

Huang Bao had opened our gate. His vigilant demeanour, his vigorous strides and his nimble, precise actions impressed me greatly. All the time we'd been inside the heated room, eating and drinking, he'd been standing outside in the cold and the snow, his nerves as taut as an armed bowstring, his eyes and ears on constant alert, concerned with only one thing—Lao Lan's safety from human and animal attack—although we, who had just dined with his boss, were collateral beneficiaries of that protection and would have done well to emulate that spirit of self-sacrifice. And there was more to his vigil than protection, for not a second went by that he wasn't prepared to respond to Lao Lan's signal—a clapping of the hands—and, in silent, spectral fashion, materialize at the man's side, ready to carry out his bidding, vigorously, to the letter, resolutely, and completely. Lao Lan's request for carp soup can serve as an example. Without any warning, he managed to set a bowl of the soup on our table in half an hour, as if it had been kept warm on a stove not far from our house and he had simply gone to bring it for us. It was so hot when it arrived that we'd have burnt our tongues if we'd eaten it too fast. Then, before it had cooled, he returned with the shark's fin dumplings. They too were steaming hot, as if they'd just been plucked from boiling water. I was amazed and found it all quite unfathomable, absolutely alien to anything I'd ever experienced. More than anything, it resembled the 'treasure transport' power of the fictional monkey of legend. Huang Bao brought in the dumplings, tranquil, hands steady, breathing relaxed, as if they'd been prepared a step away from where we sat. Laying them on the table, he turned and left. His arrivals and departures were more akin to a magician's disappearing act. At the time I entertained the thought that if I worked extra hard I could become someone like Lao Lan. But nothing I did could conceivably prepare me to be another Huang Bao. He was born to be a bodyguard, two hundred years too late to fulfil his destiny as a member of the Qing Court Palace Guard. His very existence was a reminder of classical sensibilities and a prod for us not only to reflect upon our past but also to retain our unquestioned beliefs in historical legends and tales of the marvellous.

Not until we were standing in the gateway did we realize that two big, black stallions were hitched to a roadside light post. A half-moon hung at the edge of the sky, its light muted, in contrast to the twinkling stars whose light was reflected on the animals' skin; their eyes were like pearls shining through the darkness. What I could make out of their silhouettes was insufficient to gauge how handsome they were, but I could sense that they were not run-of-the-mill animals and assumed at once that they were heavenly steeds. The blood raced through my veins, a surge of emotions filled my heart and I was overcome by a desire to run over to them, to throw my arms round one of their necks and to leap onto its back. But Lao Lan had already nimbly mounted one, with the help of Huang Bao, who then somersaulted onto the back of the other. They then carried their extraordinary riders out onto Han-lin Avenue, which ran through the centre of the village, trotting at first but then quickly breaking into a gallop that took them down the road like fiery meteors. They shot out of view and left our ears ringing with the tattoo of hooves pounding the earth.

Spectacular, truly spectacular! It was a magical evening, the most memorable evening in all my days on this earth. The significance of that evening to my family and to me in particular would become clearer over time. At that moment we could only stand there, gazing blankly through the gateway at the image of the trees frozen in a splendid golden autumn.

A breeze from the north swept across my face and cooled the alcohol's heat just below the skin. Were my parents enjoying the same sensation? I didn't know then; I'd know later. I'd know that my mother belonged to a type of drinker known as hot-and-dry. In the winter she'd drink herself into a heavy sweat and then begin to disrobe: off first was her overcoat, followed by her sweater and then her blouse. Then she'd stop. I'd know that my father belonged to a type of drinker who couldn't stand the cold—the more he drank the deeper he shrank into himself and the paler his face grew, until it resembled window paper or a whitewashed wall. Little bumps would break out over his face, like chicken skin, and his teeth would begin to chatter. When he'd had too much to drink, he shivered like a man struck with malaria; my mother, on the other hand, would break out in a sweat even on the coldest days of winter. For Father, if he was drinking, it could be the dog days of summer and he'd still have the cold shakes, like the death throes of a cicada clinging to the tip of a leafless willow after 'Frost's Descent'. And so, I assume, while we were seeing Lao Lan and Huang Bao out to the street in the wake of an evening that held such great significance for my family, that breeze comfortably caressed my mother's face whereas my father suffered under its touch, no less painful to him than the slice of a knife or the lash from a whip soaked in salt water. I don't know how it affected Jiaojiao because she'd had nothing to drink.

The sun has slipped unnoticed below the horizon, bringing darkness to the earth. Except for the field across the way, which blazes with lamplight. Fancy cars stream onto the field, flickering headlamps lighting the way, horns announcing their arrival—a scene of wealth and prosperity. The cars disgorge their loads of fashionable ladies and respectable gentlemen. Most are casually dressed, giving an initial impression of men and women of the people when, in fact, designer labels abound. While I narrate events of the past, my eyes miss nothing outside. A fireworks display lights up the inside of the temple. A gilded sheen covers the Wise Monk's face; he looks like he's been transformed into a gilded mummy. The fireworks continue, each explosion rolling my way. Every burst draws oohs and ahs from the upturned faces of observers. Just like the fireworks, Wise Monk—

Moments of enchantment are inevitably brief while those of suffering endure without respite. But that's only one way of looking at things; another is that moments of enchantment last for long periods, since they remain in the memory of the once enchanted, to be revisited at will and, over time, enhanced and improved, gaining in richness, fullness and complexity until, finally, they are transformed into labyrinths that are easy to enter but difficult to exit. Moments of suffering are, by definition, agonizing, so the sufferer avoids them like, as they say, the plague. That's true even if one suffers by accident. If avoidance is impossible, the next best thing is to soften the impact or simplify the effect or, insofar as possible, put it out of one's mind, blurring the edges until it is a puff of smoke easily blown away.

That's how I found a basis for my narrative of a night so fascinating I was loath to tear myself away from it. I could not bring myself to move forward, to relinquish the star-filled sky, the breezy winds from the north and Hanlin Avenue reflecting the light of the stars but, most of all, the wonderful smell left in the air by the two magnificent horses. My body was standing in front of our gate but my soul had left to follow Lao Lan, Huang Bao and that pair of unreal horses. I'd have stood there till dawn if Mother hadn't taken me inside. I used to think that talk of souls escaping from bodies was superstition, utter nonsense, but in the wake of that sumptuous dinner, when those magnificent horses sped out of sight, I gained a true understanding of what it was for the soul to fly away. I felt myself leave my body, like a chick emerging from its egg. I became as pliant and as light as a feather, immune to the pull of gravity. All I had to do was touch my toe to the ground to spring into the air like a rubber ball. In the eyes of this new me, the northern breezes took on form, like water flowing through the air, and I could lie out flat and let them carry me away. I could come and go at will, do whatever I pleased. If I was headed for a collision with a tree, I willed the wind to lift me high in the air and out of danger. If I couldn't avoid a head-on encounter with a wall, I willed myself into a thin sheet of nearly invisible paper and passed through a gap too small to be detected by the human eye.

Mother dragged me back into the yard and closed the gate with a loud clang, forcing my soul to reluctantly return to my body. Without fear of exaggeration I can say that my head was chilled when my soul made its way in, much like the feeling a child experiences when he slides under a warm comforter after being out in the cold. If you're looking for proof of the existence of the soul, there it is.

Father carried Jiaojiao, who had fallen asleep, to the *kang*, where he handed Mother the red envelope. She opened it and took out a fistful of hundred-yuan notes, ten altogether, and looked extremely nervous. With a glance at Father, she spat on her hands and counted the notes a second time. Still ten—a thousand yuan.

'That's too much for a greeting gift,' she said, with another look at Father. 'We don't deserve this.'

'Don't forget Xiaotong's,' he said.

'Let me have it,' she said, now angry.

I hated to but I handed it over. First she gave it a quick count, as with the other envelope, then she spat on her hands and counted it more carefully. Again, ten hundred-yuan notes, a thousand yuan.

In those days, two thousand yuan was a great deal of money, which is why the thought of lending Shen Gang two thousand yuan, never to be returned, had caused Mother such grief and indignation. Back then, you could buy a water buffalo strong enough to pull a plough for seven or eight hundred; a thousand was enough to buy a mule to pull a big wagon. Lao Lan had given Jiaojiao and me enough money to buy two mules. During the land-reform period, any family that owned two adult mules would, without question, have been counted as part of the landlord class and bad times would be waiting just round the corner.

'Now what do we do?' Mother mumbled, her forehead creased with worry, like an old woman of seventy or eighty. Her arms were stiff and her back was bent, as if what she held in her hands were bricks, not money.

'Why not return it to him?' Father said.

'How?' Mother asked, clearly worried. 'You want to do it?'

'Send Xiaotong,' he said. 'Nothing shames a child, and he won't find fault with the boy.'

'I say you *can* shame a child!'

'Then you decide,' said Father. 'I'll do whatever you say.'

'I guess we'd better hold on to it for the time being. We were supposed to be treating him to a meal. But he not only supplied us with carp soup and shark's fin dumplings, he also handed us a gift like this.'

'That shows he's serious about wanting to mend the relationship,' said Father.

'If you want the truth, he's not as petty-minded as you think. When you weren't here, he helped us out quite a bit. He sold me that tractor at scrap-metal cost and didn't ask for anything to approve the foundation of the house. Lots of people gave gifts right and left but still didn't get their approvals. If not for him, this house would never have been built.'

'All on account of me,' Father said with a sigh. 'From now on I'll be his advance foot soldier and repay a favour with a favour.'

'This money is not to be spent. Put it in the bank,' Mother said. 'We can send Xiaotong and Jiaojiao to school after the New Year's holiday.'

As dazzling fireworks briefly light up the dark sky, I'm suddenly in the grip of fear, as if I'm straddling the line between life and death, as if I'm glancing at the realms of yin and yang, of dark and light. In one of the brief illuminated moments, I see Lan Laoda meet the ancient nun in front of the temple as she hands him a bundle in swaddling clothes. 'Esteemed patron,' she says, 'Huiming has broken the bonds of this world. You must carry on as best you can.' The fireworks die out, throwing the world back into darkness. I hear the cry of a newborn child. At the next burst of fireworks I see the infant's tiny face, especially its wide-open mouth, as well the indifferent look on the face of Lan Laoda. I know that his emotions are cresting, for I see something glisten in his eyes.

Another burst of fireworks blossoms in the sky, and four red circles transmo-grify into large green characters—天下太平—spelling out 'peace on earth'. They disintegrate into dozens of green meteorites that then fizzle in the dark-ness. Another cluster quickly fills the void, illuminating the lingering smoke from the previous burst and thickens the heavy smell of gunpowder that hangs over the field and makes my throat itch. Wise Monk, I witnessed many cele-brations back when I was roaming the city streets, grand parades in daylight and fireworks displays at night, but I've never seen anything to match tonight's display of pyrotechnic words and intricate patterns. Times evolve, society progresses and the skill of fireworks artisans keeps improving, as does the art of barbecuing meat. Going back ten years, Wise Monk, the best we could manage here was lamb kebabs over a charcoal fire. But now there's Korean barbecue, Japanese barbecue, Brazilian barbecue, Thai barbecue and Mongolian barbecue. There's quail teppanyaki, flint-fired lamb's tail, charcoal mutton, pebble-roasted pork liver, pine-bough roast chicken, peach-wood roast duck, pear-wood roast goose . . . it's hardly farfetched to say that there's nothing in the world that can't be barbecued or roasted. An announcement signals the end of the fireworks display amid whoops and shouts from the spectators. Grand feasts must end some time, good times never last long, a thought that I find especially depressing. The final, and largest, pyrotechnic burst drags a fiery thread five hundred metres into the sky. Then it bursts to form a big red 肉—meat—from which sparks cascade earthward, like drip-pings from a hunk of meat as it's removed from the pot. The people's eyes— bigger, it seems, than even their mouths, which in turn are bigger than their fists—are glued to the sight, as if waiting expectantly for the 肉 in the sky to drop into their mouths. In a matter of seconds 肉 breaks up into dozens of white umbrellas that float slowly to the ground, trailing white silk streamers, before being swallowed up by the inky night. It does not take long for my eyes to adjust to the darkness, allowing me to see hundreds of barbecue stands on the open field across the street. As one, their lights snap on, each covered by a red lampshade, the red rays of light creating an air of mystery in the night. It reminds me of the ghost markets of popular legend: flickering shadows, indistinct features, pointed teeth, green fingernails, transparent ears, poorly hidden tails . . . The meat-peddlers are ghosts, the meat-eaters human. Or else the meat-peddlers are human, the meat-eaters ghosts. If not that, the peddlers and the eaters of meat are all human, or all ghosts. If an outsider were to wander into a night market like that, he'd be witness to all sorts of unimaginable things. When he thought about them later, they would send chills up his spine but would give him a wealth of things to boast about. Wise Monk, you have left the mortal world and the bitter seas of humanity, and so have escaped the stories of the ghost markets. I grew up in the gory confines of Slaughterhouse Village, and spent much of my childhood listening to those tales. Like the one about a man who walked into a ghost market by mistake and caught sight of a fat man roasting his own leg over a charcoal fire, slicing off edible pieces when it was done. 'Watch out!' the visitor yelled. 'You'll turn into a cripple!' With a cry of anguish, the man threw down his knife, knowing he was now a cripple, something that would not have happened if the visitor hadn't shouted out. Then there was the man who got up early to ride his bicycle into town to sell meat. But he lost his way. When he saw lamplight ahead, he discovered a thriving meat market where curling smoke welcomed him with an extraordinary aroma. Peddlers shouted their wares and sweat dotted the diners' foreheads. Business was lively, to the great joy of the newcomer, who set up a stall, including his butcher block, and laid out an array of aromatic, freshly roasted meat. His first shout drew a crowd of people who fought to place their orders—one jin for this person, two for that—without even asking the price. He had trouble keeping up with the demand of people who were in no mood to wait. They flung the money into his rush bag, grabbed the meat with their bare hands and began to stuff their faces. And as they chewed and swallowed, their faces underwent a hideous change and green lights began to shoot from their eyes. Realizing something was seriously amiss, the man scooped up his rush bag and fled, stumbling away and not stopping till the roosters crowed the coming dawn. Then he looked round him and discovered that he was standing in a wildwood. And when he checked his rush bag all he found was ash. Wise Monk, the barbecuing night market in front of us is an important component of the Twin Cities Carnivore Festival, and should not be a ghost market. But even if it were, would that matter? People these days enjoy nothing more than making contact with ghosts. These days it's the ghosts who are frightened by the people. The meat-peddlers out there all wear chef's hats, and they look top heavy as they busily chop meat and hail customers with their exaggerated claims. Charcoal and meat create a smell that seems to come from a time long ago, from past millennia, blanketing as much as a square kilometre. Black smoke merges with white smoke to form smoky colours that rise into the air and send birds weaving crazily in the sky. Gaily dressed young men and women happily wolf down the meat. A beer in one hand and a skewer of lamb in the other, some take a bite of meat, then a drink of beer and produce a loud belch. Others stand facing one another, man to woman, in a feeding frenzy. More daring couples hold a single piece of meat in their teeth and eat their way closer, until the end of the meat signals the beginning of a kiss, to the raucous delight of people round them. I'm hungry, Wise Monk, and I have a greedy mouth. But I took a vow to abstain from eating meat. I know that what's going on out there is your way to put me to the test, and I'll resist temptation by continuing my narration—

A number of important events occurred in our family round the Spring Festival. The first was on the afternoon of the fourth day of the new year, that is, the day after Lao Lan had dinner at our house, even before we had a chance to clean the tableware and furniture we'd borrowed for the occasion. Mother and Father were having a casual conversation as they washed dishes. Actually, it was anything but 'casual', since the talk did not stray far from Lao Lan, returning to him every two or three sentences. Once I'd heard enough, I went outside, where I peeled back the tarp covering the mortar, took out a packet of grease, and, for the last time before it was moved into the storeroom, laid on a protective coat. Now that the family had re-established friendly relations with Lao Lan, I no longer had an enemy. But that didn't remove the need to keep my weapon in good working order, if for no other reason than to remain alert to something my parents said over and over during that talk: 'No one stays an enemy for ever, and no friendships are eternal.' That is to say, an enemy today could become a friend tomorrow, and today's friend could turn into tomorrow's enemy. And there's no enemy as savage and full of loathing as someone who was once a friend. That's why it was important to keep my mortar in good working order. If the need to use it ever arose, I could put it into action immediately. I'd never consider selling it to a scrap dealer.

I began by wiping off the old coat of dust-covered grease with cotton yarn. Starting on the tube and moving down to the bipod, then from there to the gun sight and, finally, to the base plate, I cleaned it with painstaking care, reaching into every nook and cranny, including the tube, for which I used a stick wrapped in cotton yarn, back and forth hundreds of times, since my arm would not fit inside. The now-greaseless mortar had a dull, gunmetal-grey finish, and the spots eaten away by rust over the years lay exposed. Too bad, really too bad, but there was nothing I could do about that. I'd tried sanding the rusty spots with a brick and sandpaper but was afraid that I'd scrape off so much metal it would no longer be safe to fire. After removing the old grease, I spread on a new coat with my fingers, smooth and even. Every nook and cranny, of course. I'd bought this packet of grease at a little village near the airport. The villagers there, who'd steal anything, with the possible exception of an aeroplane, told me it was aeroplane-engine grease, and I believed them. A protective coat of that grease made it a very lucky mortar indeed.

My sister watched me while I tended to it. I didn't have to look to know that she was following my every move, wide-eyed. Every now and then she'd come up with a question: 'What is that thing?' 'What's a mortar used for?' 'When will you fire it?' and so on. I answered all of them because I was so fond of her. It also gave me pleasure to play the role of teacher.

I finished applying the grease but just as I was thinking of putting back the tarp, a pair of electricians from the village strolled into the compound. With startled faces and flashing eyes, they warily approached the mortar. Though they were in their twenties, their childlike expressions made them look like awkward little boys. They asked the same sorts of questions as Jiao-jiao, but they were far less sophisticated. In fact, they were ignorant, ill-informed dopes, at least as far as weapons were concerned. Which is why they didn't receive the patient responses I'd given Jiaojiao. I either ignored them or teased them. 'How far can this mortar reach?' 'Not far—about as far as your house. Don't believe me? No? Let's give it a try. I'll bet I can flatten your house with one shell.' My teasing didn't get the rise out of them I'd hoped for. Instead, they bent over, cocked their heads and squinted down the tube, as if it contained a mysterious secret. So I smacked the tube with my hand and shouted: 'Ready—aim—fire!' They nearly fell all over themselves as they scuttled away, like frightened rabbits. 'Scaredy cats!' I shouted. 'Scaredy cats!' echoed Jiaojiao. They laughed sheepishly in response.

My parents came into the yard and rolled up their sleeves, exposing pale arms for Mother and dark for Father; if not for his swarthy skin as a contrast, I'd never have realized how pale Mother's were. Their hands were red from steeping in cold water. Unable to remember the men's names, Father hemmed and hawed but Mother knew who they were. 'Tongguang, Tonghui,' she greeted them with a smile, 'it's been a long time.' Turning to Father, she explained: 'They're the sons of the Peng family, both electricians. I thought you knew them.'

The Peng brothers bowed respectfully to Mother. 'Aunty, the village head sent us to instal electricity in your house.'

'But we haven't asked for electricity!' Mother exclaimed.

'We're just following orders,' Tongguang replied.

'Will it cost a lot?' Father asked.

'We don't know,' Tonghui said. 'We just do the installing.'

'Since the village head sent you,' Mother said after a moment's hesitation, 'go ahead.'

'That's what we like, Aunty, someone who makes up her mind!' exclaimed Tongguang. 'Since we're doing this on the village head's orders, at most there'll be a modest fee for the material.'

'Maybe not even that,' Tonghui said. 'It's the village head, after all.'

'We'll pay whatever it costs,' Mother assured them. 'We're not the kind to abuse the public trust.'

'Aunty Luo is a generous person, everyone knows that,' said Tongguang with a smile. 'People say she brings home bones found in scrap heaps and boils them to feed Xiaotong.'

'Go to hell!' snapped Mother. 'Do what you came to do or get out of my yard!'

The Peng brothers giggled their way out onto the street and began moving a folding ladder, electric wiring, electric sockets, meters and other equipment into the yard. They were an impressive sight with their wide brown leather belts from which hung grips, shears and screwdrivers in a variety of colours. Mother and I once found a set of tools like that in a lane behind the city's fertilizer plant, but she took it to one of the hardware outlets behind the department store and sold it for thirteen yuan. That made her so happy she rewarded me with a meat-filled flatbread. The Peng brothers, tools at their waist, dragged the electric wire up over the eaves before going inside. Mother followed. Father squatted down to inspect the mortar.

'It's an 82 mm mortar,' he said. 'Japanese. During the War of Resistance, the most outstanding service you could perform was to get your hands on one of these.'

'You surprise me, Dieh,' I exclaimed. 'I never thought you knew stuff like that. What do the shells look like? Have you ever seen one?'

'I served in the militia and trained in town,' he said. 'They had four just like this for our use. I was the second man on a team. My job was to feed ammo to the man firing the mortar.'

'Tell me more!' I said excitedly. 'Tell me what the shells looked like.'

'They were like . . . like . . .' He picked up a stick and drew a picture of a shell with a bulging middle and a pointed tip in the sand. And tiny wings at one end. 'Like this.'

'Did you ever fire one?'

'I'd have to say yes. As Number Two, my job was to hand the shells to my comrade, who took them, and . . .' He bent, spread his legs and pretended to hold a shell. 'Then dropped them in like this, and, with a pop, they were on their way.'

Several paint-spattered men are pushing a two-wheeled flatbed wagon up to the temple door. They have only a blurred view of us, since they're in the light and we're in the shadows, but I see them clearly. One, a tall, slightly stooped old man, mumbles: 'I wonder when these people will stop eating.' 'With meat that cheap,' one of the shorter fellows answers, 'they'd be fools to stop before they have to.' 'The way I see it, the Carnivore Festival ought to be called the Waste Money and Manpower Festival,' says a man with a pointy chin. 'It gets bigger and louder every year, and more and more money is poured into it. But it's been ten years now and it's brought in neither more business nor more capital, not as far as I can see. What it does bring in are big-bellied people who eat like wolves.' 'Huang Shifu, where are we supposed to be taking this Meat God?' the short fellow asks the stooped old man. All four, if I'm not mistaken, are from a sculpture village not far from Slaughterhouse Village. The residents have a long tradition of producing fine sculptures of religious idols, not only out of clay and hemp but out of wood as well. The Wutong Spirit in this temple was probably made by their forebears. But village traditions crumbled during the campaign against superstition, and the artisans were forced to take up new occupations: they became tile masons, carpenters, house painters, inside and out. These days, with all the temples being rebuilt, their skills have grown useful again. The old man takes a look round. 'Let's leave him here in the temple for the time being,' he says. 'He'll have the Wutong Spirit to keep him company. One's hung like a horse, the other's a meat god, a match made in Heaven, wouldn't you say?' He laughs at his own witticism. 'But is that a good idea?' Pointy Chin asks. 'You can't have two tigers on a mountain or two horses at a trough, and I'm afraid two deities will be too much for a small temple like this.' 'No,' the short man says, 'these two aren't proper deities. The Wutong Spirit is the bane of beautiful women, and I hear that this one is really a boy from Slaughterhouse Village who loves to eat meat.

After something terrible happened to his parents,' sighs the fourth, lean-faced man, 'he travelled the countryside with his mysterious airs, challenging people to meat-eating contests. They say he once finished off more than twenty feet of sausage, one pair of dog's legs and ten pigtails. Someone like that would have to become a god.' All the while they're sharing opinions, the four men drag the clay idol—a good six feet in length and an arm-span in thickness— off the wagon and tie ropes round its neck and feet. Then they slide a pair of shoulder poles under the ropes and, with a shout, hoist it onto their shoulders. Bent at the waist, the four men struggle to move the idol through the narrow door and into the temple. The ropes have been left too long, so the idol's head bangs loudly against the threshold. I feel dizzy, as if it's my head and not the idol's that's been thumped against the door. But the stooped old man, who's carrying the feet, notices the problem and shouts at the others: 'Lay it down, don't drag it like that!' The two men at the front immediately take the poles off their shoulders and lay down the idol. 'This prick of a god is damned heavy!' Pointy Chin complains. 'Clean up your talk,' warns one of the others, 'or—' 'Or what!' asks Pointy Chin. 'Will the Meat God stuff my mouth full of meat?' The old man at the back shortens the rope, then gives another shout. The poles are hoisted back onto their shoulders and the four men stand up straight. The idol rises and is carried slowly into the temple, the back of its head barely brushing against the floor. In a flash, I see it nearly bang into the shaved head of the Wise Monk, but fortunately the two men at the front change direction. But then the idol's feet nearly bump into my mouth, and this time the good fortune is mine, as the men at the back change direction. I detect a mixed odour of clay, paint and wood wafting off the men's bodies. Some men and women with torches appear in the doorway, caught up in a discussion of some- thing or other. A few words later I know what they are going on about. This year's Carnivore Festival was supposed to be celebrated along with the Foun- dation-Stone-Laying Ceremony for a Meat God Temple. The spot across the way, where the festive night market is still abuzz, is where the temple was to be built. But a ranking official who's come to participate in the Carnivore Fes- tival is critical of the twin cities plan for the Meat God Temple. 'He's much too conservative,' a boyish woman with bobbed hair complains indignantly. 'He accuses us of creating gods and fostering superstition. Well, so what? Aren't all gods created by human beings? And who isn't superstitious? I hear he goes to Mt Yuntai to draw tallies, and then gets down on his knees in front of the Buddha statue to kowtow.' 'I think that's enough from you,' says Xiao Qiao, a middle-aged official. 'The main reason is there wasn't enough in his red enve-lope,' she grumbles, ignoring him. 'I said, that's enough from you, Comrade,' repeats Xiao Qiao, with a pat on her shoulder, 'Don't let your mouth get you into trouble. But she carries on, though it's increasingly hard to hear what she's saying. Their torch beams criss-cross inside the temple, the brightest swinging past the Horse Spirit's face the Wise Monk's face my face. Don't they know it's rude to shine a light in someone's eyes? The beams swing past the faces of the four men carrying the Meat God into the temple and finally pool on the face of the idol stretched out on the floor. 'What's going on here?' Xiao Qiao demans angrily. 'Why is the Meat God on the floor? Pick him up, quick!' The carriers lay down their poles, untie the ropes and take their place round the upper half of the idol's body, where each gets a handhold and then, in uni-son, they shout: 'Heave!' Not until the six-foot Meat God is on its feet do I per-ceive its immense size and realize that it's been carved out of the trunk of a single tree. I've always known that idols with long histories have been carved out of fine woods like sandalwood, but in times like these, when environmental protection and forest conservation are major concerns, it's almost impossible to find such a stately old sandalwood tree, even deep in the forest. And if you did, it'd be illegal to cut it down. So what was the Meat God carved out of? The stinking new paint on it concealed both the kind of wood it was made out of as well as any chance of the wood's natural odour providing a clue. If Xiao Qiao hadn't asked the workers that very question, I'd have never known what this god, which is so closely tied to me, was made of. 'Is this sandalwood?' he asks. 'Where could we possibly find sandalwood?' the old man replies with a smirk. 'Then what is it?' 'Willow.' 'Did you say willow? Insects love willow trees. Aren't you afraid they'll hollow the thing out in a few years?' 'I agree,' the old man replies, willow isn't ideal for carving statues, but trees this big are hard to find, and before the carving began we soaked the wood with insecticide.' 'The carving lacks proportion,' points out a young, bespectacled official, 'the boy's head is too big.' 'It's not a boy,' the old man corrects him with another smirk, 'it's a god, and the heads of gods and humans are different. Look at the Wutong Spirit. Have you ever seen a horse with a human head?' A torch beam swings over to illuminate the Horse Spirit. First the face—a captivating face—

then the neck—the spot where the human and horse necks ingeniously meet evokes seductive eroticism—and then lower, stopping at the unnaturally large genitals—testicles the size of papayas and a half-exposed penis that looks like a laundry paddle emerging from a red sheath. I hear masculine giggles in the dark. The female official shines her torch on the Meat God's face: 'This boy will definitely be a god in another five hundred years,' she says in a huff. One of her male comrades, who's shining his light on the Horse Spirit, says in a more studious tone: 'This god reveals a historical vestige of bestiality in remote antiquity. Have the rest of you heard the story of Wu Zetian engaging in sexual congress with the Donkey Prince?' 'We know you're an educated man, dear fellow,' one of his comrades responds, 'but go home and write an article instead of showing off to us.' Xiao Qiao turns to the four carriers. 'It's up to you to take care of the Meat God. His temple will be built as an expression of the people's yearnings for a good life, not to promote superstition. Meat on the table every day is an important standard of a comfortable, middle-class life.' Once again, the torch beams light up the Meat God's face. By concentrating on the boy's outsized head, I strive to find traces of myself from ten years earlier. But the longer I look, the less likely I am to find any. A round face in an oval head, slitted eyes, puffy cheeks, a dimple on each side of the mouth and big, floppy, palm-like ears is what I see. Then there's the look of joy on its face. How in the world could that be me? My memory's clear—ten years ago there was a lot more suffering, a lot more sorrow than joy or happiness. 'Section Chief,' the old man says to the official, 'we've delivered the Meat God to the temple— we've done what we were hired to do. If you expect us to take care of it after this, you'll have to pay.' 'Do you actually expect to get paid for a good deed in addition to accumulating merit?' Xiao Qiao asks. The four men burst into complaint: 'How are we supposed to live if we don't get paid for our work?'

On the afternoon of New Year's Eve, when I heard the sound of a motorbike, I had a premonition that this particular vehicle was bringing news to our family. I was right. It stopped in front of our gate. Jiaojiao and I ran out to open it and were greeted by the sight of Huang Bao, as nimble as the leopard he was named after, walking towards us with a bundle woven of hemp. We took our places on either side of the gate to welcome him like Golden Boy and Jade Girl, the Taoist attendants. Whatever was inside the bundle gave off a strong smell. He smiled and struck a pose that was part cordial, part cool and detached and part respectfully arrogant. He was a man who carried himself well. His blue motorbike, which resembled its rider— cordial, cool and detached, respectfully arrogant—rested by the side of the road. Mother came out of the house as Huang Bao reached the middle of the yard. Father followed a half dozen steps behind.

Mother smiled broadly. 'Come inside, Good Brother Huang Bao.'

'Good Sister Luo,' he said, exuding courtesy. 'The village head has sent me with a New Year's gift for your family.'

'Oh, we can't accept any gifts,' Mother said, her nervousness evident. 'We've done nothing to deserve a gift, especially from the village head himself.'

'I'm just following orders,' Huang Bao said as he laid the bundle at Mother's feet. 'Goodbye and have a wonderful Spring Festival.'

Mother reached out, as if to keep him from going, but by then he was already at the gate. 'Honestly, we can't . . .'

Huang Bao turned and waved, then left as speedily as he'd come. His motorbike roared to life, just in time for us to rush to the gate and see white smoke spurt from its tailpipe. He headed west, bumping along the pitted road until he turned into Lan Clan Lane.

We stood in stunned silence for at least five minutes, until we saw the roast-pork-peddler Su Zhou bicycling our way from the train station. His beaming smile meant that business had been good that day.

'Lao Yang,' he shouted to Mother. 'It's New Year's, you want some roast pork?'

Mother ignored him.

'What are you saving your money for,' he bellowed, 'a burial plot?'

'To hell with you,' Mother shot back. 'Burial plots are for your family.' Having got that off her chest, she dragged us back into the yard and shut the gate behind us.

She waited till we were inside and then opened the wet wrapper of Huang Bao's bundle to reveal an assortment of red and white seafood on ice. Mother took out each item, describing it for Jiaojiao and me, since we were curious and her seafood knowledge was broad; though none of the rare items she took out had ever made an appearance in our house, she was familiar with them all, and so, by all indications, was Father, though he let her be the seafood guide, content to crouch by the stove, to light his cigarette with a piece of charcoal he picked up with the tongs and sit on his haunches, smoking.

'There's so much . . . that Lao Lan . . .' Mother's cries were more like a lament. 'A guest speaks well of one's host, and a receiver of gifts respects the giver.'

'It's here, so we'll eat it,' Father said resolutely. 'I'll just have to go work for him.'

Electric light flooded our house that night, now that we'd put our days of murky lamplight behind us. We celebrated the Spring Festival under blazing lights, amid Mother's mutterings of gratitude towards Lao Lan's generosity and Father's embarrassed looks. To me it was the most sumptuous Spring Festival meal in memory. For the first time ever, our New Year's Eve dinner included braised prawns—the size of rolling pins—steamed crab—the size of horse hooves—a pan fried butterfish—bigger than Father's palm—along with jellyfish and cuttlefish—sea creatures I'd never tasted.

And I learnt something that night—that there are lots of things in the world just as tasty as meat.

The four carriers stand round the flatbed truck, drinking and feasting on meat, the truck bed serving as a dining table. I can't see any of the meat, but I can smell it, and I know they're eating two varieties: charcoal-fired lamb kebabs, heavy on the cumin, and Mongolian barbecue with cheese. The night market across the street hasn't yet closed for the day, and the first wave of diners are replaced by a second. Pointy Chin suddenly claps his hand against his cheek and lets out a howl. 'What's wrong?' the others ask. 'Toothache!' The old man sneers at him. 'I told you to watch what you were saying,' says his short comrade, 'but you wouldn't listen. Do you believe me now? The Meat God is giving you a taste of his power, and a little taste at that. Just wait!' Meanwhile, Pointy Chin can't stop moaning, holding his mouth and calling for his mother. 'It's killing me!' The old man puffs on his cigarette until the tip glows red and highlights the whiskers round his mouth. 'Shifu,' cries the suffering youngster, 'do something, please!' 'Don't you ever forget,' says the old man unsympathetically, 'that no matter what kind of wood you use, once you carve it into an idol, it's no longer just a piece of wood.' 'It hurts, Shifu!' 'Then why are you out here complaining? Get your butt into the temple, get down on your knees in front of the god and start slapping your face until it stops.' So the man hobbles into the temple, holding his hand to his face and falls to his knees in front of the Meat God. 'Meat God,' he sobs, 'I'll never do that again. Revered God, be kind and forgive me . . .' Reaching up, he gives himself a resounding slap.

Shen Gang, who'd been studiously avoiding us, showed up at our door on the afternoon of the first day of the new year. As soon as we let him in he knelt in front of our ancestral tablets, as custom dictated, and kowtowed and only then came into the living room.

'Why, it's Shen Gang!' Mother blurted out, wondering why he'd come.

Most of the time, when the shameless Shen Gang saw us, his face took on the 'a dead pig isn't afraid of boiling water' look, but now he wore a meek expression as he took a thick envelope out of his pocket and said, clearly embarrassed: 'Good Sister-in-law, I failed as a businessman and never got round to repaying the money you lent me. But last year I managed to save up a bit, and I have to repay you before anything else. There's three thousand in there. Count it, won't you?'

Shen Gang laid the envelope on the table in front of Mother and stepped back. Taking a seat on our bench, he fished out a pack of cigarettes, took out two, and, with a little bow, handed one to Father, who was sitting on the edge of the *kang*. After Father accepted it, Shen offered the second one to Mother; she declined. Her red turtleneck sweater matched her ruddy cheeks and gave her a youthful look. Charcoal briquettes burned brightly in the belly of the stove and kept the room toasty. Father's return had meant the return of the good times to our house as well as of Mother's good mood. No more scowls; even the timbre of her voice had changed.

'Shen Gang,' she said cordially, 'I know you suffered losses, which was why the loan dragged on so long. The reason I was willing to lend you this hard-earned money was because I figured you to be an upright man. In all honesty, you've caught me by surprise. I never thought I'd see the day that you'd come on your own. I'm touched, really touched. I said some things that weren't very kind. Ignore all that. We're old friends, fellow villagers, and now that the boy's father has returned we won't be strangers any longer. If there's anything we can do for you, don't hesitate to ask. After what you've done today, I'm convinced that you're a dependable person . . .'

'I'd feel better if you counted the money,' Shen said.

'All right,' Mother said. 'Bang the gong face to face, beat the drum the same, as the saying goes. Make a loan and repay a loan. I won't mind if there's too little here, but just in case you've given me too much . . .'

She removed the notes from the envelope, wet her fingers with saliva and counted them. Then she handed them to Father. 'Now you,' she said.

Father counted the notes and laid them in front of Mother. 'Three thousand exactly.'

Shen Gang stood up, looking slightly uncomfortable: 'Good Sister-in-law, could I trouble you to return the IOU?'

'It's a good thing you mentioned it or I'd have forgotten all about it. Now where did I put it? Do you remember, Xiaotong?'

'No.'

She jumped off the *kang* and searched everywhere until she found it.

Shen Gang read the IOU several times, until he was convinced it was the right one. Then he tucked it carefully into his pocket and left.

All the while the worker is slapping his face I continue with my narrative to the Wise Monk. At first I'd thought the four carriers would find my story fascinating, but their interest in the meat outstrips anything I might say. I'd thought of revealing that the Meat God was modelled after me, but I swallowed the words. I didn't think the Wise Monk would approve. Besides, even if I told them, they wouldn't believe me.

On the second night of the new year, Yao Qi, who had a very high opinion of himself and who had long dreamt of picking a fight with Lao Lan, dropped by with a bottle of Maotai liquor. We were sitting round a newly acquired dining table when this unexpected visitor arrived. Yao Qi had never stepped foot in our house, and Mother gave me a look because I hadn't obeyed her instructions to shut the gate before we began our meal. An open gate was an open invitation. Yao Qi stuck his head in through the door. Seeing us at dinner he said, 'Ah, a real feast!' but in a tone of voice that immediately annoyed me.

Father's lips parted as if he was about to say something, but he didn't.

Mother did, however: 'We're no match for you and your family, with our coarse tea and bland rice. We just eat to survive.'

'No longer,' Yao Qi remarked.

'These are leftovers from last night,' I chimed in. 'We had prawns, crab, cuttlefish . . .'

'Xiaotong!' Mother cut me off and glared at me. 'Isn't food enough to stop that mouth of yours?'

'We had prawns,' Jiaojiao said, throwing out her arms. 'And they were this big . . .'

'If you want the truth,' Yao Qi said, 'listen to a child. Youngsters, things have got a lot better since Luo Tong returned, haven't they?'

'They're the same as they've always been,' Mother said. 'But you didn't come here to quarrel with us while you're digesting your last meal, did you?'

'No, I have important business to discuss with Luo Tong.'

Father laid down his chopsticks. 'Let's go inside.'

'Worried that someone might overhear you if you stay here?' Mother glared at Father. 'You'd have to turn on the light in there, and electricity costs money.' She looked up at the overhead light.

'That comment alone shows your mettle, good Sister-in-law,' Yao Qi said sarcastically. Then he turned to Father. 'I don't care,' he said. 'I'll go outside and announce it to the whole village with a megaphone.' He put down the bottle of Maotai by the stove, took out a rolled-up piece of paper from his pocket and handed it to Father. 'This is my accusation against Lao Lan,' he said. 'Sign it and we can bring him down together. We can't let that tyrannical landlord's offspring ride roughshod over us.'

Instead of taking the paper, Father looked at Mother; she gazed down at her plate and carried on removing fish bones. 'Yao Qi,' said Father, a few moments later, 'after what I've been through this time, and how disheartened it's made me, all I want now is to live a decent life. Get someone else to sign. Not me, I won't do it.'

'I know that Lao Lan hooked your place up with electricity,' smirked Lao Yao, 'and I know he sent Huang Bao with a parcel of smelly fish and rotten shrimp. But you're Luo Tong—I don't believe he can buy you with so little.'

'Yao Qi,' Mother said as she placed a piece of fish into my sister's bowl, 'stop trying to drag Luo Tong into your hell. He teamed up with you against Lao Lan that other time, and how did that turn out? You stayed in the background with your bad advice and left him to hang from a tree like a dead cat. You want to knock Lao Lan down so you can take over as village head, isn't it?'

'I'm not doing this for myself, good Sister-in-law, I'm doing it for everyone. For that man, giving you electricity and a little seafood is nothing—one hair from nine cowhides, as they say. It's not even his money, it's the people's. Over the past few years he's secretly sold village property to an unscrupulous couple who promised to build a tech park and plant a grove of American red firs, but when no one was looking, they sold the two hundred acres to the Datun Ceramic Factory. Go see for yourself—the area's been levelled down three feet for the foundation. That was fertile farmland. How much do you think he made in that deal?'

'So he sold off two hundred acres of fallow land. He could sell off the whole village, for all we care! Anyone who thinks he's up to it can go after the man. All I know is, it won't be Luo Tong.'

'Is that right, Luo Tong, you're going to pull your neck in like a turtle?' Yao Qi shook the petition. 'Even his brother-in-law Su Zhou has signed.'

'Anyone can sign, for all I care, but not us,' Mother said with curt finality.

'You disappoint me, Luo Tong.'

'Don't play dumb, Yao Qi,' Mother said. 'Do you really believe you'd be a better village head than Lao Lan? You're fooling yourself if you think we don't know all about you. Lao Lan's corrupt, but how do we know you won't be worse? No matter what you say, he's a dutiful son, not like some people who live in big houses and stick their mothers in a grass hut.'

'What do you mean "some people", Yang Yuzhen? Watch what you say!'

'I'm just a village woman, and I can say what I want, so don't give me that "watch what you say" garbage!' Mother had regained her stride. 'I'm talking about you, you turtle spawn,' she said, now completely abandoning any semblance of politeness. 'How could anyone who treats his mother as badly as you be a friend to strangers? If you know what's good for you, you'll pick up that bottle and leave. If you don't, I've got plenty more to say that you won't like to hear.'

Yao Qi tucked his letter away and walked out, followed by a shout of 'Take that bottle with you!' from Mother.

'That's for Luo Tong, good Sister-in-law, whether or not he signs.'

'We've got our own liquor.'

'I know, and you'll get everything you want if you go along with Lao Lan,' Yao Qi said. 'But if you're smart, you'll take a longer view. "Good times don't last for ever and flowers only bloom for so long." A corrupt man like Lao Lan is doomed to self-destruct.'

'We're not going along with anyone,' Mother replied. 'We're the people, no matter who the official. Knock him down if you think you can. It's none of our business.'

Father picked up the bottle, walked out and handed it to Yao Qi: 'I appreciate the gesture but it's better you take it with you.'

'Is that all I am in your eyes, Luo Tong?' asked Yao Qi, bristling. 'Keep it or I'll smash it right here in front of you.'

'Don't be like that. I'll keep it then.' Father saw Yao Qi out to the gate, bottle in hand. 'Listen to me, Old Yao, and don't kick up a row. You live a good life, what else do you want?'

'Luo Tong, go enjoy the good life with your wife, but I'm going to do what I must. I'll knock Lao Lan down or my name isn't Yao Qi! You can tell him if you want. Tell him Yao Qi is going to take up the fight against him. I'm not afraid.'

'I wouldn't do anything as low-down as that,' Father said.

'Who knows,' Yao Qi sneered. 'It looks to me like you left your balls up in the northeast, my friend.' Looking down at Father's pants he asked, 'Does that thing still work?'

Late night. The four carriers lean against the ginkgo tree, chins on their chests, snoring loudly. The lonely female cat emerges from her hole in the tree and transfers the labourer's uneaten meat from the flatbed truck to her home, over and over until it's all safely tucked away. A white mist rises from the ground, blurring and adding a sense of mystery to the red lights of the night market. Three men with burlap sacks, long-handled nets and hammers, skulk out of the darkness, reeking of garlic. A roadside tungsten lamp that has just been turned on is bright enough for me to see their shifty, cowardly eyes. 'Wise Monk, hurry, the cat-nappers are here!' He ignores me. I've heard that some of the restaurants have created a special Carnivore Festival dish with cat as its main ingredient to satisfy the refined palates of tourists from the south. Back when I was roaming the city streets at night I spent some time with cat-napper gangs, so as soon as I saw the tools of their trade I knew what they'd come for. I'm embarrassed to admit, Wise Monk, that when I was hard up in the city I threw in my lot with them. I know that city folk spoil their cats worse than their sons and daughters. Unlike ordinary tomcats, these cats seldom leave their comfy confines, except when they're in heat or ready to mate, and then they prowl the streets and alleyways looking for a good time. People in love take leave of reason, and cats in love make tragic mistakes. Back then, Wise Monk, I fell in with three fellows and went out with them at night to lie in wait where the cats tended to congregate. Under cover of hair-raising screeches and caterwauls, we sneaked up on stupid, fat-as-pigs, pampered felines that shuddered at the sight of a mouse as they rubbed up against one another, and the second they coupled they were snagged by the fellow with the net. Then, while the trapped cats struggled, the fellow with the hammer ran up. A few well-placed thwacks and presto! we had two dead cats. The third fellow picked them out and deposited them in the sack I held. We'd slink off then, hugging the walls, heading for the next cat hangout. Our best haul was two bags full, which we sold to a restaurant for four hundred yuan. Since I wasn't a proper member of the team, more the odd-man-out, they only gave me fifty yuan. I blew it on a meal at a restaurant. I went out a second time, but there wasn't a trace of cats at the underground passageway. Since I knew I'd never find them during the day, I waited till nightfall. But the minute I arrived I was arrested by the metropolitan police. Without as much as a 'how do you do' they began to give me the full treatment. I denied I was a cat-napper, but one of them pointed to the blood on my shirt, called me a liar and began all over again. Then they took me to a place where there were dozens of owners of lost cats: white-haired old men and women, richly jewelled housewives and teary-eyed children. As soon as they heard who I was, they pounced on me, hurling tearful accusations and beating me in rage. The men kicked me in the shins and in the balls, the most painful spots, oh, Mother, how it hurt! The women and the girls were worse—they pinched my ears, gouged my eyes and twisted my nose. An old woman with shaking hands elbowed her way up to me and scratched my face. Not entirely satisfied, she then took a bite out of my scalp. Somewhere along the way I fainted. When I woke up I found myself buried under a pile of garbage. I clawed my way out frantically, stuck my head into the open air and took some deep breaths. And there I was, sitting on a pile of garbage, looking down on the bustling city streets in the distance, sore, hungry and feeling like I was at death's door. That's when I thought about my mother and my father, about my sister, even about Lao Lan, thought about how I'd been free to eat all the meat I wanted when I was a slaughterhouse workshop director, about when I could drink as much liquor as I wanted, about when everyone respected me, and the tears fell like pearls from a broken string. I was spent, resigned to dying on top of a garbage heap. Just then, my hand brushed against something soft, and I detected a familiar smell—a packet of donkey meat, a treat from the past. As soon as I tore open the wrapping and feasted my eyes on its lovely countenance, it poured out its woes to me: 'Luo Xiaotong, you be the judge. They said I'd gone past my best-eaten-by date and threw me out. But there's nothing wrong with me, I'm as nutritious as ever and I smell fine. Eat me, Luo Xiaotong, and you'll bring joy to an otherwise joyless existence.' I reached down impulsively, my mouth opened automatically and my teeth chattered excitedly. But when the meat touched my lips, Wise Monk, I remembered my vow. The day my sister died from poisoned meat, I raised a vow to the moon that I'd never eat meat on pain of an excruciating death. So I returned the donkey meat to the garbage heap. But I was famished, on the verge of starving. I picked it up again, only to be reminded of Jiaojiao's ghostly pale face in the moonlight. Just then that piece of donkey meat let out a cold laugh: 'Luo Xiaotong, you take your vows seriously. I was put here to test you. A starving man who can hold true to a vow in the face of a fragrant cut of meat is a praiseworthy individual. Based on this alone, I predict a glorious future for you. Under the right circumstances, you could even become a god and go down in history. The truth is, I'm not a cut of donkey meat, I'm imitation meat sent down by the Moon God to put you to the test. My primary ingredients are soya and egg whites, with additives and starch. So go ahead, put your mind at ease and eat me. I may not be meat, but to be eaten by a meat god is my great good fortune.' With the imitation meat's words still ringing in my ears, a new avalanche of tears poured forth. Heaven wanted me to survive! As I ate the imitation meat, whose taste was identical to the real thing, I pondered several things. When the time was right I'd cast myself out of this world of pervasive desire. If I was to become a Buddha, so be it, but if not that, then a Taoist immortal, and if not that, then a demon.

To this day I cannot forget the night when I went with Father and Mother to convey our New Year's greetings to Lao Lan. Even though nearly ten years have passed, and I'm now an adult, and even though I've tried hard to put that night out of my mind, the finer details will not let me, almost as if they were shrapnel embedded in the marrow of my bones—resisting all attempts at extrication and proving their existence with pain.

It was after Yao Qi's visit, on the second night of the new year. We'd just finished a quick dinner, when Mother turned to Father, who was enjoying a leisurely smoke. 'Let's go,' she said, 'the earlier we leave, the sooner we'll be back home.'

Father looked up through the haze of smoke. 'Do we have to?' he asked, obviously uncomfortable.

'What's your problem?' she responded unhappily. 'I thought we agreed this afternoon. What changed your mind?'

'What's going on?' I asked, curious as always.

'What's going on?' echoed Jiaojiao.

'This has nothing to do with you children,' snapped Mother.

'I think I'll stay home,' said Father, giving Mother a hangdog look. 'Why don't you go with Xiaotong and give him my regards?'

'Go where?' I asked. They'd really piqued my interest. 'I'm ready.'

'Shut up,' Mother barked angrily, then turned back to Father. 'I know how important saving face is to you, but a New Year's visit isn't going to demean you. What's wrong with villagers paying a call on their village head?'

'People will talk,' Father said, digging in his heels. 'I don't want people saying that I'm kissing Lao Lan's arse!'

'You call New Year's greetings arse-kissing?' Mother was incredulous. 'Lao Lan gave us electricity, he gave us a New Year's gift, he gave the children red envelopes—you wouldn't call that arse-kissing, would you?'

'That's different . . .'

'All those promises you made to me, they meant nothing . . .' Mother sat on the bench. The colour left her cheeks and they grew wet with tears. 'Apparently you have no intention of staying with us . . .'

'Lao Lan's a big shot!' Despite my general lack of sympathy for my mother, I hated to watch her cry. 'Dieh,' I said, 'I'm happy to go. Lao Lan's an interesting guy, worth being friends with.'

'He thinks Lao Lan's beneath him,' Mother said. 'He only wants to be friends with arseholes like Yao Qi.'

'Yao Qi's a bad man, Dieh,' I said. 'He called you names when you were away.'

'Xiaotong, stay out of adults' affairs,' Father said gently.

'I think Xiaotong's got better sense than you.' Now Mother was angry. 'After you left, Lao Lan was the only one who treated us well. Yao Qi and the others got a kick out of watching bad things happen to us. It's times like that when you can tell who's good and who's bad.'

'I'm going, too, Dieh,' Jiaojiao said.

Father heaved a sigh. 'All right, have it your way. I'll go.'

Mother went to the wardrobe and took out a blue wool tunic.

'Wear this,' she said in a tone that permitted no objection.

Father decided to say nothing. Instead, he dutifully took off his greasy, tattered jacket and put on the tunic. Mother tried to button it up for him; he pushed her hand away. But he didn't resist when she went round and straightened the back.

As a family we walked out of the house and onto Hanlin Avenue. The streetlights that had been installed shortly before New Year's were already lit. Children were out playing chase; a youngster was reading a book under one of the lights; some men were loitering under another, arms crossed, engaged in idle talk. Four young men were showing off their riding skills on brand new motorbikes, revving them up to make as much noise as possible. There was the occasional burst of firecrackers in front of houses that sported a pair of red lanterns in the doorway and a carpet of red confetti on the ground. 'All those firecrackers,' Father had muttered on New Year's Eve, 'you'd think it was the beginning of World War III.'

'More firecrackers means more money,' Mother said, 'and shows how effective Lao Lan's leadership has been.'

That's exactly how we felt as we walked down Hanlin Avenue. Within the confines of a hundred square *li*, Slaughterhouse was the only village in the area in which the roads had been paved and streetlights installed. Nearly every family lived in multistoreyed, tile-roofed houses; many even had modern interiors.

Hand in hand, our little family of four proceeded down Hanlin Avenue. It was the first time we'd appeared in public as a family. It was also the last. But I felt both proud and contented. Jiaojiao walked along happily. Father seemed less than natural. Mother was calm and unperturbed. Passers-by greeted us—Father barely mumbled a response but Mother heartily returned their greetings. When we turned into Lan Clan Lane, which led to the Hanlin Bridge, Father grew increasingly uneasy. The lane also boasted a dozen or so streetlights, which shone on the black gates and the bright red couplets pasted on them. Coloured lights on the distant Hanlin Bridge put the arch in relief. The largest village compounds were on the other side of the river, lit up holiday-bright.

I knew what was bothering Father—the bright lights. If he'd had his way, the lane would have been pitch black to hide us from view. He'd have been happiest if we'd delivered our New Year's greetings in complete darkness, hidden from public view. I also knew that Mother's feelings were the exact opposite. She wanted people to bear witness to the fact that we were bringing New Year's greetings to Lao Lan, that close bonds of friendship had developed between us, which in turn was a sign that her husband, my father, had turned over a new leaf, transforming himself from a disreputable vagrant into a respectable family man. I knew that the village was alive with talk about us, talk that centred on the virtues of my mother. 'Yang Yuzhen,' they said, 'is quite a woman. She can bear hardships, she has endurance, patience and foresight, and she's eminently sensible, all in all not one to be taken lightly. As I well knew,' they went so far as to say, 'Just watch, it won't be long before that family flourishes.'

There was nothing out of the ordinary about the gate to Lao Lan's house; if anything, it was shabbier than his neighbours'. In fact, it did poorly in comparison even with ours. We stood on the steps and banged the knocker against the gate and immediately heard the frantic barks and threatening growls of the wolfhounds on the other side.

Jiaojiao pressed up against me.

'Don't be scared, Jiaojiao,' I comforted her. 'Their dogs don't bite.'

Mother knocked again, but drew no response, except from the dogs.

'Let's go,' Father urged. 'They must be out.'

'If so, there has to be someone to watch the place,' Mother said.

She knocked again, neither too hard nor too soft. As if she were saying: I won't stop until you come out to see who's here.

Her efforts were finally rewarded. We heard the sound of a door opening, followed by a girl's crisp command to the dogs: 'Shut up!' Next, the sound of footfalls approaching the gate. Then, at last, a question—impatiently delivered—from the other side: 'Who is it?'

'It's us,' Mother replied. 'Is that Tiangua? I'm Yang Yuzhen, Luo Xiaotong's mother. We're here to wish you a happy New Year.'

'Yang Yuzhen?' The name was not familiar to the girl.

Mother nudged me to say something. Tiangua, Lao Lan's only child, had grown quite a bit, and her mother could have had a second child if she'd wanted. She hadn't. I dimly recalled someone saying that Lao Lan's wife was ill and had not been out of the house in years. I knew Tiangua, a girl with dull brown hair and two lines of snot above her mouth. She was a bigger slob than me, and couldn't begin to compare with my sister. I didn't like her one bit. So why did Mother want me to say something? Was I supposed to believe that my voice carried more weight than hers?

'Tiangua,' I said finally, 'open up. It's me, Luo Xiaotong.'

Tiangua stuck her head out through a small opening in the gate, and the first thing I noticed was that there was no snot above her mouth and that she was wearing a nice jacket. Then I saw that her hair wasn't as dull brown as I remembered, and that it was neatly combed. In a word, she was a better-looking girl than I recalled. She sized me up with a squint and a strange look, and those slitted eyes and light hair reminded me of the foxes I'd seen recently. *Again the foxes. I'm sorry, Wise Monk, I don't want to talk about them but they keep coming back to me.* Foxes, which had been raised as rare animals at first but in such large numbers that they had to be wholesaled at a deep discount to Slaughterhouse Village, where they were slaughtered and their meat mixed with dog to be sold. Our butchers didn't forget to pump the slaughtered foxes full of water, though the process was more difficult than with cows or pigs, since they were so much trickier, so much harder to work on. That's where my thoughts roamed when I heard Tiangua's say 'My dieh isn't home.'

But, led by Mother, we squeezed in through the gate and pushed Tiangua out of the way. I saw the well-fed wolfhounds jump to their feet, eyes and teeth flashing in the light, metal chains ringing out as they were pulled taut. They were as close to being wolves as dogs could possibly be, and those chains were all that kept them from tearing us limb from limb. On that earlier day, when I'd come alone to invite Lao Lan to dinner, they hadn't seemed as frightening.

'Tiangua,' Mother said once she'd elbowed her way into the yard, 'it's all right if your dieh isn't home. We're just as happy saying hello to you and your niang and chatting for a few minutes.'

Before Tiangua could react, we spotted Lao Lan, standing big and tall in the doorway of his home's eastern wing.

The three cat-nappers are merciless. One swipe of the net and the cat is caught, one swing of the club and it's out. Into the burlap sack it goes. I want to rush to the cat's rescue but I've been sitting with my legs under me so long that they've gone to sleep. 'She's just had kittens,' I shout, 'let her go!' My voice cuts through the air like a knife—even I can feel it—but they turn a deaf ear to my cry, their attention caught by the cluster of ostriches sleeping in the corner. They charge at the huddled birds excitedly, like starving wolves. Startled awake, the ostriches screech in anticipation of the inevitable fight or flight. One of the birds, a male, leaps up and strikes the net-holder in the nose with one of its powerful legs. Then the whole group, necks stretched as far as they'll go, takes off in all directions, feet flying; but they quickly come together and bolt for the highway. The thud of ostrich feet pounding the ground fades into the darkness and then vanishes altogether. The injured cat-napper is sitting on the ground holding his nose, blood seeping between his fingers. His partners help him to his feet and console him in hushed voices. But the moment they let go, he slumps back to the ground, as if his bones have turned to tendons and sinews no longer capable of support. His partners' consoling words are drowned out by his sobs and whimpers. Just then another of them discovers the three headless ostriches, and the thrill nearly throws him off balance. 'Number One,' he shouts, jumping in excitement, 'stop crying, there's meat!' The injured man stops crying and drops his hand from his nose. All six eyes are riveted to the three ostrich carcasses; the men seem frozen in place. Then the excitement claims them, including the one with the injury— he jumps to his feet. They throw the cat out of their sack—it runs in circles, mewing, a sign that the blow was serious but not fatal—and try to stuff in the dead ostriches; but they're too big, they won't fit. Plan B: forget the sack and drag the ostrich carcasses by the feet, one apiece, like donkeys pulling a wagon onto the highway. I watch them go, following the progress of their elongated silhouettes.

A pair of electric heaters warmed the eastern wing of Lao Lan's house, the thick tungsten wires burning red behind transparent covers. All those years of scavenging with Mother had taught me a lot, no lesson more valuable than how electric appliances work. I knew that his heater was not energy efficient, that the large amounts of electricity it consumed made it impractical for most people. Lao Lan was wearing a V-necked cable-knit sweater over a white shirt and a red-striped tie in a room that was uncomfortably hot. He'd shaved off his sideburns and had his hair cut short, which combined to draw attention to the mutilated ear. His freshly shaved cheeks had begun to go slack and his eyelids were slightly puffy, but none of that had any effect on my new image of him. A peasant? I hardly think so. No, clearly someone on the government payroll. His attire and demeanour put my father, with his wool tunic, to shame. Nothing in his expression indicated that he was unhappy with us for turning up without an invitation. On the contrary, he politely invited us to sit and even patted me on the head. My rear end settled comfortably into the softness of his black leather sofa, but unnaturally so, as if I was sitting on a cloud. Jiaojiao shifted her little bottom on the leather sofa and giggled. Both Father and Mother respectfully sat on its edge, so respectfully they couldn't possibly have appreciated its comforts. Lao Lan walked over to a cabinet by the wall and brought back a lovely metal box; he opened it, took out pieces of chocolate wrapped in gold foil and handed them to Jiaojiao and me. She took a bite and spat it out: 'It's medicine!'

'It's not medicine, it's chocolate,' I corrected her, displaying some of the knowledge I'd acquired while scavenging with Mother. 'Eat it. It's nutritious and it's packed with calories. All the athletes eat it.'

The look of approval on Lao Lan's face filled me with pride. But I knew a lot more than that. Scavenging is life's encyclopedia. Picking up junk and sorting it into categories is the same as reading a book of facts. The older I got, the more I grew to appreciate the wealth of knowledge I'd acquired during those years; they constituted my elementary, middle and high school, and yielded endless benefits.

Jiaojiao refused to eat another bite of chocolate, so Lao Lan returned to the cabinet and brought out a tray of hazelnuts, almonds, pistachios and walnuts, which he set down on a tea table by the sofa. Then he knelt in front of us, picked up a small hammer and cracked open a walnut and a hazelnut, carefully scooping out the meat and laying it in front of my sister.

'You'll spoil them, Village Head,' complained Mother.

'Yang Yuzhen,' Lao Lan said, ignoring her comment, 'you're a lucky woman.'

'Lucky?' Mother remarked. 'You can't be lucky with a face like a monkey.'

Lao Lan looked at Mother. 'Anyone who can denigrate herself,' he said with a smile, 'deserves my respect.'

'Village Head,' Mother said, blushing, 'this has been a wonderful New Year's for my family, thanks to you, and we're here to deliver our holiday greetings. Xiaotong, Jiaojiao, get down on your knees and kowtow to his honour.'

'No, no, no . . .' Lao Lan jumped to his feet, waving his large hands. 'Yang Yuzhen, only you could think of such an elaborate courtesy, one I hardly deserve. Have you taken a good look at the children you're bringing up?' He bent to pat us on the head. 'You have a true Golden Boy and Jade Girl here. Nothing can stop them from enjoying a wonderful future. As for us, no matter how hard we struggle, we'll always be loaches at the bottom of a ditch. Not a dragon among us. But them, they're different. I may not know my horses but I do know my people.' He reached out, cupped our chins and looked closely into our faces. He then glanced up at our parents: 'I want you to take a good look at these remarkable faces. I guarantee that these two will make you proud.'

'They don't deserve such a compliment, Village Head,' Mother demurred. 'They're only a couple of children who hardly understand a thing.'

'Village Head,' Father added, 'dragons beget dragons, and phoenixes beget their kind. With a dieh like me—'

'That's no way to talk!' Lao Lan interrupted. 'Lao Luo, we peasants have muddled along for decades, until even we have no respect for ourselves. Ten years ago, I walked into a restaurant in town and didn't know how to order a single thing off the menu. The waiter, an impatient man, tapped the edge of the table with his ballpoint pen and said, "What do you peasants know about ordering food? Here's my recommendation: order a meat and vegetable stew. It's cheap and it's filling." "Stew?" I said. "You mean leftovers you toss in the pot and heat up?" One of of my companions urged me to obey but I refused.

"What do you think we are, a bunch of pigs, only good for eating other people's trash?" Whether or not he liked it, I wanted some specialities of the house, so I ordered a "Green Dragon Lying in Snow" and "Fried Pork with Celery Sprouts". But when they arrived from the kitchen, Green Dragon Lying in Snow was nothing but a cucumber in a bed of sugar sprinkles. So I complained to the waiter. He simply rolled his eyes and said, "That's Green Dragon Lying in Snow," and then turned to leave, but not before I heard him swear: "Hick turtles!" That made me so mad that smoke nearly came out of my ears, but I swallowed my anger. I also made a vow that, before too long, this country turtle would control the lives of those city tortoises!'

Lao Lan took two Zhonghua cigarettes from his tin case, tossed one to Father and lit the other for himself, striking a dignified pose with each puff.

'Back in those days . . .' Father stammered in his attempts to stay in the conversation, '. . . that's the way things were . . .'

'So, you see, Lao Luo,' Lao Lan said sombrely, 'it's important to go out and make money. In times like these, a man with money is the patriarch—a man without it is a grandchild. With it, you stand straight and tall—without it, you have no backbone. Being the head of this little village doesn't mean a thing to me. Have you checked out the Lan clan lineage? With those who got official titles, even the lowest was at least a circuit intendant. I'm not content with what we once were. I want to lead people onto a path to riches. Not only that, I want to make this a rich village. We already have paved roads and streetlights and we've repaired the bridge. Next, we need to build a school, a pre-school and a retirement home. Of course, I have personal reasons for wanting a school, but it's more than that. I'm committed to restoring the Lan manor to its original grandeur and then opening it to the public as a tourist attraction, the proceeds all going to the village, of course. Lao Luo, a long friendship has existed between our families. Your grandfather, a beggar who stood outside our gate cursing all day long, became one of my grandfather's best friends. When my third uncle and his family fled to the Nationalist area during the Civil War, it was your grandfather who took them in his wagon. That's an act of friendship we Lans will not dare forget. So, my good brother, there's no reason for you and me not to join forces and do important things. I have big plans and the confidence to see them through!' Lao Lan paused for another puff: 'Lao Luo, I know you disapprove of how the butchers inject water into animal carcasses. But you need to look beyond our village. Where will you find another village in the county, in the province, in the whole country, where water isn't injected into the meat? If everyone else does it but we don't, we'll not only fail to earn a living but also wind up in the red. If no one else did it, we wouldn't either, of course. We live in an age that scholars characterize as that of the primitive accumulation of capital. Just what does that mean? Simply that people will make money by any means necessary, and that everyone's money is tainted by the blood of others. Once this phase has passed, moral behaviour will again be in fashion. But during times of immoral behaviour, if we persist in being moral we might as well starve to death. Lao Luo, there's much more to discuss, so you and I will sit down one day and have a good long talk. Oh, what's wrong with me! I forgot to pour tea. You'll have some, won't you?'

'No tea for us,' Mother said. 'We've already taken up too much of your time. We'll just sit a moment longer and then be on our way.'

'You're already here, so what's the hurry? Lao Luo, seeing you here is a rare treat. Of all the men in the village, you're the only one who never dropped by, until today.' He stood up, went across to the cabinet and selected five long-stemmed glasses. 'Instead of pouring tea, let's have a drink. That's how the Westerners do it.'

He took out a bottle of imported liquor—Remy Martin XO, brandy that sold in the mall for at least a thousand yuan. Mother and I once bought some for three hundred yuan a bottle in the city's infamous Corruption Lane, then resold it to a little store near the train station for four-fifty apiece. We knew that the people who sold them to us were relatives of officials who'd received them as gifts.

Lao Lan poured brandy into all five glasses.

'Not for the children,' Mother said.

'A little taste won't hurt.'

The amber liquid created a strange light show in the glasses. Lao Lan held out his glass; we did the same. 'Happy New Year!'

Our glasses clinked, a crisp, pleasant sound.

'Happy New Year!' we echoed.

'Well, how do you like it?' he asked as he swirled the liquid in his glass, watching it closely. 'You can add ice, you can even add tea.'

'It has an interesting aroma,' Mother said.

'How's a farmer supposed to tell good from bad?' asked Father. 'It's wasted on us.'

'Don't say things like that, Lao Luo,' responded Lao Lan. 'I want you to be the Luo Tong before he went to the northeast, not this passive shell of a man. Stand straight, my brother. Once a bent back becomes a habit, it's impossible to break.'

'Lao Lan's right, Dieh,' I said.

'Xiaotong, who do you think you are,' Mother bawled at me as she gave me a slap, 'calling him Lao Lan?'

'Great!' Lao Lan said with a smile. 'That's exactly what I want you to call me. From now on it's Lao Lan. I love the sound of it.'

'Lao Lan!' Now it was Jiaojiao's turn.

'Terrific!' said Lao Lan excitedly. 'Just terrific!'

Father held his glass out, tipped his head back and drained his glass. 'Lao Lan,' he said, 'I have only one thing to say. I work for you.'

'No, you don't—we work together. I'll tell you what I'm thinking. We can take ownership of the one-time commune canvas factory and refit the buildings for a meatpacking plant. My sources tell me that officials in town are up in arms over the injection of water in the meat and are about to mount a "safe meat project". The next step will be to outlaw independent butchers, which will put an end to our prosperity. We need to act before that happens by opening a meatpacking plant. We'll welcome any villager willing to join our consortium. As for the rest, well, we'll never have a shortage of manpower, since unemployment is rampant in all villages . . .' The phone rang. He picked it up, dealt briefly with his caller and then hung up. 'Lao Luo,' he said, looking up at the digital clock on the wall, 'something's come up, so we'll have to continue this another day.'

We stood up and said our goodbyes, but not before Mother reached into her black, faux-leather bag, took out the bottle of Maotai and placed it on the tea table.

'Yang Yuzhen,' Lao Lan said, looking displeased, 'what's this?'

'Don't be angry, Village Head, this isn't a gift,' Mother said, smiling meaningfully. 'Yao Qi brought this to our house last night as a gift for Luo Tong. How could we presume to drink anything as expensive as this? We'd rather you had it.'

Lao Lan picked the bottle up and held it close to the light to get a better look. Then he smiled and handed it to me. 'Xiaotong, you be the judge. Is this the real thing or a knock-off?'

Without even looking at the bottle, I said with complete assurance: 'A knock-off.'

Lao Lan tossed the bottle into a bin against the wall and laughed heartily. 'You are very discriminating, worthy Nephew!'

Tongue stiff, cheeks numb, eyes dull and heavy, one yawn after another. I fight to keep going, muddling along with my tale . . . a car horn startles me awake. Morning sunlight streams into the temple; there's bat guano on the floor. An ambiguous smile adorns the little, basin-like face of the Meat God; just looking at it gives me a sense of pride, mixed with remorse and trepidation. My past is a fairy tale or, more accurately, a big lie. I stare at him, he stares back, lively and expressive, almost as if he's about to speak to me. I feel as if I could animate him with a single puff of air, send him running happily out of the temple over to the feast and the meat forum to eat his fill and join the discussion. If the Meat God is really anything like me, then he's someone who can talk and talk and talk. Wise Monk continues to sit, lotus position, on his rush mat, unchanged. He casts a meaningful look at me before shutting his eyes. I recall my sleep being interrupted by pangs of hunger in the middle of the night, but when I awoke this morning I wasn't hungry at all. I'm now reminded of how, I think, the woman who resembles Aunty Wild Mule nourished me with her spurting milk. I lick my lips and detect its sweet taste again. This is the second day of the Carnivore Festival, when forums and discussion groups on a variety of topics will take place in guest houses and restaurants in the twin cities, followed by all manner of banquets. Barbecue stands will continue in operation in the field across the temple, albeit with a new batch of cooks. At the moment, none of them and no prospective customers have arrived. No one but fast-moving clean-up crews are up and working at this hour, busy as battlefield mop-up units.

My parents sent me to school soon after New Year's, not the normal time to begin. But, thanks to Lao Lan's intervention, the authorities were happy to let me enrol. They also enrolled my sister in the Early Red Academy, or, as it's called now, preschool.

The school gate was just outside the village, a hundred metres on the other side of Hanlin Bridge. The one-time manor of the Lan family, it had fallen into a state of rot and disrepair. The buildings, with green brick walls and blue tiled roofs, had once heralded the glories of the Lan family to all who laid eyes on them. Locally, the Lans were not thought of as rustic rich. Members of Lao Lan's father's generation had studied in America, which gave him something to be proud of. Four metal characters in red—翰林小学—that spelt out 'Hanlin Primary School' were welded onto the cast-iron arch spanning the gate. Already eleven, I was placed in the first grade, which made me nearly twice the age of, and a head taller than, my classmates. I was the centre of attention for students and teachers alike during the morning flag-raising ceremony, and I'll bet they thought that a boy from one of the upper classes had mistakenly lined up with them.

I was not cut out to be a student. It was sheer agony to sit on a stool for forty-five minutes and behave myself. And not just once a day, but seven times, four in the morning and three in the afternoon. I began to feel dizzy at about the ten-minute mark and wanted nothing more than to lie down and go to sleep. I could hear neither my teacher's murmurs nor my class-mates' recitations. The teacher's face faded from view and was replaced by what looked like a cinema screen across which danced images of people, cows and dogs.

My homeroom teacher, Ms Cai, a woman with a moon face, a head of hair like a rat's nest, a short neck and a big arse—she waddled like a duck—hated me from the beginning but chose to ignore me. She taught maths, which invariably put me to sleep. 'Luo Xiaotong!' she shouted once, grabbing me by the ear.

Eyes open but brain not yet in gear, I asked: 'What's wrong? Someone die at your house?'

If she interpreted that as a curse that augured a death in her family, she was wrong. I'd been dreaming of doctors in white smocks running down the street shouting: 'Hurry, hurry, hurry, someone's died at the teacher's house.' But, of course, she couldn't know that, which is why she interpreted my shout as a curse on her. If I'd said that to one of the less civilized teachers at the school, my ears would have been ringing from a resounding slap. But she was a cultured woman; she merely returned to the front of the room, her cheeks flushed, and sniffled like an ill-treated girl. Biting her lip, as if to pluck up courage, she said: 'Luo Xiaotong, there are eight pears and four children. How do you divide them up?'

'Divide them up? You fight over them! This is an age of "primitive accumulation". The bold stuff their bellies, the timid starve to death and the biggest fist wins the fight!'

My answer got a laugh out of my dimwitted classmates, who could not possibly have understood me. They just liked my attitude, and when one laughed the others followed, filling the room with laughter. The boy next to me, whom everyone called Mung Bean, laughed so hard that snot spurted from his nose. Under the guidance of a dimwitted teacher, that pack of dimwits was growing even more dimwitted. I stared at the teacher with a triumphant look but all she could do was bang the table with her pointer.

'Stand up!' she demanded angrily, her face turning deep red.

'Why?' I asked. 'Why should I stand when everyone else stays in their seat?'

'Because you're answering a question,' she said.

'I'm supposed to stand when I answer a question?' My voice dripped with sarcasm and arrogance. 'Don't you have a TV at home? If you don't, does that mean you've never watched TV? Have you never seen a pig walk just because you've never eaten pork? If you've watched TV, have you ever seen a press conference? The officials don't stand up to answer questions—the reporters stand up to *ask* the questions.'

That drew another laugh from my dimwitted classmates, who, once again, could not possibly have understood me. Not a clue! They might watch TV but cartoons only—never serious programmes, like I did. And never, not in a million years, would they be able to understand world affairs like I did. Wise Monk, even before that year's Lantern Festival, we had a Japanese 21-inch colour TV with a rectangular screen and a remote. A TV like that these days would be considered an antique, but then it was ultra-modern; and not onlu in our village but even in cities like Beijing and Shanghai. Lao Lan had sent it over with Huang Bao and, when he took it out of the box, all black and shiny, we were absolutely amazed. 'It's gorgeous, absolutely gorgeous,' was Mother's comment. Even Father, never one to beam with happiness, said: 'Would you look at that! How in the world did they make something like that!' Even the Styrofoam packing elicited whoops of surprise from him—he found it incredible that something useful could be so light and airy. It was nothing to me, of course—we'd seen plenty of it on our scavenging route, but we never gave it a second thought because none of the recycling centres would take it. Besides the TV set, Huang Bao brought along a herringbone antenna and a seamless 15-metre metal pole coated with anti-rust material. When we stood it up in the yard it made our house look like a crane amid chickens, towering over the neighbourhood. If I could have climbed to the top of the pole, I'd have had a bird's-eye view of the whole village. Our eyes lit up when the first gorgeous images flashed across the TV screen. That TV raised the standing of our family to a new level. And I grew a lot smarter. Enrolling me in school—in the first grade, no less—was little more than a joke of international proportions. Slaughterhouse Village could boast two individuals who were knowledgeable and well informed: Lao Lan and me. Written words were a stranger to me, but I was no stranger to them, at least that's how it felt to me. There are lots of things in this world that do not need to be studied, at least not in a school, in order to be learnt. Don't tell me you have to go to school to be able to know how to divide eight pears among four children!

My response rendered the teacher speechless. I saw something glitter in her eyes and knew that when they finally spilt they'd be tears. I was proud of myself but I was also frightened. I knew that a student who made his home-room teacher cry would be seen as a bad seed, although, paradoxically, people would know he had a bright future with endless possibilities. If his development went in the right direction, a child like that was virtually guaranteed an official position; if not, we're talking big-time criminal. But one way or other, he'd be special. Sad to say, but thank goodness, those glittering objects in the teacher's eyes did not spill.

'Leave the room,' she said, softly at first, and then shrilly: 'Roll that fanny of yours out of here!'

'A ball's the only thing that can roll out of here, Teacher, except a hedgehog, when it rolls itself into a ball. I'm not a ball, and I'm not a hedgehog, I'm human, so I can walk out of here or run out of here or, of course, crawl out of here.'

'Then crawl out of here.'

'But I can't do that either,' I said. 'If I hadn't learnt how to walk yet, then I'd have to crawl. But I'm a big boy now, and if I start crawling it'll mean I've done something wrong, but since I've done nothing wrong I can't crawl out of here.'

'Just get out of here, get out . . .' She was almost hoarse from shouting. 'Luo Xiaotong, you make me so angry I could burst . . . you and that perverse logic of yours . . .'

In the end, those glittering objects did spill from of her eyes and onto her cheeks and became tears, creating such an abruptly solemn feeling in me that my eyes grew moist too. Under no circumstances was I going to allow the wetness in my eyes to spill out onto my cheeks and turn into tears, not if I wanted to retain my dignity in front of my dimwitted classmates and not lose every last shred of significance in my verbal battle with the teacher. So I stood up and walked out of class.

I went through the gate and out onto Hanlin Bridge, where I leaned over the railing to watch the green water flowing below. There I saw little black fish not much bigger than mosquito larvae swimming along, their numbers greatly diminished when a much larger fish surged through with its mouth open. A comment I'd once heard popped into my head: Big fish eat little fish, little fish eat shrimps, shrimps eat silt. The only way to keep from being eaten is to be bigger than others. I sensed that I was already one of the big ones, though not big enough. I had to grow, and grow quickly. My eye caught a cluster of tadpoles, a tight, black, quivering mass rushing through the water, like a black cloud. Why had the big fish dined on little fish but not the tadpoles? Why, I wondered, do people, cats, kingfishers, with their long beaks and short tails, and lots of other creatures eat little fish but not tadpoles? Basically, I figured, because they don't taste good. But how would we know they don't taste good if we never tried them? Once again, basically, because of their appearance. Ugly creatures don't taste good. On the other hand, snakes, scorpions and locusts are ugly things and yet people fight over them. No one ate scorpions till the 1980s, when people began to treat them as gourmet food and they appeared on all the finest tables. My first taste came at one of Lao Lan's banquets. I want everyone to take note that, in the wake of our New Year's visit to Lao Lan, I became a regular guest at his home, spending lots of leisure time there, alone or with my sister. His wolfhounds treated us almost as family: now, when we walked in, we were greeted with wagging tails instead of menacing barks. But back to my original question: Why don't people eat tadpoles? Could it be because they're slimy, snotty-looking things? But so are snails, and people love them. Or is it because tadpoles come from toads, and toads are poisonous? But tadpoles come from frogs, too, and many consider frogs a delicacy. And not just people—there's a cow in our village that loves frogs. So why don't people eat the young creatures that will grow into frogs? I couldn't make sense of it, and couldn't help thinking that the world was a very puzzling place. But if there's one thing I knew, it was that only well-informed youngsters like me contemplated these complex issues. I was faced with a great many questions, not because I *lacked* knowledge but because I *possessed* it. I didn't think much of my homeroom teacher, but was grateful to be the target of that last comment of hers—perverse logic. I felt that her evaluation of me was quite fair. What sounded like a curse was, in truth, lavish praise. My classmates knew the meaning only of one part—perverse—with no chance of grasping the whole idea—perverse logic. To take it a step further: How many people in the village knew the meaning of perverse logic? I did, and without recourse to a teacher. In essence, perverse logic is a perverse way of thinking about things.

In accordance with my perverse logic associated with tadpoles, I began thinking about swallows. Actually, the thought about swallows didn't come out of nowhere. Some were flying low over the river at the moment, and they were so beautiful in flight. They skimmed the surface, raising tiny waves with their bellies and sending ripples to the banks. Others stood on the banks and dug their beaks into the mud. This was the season for building nests—apricot trees were in bloom, and buds on peach trees were waiting their turn to flower. There were new leaves on riverside weeping willows, and cries of cuckoos came on the air from afar. Everyone knew it was time for planting, but no one in Slaughterhouse Village worked the fields any more—it was a tiring, sweaty way to make a meagre living. Who but a moron would do that? There definitely were no morons in Slaughterhouse Village, where the fields were left fallow. When he returned home, my father planned to take up the plough, but that never happened. Lao Lan had given him the responsibility of managing the United Meatpacking Plant, while he himself was chairman and general manager of its parent company, the newly created Huachang Corporation.

Father's plant was half a *li* east of the school, within sight of the bridge. Originally housing a number of canvas-production workshops, the buildings had been restructured for animal slaughter. Every creature that entered one of the buildings, except for the humans, went in alive and came out dead. I was much more interested in the plant than I was in school, but Father would not let me near it. Nor would Mother. He was the plant manager, she its book-keeper and many of the village's independent butchers its workforce.

I sauntered towards the plant. After being thrown out of class, I experi-enced a sense of unease over what I considered to be a smallish mistake—at first, that is. But that feeling left me as I strolled along on that glorious spring day. How incredibly foolish to sit cooped up inside a room listening to a teacher chatter away during that wonderful season. No less foolish than going out to tend a field day after day, knowing it only put you deeper in debt. Why should I have to go to school? The teachers didn't know any more than I did, perhaps even less. And while I knew practical, useful things, everything they knew was useless. Lao Lan had been right about everything except when he told my parents to send me to school. It was also a mistake to have them enrol my sister in preschool. I was tempted to rescue her from her ordeal and explore the secrets of nature with her. We could fish in the river with our bare hands, we could climb trees and trap birds, we could pick wildflowers in open fields. There was no limit to the things we could do, and every one of them was better than being in school.

From my hiding place behind a riverside willow tree, I surveyed Father's plant, a large compound surrounded by a high wall topped with barbed wire. It looked more like a prison—rows of high-ceiling factory buildings inside the wall, with a row of squat buildings in the southwest corner in front of a massive smokestack belching out thick smoke. That, I knew, was the plant's kitchen, the source of the meaty aroma that frequently assailed my nostrils, even when I was in class. When that happened, my teacher and my class-mates ceased to exist and my mind filled with beautiful images of meat that expelled bursts of heated fragrance as it lined up and hopped along a road paved with garlic paste and coriander and other spices, heading straight for me. I could smell it now. I had no trouble picking out the smell of beef, of lamb, of pork and of dog, and beautiful visions swam in my head. Yes, in my head, where meat always has form and is imbued with language; meat is a richly evocative living thing with which I enjoy a close relationship. These meats call out to me: 'Come eat me! Come eat me, Xiaotong, and hurry.'

The gate was shut, even though it was midday. Unlike the school gate, which was made of finger-thin steel bars with gaps wide enough to allow a young calf through, this was a sturdy double-panelled gate made of two iron plates that would require a pair of strong young men to push it open and pull it shut, two extremely creaky operations. Later, when I watched it being opened and shut, it was just as I'd assumed.

The smell of meat drew me down off the riverbank and across the broad paved road, where I waved to a black dog out for a stroll. It looked up and gazed at me with the eyes of an old man living out his sad days, then made its way over to a roadside building, turned and lay down in the doorway, where a wooden sign, painted white with writing in red, hung on a brick wall. I didn't know those words but they knew me. The place, I knew, was the plant's new inspection station. All the meat from Father's plant passed through here. Once it received the blue stamp of approval, it was on its way to wholesalers throughout the county, the province and beyond. No matter where it went, that stamp was all it needed to be sold on the open market.

I barely paused in front of this building, since it wasn't occupied. Looking through one of the dirty windows, I spotted a pair of desks and a disorderly array of chairs. All brand new, they had yet to be cleaned of factory dust. A disagreeable paint smell seeped through gaps in the window and set me off on a sneezing fit.

But the main reason I chose not to dally was the captivating aroma of meat in the air. Admittedly, after the Spring Festival passed, meat dishes had stopped being a rarity at our table, but the devilish attraction of meat created an insatiable appetite, the sort of effect women have on men. You can eat your fill today and still hanker for more tomorrow. If one meaty meal some-how satisfied people's appetites for all time, Father's meatpacking plant would have had to shut down. No, the world is the way it is because people are in the habit of eating meat, and their nature is to return to it meal after meal.

Four barbecue stands have been set up in front of the temple. Four ruddy-faced cooks in tall chef's hats are standing under white umbrellas. More stands have been set up in the field on the north side of the highway, where the line of white umbrellas reminds me of the beach. By all appearances, today promises to be bigger than yesterday, with greater numbers of people who want to eat meat, who have the capacity for it and who can afford it. Despite the daily media blitz against a meat diet and the call to replace it with vegetarian fare, how many people will willingly give up eating meat? Look, Wise Monk, here comes Lan Laoda. I count him among my acquaintances, even though we're yet to have a chance to talk. But that day will come, I'm sure of that, and we'll become fast friends. In the words of his nephew, Luo Lan: 'The friendship between our two families goes back generations.' If not for my father's grand-father, who braved chilling dangers to take him and his siblings through a blockade and deliver them to the Nationalist area by horse cart, there'd be no glories for his descendants. Lan Laoda wields enormous power, but I, Luo Xiaotong, am a man of unique experience. Just look at the Meat God standing there. That's me in my youth. The youthful me has been transformed into a god. Lan Laoda is being carried in a simple sedan chair patterned after those Sichuan litters, its passage marked by a series of languid creaks. A fat child who's fast asleep, snoring loudly and drooling copiously, occupies another sedan chair behind him. Bodyguards are arrayed, front and back; there's also a pair of loyal, dependable middle-aged nannies. Lan Laoda's chair is set down and he steps out. He's put on weight since I last saw him, and he has bags under his eyes. He's also not as energetic as before. The second chair touches the ground, but the boy sleeps on. When the nannies move to awaken him, Lan Laoda stops them with a wave of his hand; he then tiptoes up to the sleep-ing boy, takes a silk handkerchief from his pocket and wipes away the spittle. The boy wakes up and gazes at him with a blank look before opening his

mouth and bawling. 'Don't cry,' Lan Laoda says soothingly, 'that's a good boy.'
But he cries on, so one of the nannies twirls a little red rattle-drum in front of
him. The boy takes it from her, twirls it a time or two and throws it away. More
tears. The other nanny says to Lan Laoda: 'The young master must be hungry,
sir.' 'Then get him some meat!' he says. At the prospect of business, the four
cooks bang their utensils and begin to yell:

'Barbecue, Mongolian barbecue!'

'Barbecued lamb kebabs, genuine Xinjiang lamb kebabs!'

'Beef teppanyaki!'

'Barbecued goslings!'

At a wave of Lan Laoda's hand, the bodyguards shout in unison: 'One of
each, and hurry!'

Four large platters of fragrant, steaming, sizzling, grease-dripping meat
are brought up to one of the nannies, who hurriedly sets up a folding table and
places it in front of the boy. The other woman ties a pink bib, with a little
embroidered teddy bear, under his chin. The table is only big enough for two
platters, so the bodyguards stand holding the other two, waiting to replace
the first two as soon as they're empty. The nannies stand on either side to help
the boy eat, which he does with his hands. He stuffs the meat, piece after piece,
into his mouth. His cheeks bulge so much I can't see him actually chew, but I
envision the chunks of meat working their way down his outstretched neck
like little mice. I'd always considered myself a champion carnivore, and seeing
this child putting meat away is like seeing a carnivorous twin, though I've
taken a vow to never eat meat again. This boy is a carnivorous genius, way
ahead of where I was as a youngster. I could eat meat, but I had to chew it
awhile before swallowing it. There's no chewing with this five-year-old—he
just stuffs it into his mouth. Two large platters of barbecued meat are gone in
no time—he's definitely earned my respect. No matter how good you are,
there's always someone better—how true that is! The nannies whisk away the
empty platters and the bodyguards lay the next two onto the table. The boy
wastes no time in grabbing a goose drumstick. His teeth are so sharp they
clean away tendons better than any knife. Lan Laoda's eyes don't leave the
boy's mouth for a moment. Unconsciously, his mouth moves along with the
boy's, as if he too were eating. That movement epitomizes his deep feelings

for the child. Only one's flesh and blood could inspire such a depth of emotion.
At this point I conclude that the young carnivore is the son of Lan Laoda and
the now cloistered Shen Yaoyao.

As I mulled the relationship between man and meat, I arrived at the
entrance to Father's meatpacking plant. The main gate was closed and so was
a smaller side gate. I knocked on the latter, which made a loud, scary noise.
Since school was still in session, Father and Mother would not have been
happy to see me, no matter what excuse I came up with. Lao Lan had already
poisoned their minds into thinking that only by attending school could I rise
above others, something they assumed was a foregone conclusion. They
couldn't possibly understand me, even if I revealed everything that went on
in my head. That, in essence, is the agonizing cost of genius. This was no time
to show up in front of my father's plant but I was defenceless against the smell
of meat rushing at me from the kitchen. I looked into the sunny blue sky and
saw that it wasn't yet time for a meal at Lao Lan's. Why go to his house for
lunch? Neither Father nor Mother went home to eat. Nor did Lao Lan.
Instead, he had Huang Biao's daughter-in-law do all the cooking and look
after his invalid wife. Lao Lan's daughter, Tiangua, was a third-grader in
school. I'd never much cared for the light-haired girl, although that had now
changed, for the simple reason that she was a dimwit. Her thoughts were
always remarkably shallow, and getting as much as one question wrong in an
exam had her in tears, the moron. Jiaojiao always joined me for lunch at Lao
Lan's. She too was gifted. And, like me, she was in the habit of falling asleep
in class. And, like me, going without meat at even one meal made her listless.
But not Tiangua—not only did she not eat meat, she actually called us rav-
enous wolves when she saw how much we enjoyed it. In return, we took one
look at her pathetic vegetarian fare and called her a goat. Huang Biao's wife,
a shrewd woman with fair skin and big eyes, wore her hair short and had a
pretty mouth—red lips over white teeth. She was always smiling, even when
she was alone in the kitchen doing the dishes. She knew that Jiaojiao and I
were there to eat but, since Tiangua and her mother were her primary
responsibility, she mainly prepared vegetarian food. Only occasionally did
she prepare a meat dish, invariably bland and tasteless, something simply
thrown together. Needless to say, eating at Lao Lan's house was no treat, but
it was all right, since a good meaty dinner awaited us at home in the evening.

The changes in our lives during the six months Father had been back were monumental. Things I hadn't dared dream of in the past had now become realities. Both he and my mother were different people, and issues that had led to quarrels in the past were now brushed away as trivial. I knew that their transformation had come about because of the new relationship with Lao Lan. Honestly, a person takes on the colour of his surroundings. You learn from those nearest you. If it's a witch, then you learn the dance of a sorceress.

Though Lao Lan's wife was an invalid, she managed to retain her poise through her illness. We were never told what she suffered from, but she had a sickly, pale complexion and was extremely frail. For me, the best comparison was of potato sprouts in a dank cellar. We often heard moans coming from her bedroom, but they stopped abruptly when she heard footsteps. Jiao-jiao and I called her Aunt, and she gave us the funniest looks, with hints of a mysterious smile at the corners of her mouth. We couldn't help noticing that Tiangua didn't act like a dutiful daughter round her, almost as if she wasn't her real mother. I was well aware that mysterious relationships often infect the homes of influential people, and Lao Lan was an influential man whose home gave rise to matters most people could never comprehend.

So I left that small iron gate, the thoughts galloping through my mind like wild horses and, hugging the wall, made my way to the kitchen. As the distance shrank between me and the meat being cooked inside, the aroma intensified and I could visualize great hunks of the lovely stuff stewing in a big pot. The already high wall seemed to tower over me as I stood there looking up. Not even a grown-up—let alone a child my size—could scale a wall that high, especially since it was topped by barbed wire. But, as they say, where there's a will there's a way. Just as I was about to give up, I spotted a sewage ditch for funnelling foul water out of the kitchen. Was it dirty? Of course it was—it was a sewer. I picked up a fallen branch and moved away pig bristles and feathers and created a passage. Any hole that could accommodate my head, as I knew from experience, was big enough to crawl through, since that's the only body part that can't be made smaller. By using the dead branch as a measuring stick, I determined that the hole was larger than my head, but before squeezing my way in I took off my jacket and my pants, then spread some dirt over the sewage to keep from getting wet. I looked round—there were no people on the street, and a tractor had just passed by; a horse cart was too far away to see what I was up to. I couldn't have asked for a better time to make my move. But even though it was larger than my head, squeezing through that little hole would not be easy. I flattened on my belly and stuck my head in. A complex mixture of smells rose out of the sewer, so I held my breath to keep the foul air out of my lungs. About half way in my head got stuck, and I panicked. But only for a moment. I had to stay calm, because I knew that panicky thoughts make your head grow bigger, and then I'd really be stuck. If that happened, this sewer was where I'd end my days, and the death of Luo Xiaotong would have been a terrible waste. My first reaction was to pull my head back out. It didn't work. I knew then that I was in trouble, but I stayed calm and turned my head until I felt it loosen up a bit. Next, I stretched out my neck to free my ears; once that was done I knew I'd made it past the hardest part. Now all I had to do was shift my body slightly and I could make it through to the other side. So I did, and a moment later I was standing inside Father's plant. After hooking my clothes on the other side with a piece of wire, I cleaned most of the sewer filth off my body with a handful of grass and got dressed. Then, in a crouch, I negotiated the narrow path between the brick wall and the kitchen. When I reached the first window, I was swathed in meaty aromas, almost as if I was immersed in a sticky meat broth.

With a piece of rusty metal I jimmied the two window sections until the last obstacle to a view of the inside fell open. A blast of meaty aromas hit me, as a huge pot atop a blazing stove about fifteen feet from the window caught my attention. Soup was boiling so fiercely that waves of it nearly splashed over the sides. Huang Biao, in a white apron and over-sleeves walked into the room. I frantically scurried away from the window so he wouldn't spot me. He picked up a long-handled hook and stirred the mixture in the pot, bringing into view sections of oxtails, pig's knuckles, dog's leg and sheep's leg. Pig, dog, cow and sheep, together in one pot. They danced, they sang, they greeted me. Their aromas blended into a heavy fragrance, though I could pick out the individual smells.

Huang Biao snared a pig's knuckle and examined it. What was he looking for? It was soft and fully cooked, and would be overdone if he let it stew any longer. But he threw it back in, picked out a dog's leg and then went through the same motions, although this time he sniffed it too. What are you doing, you moron? It's ready to eat, so turn down the heat before it turns to mush. Next came a sheep's leg, and once again it was examine and smell. Why don't you taste it, you fool? Finally, satisfied that it had cooked long enough, he pulled out the partially burnt kindling and stuffed the hot ends into a sand-filled metal pail, which sent a pall of white smoke into the air and injected the meaty fragrance with a charcoal-like odour. Now that the heat had diminished, the liquid was no longer roiling, although a few ripples remained in the spaces between the cuts of meat, whose song had softened as they waited to be eaten. Huang Biao brought up a sheep's leg with his hook and laid it on a metal platter behind a smaller stove next to the first one. Then he added a dog's leg, two sections of oxtail and a pig's knuckle. Free of the crowd, they cried out happily and waved me over. They had tiny hands, about the size of hedgehog paws. What happened next was, to say the least, entertaining. Huang Biao walked to the door, looked round, then came back in and shut the door behind him. I just knew the bastard was about to dig in and eat all the meat that had invited me to feast on it. Pangs of jealousy rose in me. But he did nothing of the sort—not a single bite (a bit of a relief—at first). Instead, he moved a stool up to the pot, climbed onto it, undid the buttons of his pants, took out a demonic tool and then released a stream of yellow piss into the meaty mixture.

The meat cried out shrilly and huddled up, trying to hide by crowding together. But there was no escape. The powerful stream subjected them to crippling humiliation. Their smell changed. They frowned and they wept. When he was finished, he put the now-contented object back inside his pants, climbed off the stool with a smirk and picked up a spade-like object, which he dipped in the pot to stir the meat, which whined as it tumbled in the fouled soup. After laying down the spade, Huang Biao picked up a small copper ladle, scooped up some of the liquid and held it under his nose. With a satisfied smile, he said: 'Just right. Now you bastards can eat my piss.'

I threw open the window, intending to voice my outrage. But the shout caught in my throat. I felt sullied and was filled with uncommon loathing. Startled by the sound, Huang Biao dropped the ladle, spun round and stared at me. As his face turned purple, he grimaced and then gave a sinister little laugh. 'Oh, it's you, Xiaotong,' he said. 'What are you doing here?'

I glared at him without answering.

'All right, boy, come here,' he said, waving me over. 'I know how much you love meat. Today you can eat as much as you want.'

I sprang through the window and landed on the kitchen floor. Huang Biao solicitously moved over a campstool for me to sit on, followed by the stool he'd stood on, and then laid a platter on it. Flashing a crafty smile, he picked up his hook and dragged a sheep's leg out of the pot, broth dripping from it as he placed it before me.

'Eat up,' he said. 'Stretch your stomach as far as it'll go. Here's a sheep's leg. There are dogs' legs in there, pig's knuckles and oxtails. Take your pick.'

I looked down at the tortured expression on the sheep's leg.

'I saw everything,' I said coldly.

'You saw what?'

'Everything.'

Huang Biao scratched his neck and released yet another sinister laugh. 'I hate those people,' he said. 'They come here every day for a free meal, and I hate them. This has nothing to do with your parents—'

'But they'll eat this too!'

'Yes, they will,' he said with a smile. 'The ancients have said, "What the eye does not see cannot be dirty." Don't you agree? If you want the truth, the urine makes the meat fresher and more tender. What you saw as urine is really fine cooking wine.'

'Then you eat it.'

'Now that poses a psychological problem, because people aren't supposed to drink their own urine.' He laughed. 'But since you saw what happened, I guess I can't expect you to eat any of it.' He dumped the sheep's leg back into the pot, picked up the platter with the meat he'd taken out before urinating and set it down in front of me. 'You saw that this meat was taken out before the "cooking wine" was added, old friend, so you can eat it with no worries.' Next he picked up a bowl of garlic paste off the chopping board and set it in front of me. 'Dip the meat in this. Your Uncle Huang cooks the best meat. Fully cooked but not mushy, fatty but not greasy. They hired me for one reason alone—so they could enjoy the meat I prepare.'

I cast my eyes at the platter brimming with joyous promise, observed the expressions of excitement, marvelled at the little hands that quivered like tendrils on a grapevine and listened to the mellifluous buzzing of speech, all of which moved me to my soul. It spoke softly, but what it said was clear and distinct, each word a gem of comprehensible speech. It called my name and described itself as wonderful, it revealed to me how pure and untainted it was, it spoke to me of its youth and beauty: 'We were once part of a living dog or a cow or a pig or a sheep,' it said, 'but we were washed three times and then steeped in boiling water for three hours and we are now independent living beings with powers of thought and, of course, emotion. The infusion of salt imbued us with souls, the injection of vinegar and alcohol supplied us with emotions and the addition of onions, ginger, anise, cinnamon, cardamom and pepper imbued us with expression. We belong to you, to you alone, you are whom we sought. We called out to you when we were suffering the agonies of boiling water, we longed for you. We want you to eat us and we are fearful of being eaten by anyone but you. Yet we have no say in the matter. A woman has the ability to end her life to preserve her chastity but even that is denied us. We were born in debased circumstances and are resigned to our fate. If you had not come to feast upon us, who knows to which low and vulgar mouths that privilege would be granted. They might take a single bite before tossing us onto a table to soak in cheap liquor spills. Or they might stub out their cigarettes on our bodies and poison our souls with nicotine and pungent smoke. Together with the skins of shrimp and crabs and soiled paper napkins, they will sweep us into garbage pails. The world can boast a handful of individuals like you, people who love, understand and appreciate meat, Luo Xiaotong. Dear Luo Xiaotong, you love meat and meat loves you. We love you, so come eat us. Being eaten by you makes us feel like a bride being taken by the man she loves. Come, Xiaotong, our virtual husband, what are you waiting for? What is bothering you? Come, don't waste another minute. Tear us apart, chew us up, send us straight down into your guts. Whether or not you know it, all the meat in the world longs for you, it admires you. All the meat in the world considers you its lover, so what is holding you back? Ah, Luo Xiaotong, our lover, might you be worried that we're unclean? Worried that when we were still attached to dogs, cows, sheep and pigs, we were contaminated by feed that included growth hormones, lean meat powder and other poisons? You are right to be concerned about this cruel reality. Unadulterated meat is a rarity in this world—you can look high and low and still be frustrated in your search for animals untainted by poisons in their sheds cotes sties and pens, finding instead only hormonal cows, chemical sheep, garbage pigs and prescription dogs. But we are clean, Xiaotong, we have been brought here from deep in South Mountain by Huang Biao on orders from your father. We are we are cows and sheep that have grown to maturity grazing grassy fields and drinking spring water, we are pigs that ran wild in remote mountain ravines and we are local dogs that have grown to adulthood eating bran and wild plants. Not once, either before or after being slaughtered, were we subjected to the injection of water, and we never came into contact with a drop of formaldehyde. You will not easily find meat as pure and uncontaminated as us. So hurry up and eat, Luo Xiaotong. If you don't, Huang Biao will. Though he pretends to be a dutiful son, though he treats a cow as his mother and though he supplies his dogs, his hormonal animals, with her milk, he injects his butchered dogs with water and he's the last person we want to eat us . . .'

I was nearly moved to tears by how the meats poured out their hearts to me. But before I could cry, anguished wails erupted from their counterparts in the pot. 'Luo Xiaotong,' they said, 'please eat us too. Even though that bastard Huang Biao doused us with his urine, we're still much cleaner than any meat on the street. We are free of toxins, we are highly nutritious, we are clean. Please eat us, Xiaotong, we beg you . . .'

That did it—my tears dripped onto the pieces of meat on the platter, and that made them even sadder. They rocked back and forth in anguish, causing the platter to bounce on the stool and nearly breaking my heart. That's when I finally grasped the reality that the world is a very complicated place. No matter what he's dealing with, even if it's a piece of meat, a person must let love flow from his heart if he is to be repaid in kind—that is the only way to truly appreciate what is good and decent. In the past, I'd hungered for meat but had not loved it enough, even though meat had been so good to me, the person it had picked out of the vast sea of humanity to be its friend, to my enduring shame. I surely could do better. All right, meats, dear meats, the time has come for me to feast on you so as to be worthy of your abiding love.

To be loved and respected by such fine, uncontaminated meat has made Luo Xiaotong the world's happiest person.

With tears in my eyes, I began eating you. I heard you cry in my mouth but I knew that you were shedding tears of joy. Tearfully I ate the tearful meats, and felt that we had embarked on the path to spiritual awakening. This was a first for me, and my relationship with meat underwent a fundamental change. As did my approach to my fellow humans. I heard an old greybeard from deep in the mountains say to me: 'There are many paths a human can take to achieve immortality.' 'Is eating meat one of them?' I asked. 'Yes,' he replied with a sneer, 'and so is eating shit.' I understood everything, then. The day I found myself able to hear meat speak I knew that I was different. That was one of the reasons I'd left school. What could I learn from any teacher that I couldn't learn from meat?

While I ate, Huang Biao stood watching me like a fool. I had neither the energy nor the interest to look at him. As I continued my intimate relationship with the meat, the kitchen and everything in it ceased to exist. But when I came up for air, those glittering little demon's eyes of his were reminders that he too was a living creature.

Little by little, the plate grew empty at the same time as my stomach grew full. Soon I realized that if I ate any more I wouldn't be able to breathe. But the remaining meat kept calling out to me, while the meat in the pot continued its complaints in loud, grudging tones. My dilemma suddenly became clear—my stomach could hold only so much, but the amount of meat in this world stretched out into infinity. And all that meat longed for me to eat it, which was in perfect accord with my desires. I did not want any of it to wind up in the bodies of people who had no understanding of it but I lacked the power to see that that did not happen. In order to ensure that I continue to dine on meat thereafter, I shut my still-greedy mouth and tried to stand. I couldn't. With difficulty, I looked down at my hideously swollen belly and tried my best to ignore the meat on the platter and its sweet yet mournful appeals. I knew that I'd die if I took another bite, so I gripped the edge of the stool and somehow managed to stand. I was a little light-headed from all the meat—'meat dizzy', a not-totally-unpleasant sensation. Huang Biao held me up by the arm and, in a voice dripping with admiration, said:

'You've earned your reputation, my young friend. That performance was an eye-opener.'

I knew what he was getting at. My meat-eating ability and my hankering for it were no secret in Slaughterhouse Village.

'To be a carnivore you must have a prodigious stomach,' he said, 'and you were born with the stomach of a tiger or a wolf. The heavens have sent you down here, my young friend, for one purpose only, and that is to eat meat.'

I knew that there were two levels of meaning in his words of praise. One was that I had truly opened his eyes by my capacity for meat, and that deep down he admired me. But on another level he wanted his fine words to buy my silence over the fact that he'd pissed in the pot.

'Meat finds its way into your stomach, my young friend, the way a beautiful woman finds her way into the arms of a staunch man and the way a finely worked saddle finds its way onto the back of a gallant steed,' he said. 'Putting it into the stomachs of others would be a terrible waste. My young friend, come see me any time you desire a meal of meat. I can put some aside for you. But tell me, how did you manage to get in here? Did you scale the wall?'

Ignoring him, I opened the kitchen door, hitched up my belly with both hands and walked out with a pronounced sway. 'Tomorrow, my young friend,' his voice followed me out, 'you don't have to crawl in through the sewage hole. I'll leave some meat here for you at noon.'

My legs grew rubbery and my vision blurred, my protruding belly slowed me down. Struck by a feeling that I existed solely for the benefit of my stomach, I actually sensed the meat that lay in it. What an amazingly joyous feeling that was, flickering through my head as if I were sleepwalking. I strolled aimlessly round Father's plant, from one workshop to the next. All the doors were tightly shut, in order to keep prying eyes away from the secrets within. That did not stop me from peeking through every crack, but I saw only spectral movements in the darkness, most likely beef cattle awaiting slaughter. I was later proven right, for the buildings did in fact house beef cattle. Four buildings in the plant were devoted to slaughtering animals, one each for cattle, pigs, sheep and dogs. The two reserved for cattle and pigs were quite large, the one for sheep small and the one for dogs smaller still. I'll delay descriptions of the four buildings for the time being, Wise Monk. What I want to say now is that while I was walking through Father's plant, I forgot all about what had happened at school, thanks to a belly filled with meat. More than that, my plan to pick up Jiaojiao from her preschool and take her to Lao Lan's for lunch had been swept from my mind.

I simply enjoyed a leisurely stroll that took me up to an elegant table groaning under the weight of many, many plates and bowls filled with meat, along with an array of colourful things.

That plump, golden goose is now nothing but a pile of bones. The boy leans back his corpulent body and exhales loudly, the expression on his face one of intoxicating, after-meal contentment. Bright sunlight falling on his face paints an enchanting image. Lan Laoda walks up to him, bends over and asks lovingly: 'Have you had enough, dear?' The boy rolls his eyes and belches. Then he closes his eyes and Lan Laoda straightens up. At his signal, a nanny approaches meekly to remove the bib from under the boy's chin while her workmate gently wipes the grease from the corners of his mouth with a clean white handkerchief. Annoyed, the boy brushes her hand away and makes a few short indecipherable noises. The bearers lift the chair and head back to the highway, the nannies trotting along awkwardly, trying to keep up with the bearers' longer strides.

Father stood up, held his glass out to Great Uncle Han, and said: 'Here's to you, Station Chief Han.'

What was that all about? I quickly figured it out. Only months before, the man had been Township Dining Hall Manager Uncle Han but he now ran the meat inspection station. He was wearing a light grey uniform with red epaulettes and a wide-brimmed hat that sported a large red insignia. Seemingly reluctant to stand up, he raised his body slightly, clinked glasses with Father and sat back down. He looked funny in those clothes, like a paper cut-out.

'Station Chief Han,' I heard Father say, 'we'll need you to keep an eye out for us.'

Han took a drink before picking up a long slice of dog meat with his chopsticks and stuffing it into his mouth. 'Lao Luo,' he sputtered as he chewed, 'don't you worry. This plant may be located in your village but it serves the township, even the city. Your meat products can be found in all corners of the land, and I'm not exaggerating when I say that samples of it might even show up on the provincial governor's table when he entertains foreign dignitaries. So, how could I not give you all the help you need?'

Father glanced at Lao Lan, in the seat of honour, as if seeking help. But the man responded with what appeared to be a confident smile. Mother, who was sitting next to him, refilled Lao Han's glass, picked up hers and stood up. 'Station Chief Han,' she said, 'Elder Brother Han, please don't stand. Congratulations on your promotion. Cheers.'

'Young sister,' Lao Han replied as he got to his feet, 'I can remain sitting with Luo Tong but not with you.' He continued meaningfully, 'Everyone knows that Luo Tong has got this far because of you. He's the nominal head of this plant but you're the one in charge.'

'Chief Han,' Mother replied, 'please don't say that. I'm just a woman, and, even though we can make a difference here and there, important matters are best left to you men.'

'You're much too modest!' Lao Han said as he clinked glasses with her— loudly—and then drained his. 'Lao Lan,' he said, 'while we're all here together, I want you to know exactly what's going on. The township government did not decide to assign me to this position lightly, but only after careful thought. Interestingly, they did not have the authority to appoint, only to recommend. The municipal government had the final word.' He stopped and looked round the table, then went on self-importantly, 'So why did they choose me? Because I know Slaughterhouse Village inside and out, and because I'm an authority on meat. I can tell good meat from bad, and if my eyes can't spot the difference my nose can. I know precisely how Slaughterhouse Village got rich and know all about your shady deals. And it's not just me. People in the township and municipal governments are well aware that you injected water and chemicals into your meat. You also treated meat from diseased animals and sold it in the city. Have you made enough off your unlawful earnings by now?' Lao Han looked at Lao Lan, who just smiled. 'Lao Lan,' he went on, 'you've succeeded where others have failed because of your ability to see the big picture—you realized that these underhand tactics were no good for the long haul. So you took the initiative of doing away with independent butchers and founded this plant before the government stepped in. It was a wise and clever move. You scratched the leaders where they itched. Their blueprint is for us to become the largest meatpacking enterprise in the province, the industry's base from where meat is sent everywhere in the province, in the country, in the whole world. Goddamn it, Lao Lan, like a gangster's gangster, you never do anything small. I could see you stealing from the Emperor's treasure house or taking liberties with the Empress herself. Go small, and it's like a mouse stealing a bit of grease, not worth talking about. So I want to thank you. If there were no United Meatpacking Plant, there'd be no inspection station, and without that, obviously, there'd be no department-level position of Station Chief. Here's to you!' Lao Han stood up and touched glasses with everyone round the table. Then he tossed down his drink. 'Good stuff!' he complimented.

Huang Biao walked in with a steaming platter containing half a pig's head covered in a reddish brown sauce. The aroma filled nostrils at the table, although the taste had been overwhelmed by spices and would not have appealed to a true connoisseur.

Lao Han's eyes lit up. 'Has this pig's head been injected with water, Huang Biao?'

'Station Chief Han,' Huang Biao replied respectfully, 'what you see here is the head of a wild boar the manager sent me to buy in South Mountain. Not a drop of water has been added. Taste it and see for yourself. We might be able to pull something over your eyes but not your mouth.'

'I like the sound of that.'

'You're the expert where meat's considered. I'd never show off in front of you.'

'All right, I'll give it a try.' Lao Han picked up his chopsticks and stuck them into the flesh; it immediately fell away from the bones. He chose a piece of lean meat from the cheek, about the size of a mouse, and put it in his mouth. He blinked, he chewed, he swallowed. 'Not bad,' he said, dabbing his lips with a napkin, 'but no match for Wild Mule's.'

Father's face flushed bright red. Mother's face grew pinched.

'Eat, everyone,' Lao Lan said loudly, 'eat it while it's hot. It's no good cold.'

'Yes, eat it while it's hot,' said Han in immediate agreement.

Huang Biao slipped away while the diners were sticking their chopsticks into the pig's head. He didn't see me hiding outside the window but I saw him. His servile smile on the way in was replaced by a crafty, malicious smirk on the way out, an alarmingly swift transformation. 'All right, people,' I heard him say under his breath, 'now's the time for you to get a taste of my piss!'

It seemed like such a long time since Huang Biao had pissed in the pot of meat that it had become illusory, unreal, like a dream. It no longer seemed important that a beautiful, succulent pig's head had soaked in the man's urine. My father ate it, my mother ate it. Nothing happened. There was no need to tell them that the meat had been enhanced by Huang Biao's piss. They were getting the meat they deserve. Truth is, they loved it. Their lips glowed like fresh cherries.

It didn't take long for them to eat and drink their fill or for their faces to reflect the contentment that comes only after a satisfying meal.

Huang Biao cleared the table. The uneaten meat that had turned cold—choice cuts that had gone to waste—he tossed to the dog tied up outside the kitchen. Sprawled lazily on the ground, it carefully picked out the pieces that appealed to it and ate only those few. How infuriating, how galling! Whoever heard of a lowly mutt turning up its nose at meat when there are people in this world for whom it is beyond their reach?

But, having no time to waste on an ill-bred dog, I turned back to watch the adults in the other room. Mother wiped the table with a clean rag and then covered it with a sheet of blue felt. Then she fetched a yellow mah-jongg set from a cabinet against the wall. I knew that villagers played mah-jongg, that some even gambled on it. But Father and Mother had been quite hostile towards the game. Once, when we were walking down an alley, Mother and I passed by the eastern wing of Lao Lan's house and heard the swishing of mah-jongg tiles. With a sneer, she'd said softly: 'Son, everything is worth learning, everything but gambling.' I can still see the stern look on her face, but she was obviously no stranger to mah-jongg.

Mother, Father, Lao Lan and Lao Han sat round the table, while a young man wearing the same uniform as Lao Han—his nephew and his aide—poured tea for all four players and then retired to the side to sit and smoke. I spotted several packs of high-quality cigarettes on the table, each costing as much as half a pig's head. Father, Lao Lan and Lao Han were heavy smokers. Mother didn't smoke, but she made a show of lighting up and, with a cigarette dangling from her lips, expertly arranged her tiles. She looked a bit like one of those femme fatales you see in old films, and I could hardly believe how much she'd changed in a few short months. The poorly dressed and unkempt Yang Yuzhen who'd spent her days dealing in junk had ceased to exist. It was as miraculous a change as a caterpillar turning into a butterfly.

These were not your typical mah-jongg players. No, this was high-stakes gambling. Each player sat behind a stack of money, with nothing smaller than a ten-yuan note. The money fluttered when the tiles were mixed. Lao Han's pile grew as the rounds progressed, those in front of the other three shrank. He had to stop to wipe his sweaty face from time to time and frequently rolled up his sleeves to rub his hands. He had removed his hat and tossed it onto the sofa behind him. Lao Lan never stopped smiling. Father wore a detached look. Mother was the only animated one among them, muttering to herself. There was something about her unhappiness that didn't seem quite real—it was really a ploy to let Lao Han savour his winning ways.

'No more,' she said after a while, 'that's it for me. I've had terrible luck.'

Lao Han straightened his pile of money and counted it. 'How about taking some of mine?'

'Not on your life! Lao Han! Thanks to me you've done well today. Next time I'll win it all. Even take that uniform off your back.'

'Big talk,' Han said. 'Unlucky in love, lucky at the table. Since I've never had any luck in love, I'll always win at the table.'

My eyes were glued to Lao Han's hands as he counted his money. In two hours he'd won nine thousand.

Smoke rises, fires blaze and crowds buzz at the barbecue stands across the road, a scene of frenetic activity. But only Lan Laoda's bodyguards are standing, arms folded, in front of the four barbecue stands in the temple yard, while he paces at the gate. He's frowning, as if weighed down with daunting concerns. Hungry participants at the festival glance at us as they come and go but no one approaches us. The cooks keep flipping the meat on the grill, which has begun to smoke. I see they're growing annoyed, but their scowls turn to fawning smiles whenever one of the bodyguards looks their way. The cook who's grilling goslings cups a cigarette and takes a drag when no one's looking. The sound of singing from across the way comes to us on the wind. They're the songs a Taiwanese chanteuse sang some thirty years ago. They were popular when I was a little boy, travelling across China from city to town to village. Lao Lan said that his third uncle had been the singer's sole patron. Now her songs have returned and the clock has turned back. In a black dress under a white vest, she's cut her bangs just above her eyebrows; like a lovely swallow, she comes flying across the road and throws herself into Lan Laoda's arms. 'Big Brother Lan,' she mews coquettishly. He picks her up, twirls her round a time or two and then flings her to the floor. She falls upon a thick wool carpet on which are embroidered a male and female phoenix frolicking amid peonies—a spectacularly colourful display. The singer's now-naked body lies in the light of a crystal chandelier, her eyes glazing over. With his hands clasped behind his back, Lan Laoda takes several turns round her, like a tiger circling its prey. She gets to her knees and says, flirting: 'Come on, Big Brother.' He sits on the carpet and crosses his legs to scrutinize her figure. He's in suit and tie, she hasn't a stitch on, a wondrous contrast. 'What do you plan to do, Lan Laoda?' she pouts. 'I had lots of women before you,' he says, almost to himself. 'My boss gave me fifty thousand US dollars every month for expenses, and if I couldn't spend it all he called me a stupid arse.' I can't divulge his name to you, revered Wise Monk, and I swore to Lao Lan that if I ever told a soul I'd die with no offspring. 'It didn't take me long to learn how to throw money about like dirt,' he says. 'I went from woman to woman like a carousel. But since I found her, you're the first woman to take her clothes off for me. She's the line of demarcation, and since you're the first woman on this side of that line you deserve an explanation. I'll never say this to anyone again, not ever. Are you willing to be her stand-in? Are you willing to call out her name while I'm screwing you? Are you willing to pretend to be her?' The singer mulls that over for a moment. 'Yes, Lan Laoda,' she says thoughtfully, 'I am. Whatever makes you happy. I wouldn't flinch if you told me to kill myself.' Lan Laoda takes the singer in his arms and cries out emotionally, 'Yaoyao . . .' After they roll and writhe on the carpet for an hour or so, the singer—hair askew, lipstick gone, a woman's cigarette dangling from her lips—sits on a sofa with a glass of red wine, and when two streams of white smoke emerge from her mouth the signs of age on her face cannot be erased. Wise Monk, why has this singer's *youth vanished after having sex with Lan Laoda for only an hour, and why does she have the face of an old woman? Could this be a case of 'Ten days in the mountains are a thousand years on earth'? Lao Lan has said that Shen Yaoyao was in love with his third uncle. So was the singer. Enough women to form a division have been in love with him. I know that Lao Lan was boasting, Wise Monk, so just laugh off what I'm saying.*

Father and Mother woke up early in the morning on the day the United Meat-packing Plant formally opened for business and got Jiaojiao and me out of bed. I knew this was a day of great importance for Slaughterhouse Village, for my parents and for Lao Lan.

When the Wise Monk purses his lips, a vapid smile forms on his face, which must mean that he has seen the same scene and heard the same words as me. Then again, that smile may have nothing to do with what I saw and heard and may simply be a reflection of his thoughts and whatever he finds funny. But one way or other, let's you and me, Wise Monk, enter a scene of greater splendour. The street beyond the gate of Lan Laoda's mansion is crowded with luxury automobiles, whose drivers are being respectfully directed to parking spots by a gatekeeper in a green uniform and spotless white gloves. The brightly lit foyer is packed with gorgeous women, high-ranking officials and wealthy men. The women are resplendent in evening dresses, like a flower garden in a riot of competing colours. The men are wearing expensive Western suits, all but one old man—supported by a pair of jewelled women—who is wearing a tailored Chinese robe. His long white goatee shimmies, the mystique of an immortal. An enormous scroll with the golden character 壽 , for longevity, hangs in the great room; an array of birthday gifts is stacked atop a long table beneath the scroll, beside a basket overflowing with pink-lipped peaches of immortality. Placed strategically about the room are vases full of camellias. Lan Laoda wears a flashy white suit and red bow tie; his thinning hair is neatly combed and his face is glowing. A group of gorgeously dressed women rushes up, like a bevy of little birds—chirping, laughing and planting kisses on his cheeks until they are covered with lipstick. Now truly red-faced, he walks up to the goateed old man and bows deeply: 'Patron, your nominal son wishes you a long life.' The old man taps him on the knee with his cane and enjoys a hearty laugh. 'How old are you now, my boy?' The old man's voice

is as melodic as a brass gong. 'Patron,' Lan Laoda replies modestly, 'I've managed to reach the age of fifty.' 'You've grown up,' the old man says emotionally,
'you're a man, and I don't need to worry about you any longer.' 'Patron, please
don't say things like that,' pleads Lan Laoda. 'Without you to worry about me,
I'd lose the pillar of my existence.' 'Aren't you the crafty one, young Lan!'
laughs the old man. 'An official career is not in your future, young Lan, but
riches are. And you'll be lucky in love.' Pointing his cane at the beautiful women
swarming behind Lan Laoda, he asks: 'Are they all your lovers?' 'They are all
loving aunts who watch over me,' replies Lan Laoda with a smile. 'I'm too old,'
says the old man, his voice heavy with emotion. 'The spirit's willing but the flesh
is weak. You take good care of them, for my sake.' 'Don't you worry, Patron,
satisfying them is something I'm committed to.' 'We're not satisfied, not even a
little!' the women complain coquettishly. 'In the old days,' the old man remembers with a smile, 'the emperor had women in three palaces and six chambers,
a harem totalling seventy-two concubines, but you've outdone that, young
Lan.' 'I owe it all to my Patron,' replies Lan Laoda. 'Have you mastered the
martial skills I taught you?' the old man asks him. Lan Laoda backs up a
few steps and says: 'You tell me, Patron.' Seated on the carpet, he slowly
folds his body into itself until his head is hidden in his crotch, his arse sticks
up in the air, like the rump of a young colt, and his mouth is touching his
penis. 'Excellent!' the old man exclaims as he taps the ground with his cane.
'Excellent!' echoes the crowd. The women, likely recalling some intimacy, cover
their mouths, blush and giggle. A few in the crowd react with open-mouthed
guffaws. 'Young Lan,' says the old man, sighing, 'you have gathered all the
city's flowers in a single night and I can do nothing but touch their pretty
hands.' And his eyes brim over with tears. The emcee, who is standing beside
Lan Laoda, shouts: 'Strike up the band and let the dancing begin!' The musicians, waiting patiently in the corner, begin to play—cheerful, light-hearted
music followed first by lilting melodies and then by passionate numbers. Lan
Laoda takes turns dancing with members of his female entourage while the
most seductive among them winds up in the arms of the old man, who shuffles
his feet so slightly it looks more like scratching an itch than dancing.

Mother's persistence worked: Father put on his grey suit and, with her
help, knotted a red tie. The colour reminded me uncomfortably of blood
gushing from the throats of butchered animals. I'd rather he wore another

but I kept that to myself. To be perfectly honest, Mother wasn't much good at knotting the tie. Lao Lan had made the actual knot and now she merely pushed it up under Father's chin and tightened it. He stretched his neck out and shut his eyes, like a strung-up goose. 'Who the hell invented this stuff?' I heard him grumble.

'Stop complaining,' Mother said. 'You're going to have to get used to this. From now on there'll be many occasions when you have to wear a tie. Just look at Lao Lan.'

'There's no comparison. He's the chairman and general manager.' Father's voice sounded strange.

'You're the plant manager,' Mother reminded him.

'Plant manager? I'm just another worker.'

'You really need to change the way you look at things,' Mother said. 'Times like this, you change or you get left behind. Again, look at Lao Lan, the perennial bellwether. A few years back, during the 'age of independents', he was the first to get rich in the butcher trade. Not only that, he helped the village get rich too. And just when the independent butchers began to get a bad name, he founded the United Meatpacking Plant. We've done well by keeping up with him.'

'I can't help seeing myself play-acting like a monkey in a cap,' Father remarked glumly. 'And this outfit makes it worse.'

'What am I going to do with you?' Mother said. 'Like I said, learn from Lao Lan.'

'He's a monkey in a cap too, as I see it.'

'Who isn't? And that includes your friend Lao Han. No more than a few months back, wasn't he only a no-account mess cook? But then he put on a uniform and turned into a hypocrite.'

'Niang's right,' I said, thinking it was time I said something. 'The old saying "A man's known by his clothes, a horse by its saddle" got it right. As soon as you put on a suit, you became a peasant-turned-entrepreneur.'

'These days there are more of those than fleas on a dog,' Father said. 'Xiaotong, I want you and Jiaojiao to study hard so you can leave this place and get a decent job out there somewhere.'

'I've been meaning to talk to you about that, Dieh. I want to quit school.'

'What?' He grew very stern. 'Just what do you plan to do?'

'I want to work at the meatpacking plant.'

'What's there for you to do?' he said unhappily. 'For years it was me who kept you from going to school. Now you must cherish this opportunity if you're to have any hope for a decent future. Don't throw your life away like I did. No, go to school and work hard. Education is the path to success. Everything else will lead you astray.'

'I don't agree with you, Dieh! First, I don't think you threw your life away. Second, I don't believe that education is the only path to success. Third, and most importantly, I don't think I can learn anything useful in school. My teacher doesn't know as much as I do.'

'I don't care,' he insisted, 'I want you to stick it out for a few years.'

'Dieh, I have strong feelings for meat. And I can help you with lots of things at the plant. I can hear the meat speak to me. Did you know that it's a living organism? I can see it wave to me with all its little hands.'

Father stared at me, as if he'd been strung up by his tie. Then he and Mother exchanged looks. I knew they thought I must be losing my mind. I'd assumed that Father, if not Mother, would understand my feelings. He, at least, had a vivid imagination. But, no. His imagination, it seemed, had dried up.

Mother walked up and rubbed my head, both to show her concern and to to see if I had fever. If I did, then she knew that what she'd heard was wild talk, delirium. But I wasn't running a fever, I was absolutely all right. There was nothing wrong with me or my mind, not a thing.

'Xiaotong,' she said, 'don't be silly. You have to go to school. I was so obsessed with money all this while that I never stopped to think about your education. But now I understand that the world offers many things more valuable than money. So do as we say and go to school. You may not want to listen to your father and me, but you'll listen to Lao Lan, won't you? It was he who made us realize that you and your sister belong in school.'

'I don't want to go either,' protested Jiaojiao. 'The meat speaks to me too, and waves to me with all its little hands. And sings, and has feet. Its hands and feet are like kittens' paws, clawing and moving . . .' She gestured in the air as she tried to demonstrate how the meat moved before.

I was impressed by her vivid imagination. Only four, and from a different mother, but our hearts beat in unison. I'd never mentioned that meat spoke to me or that it had hands, but she knew what I meant and gave me the support I needed.

Frightened by our strange talk of meat, our parents could only stare at us blankly. If the phone hadn't rung at that moment they'd have stood there all day, still staring. Oh, yes, I forgot to mention that we'd had a telephone installed, though it was for internal use only and controlled by a switchboard at the village headquarters. Still, it was a telephone, one that connected our house with Lao Lan's and the houses of several local cadres. Mother moved to answer it.

I knew it was Lao Lan.

'Lao Lan wants us to go to the plant right away,' she said to Father after hanging up. 'People from the county propaganda office are bringing along representatives from the provincial TV station and some newspaper reporters. We're to entertain them till he gets there.'

Father adjusted the knot in his tie, then swivelled his neck up and down and from side to side. 'Xiaotong,' he said hoarsely, 'and Jiaojiao, we'll talk more tonight. But you're both going to school. Xiaotong, I want you to set a good example for your sister.'

'Not today,' I said, 'no one's going to school today. It's too big a day, a day of celebration, and we'd be the biggest fools if we spent it in school.'

'I expect big things from you two,' Mother said as she touched up her hair in the mirror.

'And that's what you'll get,' I said. 'But going to school is not one of them.'

'Not one of them,' echoed Jiaojiao.

'Bring it out! Bring it out so I can see it!' A man whose forehead looks like shiny porcelain stands in the yard barking commands to his underlings. He's clearly not a happy man. His smartly dressed assistants echo his command like parrots: 'Bring it out! Bring it out so Governor Xu can see it!' Wise Monk, that's the provincial lieutenant governor. It's customary in official circles for his subordinates to call him Governor. The four paint-spattered labourers run out from behind a large tree and enter the temple at a crouch. They pass by us and stop in front of the idol. Without exchanging a word, not even a glance, they work together to lay the Meat God on the floor. I hear the Meat God giggle like a child being tickled. They tie yesterday's ropes under its neck and feet, slip the two shoulder poles under the ropes, crouch to lift the poles and, with a shout—four voices at once—straighten up and gently carry their load outside. The Meat God's giggles get louder as it jiggles, loud enough, I think, for the people in the yard—Lieutenant Governor Xu and his underlings—to hear. Can you hear, Wise Monk? Outside, the Meat God lies on the ground. Then the ropes are removed. 'Stand it up, stand it up!' shouts a Party cadre with a full head of hair from behind the lieutenant governor. That's the local mayor, Wise Monk. He and Lao Lan are thick as thieves; some people say they're sworn brothers. The four labourers try to lift the idol by the neck but all they accomplish is to slide it along the ground by its feet. It doesn't want to stand. It's clearly being naughty, the sort of thing I did as a boy. The mayor glares at the men behind him, displeased but unwilling to throw a tantrum in front of the lieutenant governor. That look is not lost on his subordinates, who rush to lend a hand. While some keep the feet from moving, the others line up behind the straining labourers and push. Far from a smooth operation, the giggling idol is nevertheless manoeuvred into an upright position. The lieutenant governor takes a few steps back and squints at it. It's impossible to decipher the enigmatic look on his face. The mayor and his entourage have

their eyes on the lieutenant governor but without making it obvious. His scrutiny complete, the man steps up and pokes the Meat God in the belly, extracting shrieks of laughter. Next, he jumps up to rub the idol's head, just as a gust of wind raises havoc with his own few strands of hair. The loose comb-over slips over his ear and hangs there comically, like a little braid. Then the mayor's head of thick black hair slides off his head like a rat's nest and, landing on the ground, rolls at the mercy of the wind. The men behind him are evenly split between those who look on, mouths agape, and those who cover their mouths to stifle a laugh. A coughing spell is the concealment tactic of choice. But none of this gets past the watchful eye of the mayor's secretary, who will make a list of those who laughed and place it on his boss' desk that evening. A quick-witted middle-aged employee runs down the mayor's fleeing hairpiece at a speed that belies his age. Its red-faced owner doesn't know what to do. At the same time, the lieutenant governor lays his errant swatch of hair back in place, eyes the mayor's patchy scalp and jokes: 'You and I are brothers in adversity, Mayor Hu.' The mayor rubs his scalp. 'My wife's idea,' he says with a little laugh. 'Hair doesn't grow on clever heads,' observes the lieutenant governor. The fleet-footed employee hands the hairpiece back to the mayor, who throws it away. 'Out of my sight, damn you. I'm no movie star!' 'Eight out of ten movie stars and TV hosts wear toupees, you know,' says the helpful junior. 'Only a bald mayor truly looks the part,' adds the mayor by way of encouragement. 'Thank you, Governor,' responds the now-pacified and radiant mayor. 'Won't you please share your thoughts with me?' 'No, I think this is fine. Many of our comrades are too conservative. There's nothing wrong with a Meat God and a Meat God Temple. They have rich implications and lasting appeal.' His comment is met with applause, the mayor taking the lead, continuing for a full three minutes despite attempts by the lieutenant governor to end it. 'We must be bold,' he continues, 'give rein to our imagination. In my view, there should be no restrictions on things that benefit the people.' He points to the inscribed board above the decrepit little temple entrance. 'Take this Wutong Temple,' he says. 'I think it should be restored. A local gazetteer I looked at last night indicated that this little temple once thrived with many pilgrims, up until the Republican era, when a local official handed down an order that people were no longer permitted to worship here. That was the beginning of the temple's decline. Paying respects to the Wutong Spirit shows that the masses yearn for a healthy, happy sex life, and what's wrong with that? Allocate some funds and refurbish it while you're building the Meat God Temple. Here you have two bright spots that will boost the economic development of the twin cities, so don't let other provinces come in and steal your thunder.' The mayor steps up with a glass of fifty-year-old Maotai: 'Governor Xu,' he says, 'I toast you on behalf of the twin cities!' To which the senior official replies: 'Didn't you just do that?' 'No,' replies the mayor, 'that was on behalf of the people of the city in gratitude for approving the construction of a Meat God Temple and the refurbishing of the Wutong Temple. Now on behalf of the people of the city, I want to thank you ahead of time for personally writing the words for the board.' 'I wouldn't dare try,' responds the lieutenant governor. 'But Governor Xu, you are a famous calligrapher and the authority who has approved the Meat God Temple. If you don't inscribe the words, the temple won't be built.' 'Now you're driving the duck onto its perch,' says the lieutenant governor. A local Party man rises: 'Governor Xu, people feel that you ought to be a professional calligrapher, not a governor. If you'd chosen calligraphy for a career, you'd be a millionaire many times over.' The mayor carries on the train of thought: 'Now you see why we are resorting to well-meaning extortion to get you to honour us with your writing.' The lieutenant governor blushes; he wavers. 'For Wu Song, warrior hero of Mt Liang, the more he drank the greater his bravery. For me, the more I drink the greater my vitality. Calligraphy, ah, calligraphy, the essence of a man's vitality. Bring me brush and ink.' The lieutenant governor takes a large-handled writing brush, dips it into a thick, inky mixture, holds his breath, and, in the wake of one magical sweep, three large, wildly haughty characters—肉神廟, Meat God Temple—leap onto the paper.

Water-injected and spoilt meat—beef, pork and mutton—was stacked atop kindling in the drainage ditch that ran past the inspection station. It reeked terribly, it grumbled loudly and its mouldy little hands waved angrily. Xiao Han, in full uniform and looking quite sombre, walked out with a bucket of kerosene and splashed it over the exposed meat.

A big-character slogan banner hung between two poles in the simple meeting site that had been erected just inside the plant's front gate. The same old stuff. I didn't know the words but they knew me. I didn't have to be told that they spelt out a congratulatory message for the plant's formal opening.

The gate, which was usually shut, had been thrown open, sandwiched between a pair of brick columns on which hung celebratory scrolls in red. Those words knew me as well. Several long tables with red tablecloths had been set up beneath the banner. Chairs were lined up behind the tables, colourful flower baskets were arranged in front.

Jiaojiao and I ran hand-in-hand between these two soon-to-be-bustling spots. Most of the village had turned out to stroll through the area. We spotted Yao Qi but the look on his face was hard to read. We also spotted Lao Lan's brother-in-law, Su Zhou, squatting on the riverbank and gazing at the meat in the drainage ditch.

Some vans drove down the road that separated these two spots, and out jumped people with video equipment or with cameras round their necks. Reporters, people you never want to offend. They seemed pleased with themselves as they emerged from their vans. Lao Lan strode out through the gate to greet them, Father at his heels. Lao Lan smiled and shook hands. 'Welcome,' he said, 'a hearty welcome.'

Father, also smiling, shook hands. 'Welcome,' he echoed, 'a hearty welcome.'

The reporters, as was their wont, went right to work. After filming and photographing the pile of spoilt meat that was to be burnt, they turned their cameras to the main gate and the outdoor meeting site.

Then they interviewed Lao Lan.

Speaking volubly into the camera, and gesturing as he spoke, he was poised and at ease. 'In days past,' he explained, 'Slaughterhouse Village families were independent operators. And despite being law-abiding citizens, they did indulge in the illegal injection of water into meat. To facilitate management and to offer fresh, choice cuts of meat that are not water-injected to city customers, we have shut down independent butcher operations and formed the United Meatpacking Plant. At the same time, we have asked our superiors to create an inspection station. Citizens in the county and provincial cities can be assured that our products have been thoroughly inspected and are of the highest quality. To guarantee this standard, we will not only subject the meat that emerges from the plant to the most stringent inspection but also subject the animals that enter the plant to the same standard. To do this we are setting up production centres for live pigs, beef cattle, sheep and dogs as well as breeding farms for less common fowl and animals, like camels, sika deer, foxes, boars, wolves, ostriches, peacocks and turkeys, to meet the gustatory demands of urban consumers. In a word, the day will come when we will be the centre of meat production in the province, providing the masses with a virtually endless supply of top-quality meat. And we won't stop there. In the near future, we will begin exporting to the world, even beyond Asia, so that people in all countries will be able to enjoy our products . . .'

After concluding the interview, the reporters turned to Father, who couldn't stop fidgeting and swaying from side to side, as if looking for something to lean on—a wall, a tree, something. But nothing came to his rescue, and his eyes darted this way and that, looking everywhere but into the camera. The woman holding the microphone said: 'Manager Luo, try not to move so much.'

He froze.

Then she focused on his eyes. 'Manager Luo, don't keep looking to the side.'

He stared straight ahead.

The answers he gave bore little relevance to the reporter's questions.

'You have my word that we will not inject our meat with water,' he said.

'We are going to supply city residents with top-quality meat products,' he said.

'We invite you to come often to supervise our operations,' he said.

Those few statements were repeated by him over and over, regardless of the question. Finally, the reporter let him go with a good-natured smile.

A dozen or so automobiles—some black, some blue, some white—drove up, and out stepped men in suits and ties and highly polished shoes. Officials, clearly. The leading VIP, a short, thickset, ruddy-faced man, smiled radiantly. All the others lined up behind him and made their way towards the plant gate. The reporters quick-stepped their way ahead of the approaching officials and then walked backward to film and photograph them. The video cameras were silent but the still cameras clicked with each shot. Their subjects, well used to the attention, talked and laughed and gestured, perfectly naturally, unlike my father who shrank from the cameras, unnerved by the limelight. I thought the men surrounding the leading official looked familiar. Perhaps I'd seen them on TV. They stuck close to him, leaning his way and vying to get a word in. Saccharine smiles seemed in danger of dripping off their faces.

Lao Lan trotted out through the gate, followed by my father. They'd seen the official and his entourage arrive but had waited for the right moment to step out and to be photographed and filmed, just as they'd rehearsed an hour earlier at the municipal propaganda office under the supervision of one of the secretaries.

Mr Chai, a gaunt beanpole of a man with a small head, had a vegetative appearance. But for all that, he owned a booming voice. 'You there, Yang Yuzhen,' he instructed Mother, and then turned to the girls who were to be hostesses. 'You, you and you, you three girls pretend that you're members of the official contingent approaching the gate. Yang Yuzhen, Lao Luo, you wait behind the gate. When the group reaches the chalk mark, come out to receive your guests. OK? Let's give it a try.' Secretary Chai stood by the gate. 'Yang Yuzhen,' he shouted, 'lead them this way.' The girls behind Mother giggled, holding their hands over their mouths. That made Mother laugh. 'What's so funny?' Chai barked. With a dry little cough, Mother managed to stop and assume a stern look. 'That's enough,' she said to the girls. 'No more giggles. Let's go.' Jiaojiao and I watched as Mother, dressed in a blue blouse and skirt, with an apple-green scarf round her neck, threw out her chest and held her head high. She looked the part. 'Not so fast,' Chai called out, 'slow down! Pretend you're talking. Good, that's it, now keep walking. Lao Lan, Lao Luo, get ready. OK, now! Go on, walk, Lao Lan in front, a little more natural, speed it up, shorter steps, don't run. Raise your head, Lao Luo, don't look down like you've lost something. OK, good, now keep walking.' Taking their cues from Secretary Chai, Lao Lan and Father were all smiles as they met Mother's contingent at the chalk mark. Lao Lan shook hands with Mother. 'Welcome,' he said, 'a hearty welcome.' Secretary Chai said: 'Now one of the staff will make the introductions. Lao Lan, you have to let go of the official's hand. Once you've shaken his hand, move to the side to let Lao Luo shake hands with Lao Yang, no, not Lao Yang, I mean the VIP. Let them shake hands.' Lao Lan let go of Mother's hand and, laughing, moved to the side, leaving Father and Mother standing face to face, both looking quite uncomfortable. 'Lao Luo,'

Chai said, 'offer her your hand. She's a VIP, not your wife.' Grumbling under his breath, Father reached out, shook Mother's hand and shouted angrily: 'Welcome, a hearty welcome! That'll never do, Lao Luo,' scolded Chai. 'What kind of a welcome is that? You sound like you want to start a fight!' 'I won't do it like that with a real official,' Father responded, his temper rising. 'What the hell is this, a circus?' Secretary Chai smiled understandingly: 'Lao Luo, you're going to have to get used to this. Who knows, before long your wife might become an official and your boss.' Father's response was a snort of disdain. 'OK,' Chai said, 'that wasn't bad. Let's try it again.' 'That's all for me,' Father complained. 'We could do it ten more times and nothing would change.' 'Me, too,' Mother said, 'I'm done. Being an official is hard work.' She wiped her face with her hand. 'Look at my sweaty face,' she said exaggeratedly. 'We can stop here, Secretary Chai,' Lao Lan said, 'we know our parts. Don't worry, we'll get it right.' 'All right, then,' Chai said. 'Just be as natural as you can, and outgoing. You need to treat the VIPs with respect, but don't come across as a lackey.'

Despite the rehearsal, Father was stiff and unnatural; when the time came he was, if anything, worse. I felt deeply embarrassed. Just look at Lao Lan—standing straight, chest out, a broad smile on his face, making a wonderful impression. One look told you that he was a man of the world yet one who remained simple, honest and trustworthy. But then my father followed him, head down, shifty-eyed, evasive, like a man harbouring sinister thoughts. He stepped on Lao Lan's heel at least once as he stumbled along, and it looked as if an invisible brick in the road had tripped him. His arms were like clubs hanging from his shoulders, incapable of bending or moving. It was almost as if he was wearing a suit of armour. His expression was something between a laugh and a sob, a sorry sight to behold, and all I could think was how much better a job Mother would have done, or, me, for that matter. I'd have done better, perhaps even outdone Lao Lan.

Lao Lan grabbed the leading official's hand with both of his and shook it hard. 'Welcome, a hearty welcome!'

A minor official introduced Lao Lan to his superior: 'This is Lan Youli, Chairman of the Board and General Manager, Huachang Corporation.'

'A peasant-turned-entrepreneur!' said the man with a smile.

'A peasant, yes,' Lao Lan said modestly, 'but hardly an entrepreneur.'

'Just do a good job,' said the official. 'I don't see a Great Wall separating peasant and entrepreneur these days.'

'Our leader is very wise,' Lao Lan said. 'We will, as you say, do a good job.'

Lao Lan shook the official's hand a second time before relinquishing his spot to Father.

'This is Luo Tong,' introduced the minor official, 'the plant manager, an expert on meat. He has an unerring eye, like the legendary chef Pao Ding.'

'Really?' the official remarked as he shook Father's hand. 'I guess in your eyes there's no such thing as a living cow—just an accumulation of flesh and bones.'

Father glanced down at the tips of the minor official's shoes as his face turned red and he muttered unintelligibly.

'Pao Ding,' official said to him, 'it's up to you to see that no water is injected into the meat.'

Finally Father managed a few words: 'I guarantee . . .'

Lao Lan led the VIP and his entourage into the plant compound. As if a great weight had been lifted from his shoulders, Father moved away and watched the party pass by.

His inability to perform in the limelight made me feel terrible. I'd have liked to run up, grab hold of his tie and throttle him till he snapped out of his muddle-headedness, till he stopped standing at the side of the road like some moron. All the spectators followed the VIPs through the gate but Father stayed where he was, looking lost. When I couldn't take it any longer, I went up to him; to avoid destroying the last vestige of his dignity, I did refrain from grabbing his tie. I just nudged him in the waist and said: 'Don't stand here, Dieh. You need to stand next to Lao Lan. You have to give the guided tour.'

'Lao Lan can handle it by himself,' he replied, looking timid.

Pinching his leg savagely, I whispered: 'You really disappoint me, Dieh!'

'You're stupid, Dieh!' Jiaojiao remarked.

'Now go!' I said.

'You're just children.' Father looked down at us. 'You can't understand how your father feels . . . but all right, I'll go.'

He strode off towards the meeting site, as determined as I'd ever seen him, and I saw Yao Qi, who was standing by the gate, arms folded, reward him with a meaningful nod.

The ceremony finally got underway and, as Lao Lan loudly made the opening remarks, Father walked over to the drainage ditch in front of the inspection station. He then lit a torch, held it high and waved it for the benefit of the spectators. Reporters rushed up and aimed their cameras at the torch in his hand. He spoke, though no one asked him to: 'I guarantee that we will not inject our meat with water.'

With that he flung the torch onto the pile of rotting, reeking kerosene-soaked meat.

Seemingly before the torch actually touched it, flames roared into the sky and shrill screeches—a mixture of excitement and agony—emerged from the conflagration, carrying with them a sweet yet disagreeable smell. The flames leapt high into the sky, and twisting columns of black smoke accompanied the sound and the smell. The flames, a deep red, looked especially dense, and my thoughts were taken back a year or so, to the fires Mother and I set to burn discarded rubber tyres and plastic waste. There was a definite resemblance with the fire in front of me now, but also a fundamental differ-ence. The fires back then had been industrial burns—plastic, chemical, toxic—while this fire was agrarian—animal, life, nutrients. Though spoilt, it was still meat, and incinerating meat like this made me hungry. I knew that Lao Lan had told my parents to buy it at the local market and then store it inside to let it rot. It had not been purchased for consumption but to be burnt, to play the role of an inferno. Which is to say, it was edible when my parents sent someone to buy it. Which is also to say, if they hadn't sent some-one to buy it, someone else would have consumed it. Had fortune smiled upon the meat or hadn't it? The most cherished fate for meat is to be eaten by someone who both understands and loves it. The least cherished fate is to be incinerated. And so, as I watched it curl up in agony, struggle, moan and shriek in the flames, solemn and tragic feelings rose up in me, creating the illusion that I was that meat, that I was sacrificing myself for Lao Lan and my parents. The sole purpose of the spectacle was to show that we, the residents of Slaughterhouse Village, would never again produce water-injected or otherwise corrupted meat. The fire was the concrete expression of that resolve. Reporters filmed and photographed it from all angles, and the flames attracted a crowd round the plant gate. Including a fellow from a neighbouring village with the unusual name of October. People said he was a mental midget but he didn't seem stupid to me. He elbowed his way up to the fire and stabbed a hunk of meat with a steel pike. Then he ran off, holding the flaming meat over his head, like a torch. Shaped like a large shoe, it dripped grease, tiny, sizzling drops of liquid fire as October shouted excitedly and ran up and down the street. A young reporter snapped his picture, although none of the video cameras turned towards him.

'Meat for sale,' he shouted, 'cooked meat for sale . . .'

October's performance made him the centre of attention, even as the grand opening ceremony was in progress and the VIP in the middle of his speech. The reporters rushed back with their cameras, though I'd have bet that the younger ones would have preferred to film October's antics. Professional diligence, however, did not allow for impetuous actions.

'The creation of the United Meatpacking Plant is a historic event . . .' The VIP's amplified voice swirled in the air.

October twirled the skewer over his head, like a spear-wielding actor in an opera. The chunk of flaming meat popped and crackled, sending hot drops of grease flying like tiny meteors. A spectator screamed as grease spatter landed on her cheeks. 'Damn you, October!' she cursed.

People ignored her, preferring to watch October and reward him with the odd encouraging shout of 'Bravo, October, bravo!' People in the crowd jumped out of the way with a skill and a vigour to match his.

'In line with our goal to supply the masses with worry-free meat, we have created the Huachang brand and ensure its reputation . . .' Lao Lan was speaking now.

I took my eyes off October, just for a moment, to see if I could find my father. In my mind, the plant manager ought to be on the speaker's platform at this important moment, and I fervently hoped he wasn't still hanging round the fire. I was in for another disappointment, for that's exactly where he was. The attention of most of the people there had been drawn by October, all but a few old-timers hunkered down alongside the drainage ditch and close to the fire, probably trying to keep warm. Two people were standing: one was my father, the other a uniformed man who worked for Lao Han and who was poking the flaming pile with a steel pole as if it were a sacred duty. My father's unblinking eyes were fixed on the flames and the smoke as he stood almost reverently, his suit curling from the heat. From where I stood he looked like a charred lotus leaf that would crumble at the slightest touch.

All of a sudden I felt very afraid. Was there something wrong with his mind? I was suddenly afraid that he'd throw himself onto the pyre and join that meat in its martyrdom. So I grabbed Jiaojiao's hand and ran towards the burning pile as shouts of alarm erupted behind us, followed by uproarious laughter. Instinctively, we turned to see what had happened. Apparently the meat on October's pike had flown off like a leaping flame and landed on top of a parked luxury sedan. The driver shrieked in alarm, he cursed, he jumped, he tried desperately to knock the flaming meat off his car but carefully for fear of being burnt. He knew the car could go up in flames, perhaps even explode. Suddenly he took off one of his shoes and knocked the meat to the ground.

'We are committed to putting in place a system of checks that will enable us to carry out our sacred duty, ensuring that not a single piece of non-standard meat ever leaves this plant . . .' The passionate voice of Lao Han, chief of the Inspection Station, momentarily drowned out the noises on the street.

Jiaojiao and I reached Father, then we pushed and shoved and pinched him until he reluctantly took his eyes of the pyre and gazed down at us. In a hoarse, raspy voice—as if the flames had seared his larynx—he asked: 'What are you children doing?'

'Dieh,' I said, 'you shouldn't be standing here.'

'Where do you think I should to be standing?' he asked, a bitter smile on his lips.

'Over there.' I pointed to the meeting site.

'I'm beginning to get annoyed, children.'

'Please, Dieh,' I said. 'Take a page out of Lao Lan's book.'

'Do you really want me to turn into someone like him?' he asked darkly.

'Yes,' I said, with a look at Jiaojiao. 'But better than him.'

'That's a tune I can't sing, children,' he said. 'But for your sake, I'll try.'

Mother ran up breathlessly. 'What's the matter with you?' she hissed. 'You're up next. Lao Lan says to come now.'

With one last reluctant look at the fire, Father said: 'All right, I'm coming.'

'And you two, don't get close to that fire,' Mother warned.

Father strode purposefully towards the meeting site. Mother walked away from the fire, and we followed her. On the way we spotted the young driver, who had put his shoe back on, kicking the flaming chunk of meat as far as he could. He then ran up to 'madman' October and kicked him in the shin. October yelped and staggered but didn't fall.

'What the hell are you up to?' the driver cursed.

Terrified by the attack, October gaped at the man for a moment before raising his pike and, with an eerie shout, swinging it at his head. The man ducked, and the pike merely glanced off his cheek. Pale with fright, he managed to grab it before uttering a stream of curses, assuring October that he'd make him pay. Spectators rushed up and held him back. 'Forget it, comrade,' they urged. 'You don't want to get into a dispute with someone who's not right in the head.'

The driver let go of the pike and stormed off angrily. Then he opened the car's trunk, took out a rag and began to clean the grease off the top of the car.

October walked off, dragging his pike behind him, limping slightly.

Suddenly, we heard Father's voice over the loudspeakers: 'I guarantee that we will not inject our meat with water.'

The people on the street looked up, trying to locate the source of his voice.

'I guarantee that we will not inject our meat with water,' he repeated.

'Movie star Huang Feiyun, a beauty for the ages, was my third uncle's lover.'
Or so Lao Lan told me more than a decade ago. 'If you could gather up all the
newspapers, magazines and posters with her pictures, there'd be enough to
fill the hold of a ten-thousand-tonne freighter,' Lao Lan said on several occasions back then. I tell you, Wise Monk, he wove a riotous romantic history of
his third uncle for us. Of course I'm familiar with this Huang Feiyun—her
somewhat boyish look hangs before my eyes like a beaded curtain. Though
she's retired from public life, and is now the wife of a very rich man, the mother
of his children and the hostess of his extravagant villa on Phoenix Mountain,
she continues to be an important target of the paparazzi. When she drives her
luxury sedan, with its tiny figure of a man as a hood ornament, out of the
villa's underground garage, she keeps her foot on the accelerator and races
down the winding mountain road. From a distance, it looks like the car is
plummeting from the heavens. Her drives down the mountain have been
labelled 'The Descent of the Heavenly Fairy to the Mortal World' by scandal-
mongering tabloid reporters. She steps out of the car, wearing dark glasses
and attended by a maidservant who carries her dogs, Napoleon and Vivian
Leigh, of a famous breed little known to the average person. She moves quickly
through the chandelier-graced hotel lobby, her designer dress reflected off the
mirror-like surface of the granite floor (an aspect of the hotel that has been
roundly criticized but that attracts a multitude of stars). The concierge knows
exactly who she is but dares not make her identity known. He keeps his eyes
on the hem of her skirt as she glides across the floor. At the bank of lifts she
gestures for her dog-carrying maid to wait in the lobby. Then she steps into a
lift, and her progress up to the twenty-eighth floor is observed through the
glass in its exterior. She knocks on the door of the Presidential Suite, so
luxurious it could cause a public revolt. A young man answers the door and
asks who she's looking for. She brushes past him and enters the enormous,
flower-festooned living room. Stepping on the rare black peonies strewn across

the floor, she heads straight for the oft-visited master bedroom, where there is a bed so frightfully big you could ride a bicycle on it. The bed is vacant but watery sounds emerge from the bathroom. She kicks the door open, and steam billows out accompanied by the sounds of splashing water and feminine giggles. As the steam dissipates, an enormous whirlpool tub comes into view, water gurgling from its sides like a wellspring. Four virginal-looking girls surround Lan Laoda in water covered by flower petals. The star takes a black bottle from her purse and tosses it into the tub. 'Sulphuric acid', she says softly. Then she turns and walks out. The girls shriek and clamber out of the tub, their fair bodies suddenly turned black—but only their bodies; their faces are still white. Lan Laoda, on the other hand, stretches out in the tub, shuts his eyes and says: 'Dinner tonight, third floor, Huaiyang Chun'. As she walks out of the bedroom she says: 'You should invite classier girls'. 'They're all younger than you', he replies from the bath. We see the star retrace her steps through the living room, spitting on the flowers beneath her feet. The young man who'd opened the door can only stand still and stare. The doorbell rings in loud bursts and then a two-man security detail enters. 'What's going on here?' they demand. The star picks up a bunch of black flowers and smacks one of them across the face. He backs away, clutching his cheek. Bells ring out in the corridor.

One night, soon after the United Meatpacking Plant began operations, Father, Mother, Lao Lan, Jiaojiao and I were sitting round our table, steaming platters of meat glowing beneath the electric lights. There was a bottle and several glasses filled with wine as red as fresh cow's blood. The adults were drinking more than they were eating, unlike my sister and me. Truth be known, the two of us had a respectable capacity for liquor but Mother wouldn't let us drink. At some point, Jiaojiao began to snore; I was quite sleepy myself, which was usual after a big, meaty meal. After putting Jiaojiao to bed, Mother said: 'You get some sleep too, Xiaotong.'

'No. I want to talk to you about school.'

'Boss Lan,' Mother said, 'the boy doesn't want to go to school. He wants to work at the plant.'

'Is that so?' His eyes narrowed into a smile. 'Why?'

Snapping awake, I began to explain: 'Because the things they teach in school are useless and because I have feelings for meat. I can hear it talk.'

Surprised at my unexpected response, Lao Lan burst out laughing. 'You're a true wonder. I'd better not offend you because, who knows, you might really have extraordinary powers. But you still need schooling.'

'I'm not going,' I said. 'Forcing me to attend school is a waste of my life. I sneak into the plant through the sewer ditch every day, and I've discovered lots of problems. If you let me work there, I can help you solve them for you.'

'Enough of this nonsense,' Father said, impatiently. 'Go to bed. We have things to discuss.'

I could have carried on, but the look on Father's face stopped me. 'Xiaotong!' he roared.

So I went into the bedroom, grumbling to myself, and sat in a mahogany chair we'd just bought, intent on watching and listening to the adults in the other room.

Lao Lan swirled the wine in his tall-stemmed glass. 'Lao Luo, Yuzhen,' he said unemotionally, 'what's your view? Will we make or lose money?'

'If the price of meat doesn't rise, then we're bound to lose,' Mother said, clearly worried. 'They won't give us a higher price just because we don't inject water into our meat.'

'That's why I want to talk to you,' Lao Lan said as he sipped his wine. 'Over the past few days, Huang Biao and I have visited meatpacking plants in several nearby counties, pretending to be meat-sellers. We discovered that they all inject their meat products with water.'

'But we broadcast our assurance in front of those dignitaries,' Father said softly. 'That was only a few days ago. Our words are probably still ringing in their ears.'

'My friend, our hands are tied. The way things are these days, even though we're unwilling to inject our meat with water, others aren't. So soon we'll not only lose money but also be out of business.'

'Can't we think of something?' Father asked.

'Like what? What are our options? There's nothing I want more than to do business the way it ought to be done. If you can figure out a way of staying in business without injecting water, I'm all for it.'

'We can report them to the authorities,' Father said weakly.

'Is that what you call a good idea? The authorities know exactly what's going on but there's nothing they can do about it,' he said coldly.

'Crabs go where the currents take them,' Mother said. 'If others inject water and we don't, the only thing that proves is how stupid we are.'

'We can try another line of work,' Father offered. 'Who says we have to be butchers?'

'That's all we know,' Lan said with a caustic laugh. 'It's what we're good at. Your ability to evaluate beef on the hoof, for instance, is part of the butcher system.'

'What good am I anyway?' Father said. 'I have no talents.'

'None of us have any talents, except this,' Lan said. 'But we've got an edge, and if we inject our meat with water then we'll do a better job of it than the rest.'

'You have to do it, Luo Tong,' Mother said. 'We can't operate at a loss.'

'If that's what you both want to, then go ahead,' Father said. 'The key is Lao Han at the Inspection Station—will he give us trouble?'

'He wouldn't dare,' Lao Lan said. 'He's a dog we feed.'

'When the monkeys attack, the dogs grow fangs,' Father said.

'You two do what you have to, and I'll take care of Lao Han. It won't take more than a few rounds of mah-jongg. I'm sure he remembers that his station is a product of the meatpacking plant—it wouldn't exist if not for us.'

'There's nothing I can say,' Father conceded, 'except that I hope we don't inject our meat with formaldehyde.'

'That goes without saying,' Lao Lan responded solemnly. 'It's a matter of conscience. Most of our customers are ordinary citizens, and we have a responsibility to safeguard their health. We'll inject only the purest water. Of course, adding a trace of formaldehyde would pose no danger—it could even protect them against cancer, slow the ageing process, prolong their life. But we've vowed not to add formaldehyde. We have long-range goals. We have moved beyond the independent butcher system. Now that we've come together as a united slaughterhouse, there are limits to what we do, and that includes not experimenting with the people's health.' Smiling, he continued: 'Before too long we'll evolve into a major enterprise with an automated production line—a living animal in one end and sausage and canned meats out the other. By then the water issue will be irrelevant.'

'Under your leadership, we're certain to achieve that goal,' declared Mother, charmed by his words.

'Dream on, you two,' Father said in icy tones. 'But let's come back to the water issue. The question is: How do we do it? And how much? And what do we do if someone reports us? In the past, it was every family for itself. But now there are more mouths than we can control . . .'

I walked into the room. 'Dieh,' I said, 'I know an ideal way to inject water.'

'What are you doing out of bed?' he demanded. 'Don't stick your nose where it doesn't belong.'

'I'm not!'

'Let's hear what he has to say,' Lao Lan said. 'Go ahead, Xiaotong, what's your brilliant idea?'

'I know how it's done. I've watched every family in Slaughterhouse Village do it. They attach a high-pressure hose to the heart of a newly slaughtered animal. But since the animal is dead, its organs and cells can no longer absorb the water and half of it is lost. Why can't we inject water when the animal is still alive?'

'Makes sense,' Lao Lan said. 'Go on, my young friend.'

'I watched a doctor administer an IV once, and that gave me an idea. We'll do the same with the animals before they're slaughtered.'

'But that's so slow,' said Mother.

'It doesn't have to be an IV,' Lao Lan volunteered. 'There are other ways. It's a great idea, no matter how you look at it. Injecting water into a living animal and into a dead one are radically different concepts.'

'Adding water to a dead animal is injection,' I said. 'But adding it to a living animal is something different. It's cleansing their organs and their circulatory system. If you ask me, this meets both your output goals and your standard for high-quality meat.'

'Worthy Nephew Xiaotong, I'm impressed,' Lao Lan said. His fingers shook as he took a cigarette out of his case, lit it and took a drag. 'Were you listening, Lao Luo? Your son puts us old-timers to shame. Our brains are stuck in a rut. He's right, we wouldn't be injecting meat with water—we'd be cleansing our cows of toxins and improving the quality of their meat. We can call it meat-cleansing.'

'Does this mean I can work in the plant?' I asked.

'In theory you don't have to go to school, since you could cause Teacher Cai to die of apoplexy. But your future is at stake, and you're better off listening to your parents.'

'I don't want to listen to them—I want to listen to you.'

'I'm neutral on this,' he said evasively. 'If you were my son, I wouldn't force you to go to school. But you're not my son.'

'So you're in favour of my working in the plant?'

'What do you say, Lao Luo?' Lao Lan asked.

'No.' Father was adamant. 'Your mother and I both work there, and that's enough for one family.'

'This plant will never succeed without me,' I said. 'None of you has an emotional attachment to meat, so you can't produce a top-quality product. Try me out for a month? If I don't do a good job, you can fire me and I'll go back to school. But if I do a good job, I'll stay on for a year. After that, I'll either return to school or go out on my own and see what the world has in store for me.'

A gourmet spread of a dozen delectable dishes has been laid out on a table three feet in diameter in a private room at the Huaiyang Chun restaurant on the third floor of a luxury hotel. Directly opposite the door, on the red velvet wall, hangs a 'good fortune' tapestry with a dragon and phoenix. Twelve chairs are arranged round the table, only one of which is occupied—by Lan Laoda. His chin rests in his hands and he has a melancholic air. Threads of steam waft from some of the delicacies on the table in front of him but the rest have grown cold. A waiter in white, led into the room by a young woman in a red suit, is carrying a gold-plated tray on which rests a small plate of food dripping with golden-yellow gorgon oil and emitting a strange aroma. The woman takes the plate from the tray and places it in front of Lan Laoda. 'Mr Lan,' she whispers, 'this is the nasal septum from one of Heilongjiang's rare Kaluga sturgeons, known popularly as a dragon bone. In feudal times, the dish was reserved for the enjoyment of the emperor. Its preparation is very complicated. Steeped for three days in white vinegar, it is then stewed for a day and a night in a pheasant broth. The owner personally prepared this for you. Enjoy it while it's hot.' 'Divide it into two portions,' Lan Laoda says indifferently, 'and wrap them to go. Then send them to the Feiyun Villa on Phoenix Mountain—one for Napoleon and one for Vivian Leigh.' The woman's long, thin brows arch in astonishment but she dares not say a word. Lan Laoda stands up: 'And send a bowl of plain noodles to my room.'

Lao Lan put me in charge of the meat-cleansing workshop after consulting the calendar to select my first day on the job.

My initial managerial recommendation was to combine the dog and sheep kill rooms to free up one for a meat-cleansing station. All the animals would have to pass through the station on their way to the kill rooms. Lao Lan considered my suggestion for only a minute before agreeing, his eyes sparkling golden with excitement.

'I like it!' I said and on a sheet of paper, using a red-and-blue pencil, I quickly sketched out my plan. Finding nothing to criticize or change, Lao Lan gave it an appreciative look. 'Do it!' he announced.

Father, on the other hand, had a number of objections. Although he claimed it to be a terrible idea, I did note a look of admiration in his eyes. There's an old saying that goes: 'No one knows a boy like his father.' But you could also say, 'No one knows a man like his son.' I could read my father like a book. When he saw me announce to the one-time independent butchers, now employees of the plant, the new procedures, his misgivings were also tinged with pride. A man can be jealous of anyone but his own son. His unease stemmed not from any sense that I'd upstaged him but that I had the mind of an adult in a child's body. The villagers believed that precocious youngsters were fated to die before their time. My quick wits and my intelligence filled him with pride and his father's hope for his son soared high. But, according to local superstition, those same qualities enhanced my chances of dying young. Hence his emotional predicament.

As I think back, it seems almost miraculous that, as a twelve-year-old boy, I was able to devise a method for injecting water into living animals, to redesign a workshop, to be in charge of a few dozen workers and to successfuly increase the plant's production. When I recall those times I can't help thinking that I was quite a remarkable fellow back then!

Wise Monk, now I'm going to tell you exactly how remarkable I was. I'll describe for you the layout of the meat-cleansing station and what I did, and you'll see that I'm not exaggerating.

Security at the plant was tight in order to protect it from the prying eyes of competitors and sneaky reporters. We maintained our secrecy with the claim that we were trying to prevent outsiders from contaminating our products. Though my innovation turned the water-injection process into 'meat-cleansing', if the reporters—who thrive on misrepresentation—got wind of it, there's no telling what they'd feed their readers. (My handling of the reporters, which I'll describe later, is one of the highlights of my recollections.)

On my first day on the job, Lao Lan announced that I was in charge. That done, I addressed the workers: 'If you think I'm just a child, you are sadly mistaken. I may be a head shorter and several years younger, but I know more than any of you. I'll be watching you and taking note of your performance. I'll report everything to Lao Lan. I may not scare you but Lao Lan's a different story.'

'You needn't be scared of me either,' Lan Lan spoke to them next. 'You are working for yourselves, not for me, not for Luo Tong and not for Luo Xiaotong. We have given him heavy responsibilities because he has room in his head for new and original ideas that can bring vitality to our plant. Now that may not mean much to you but you know the meaning of money, and that is what vitality equals—money. When the plant makes a profit, the money winds up in your pockets and that equals good food and fine liquor, new houses, improved prospects for your sons' brides and richer dowries for your daughters. In a word, it's what will make you stand straight and tall. You all know that operating as an independent butcher has been outlawed. I wouldn't have created this plant otherwise. If you decide to do some private butchering on the side and get caught, at the very least your family will suffer from a heavy fine. At the very worst, you'll serve jail time. This plant was created for all of us, since the one thing our village knows is how to slaughter livestock. You are all pros at butchering and amateurs at everything else. Even if some of you decide to breed livestock or work with processed meat, at the end of the day you're still involved with slaughter. There can be only one conclusion—if the plant does well, we all do well, and if it doesn't then we all go hungry. How do we see that it does well? By working as a team. The flames rise higher when everyone feeds the fire. United, we can move mountains. The Eight Immortals crossed the sea by calling on everyone's talents. Hard work will be rewarded. In the eyes of most, Xiaotong is just a boy. But in my eyes he's a talented resource, one we must make use of. I'm not talking iron rice bowl here. He'll stay on as long as he performs well. If he doesn't, he'll be out. Director Xiaotong, give the order.'

I'm no longer young, and public speaking makes me nervous. But back then I was almost fanatical in my desire to put on a show—the bigger my audience the better. Well, I put those plant employees through their paces like a fearless cowherd tending a field full of dumb animals. My first task for them was to build a structure in the workshop. In accordance with my design, they were to erect two tall towers—metal posts held together with steel struts, one on each side of the workshop and fitted on top with a galvanized steel water vat. Iron pipes leading from the vats' bases stretched along the width of the workshop with a water tap connected to a rubber hose every six feet. That, in all its simplicity, was the meat-cleansing station. Complicated designs are ineffective, effective designs are uncomplicated. Some of the men made faces as they worked, some sniggered. 'What the hell are we doing?' one of them muttered under his breath, 'Making cricket cages?'

'Right,' I said loudly, without caring whose feelings I hurt. 'I plan to put cows into cricket cages!'

I knew that these workers—not long ago the village's most unruly residents and most of them illegal butchers—had no interest in carrying out my orders. Putting me in charge of a workshop was, in their view, a stupid mistake by Lao Lan and one further compounded by my drawings and my instructions. I'd have wasted my time trying to explain things to them, so I thought I'd let the results speak for themselves. 'Just do as I say,' I ordered. 'And think whatever you want.'

Once the structure was complete, the workers backed off to smoke or woolgather while I gave Father and Lao Lan a guided tour. After pointing out the features and their uses, I turned to the smoking workers. 'If you light up in this building tomorrow, I'll fine you two-weeks' pay.'

Their eyes blazed with fury at my threat but they did stub out their cigarettes.

Early the next morning, six men filled the two overhead reservoirs. I could have had them hook up a hose to an electric pump but that would have been expensive and, as I saw it, unexciting and dull. I preferred the view of six men labouring to and from the well, time after time.

When the reservoirs were full, the six men walked over to the entrance and laid down their shoulder poles for a rest. 'Once the process begins,' I said, 'it's your job to see that there's always water in the reservoirs. There can be no interruptions.' 'No sweat, Director,' they said as they thumped their chests, apparently in high spirits. I knew why. I'd known from the very beginning that only four men were needed to keep the reservoirs full, but I'd added two more just to spice things up.

Before the formal work day began, my father and mother, along with Lao Lan, showed up for the guided tour. As I spiritedly explained the technical aspects, I really looked the part of a water-station manager, at least I thought so. Over the past few days Jiaojiao had followed me everywhere, carrying my army canteen—another item Mother and I had found scavenging—filled with sugar water. Every time I'd hand out an order, she'd raise her thumb and say, 'My brother's great!' Then she'd unscrew the cap and hand me the canteen: 'Here, drink.'

After the guided tour, it was time to start work. I stood on a chair by the entrance so I could see everything in the building.

'Is everyone ready?' I shouted.

They stared blankly for a moment, but then quickly responded in unison, the way we'd practiced: 'Ready! We await the director's instructions!'

Their false show of enthusiasm turned what was ceremoniously serious into something akin to farce, and I saw the smirks on the faces of the less sincere workers. But I let it go. I'd worked things out carefully and I knew my plan was all right.

Time to give the order: 'Bring the first beef cows in from the cattle pens.'

The men picked up their halters and ropes: 'Got it!'

'Go!' I made a chopping motion, the way I'd seen film toughs give commands.

The men's faces froze. I knew that if Lao Lan and my parents hadn't been there then they'd have burst out laughing. Instead, they ran to the door, bumping into one another on their way out. Since we'd rehearsed the drill, they knew what to do and so ran straight to the cow pen in the plant's southeast corner. A hundred head of recently purchased cattle had been herded into a circular pen. Local peasants had brought some to us, others had been driven over by cattle merchants, there were even some that the cattle thieves had delivered in the middle of the night. Mixed with the cattle were ten donkeys, five ageing mules and seven old nags, plus some camels with patchy hides, like old men with padded jackets draped over their shoulders in early summer. We happily accepted any and all livestock that could be turned into meat. We'd also built a sty nearby for, in addition to pigs, a quantity of sheep and goats, including milch goats. And dogs. Fed an enhanced diet, our dogs looked like young hippos, their movements slowed by bloated bodies. No longer agile and intelligent, they had lost all their canine traits and become dull, stupid animals who were useless as watchdogs—they'd wag their tails in welcome at thieves and snarl at their owners. All these animals, without exception, were scheduled to pass through our meat-cleansing station. But let's start with the cows, since they were our main concern. We were the official suppliers to farmers' markets and restaurants in town. Urbanites tend to be faddish diners and their tastes change like the wind. At the time, the newspapers were reporting on the nutritional value of beef being higher than that of other meats. Hence, a beef craze. Hence, cows were what we slaughtered. Some time later the newspapers would report that the nutritive value of pork was higher. Hence, the pork craze. Hence, pigs were what we slaughtered. Lao Lan was the first peasant-turned-entrepreneur to realize the importance of the media. 'When profits from plant operations are high enough,' he said one day, 'we'll start our own newspaper, *Meat Digest*, and advertise our own products every day.' But, back to our workers. Each led in a pair of cows from the pen. Some obediently trotted behind the men who held their halters, some others were less well behaved and veered this way and that and slowed things down. A black bull broke loose, raised its tail and ran, hoofs flying, to the gate, which was now shut. 'Stop it!' someone yelled. 'Stop that bull!' Now who would be *that* foolish? Anyone who got in the way of those horns would be tossed into the air and land with a thud, a mangled mess. Though I was apprehensive, I was still in control. 'Out of the way!' I shouted. The raging bull ran headlong into the steel gate and we were deafened by the sound of the collision. Its neck twisted as it bounced into the air and then landed hard on the ground. 'All right!' I shouted. 'Now tie it up.' The man with the empty halter walked over tentatively and bent down, legs slightly bowed, ready to flee at a moment's notice. But the bull let itself be haltered, then obediently got to its feet and dutifully followed the man up to the workshop door. Its head was bleeding and it wore a sheepish look, like a schoolboy caught misbehaving. Though only a minor episode, it livened up the atmosphere—a good thing, nothing wrong with that. In a matter of minutes, men and beasts were in position at the door and the cows eager to get in, perhaps because they smelt the fresh water in the reservoirs. The six water-carriers standing by the door lazily observing the goings-on were nudged aside; their buckets clattered loudly against each other. 'What's the hurry?' I shouted. 'This isn't a race to mourn your dead fathers! Bring them in slowly, one at a time.' I had to remind the men to treat these beasts with a little kindness during their last minutes on earth. They needed to be cajoled, tricked even, so they'd remain calm and contented. An animal's mood has a direct effect on the quality of its meat. One that's terrified just before it's slaughtered produces sour meat; only an animal that dies peacefully produces fragrant meat. I told them to treat the beef cattle with special care, since they were in the minority; most of the animals had contributed to humanity by working in the fields. We may have been different from Huang Biao, who treated an old cow as the reincarnation of his mother, but we still needed to show them a degree of respect. In today's words: we wanted to let them die with dignity.

The workers lined up their charges in two rows at the door, an impressive column of forty head of cattle. I've never been someone to shout his successes from the rooftops but watching my vision being transformed into a reality was a proud moment indeed. The first man up was Yao Qi, which only made me prouder, as I recalled how he'd brought my father that bottle of fake Mao-tai, which Mother had then given to Lao Lan. He'd also said filthy things about Aunty Wild Mule, including that he'd like to take her to bed. A perfect example of 'Ugly toad wanting to eat swan meat'. I had no reason to treat a bum like him with kid gloves. I was hostile to anyone who slandered Aunty Wild Mule. Joining as an ordinary worker at the meatpacking plant—was it a sign of a wise Yao Qi toeing the line? Or was it more a case of enduring hardships in order to seek revenge? This could be a problem, I thought to myself. But not Lao Lan, who stood in front of me. He nodded to Yao Qi and smiled. Yao Qi smiled back. The nods and smiles hinted at a unique relationship between the two men. Lao Lan was a broad-minded man, and someone like that cannot be taken lightly. Yao Qi was a man who could demean himself in front of others. Someone like that cannot be taken lightly either.

Yao Qi was holding the leads of two brown Luxi cows, the best-looking animals in the pens. I'd been present when they were sold to us. Father's eyes had lit up as he circled them, examining them carefully, and I could imagine how the legendary Bo-le must have felt when he discovered a fine steed . . . 'Too bad,' Father sighed, 'what a pity.' 'Lao Luo, you can stop the phony dramatics,' the cattle merchant snickered. 'Do you want them or don't you? If not, I'll take them back with me.' 'No one's stopping you,' replied Father.

'Go ahead, take them.' The cattle merchant gave an embarrassed little laugh: 'We're old friends. If the goods die at the wharf, that's where they stay. You and I will be doing more business in the future . . .'

Yao Qi wore a pompous smile as he stood at the head of the line with the two handsome cows and I must say I was impressed. To be at the head of the queue he must have raced to the cow pens, forced halters onto the two most powerful animals and then walked them over, no easy task for someone that fat. That he had beat all those younger and stronger men to the first spot was testimony to the power of a man's will. The Luxi cows' eyes were clear and bright and their muscles rippled beneath their satiny hides. They were in their prime, at an age when they could pull a plough with speed and power—a glance at their shoulders was proof enough. The West County cattle merchants were cattle thieves, part of an organized gang that stole cattle for others to sell. They had a special arrangement with the train station that promised a worry-free delivery of stolen cattle to our village. But things had begun to change. The cattle we bought from West County for the plant came not in cattle cars but in trucks, long semis covered with green tarps, gigantic, intimidating vehicles that could have been transporting anything, even military hardware. The animals emerged from the trucks on such unsteady legs you'd think they were drunk. The merchants were pretty unsteady too, and they were most certainly drunk.

Yao Qi entered the station with his Luxi cows, followed by Cheng Tianle, a one-time independent, conservative pig butcher. In the 1960s, butchers in our village began to skin the pigs they slaughtered because the hides were worth more, pound for pound, than the pork—they could be turned into fine leather. Cheng Tianle was the only one who refused to do so. He kept an oversized cook pot in his kill room, covered by a thick plank; the sides of the pot and the plank were covered with pig bristles removed the old-fashioned way. He'd cut a hole in one of the rear legs and open several passages with a metal rod, then put his mouth up to the hole and blow, puffing the carcass up like a balloon and creating a space between the hide and the flesh. Then he'd pour hot water over the skin causing the bristles to simply fall off. This method produced the best-looking meat; it was sold still enclosed in its shiny skin and looked so much more appealing than stripped pork. Blessed with powerful lungs, Cheng Tianle could inflate a whole pig with a single breath. His meat was popular with those who enjoyed the crunchy texture and appreciated the high nutritional value. But now, here he was, a man uniquely skilled to produce fine, crunchy meat by blowing air under the hide, looking as mournful as can be, leading two head of cattle into the building. It was as sad as putting a master shoemaker on a shoe assembly line. I'd always had a soft spot for him, a good and decent man who remained true to his ways. Unlike so many craftsmen who liked to show off in front of the young, Cheng Tianle, a modest man, treated me with kindness; he greeted me warmly whenever I dropped by in the old days and sometimes even asked if there was news of my father. 'Xiaotong,' he'd say, 'your father is an upright man.' And when I went to buy his bristles (I resold them to make brushes), he'd say: 'You don't have to pay for those, just take them.' Once he even gave me a cigarette. He never treated me like a child but always with respect. And I intended to repay his kindness within the limits of my authority.

Cheng Tianle led a big black local animal—it had a sagging belly that swayed from side to side, like a sack of ammonia. It was long past its working age, and either its owner or a merchant who specialized in old animals had fattened it up with hormone-laced feed. No good meat with high nutritional value could come from that. But the taste buds of the city-dwellers had deteriorated to such a point that they could no longer distinguish good meat from bad. There was no sense in giving them high-quality meat—it was wasted on their inferior palates. They were easy marks too. If we told them that the meat of a chemically fattened animal came from one raised on grazing land, with an abundance of spring water, they'd smack their lips and say how good it tasted. I had to agree with Lao Lan, who had nothing good to say about the city-dwellers; he said they were evil and stupid, and that gave us the right to feed them as full of lies as we wanted. We weren't happy about that; but they didn't want to hear the truth and were prepared to take us to court if we so much as tried.

The second animal Cheng Tianle led up was a milch cow with a spotted belly, also well up in years. Since it was too old to produce milk, the dairy owner had sold it as a beef cow. Beef from a milch cow is as poor as pork from a breeding sow—tasteless and pulpy. The sight of those loose, dried-up teats saddened me. An old milch cow and an old draft cow, two animals that had served man and served him well. They should have been put out to pasture to live out their lives and then been properly buried, with a marker if possible, perhaps even a headstone.

There's no need for me to describe all the animals that followed. During my tenure, thousands of cows made their death march through the meat-cleansing building, and I remember each of them, body and face. As if a set of drawers in my head contains each of their photographs. They are drawers I don't like to open.

The men knew the drill. So after leading the animals into the enclosures, they barricaded them in, with steel rods in the rear, to keep them from backing out during the treatment. If we'd set up a trough in front of the cages, our meat-cleansing station would have looked like a bright, spacious feed building. But there were no troughs in front of these animals, and they were not there to feed. I doubt that many of them knew what lay in store—most were blithely ignorant of their imminent death (which is why they stopped to graze before entering a slaughterhouse). It was time to inject the water, so I reminded the men to keep at their jobs. To dispel any misgivings, I reminded them that we were cleaning the animals' inner organs—not pumping them full of water.

The workers began by inserting rubber hoses up the animals' noses, down through their throats and into their stomachs. The animals could shake and twist their heads as much as they wanted but the hoses stayed in place. The job required two men, one to raise the animal's head and the second to insert the hose. Some of the animals reacted violently to the invasion, others remained docile. But all resistance ceased once the hose was in—perhaps they finally realized it was too late. Hoses inserted, the men stood in front of the cows and awaited my order.

'Start the water,' I said, unemotionally.

The taps were turned on. Two hundred and fifty, give or take ten, gallons over twelve hours.

The system still had a few defects, as we discovered that first day. Some of the cows collapsed after taking in water for hours, others had coughing fits and vomited. But, whatever the problem, I always found a solution. To keep the animals from collapsing, I had the men insert a frame of steel rods under their bellies. And to keep them from vomiting, I had the men cover their eyes with a black cloth.

The cows released a watery mess from their rear ends during the entire process. 'Look!' I said proudly to the men, 'That's what this is all about. Our water is cleaning the filth inside them. Every cell in their bodies is being washed. Now you see why I said that we're not filling them with water—we're cleansing their internal organs. Filling them with water ruins the meat but what we're doing improves it. Even meat from sick and ageing cows will be tender and nutritious after such a thorough cleansing.'

Finally, they were happy. I'd won them over. I'd taken the first major step in establishing my authority.

The animals were to be taken to the kill room once the cleansing was complete. But the long hours spent standing in the cages caused their legs to buckle after only a few steps and then they collapsed like bulldozed walls. There was no way in which they were going to be able to get back on their feet. The first time that happened, I asked four men to lift the animal off the floor. They struggled until they were gasping for breath and sweating profusely but the animal hadn't budged an inch. It just lay there, panting, its eyes rolled back in its head and water shooting out of its mouth and nose. I called over four more men, then stood behind them and shouted: 'One, two, three—lift!' They bent, arses raised and lifted with all their might. The cow was finally upright. It took a few unsteady steps and promptly fell down again.

I was embarrassed—this was not something I had anticipated. The workers began to smirk again. But Father came to my rescue. He told the men to go into the kill room and bring back some of the logs. Once they were laid out on the floor, he sent a man to get some rope, which was then tied round the animal's horns and legs. One lot of men were ordered to pull while two of the strongest were ordered to use a level on the animal's rump and push with all their might. As the animal moved forward, those who were fast on their feet picked up the logs that had been passed over and then placed them up at the front. And so, with this primitive method, we rolled the cow straight into the kill room.

I fell into a funk.

'Don't let it get to you, youngster,' Lao Lan said, trying to make me feel better. 'You did fine. What happened after the water-injection—no, I mean, the meat-cleansing—wasn't supposed to be your responsibility. So let's figure this out together. We need to come up with a simple, convenient means of transporting water-treated cows into the kill room.'

'Lao Lan,' I said, 'give me half a day.'

He glanced at my parents. 'Xiaotong's afraid we'll steal his thunder.'

I shook my head. 'I'm not worried about who steals who's thunder. I need to prove myself.'

'All right,' Lao Lan said, 'I trust you. Come up with a bold idea, and don't worry about the expense.'

Accompanied by his staff, the lieutenant governor walks to the street and climbs into his Audi A6. With a police car leading the way and a caravan of a dozen or so Red Flags and VW Santanas, he speeds away to attend a banquet filled with imagination. As they leave the temple grounds, the worker suffering from toothache runs over to the outer wall. Retrieving Mayor Hu's hairpiece, he claps it onto his head. The change is startling. 'I'll never be a mayor,' he says, 'but this makes me look like one.' 'More like a hapless fool, if you ask me,' his short co-worker mocks. 'The more hapless the official,' the first fellow says confidently, 'the better off the people. Now, is getting hold of a stinking rug any cause to be so pleased with yourself?' With that, the short one reaches under his jacket and—presto change-o—brings out a fine black satchel. 'Look what I've got!' he says, waving it proudly. He unzips it and then empties it of its contents, one object at a time. First out are a little red notebook and a brand-name gold pen. Next, a cellphone, and then a white vial. Finally, two expensive condoms. The worker unstops the vial and shakes out some light blue, diamond-shaped pills. 'What's this?' he wonders aloud. The fellow who's stayed out of the conversation thus far, a young man with the look of a rural schoolteacher, sneers. 'Those are one of the two magic items all venal officials never leave home without. They're called Viagra.' 'What's Viagra?' The young fellow smiles. 'Selling Viagra in front of the Wutong Temple is as foolish as reading the Three Character Classic in front of a Confucius Temple.' 'Big Brother Lan,' a bald fellow says conspiratorially as he hands a small white vial to Lan Laoda, 'this is something I brought back from the US as a humble gift for you.' Lan Laoda takes the vial. 'What is it?' 'It's more effective than any Indian Magic Oil or Thai Invigorates,' the bald fellow replies. 'A golden spear never tips over, they say.' 'What am I supposed to do with something like this?' Lan Laoda says as he throws the vial to the ground. 'I can go non-stop for two hours,' he boasts. 'Go home and ask that sister-in-law of yours how many times she came. I can make a stone maiden go wet.' 'Big Brother Lan is an *immortal,' pipes up a red-faced man, 'who does as he pleases, comes and goes at will, the last man who needs something like that.' The bald fellow picks up the vial and tucks it away. 'If you really don't want it, Big Brother,' he says, 'I'll put it to good use.' 'Take it easy, Baldy,' warns the red-faced man. 'Too much of that can make you nearsighted.' Baldy doesn't miss a beat. 'Nearsighted? I don't care if they made me blind.' A desk clock in the corner chimes two, and a pale-faced woman comes into the main room followed by a trio of tall young women. 'They're here, Mr Lan,' she says softly. The young women, faces devoid of expression, follow their leader into the bedroom. 'Showtime,' announces Lan Laoda. 'Anyone want to watch?' 'Who wouldn't want to watch the finest show in town?' laughs Baldy. 'You're all welcome,' says Lao Lan, also laughing, 'no tickets necessary.' Then he steps into the bedroom and, in a matter of minutes, come the sound of flesh pounding flesh and a woman's moans. Baldy tiptoes to the bedroom door and peeks inside. 'That isn't a man in there,' he says to the red-faced fellow, 'that's the legendary Wutong Spirit!'*

I snuck into the kitchen and sat on my low stool. Huang Biao, attentive as always, set the taller stool in front of me. 'What would you like, Director Luo?' he asked, fawning.

'What do you have today?'

'Pork rump, beef tenderloin, sheep leg, dog cheek.'

'I need to keep my wits about me today, so none of those.' I twitched my nose. 'Got any donkey? Donkey always gives me a clear head.'

'But . . .'

'But what?' That did *not* please me. 'You can pull the wool over my eyes but you can't pull it over my nose. I smelt donkey the minute I walked in.'

'There's no putting anything over you,' Huang Biao said. 'I do have donkey, but it's for Boss Lan. He's entertaining some VIPs from the municipal government tonight.'

'Donkey? For the VIPs? Is it that little black donkey over from South Mountain?'

'Yes. Meat so good I could eat half a pound of it myself—raw.'

'And you plan to give it to those men? What a waste!' I was beside myself. 'Cook up a couple of chunks of camel. Their mouths and tongues will be so numb from liquor and cigarettes that they won't be able to tell the difference.'

'But Boss Lan will . . .'

'Take him aside and tell him you fed the donkey to Xiaotong. He won't mind.' I was not interested in making things easy for Huang Biao.

'I'm not happy about feeding this meat to those louts either. I'd rather feed it to that dog in the doorway.'

'Is that snide comment meant for me?'

'Oh, no,' Huang Biao rushed to his own defence. 'You could give me two more gonads and I still wouldn't have the balls to do that. Besides, we've been friends for a long time. And the only reason I've been able to keep my job here is because I've got you, a gourmand, to back me up. My cooking skills have not gone to waste if they've managed to make you happy. Just watching you eat meat—I'm not just saying this—is a true pleasure, more satisfying than embracing my wife in bed—'

'Enough sweet talk,' I said impatiently. 'Bring out the donkey meat.' I loved being flattered but I didn't want to show it. I couldn't let any of those petty individuals see what made me so special. No, I had to remain a mystery to them, full of complexities. I had to make them forget my age and remember my authority.

Huang Biao went over to a cupboard behind the stove and brought out the portion of donkey meat, lovingly wrapped in a fresh lotus leaf, and placed it on the stool in front of me. What I need to make clear here is that, given my special status and position, I could have had him deliver the meat to me in my office. But I've always been particular about my surroundings when I eat, like the big cats that take their kill back to their lairs and then eat it an unhurried pace. A tiger takes its kill to its den, a panther to the crotch of its favourite tree. An unhurried meal in a safe and familiar spot is the height of enjoyment. Ever since the day I first stole into the plant's kitchen through the sewage ditch, and was rewarded by a truly satisfying meal, I'd developed a fondness for this spot, like a conditioned reflex. Other comforts included sitting on the same low stool, having the same tall stool in front of me and eating out of the same bowl while keeping an eye on the same pot. I must admit that my motivation for wanting to work at United, and then for working as hard as I did, was so that I could sit in the kitchen and enjoy a proper meal of our meat products whenever I wanted. So that I never had to steal in through the sewage ditch like a dog, sneak a bowlful of meat and then sneak out the same way. Imagine wallowing in the sewer after finishing off a bowlful of meat—now you know why I set my sights on the job.

Huang Biao started to peel away the lotus leaf but I stopped him. He was too stupid to realize that peeling away the meat's wrapping gave as much pleasure to me as disrobing a woman did to Lan Laoda.

'I've never disrobed one of my women myself,' Lan Laoda says unemotionally. 'They take off their own clothes. That's how it has to be,' he says behind me. 'After the age of forty, I no longer touched their breasts nor kissed them nor took them in the missionary position. Doing so would have stirred my emotions and that would have made my world collapse.'

A cloud of white steam rose from the meat as I peeled away the lotus leaf, scorched black by the heat. Donkey, ah, donkey, dear, dear donkey. The aroma brought tears to my eyes. I tore off a piece but, before I could put it in my mouth, Jiaojiao stuck her head in the doorway. As greedy and as knowledgeable, if not as well informed, a meat-eater as I, her tender age meant that she had a much deeper appreciation for meat than most people. Usually we ate together, but that day I had to mull something over and didn't want her sitting across from me and interfering with my train of thought. I waved her in, tore off a hunk of meat twice the size of my fist and offered it to her: 'There's something I need to think over, so take this and enjoy it.'

'All right,' she said. 'There's something I need to think over too.'

She left. I turned to Huang Biao: 'You can go too. Leave me alone for the next hour.'

With a nod, he walked out.

I looked down at the beautiful meat and listened to its contented whispers. Squinting, I could envision the way this piece had been taken off of the lovely, clever little black donkey. Like a butterfly that had flown off its body and fluttered into the pot, from there to the cupboard and finally, here, to me. The whispered words that came through most clearly were: 'I've been waiting for you . . .'

'Eat me now, don't waste a minute,' it then gushed softly. 'I'll grow cold if you don't hurry, and stringy . . .'

Whenever I hear meat passionately urging me to eat it, my heart soars and my eyes begins to water. If I'm not careful I may even burst into tears. I've made a fool of myself more than once in the past—sitting in a crowd, eating meat and crying like a baby. But that's ancient history. The weepy carnivore Luo Xiaotong was grown up now. Enjoying a meal of emotional, sensitive donkey meat, he was busy trying to figure out how to transport live, water-treated animals from the meat-cleansing workshop to the kill rooms, a technological problem with momentous impact on United's meat production.

My first brainstorm was about a series of conveyor belts from the injection station to the various kill rooms. But I rejected that. Even though Lao Lan had said not to worry about the cost, I knew that the plant's finances were tight and I didn't want to add to my parents' money worries. I was also aware that the plant had inherited its electrical system from the canvas factory and that its old, frayed wires and transformers were already overloaded. The system would collapse it it had to power conveyor belts carrying tonnes of cows. Next, I considered sending the animals into the kill rooms on the hoof, that is, perform the treatment there and then slaughter. But that would put the newly created meat-cleansing building out of commission even before it was up and running. And I'd be out of a job. Even more important was the fact that the animals receiving the water treatment continuously emptied their bowels and their bladders. Slaughtering them amid all that filth would affect the quality of the meat. Every animal sent out from the meat-cleansing workshop was supposed to be clean, inside and out; that was what separated United from independent butchers and all other meat-packing plants.

The donkey meat sang in my mouth as my brain went into high gear, each discarded idea quickly replaced by a new one. In the end, I came up with a solution that both suited local conditions and was simple and cheap. Lao Lan's eyes flashed in excitement when I explained it to him: 'You really are something, youngster!' he said with a pat on the shoulder. 'I approve. Put it into operation.'

'I guess that's what we'll have to do,' said Father.

At the workshop's exit, I had a team of workers build a rack with five thick fir posts. Then a hoist atop the rack with a block and tackle, christened

the 'lifting gourd'. Another team joined two flatbeds to make a moveable platform. With that device, when the workers led or dragged a water-treated cow
or some other large animal to the exit—standing if possible, lying if not—a
rope was placed under its belly to hoist it up onto the platform, which was
then pushed and pulled—two men on each end—rumbling straight into one
of the kill rooms.

What happened to it there was not our concern.

Water-injected large livestock no longer presented a problem. As for
pigs, sheep, dogs and other domestic animals—well, they're not even worth
a mention.

My narrative is cut short by the wail of ambulance sirens, one from West City and another from East City. Then two more out from each, making it a total of six. When they meet on the highway, two turn onto the grass field, leaving the remaining four in the middle of the road. Their flashing red and green lights heighten the tension and terror in the air. EMTs in white smocks, white caps and blue masks, some carrying medical bags, others lugging simple stretchers, rush out of the ambulances in the direction of the meat-vendors, where people have formed a dozen or more tight circles. The medics push people out of their way to get to the stricken—some lying unconscious, some rolling on the ground, some others bent over, vomiting. People pat the backs of their retching friends, and family members kneel beside the unconscious and anxiously call out their names. The medics first examine and tend the unconscious and those rolling on the ground. Then up onto the stretchers they go, to be carried off to the ambulances. There are not enough stretchers so an EMT asks for help to carry or help poison victims to the ambulances. The medical vehicles halt traffic from both directions and, in no time, more than forty cars are stopped, bumper to bumper. They do not suffer in silence, however, and announce their displeasure with a barrage of blaring horns. It's the worst noise in the world. If I were king of the world, Wise Monk, I'd destroy every single horn and horn-blower. Now come the police cars and the police. A policeman drags a truck-driver out of his cab because he refuses to stop honking. The driver resists, and his surly manner so angers the policeman that he grabs the man by the throat and throws him into a ditch. The driver crawls out, soaked, and screams in a heavy accent: 'I'll sue, damn it! All you cops are thugs!' The policeman takes a step in his direction and the driver jumps back into the ditch. With the police directing traffic, the ambulances bearing the poison victims drive onto the temple grounds, then turn and speed off to their respective hospitals through the slender spaces between the lines of cars. The *police cars lead the way. A policeman sticks his head out the window and orders the drivers to clear a path. Another group of poison victims has collected on the grassy field, the sound of their retching and moaning merging with the shouts of the police directing traffic. The police have commandeered several private vans to take the sick into town, ignoring the drivers' complaints. 'Who told those people to eat so much?' grouses a low-ranking Party official. His comment draws a glare from a large, swarthy policeman. Thus silenced, he stands by the road and lights a cigarette. Now van-less drivers begin to congregate in our compound. Some poke their heads inside the temple, others gape at the Meat God lying out in the sun. One of them, delighted at the calamity that has struck the enviable Carnivore Festival, says: 'Well, folks, I think we're witnessing the end of the Carnivore Festival.' 'The whole thing's ridiculous,' another agrees. 'Baldy Hu was looking to make a big splash. It was a terrible idea but his superiors think the world of him and let him go ahead. He's in big trouble now, and he'll be lucky if no one dies. If lots of people die—' A woman with piercing eyes steps out from behind a tree and interrupts in a severe tone of voice: 'If lots of people die, Chairman Wu, what good will that do you?' 'I was just thinking aloud,' the man replies, obviously embarrassed, 'and I apologize. We were about to phone the hospital to send help for you.' The woman, a cadre herself, shouts into her cellphone: 'It's beyond urgent! To hell with the cost! Mobilize everything you've got, personnel, money, everything. Punish anyone who stands in the way!' A small fleet of Audi A6s drives up with a police escort, and Mayor Hu steps out of the car. On-site cadres rush to report. The mayor's face grows grave at the enormity of the situation and he walks towards some of the stricken individuals.*

With Father (actually, with me) in command, the United Meatpacking Plant began production as scheduled.

I was enjoying a meal in the kitchen.

'Your father's the plant manager,' Huang Biao said, 'but you run the show.'

'I'd be careful with what I say, Huang Biao,' I replied sternly although I was secretly pleased with his words. 'My father won't be pleased that thought.'

'It's not just what I think, my young friend. It's what everyone thinks. I can't help repeating what I hear. It's my nature. I just thought you'd like to know.'

'What else do they think?' I said, trying to sound casual.

'That sooner or later Lao Lan will fire your father and hire you in his place. If you ask me, there's no need to be humble when that day comes. Having officials for parents is never as good as being one yourself.'

I turned my attention back to the meat in front of me and ignored him but I didn't ask him to stop. His flattering remarks—half true, half false— were like spice for the meat, stimulating my appetite and giving me a sense of true comfort. When I finished the meat, I felt replenished and sated. It now lay in my stomach, waiting to be digested, as I drifted off into a state of suspended animation, as if afloat in the ether. Thinking back now, those were among the happiest days of my life. When I first went to the plant kitchen to feast on meat during working hours, I did so on the sly so as not to be seen. But the day came when I could openly enjoy my meals. When we were gearing up for production in the workshop, I'd say: 'Yao Qi, take over while I go to the kitchen to think.'

'Go ahead, Director, leave everything to me,' he'd reply deferentially. 'I'll let you know if there are problems.'

I gave such heavy responsibilities to Yao Qi not to patch up relations between him and my parents but because he'd become such a good worker— it was the right thing to do. I had no authority to give him an official title or status but he was the de facto director when I was away. I'd also planned to repay the kindnesses of Cheng Tianle, but he had changed and not for the better. He walked about with a frown and never said a word, as if people owed him money and refused to pay it back. My good opinion of him was pretty much a thing of the past.

It was clear that many of the men, including Yao Qi, resented the fact that I ate in the plant kitchen during working hours. I had no way of knowing what truly lay behind the the sweet words and smiles with which he greeted me. But I had no time to waste worrying about that. Why should I? Meat was my life, my love; the meat that went into my stomach, and only that meat, was mine. Meat in my stomach made me carefree and happy, and if the men were unhappy, if they were envious, if they drooled at the thought of it, even if they were downright angry, that was no concern of mine. They could drop dead for all I cared.

I told Lao Lan and my parents that the way to ensure that United flourished was to see that I remained strong and vigorous and that my creative juices kept flowing. An endless supply of meat guaranteed both. The only thing that kept my brain functioning was a bellyful of meat. Without it, my brain was like rusty machinery. My parents withheld their response to my request but Lao Lan roared with laughter.

'Luo Xiaotong,' he said, 'Director Luo, is there even a remote chance that this plant could not supply you with the meat you desire? No, I want you to eat. Eat as much as you can, set a new standard of eating, create a model of eating and, in the process, establish the prestige of our plant.' He turned to my parents. 'Lao Luo, Yang Yuzhen, meat-eaters are fated to enjoy prosperity and power. Paupers are not blessed with a well-developed digestive system. Do you believe that? Well, I do. The quantity of meat any individual is slated to eat is predetermined at birth. For you, Luo Xiaotong, the quantity is probably twenty tonnes, and the King of Hell will see that you eat every bit of it.' Another hearty laugh, this time joined in by my parents.

'We're lucky United Meatpacking is in financial good shape,' Mother said. 'Any other plant would have gone bankrupt!'

'Why don't we organize a meat-eating competition?' said Lao Lan in a burst of inspiration. 'We can hold it in the city, even show it on TV. Then, when Xiaotong takes first place, United gets free advertising.' Waving his fist excitedly, he carried on. 'It's great idea! Think about it—a mere boy finishes off a platter of meat! But that's not all—he can hear meat talk, he can see its face. He can't lose, and the image of him destroying the competition is beamed into thousands and tens of thousands of living rooms. The impact will be mind-boggling! Xiaotong, you'll be famous! And as you, director of a workshop at United Meatpacking, will be feasting on our meat products, we'll be famous too. Huachang meats will be the best brand of all, and all the consumers will trust only our meat. Xiaotong, eating meat will be your finest contribution, and the more you eat the greater the contribution.'

'First place in meat-eating?' Father shook his head. 'He'll be seen as nothing but an empty vessel for food and drink.'

'Lao Luo, your backsliding has become serious,' commented Lao Lan. 'Don't you watch TV? Contests like this are all the rage—beer-drinking, meat-pie-eating, even leaf-eating. In fact, everything *but* meat-eating. No, we're going to do it. The effect will be felt not only in China but worldwide. Our meat products will show up in shops all over the world. Everywhere, people will be able to enjoy Huachang meats—meats you can trust. And when that happens, Luo Xiaotong, you'll have achieved international fame.'

'Lao Lan,' Mother said with a smile, 'have you got drunk on meat, like Xiaotong?'

'Not having your son's talent or luck, I don't know what it feels like to be drunk on meat. But I can, unlike you two, appreciate his vivid imagination. Your biggest problem is that you see your son through the eyes of parents. That's a mistake. First, forget he's a child, and second, forget he's your son. If you can't do that, you'll never be able to discover his value, his unique gift.' Lao Lan turned to me: 'Worthy Nephew, let's settle this here and now. We'll organize a meat-eating contest, if not in the next six months then some time later in the year, and if that fails then next year. Your sister is a talented meat-eater, too, isn't she? She can be a part of what will be a true sensation . . .' There were tears in his eyes as he continued: 'Worthy Nephew Xiaotong, all sorts of feelings rise up in me when I'm in the presence of a boy who knows how to eat meat. There are two meat-eating virtuosos in this world, you and the son of my third uncle, who sadly died way before his time . . .'

A while later, Huang Biao was ordered to set up a new stove in the kitchen, one that could accommodate a larger pot; it was to be reserved for Luo Xiaotong's exclusive use. Huang Biao was then ordered that stock be constantly boiling in the pot and the meat cooking at all times. A ready supply of meat for Luo Xiaotong was the key to United's prosperity.

Word soon got out of my daily supply of free meat, as well as of Lao Lan's plan of sponsoring a meat-eating contest. One day, three unhappy workers confronted me at the entrance to the meat-cleansing building. 'Xiaotong,' they said, 'just because your father is the manager and your mother is the bookkeeper, and just because you're the director of this workshop and Lao Lan's protégé, does not mean that we have to kowtow to you! What makes you so special anyway? You can't read—a blind man can open his eyes but he still can't see—which makes filling that big belly of yours with meat your only talent.'

'First of all, I'm not Lao Lan's protégé,' I interrupted. 'Next, I know enough characters to read what's important. As for my talent, I'm good at eating meat but I don't have a big belly. Tell me, would you call this a big belly? Eating lots of meat with a big belly is nothing to boast of. Eating the same quantity with a small belly is. If you don't want to kowtow to me, go tell Lao Lan. We can have a contest. If I lose, I'll step down as workshop director and leave the plant for good. I'll go out into the world or back to school. Of course, if I lose, someone else will have to enter the contest, maybe one of you.'

'It won't do us any good to go tell Lao Lan,' they said. 'You may deny you're his protégé but it's obvious you two have a special relationship. Otherwise, there's no way he'd have appointed a boy without a hair on his crotch as workshop director and given him the right to eat all the meat he wants.'

'If you want to out-eat me, I accept the challenge. There's no need to disturb Lao Lan over something so silly.'

'That's exactly what we want,' they said. 'To see who's the champion meat-eater. You can count us as your drill squad. If you can't beat us, you can forget about entering a real contest. It would be humiliating, and not just for you. The plant would suffer, and that would include us. So we challenge you to a contest, at least in part as an expression of fairness.'

'Good,' I said. 'We can start tomorrow and, since public spirit has entered the picture, I'm going to take this very seriously. Now we must inform Lao Lan, but don't worry, I'll assume full responsibility. And we need to establish ground rules and conditions. First, of course, is quantity. If you eat a pound and I eat eight ounces, that's simple, I lose. Next, speed. If we both eat a pound but I finish in half an hour while it takes you an hour, I win. Third, post-contest. Anyone who throws up what he's eaten can't win. Style points are received only by keeping down what you've eaten. Oh, and one more thing. One round won't be enough—the contest must stretch over three days, or five, even a week or a month. In other words, all contestants have to come back day after day. Someone might be able to eat three pounds the first day but only two the next and by the third day he's lucky if he can get down one. A person like that isn't a true meat-eater and definitely not a meat-lover. Meat-lovers have an ongoing relationship with meat, day after day. We never tire of eating it—'

'That's enough! You're can't scare us off with bluster. All we're talking about here is stuffing meat into your mouth. So, whoever eats the most in the shortest time without puking wins, right?'

I nodded.

'Then go talk to Lao Lan. We'll be waiting to begin. I'd like to start today,' said one of them, patting his stomach. 'This belly hasn't been greased in a long time.'

'It's best to ask your un-patron to lay out plenty of meat,' said one of his companions, 'I can eat half a cow at one sitting.'

'Half a cow? That's nothing!' another retorted. 'Half a cow will just get me started. I can finish off the whole thing.'

'All right! Wait here. And try not to eat anything until the contest so you can start with an empty stomach.'

'Don't worry,' they laughed, patting their stomachs, 'they're empty all right!'

'And I think you'd better go home and make arrangements with your families. Too much meat can be fatal for some.'

Their eyes blazed with contempt for a moment and then they burst out laughing. 'Not to worry, youngster,' one of them said. 'Our lives aren't worth anything.'

'And even if it's fatal,' said another, 'at least we'll die happy!'

The enormous hulk that was Lan Laoda's son, surrounded by fresh-cut blooms, lies not so much on the bier as on a bed of flowers. Dozens of mourn-ers—all in black—walk round it amid the soft sounds of funereal music. Lan Laoda stands, bent at the waist, looking down into the face of his son. Then he straightens up, raises his head and faces the mourners with a broad smile. 'From the day he was born,' he says, 'my son lived in the lap of luxury. He knew neither suffering nor worry. His only wish in life was to eat meat, and that wish was never denied him.' Looking down at the hillock that was his son's belly, then continues: 'After consuming a tonne of meat, he slipped away pain-lessly in his sleep. His was a happy life, and I carried out all the responsibilities of a father. What I find most gratifying is that I was with him when he died and that I am now giving him the finest funeral possible. If a nether-world exists, my son will never know an unhappy moment, and now that he is gone I have no more concerns. I am hosting a banquet at the manor tonight, to which you are all invited. Please come in your finest clothes and bring lovely women with you to share the best food and drink money can buy.' At the manor that evening, Lan Laoda raises an amber glass of VSOP brandy, immersed in the aromas of gourmet dishes, the liquor swirling in his glass, and announces grandly: 'To my son, who knew the best that life has to offer and who then passed away peacefully!' Grief seems not to have touched him, not at all.

An outdoor contest between the three workers and me commenced in front of the plant kitchen.

The episode occupied my reveries in the days and months that followed, and never failed to make my mind wander far from whatever I was doing or thinking at the moment. It would always be that day all over again.

The contest was set for six in the evening. It was the end of the day shift, and time for the night-shift workers to arrive. It was midsummer, the longest day of the year. The sun was still high in the sky, and the peasants had not yet come home from the fields. The wheat harvest was in and the smell lingered in the air. New wheat lay drying in the sun on the road in front of the plant gate and the occasional gust of wind carried the smell of farmland into the compound. Though we continued to live in the village and were listed as village residents, we were no longer a peasant household. We water-injected the animals in the day and slaughtered them in the night. The inspectors added their blue stamps to the meat and we sent the meat into town. Uncle Han's meat inspector showed up dutifully, ready to stamp the meat, a paragon of responsible public service. But not for long; after the first few nights he left his stamp and inkpad in the kill room for us to do it ourselves. In order to prevent the injected water from leaking out and lowering the weight and, more importantly, the quality, of the meat, we sprayed its surface with an anti-leak substance (which neither protected nor endangered the health of the consumer). Since we hadn't yet installed cold-storage rooms, the meat had to be delivered the same day the animals were slaughtered. We owned three delivery trucks that had been modified to carry fresh meat, and which were driven by ex-servicemen hired for their ace driving skills, their take-no-prisoners attitude and their alarming appearance. You wouldn't want to mess with these men. At about two every morning, a pair of ageing gatekeepers pushed open United's loudly creaking steel gate and the delivery trucks, loaded with trustworthy meat, slipped out of the compound, one after the other, made quick turns and then slid onto the highway. Their breathing adjusted, like spirited horses, they then gathered speed and their headlights lit up the road to town. I knew that the trucks carried nothing but meat injected with clean well water to guarantee its freshness and safety. But every time I watched them slip out of the compound in the pre-dawn darkness and then speed up the highway, I would be possessed of the nagging feeling that their cargo was actually contraband—not meat but explosives or drugs.

Here I must put to rest the long-standing misconception that all water-injected meat is contaminated. Admittedly, when individual families in Slaughterhouse Village illegally injected their meat with water amid unsanitary conditions and via unsanitary procedures, much of what was produced was of an inferior quality. But at United, the move from post-slaughter to pre-slaughter injection was nothing less than revolutionary, a turning point in animal-slaughter history. Lao Lan said it best: 'One cannot overstate the significance of this revolutionary moment.' And there was another important factor that ensured that United's water-injected meat was fresher than everything else: we could have used tap water but we didn't, since it contained additives like chlorine. Our products were what we now call organic, with no chemical additives. Which is why I insisted we treat our animals with pure, crystalline well water, water superior to both its distilled and mineral counterparts. It was like fine wine. Red, puffy eyes caused by internal heat can be cured with just one bath in our spring water. Yellow urine also caused by internal heat clears up completely after two cups of the same. Since this is what we injected in our animals before their slaughter, you can imagine the superior quality of the meat they produced. If you could not eat our meat with complete confidence, then you were a pathological worrywart. Everyone complimented us on our products, which were sold exclusively in urban supermarkets. I hope that when people hear about water-injected meat, they won't think of putrid meat produced in filthy, illegal butcher sites. Our meat was succulent, bursting with flavour and glowing with the air of youth. Too bad I can't show you any of our water-injected meat, too bad I can't recreate my sterling achievements, too bad I can only experience my, as well as United Meatpacking Plant's, glorious history by calling upon my memories.

When the rest of the workers heard about the meat-eating contest, the day-shifters stayed back and the night-shifters showed up early. A crowd of more than a hundred filled the yard outside the kitchen to see the spectacle unfold . . . At this point in my narrative, I need to stop and talk about something else. Back in the day of street-corner storytellers, this is what they called 'one plant, double stems, two flowers, focusing on one first'.

During a rest period back in the commune era, when the villagers combined their labour, two individuals took part in a chilli-pepper-eating contest. The winner was to receive a pack of cigarettes, donated by the production team leader. The competitors were my father and Lao Lan. Both were fifteen or sixteen at the time—no longer boys, not yet men. The peppers chosen for the contest were no run-of-the-mill variety but of a special type known as goat horns. Each contestant was given forty long, thick, purple peppers, just one of which was capable of reducing most men to crying for their mothers. The team leader's pack of cigarettes would not be easily won. Not knowing what my father and Lao Lan looked like back then, I've had to rely on my imagination. They were friends but they were also rivals, each trying to outdo the other at activities like wrestling, usually without a clear winner or loser. It does not take much imagination to conjure up a picture of two men eating forty peppers each; on the other hand, it's a scene impossible to describe. Forty goat horn peppers create a substantial pile, tipping the scales at two pounds at least. No clear winner emerged after the first round of twenty, nor after the second. The judge, their production team leader, observing how red the combatants' faces had grown, fearfully called it a draw and offered each a pack of cigarettes. They would have none of that. So, on to the third round, with twenty more peppers. When they were halfway through the seventeenth pepper, Lao Lan tossed it along with his last two to the ground and conceded defeat. Almost immediately he bent over, his arms wrapped round his stomach, his face covered with sweat, and spewed out a stream of green—some said purple—liquid. My father finished his eighteenth pepper but, before he could bite into the nineteenth, blood began to seep out of his nostrils. The production leader sent a member of his team to buy two packs of the most expensive cigarettes. That contest became one of the village's most significant events of the commune era, and no talk of an eating competition ever ended without its mention. A few years later, a fritter-eating contest was held at the station restaurant between one of the porters—a man so well known for his appetite that he was nicknamed Big Belly Wu—and my father, then eighteen. Father was delivering beets to the station with other members of his team. Big Belly Wu was strutting up and down the platform, patting his belly and daring one of them to take him up on his challenge. Disgusted by the man's behaviour, the team leader asked what the challenge entailed. 'Eating!' Wu replied. 'I can out-eat anyone!' 'That's a boast I don't think you can back up,' laughed the team leader. 'That's Big Belly Wu!' someone sidled up to him and whispered. 'This is his hangout, and this is how he gets free meals. He can eat so much at one sitting that he doesn't have to eat again for three days.' The team leader glanced at my father and gave another little laugh. 'My friend, there's always a better man and a higher heaven.' 'I'm ready to find out if you are,' grinned Wu. 'What are you eating?' asked the team leader, not willing to pass up a chance at some excitement. Big Belly Wu pointed to the station restaurant. 'They've got stuffed buns,' he said, 'fritters, noodles with shredded pork and steamed bread. You choose. The loser pays, the winner eats free.' The team leader looked again at my father: 'Luo Tong, do you feel like taking him down a peg?' 'Fine with me,' replied Father in a muffled voice, 'but what if I lose? I don't have any money.' 'You won't lose,' his team leader assured him, 'but don't worry if you do. The money will come from the production team.' 'I'll do it then,' my father said. 'I haven't eaten a fritter for a very long time.' 'All right,' Wu said, 'fritters it is.' The crowd noisily made its way over to the restaurant. Wu took my father's hand and led him in, to all appearances a friendly gesture between old friends. Truth be known, he was afraid that Father would back out. A shout of 'Big Belly Wu's back!' from a waitress greeted them as they entered. 'What's on today's contest menu, Big Belly?' 'Who are you to call me Big Belly?' Wu complained. 'You should be calling me Grandpa.' 'Hah! And you can call me Aunty!' The other employees rushed over to watch as soon as they heard that Big Belly Wu was putting on another eating contest. The few diners looked on wide-eyed. The assistant manager walked up, wiping his hands on his apron: 'Wu, what'll it be this time?' After a quick glance at my father, Wu said: 'Fritters. We'll start with three pounds apiece. How's that, young fellow?' 'Fine with me,' my father muttered. 'I'll match you pound for pound.' 'That's pretty big talk from a pipsqueak like you,' retorted Wu. 'I've hung round this station for more than a decade and defeated at least a hundred challengers.' 'Well, you've met your match today,' said the team leader. 'This young fellow's polished off a hundred eggs at one sitting, then topped it off with a whole hen. Three pounds of fritters won't make a dent in his appetite, isn't that so, Luo Tong?' 'We'll see,' my father said, keeping his head down. 'I'm not one to brag.' 'Good!' Big Belly said excitedly. 'Bring out the fritters, girls, straight out of the oil.' 'Not so fast, Wu,' said the assistant manager. 'You'll have to pay up front.' 'Talk to them,' said Wu, pointing at the team leader, 'since they're going to have to come up with the money sooner or later.' 'Says who, Big Brother? We can afford to pay for six pounds of fritters, three each, but there's that saying: "Eating a pile of shit is no big deal, except for the taste." How can you be so sure we're going to lose?' Wu wiggled his thumb in the team leader's face: 'All right, maybe I've been a little rude and have offended you. How's this: we'll each take out enough for six pounds of fritters and lay it on the counter. The winner can pick his share and walk out, the loser can walk out but leave his share behind.

Does that sound fair?' The team leader thought it over for a moment: 'Yes, it's fair. But our villagers are pretty gruff people who don't mince their words, so don't make a scene.' Wu fished out some greasy notes and laid them on the counter. The team leader did the same. Then a waitress covered the stacks with upside-down bowls to keep them from flying away. 'Can we start, ladies and gentlemen?' Wu asked. The assistant manager turned to the waitresses. 'Go on, bring out the fritters for Master Wu and this fellow, three pounds apiece, and let the yardarm stick up a bit.' 'You scoundrels always shortchange your diners,' laughed Wu, 'but for a contest you want the yardarm to stick up a bit. I want you all to know that anyone who comes here either to throw down or to accept a challenge is no pushover. As the saying goes: "You don't swallow a sickle unless you've got a curved stomach." If it's an eating contest, what difference does it make if the yardarm is up or down. Isn't that right, young fellow?' My father ignored him. While Wu was holding forth, waitresses carried out a pair of enamel trays piled high with oil fritters and laid them on the table. Obviously fresh, they were big and fluffy, fragrant and steaming hot. 'Can I start?' my father asked the team leader politely. Before the team leader could give the OK, Wu had picked up one of the fritters and bitten off half. With bulging cheeks and moist eyes, he stared at the tray, his hunger clearly raging. My father sat down. 'If you'll excuse me,' he said to the team leader and the villagers, 'then I'll start.' With an apologetic look at the spectators, he began to eat at an easy, steady pace, taking ten bites to finish a foot-long fritter and chewing slowly before swallowing. Not Wu, who was not so much eating the things as stuffing them down a hole. The piles shrank. By the time five remained on Wu's tray and eight on my father's, each swallow took longer and caused greater distress. That they were suffering was obvious. Then there were only two left on Wu's tray, and the pace had slowed to a crawl. There were also two left on my father's tray. The end game had arrived. They ate their last fritters at the same time, after which Big Belly Wu stood up. But he sat right back down, weighed down by his body. The contest had ended in a draw. Suddenly my father said: 'I can eat one more.' The assistant manager turned to a waitress: 'Hurry,' he said excitedly, 'this fellow says he can eat one more.' The waitress fished one out of the oil with her chopsticks, looking jubilant. 'Are you all right, Luo Tong?' the team leader asked. 'If not, just stop. We don't care about the little bit those fritters cost.' Without a word, my father took the fritter from the waitress, tore it into little balls and put them into his mouth, one at a time. 'I want another one, too,' Big Belly called out. When the waitress handed it to him, he put it up to his mouth, ready to take a bite but unable to. Agony was written all over his face and tears ran from his eyes. He laid it back on the table and said feebly: 'I lose . . .' He tried to stand again, and did so for a moment before sitting down so heavily the chair groaned and squealed before collapsing under his weight.

The contest over, Big Belly Wu was sent to the hospital, where he was opened up and the half-eaten fritters labouriously removed from his stomach. My father was not sent to the hospital, but he paced the riverbank all night long, stopping to bend over and vomit every few steps, leaving behind a partial fritter each time. A pack of half-starved dogs, eyes ravenously blue, followed him, eventually joined by dogs from neighbouring villages. They fought tooth and nail over my father's regurgitated fritters, from the top of the riverbank down to the river itself and back up. I didn't witness the events, of course, but they have created a vivid scene in my imagination. It was a frightful night, and my father was lucky the dogs didn't eat him too. If they had, I wouldn't be here. He never did describe to me what it felt like to throw up all those fritters. Whenever my curiosity got the better of me and I asked about his chilli and fritter contests, his face would redden. 'Shut up!' he'd snap. I'd obviously be touching a nerve, a very painful one. Though he never said so, I knew he'd suffered grievously over those fifty-nine chilli peppers and the three pounds of oil fritters. Back then, people added alum and alkaline to the flour along with sodium carbonate. The unrefined cottonseed oil they used was so black it was almost green, and highly viscous, like tar. And it was loaded with chemicals like gossypol, DDVP and benzine hexachloride, pesticides that do not easily break down. My father's throat must have felt like it had been scraped raw and his stomach must have bulged like a taut drumhead. Unable to bend over, he must have taken painfully slow steps, holding his belly tenderly with both hands, as if it might explode. He must have seen the flashing eyes of the dogs behind him, green like will-o'-the-wisps. I'll bet he thought that those dogs could hardly wait to rip open his belly to get at the fritters inside, and that thought led to another, that once they'd finished off all the fritters, they'd turn on him, starting with his internal organs, then his flesh and finally his bones.

Given that history, Father frowned at my report to him and Lao Lan about the meat-eating contest between the three workers and me. 'No,' he said sternly. 'Don't get involved in anything that shameless.' 'Shameless?' I retorted. 'How? Don't people tell the story of the pepper-eating contest between you and Lao Lan with admiration?' Father banged his fist on the table. 'We were poor,' he said, 'do you understand?' 'Poor!' Lao Lan tried to cool the air: 'It was more than that. You took the challenge to eat fritters because you loved the things, but the chilli-eating contest between you and me was for more than just a crummy pack of smokes.' Lao Lan's words took the edge off of Father's anger. 'There's nothing wrong with contests,' he said, 'except for eating contests. A person's stomach can only hold so much but the supply of good food is limitless. Even if you win, you're gambling with your health. However much you eat is how much you have to throw back up.' That made Lao Lan laugh. 'Lao Luo,' he said, 'don't get carried away. If Xiaotong thinks he's up to it, I don't see anything wrong in organizing a preview for the meat-eating contests.' My father calmly stood his ground. 'No,' he said, 'I can't allow it. You have no idea how it felt.' My mother's anxieties arose out of a different concern: 'Xiaotong,' she said, 'you're a growing boy, and your stomach is no match for those young men. It wouldn't be a fair fight.' 'Well, since your parents don't want you to do it,' Lao Lan said, 'then forget it. I couldn't bear it if something happened.' But I refused to back down. 'You don't understand me, none of you. I have a special relationship with meat and a special ability to process it in my digestive system.' 'I agree,' Lao Lan said, 'you're a meat-boy but it's too risky. You need to realize that you're our hope for the future. We're counting on you to implement many innovations for United.' 'Dieh, Niang, Uncle Lan,' I said, 'I know what I'm doing, you don't have to worry. First, take my word for it, they can't win. Second, I'm not about to gamble with my health. Actually, I'm worried about them and suggest that we get them to sign waivers so we're not responsible for any consequences.' 'That's something we can do if you insist on going through with this contest,' Lao Lan said, 'but I want a guarantee that you'll be in no danger.' 'I can't say this about everything,' I said reassuringly, 'but I have absolute confidence in my digestive system. Do you have any idea how much meat I put away every morning in the plant kitchen? Go ask Huang Biao.' Lao Lan turned to my parents: 'Lao Luo, Yang Yuzhen, why don't we let him go ahead? My worthy nephew's capacity for meat is the stuff of legend, and we know that his reputation is based on eating and not boasting. We can take the precaution of having a doctor sent over from the hospital to deal with any emergency.' 'Not for my sake,' I said, 'but it's a good idea to have one on hand for the safety of my rivals.' 'Xiaotong,' my father said sternly, 'in the eyes of your mother and me you're no longer a child, so you're responsible for your actions.' 'Dieh,' I said with a laugh, 'what are you so worried about? What are we talking about here?—a meal. I eat every day—I'll just eat a little more for the contest. And I may not even have to. If they throw in the towel early, it's possible I'll end up eating less than usual.'

My father was hoping that the contest would be a low-key event but Lao Lan said: 'If we go ahead with this, then it has to be a public affair. Otherwise, it's a waste of time.' Needless to say, I was hoping for a larger audience and not just the workers in the plant. Ideally, we'd put up posters or blare it over PA systems to attract people from the train station, from the county and township and other villages. The bigger the crowd the greater the people's emotional involvement. What I really wanted was to establish my authority at the plant and make a name for myself in the world. I wanted to win over all those people who had doubts about me, and then have them admit that Luo Xiaotong's reputation was not undeserved but earned one bite at a time. And I wanted to show my three rivals that they had thrown the gauntlet down in front of the wrong person. They had to realize that while meat is good to eat it's hard to digest. If you aren't equipped with a digestive system specially designed for it, your troubles begin with your very first swallow.

I knew they were in trouble even before the contest began, and that their punishment would be doled out not by Lao Lan, not by my parents and not by me, but by the meat they sent into their stomachs. People in Slaughter-house Village like to say that a person has been 'bitten' by meat. That means not that meat can grow teeth, but that a steady diet of it is bad for your stomach and intestines. I was sure that my rivals were going to be badly 'bitten' soon. I know you're strutting about looking forward to a real treat. But before long you'll wish that tears were the worst you'd suffer. No doubt they feel like kings at the moment, waiting to be celebrities at the end of the contest. Even if they lose, at least they'll have a stomach full of free meat. I knew that many among the audience would have the same idea; some would even be a bit envious and kick themselves for missing out on a great opportunity. Just wait, my friends, you'll soon stop kicking and start congratulating yourselves. For you are about to see what a spectacle these three make of themselves.

My challengers were Liu Shengli (Victory Liu), Feng Tiehan (Ironman Feng) and Wan Xiaojiang (Water Rat Wan). Liu, a big swarthy man with large staring eyes, was in the habit of rolling up his sleeves when he spoke. A coarse individual, he'd started out as a pig butcher. Since he was surrounded by animal flesh all day long, you'd have thought he'd gained some insight into the nature of meat. Now, gambling on meat-eating was stupid, but that's what he wanted to do so he must have had something up his sleeve. As they say: Good tidings don't just show up, and what shows up isn't always good. I'd have to keep my eye on him. Tall, skinny Feng, with his sallow complexion and bent back, looked like a man who'd just recovered from a serious illness. People with his complexion were rumoured to possess unique and astonishing skills. I'd once heard a blind storyteller say that among the hundred and eight Ming Dynasty bravehearts were several sallow-faced ones who were blessed with extraordinary fighting skills. I'd have to keep my eye on him too. Wan, nicknamed Water Rat, was small in stature, had a pointy mouth, cheeks like a chimp and triangular eyes. A first-rate swimmer, he could catch fish underwater with his eyes open. I'd heard nothing about him or any special capacity for meat, but everyone knew he was a champion watermelon-eater, and anyone who wants to be a champion eater must gain that reputation through competitions—it was the only way. Wan Xiaojiang once put away three whole watermelons by attacking them as if he were playing a harmonica, side to side, back and forth, spitting out the black seeds as he went along. Another one to keep my eye on.

I set out for the contest site. Jiaojiao walked behind me with a teapot. Her face was set tight, her forehead beaded with sweat.

'Don't be scared, Jiaojiao,' I said with a laugh.

'I'm not.' She wiped her forehead with her sleeve. 'I know you'll win.'

'Yes, I will,' I said. 'So would you, if you took my place.'

'No,' she said. 'My stomach isn't big enough yet. But some day.'

'Jiaojiao,' I said, taking her hand, 'we were sent down to earth to eat meat. Each of us is slated to eat twenty tonnes of it. If we don't, Yama won't let us in the underworld door. That's what Lao Lan said.'

'Great,' she said. 'But let's stick around after the twenty tonnes and then go for thirty. How much is thirty tonnes?'

'Thirty tonnes.' I had to think for a minute. 'It would make a little mountain of meat.'

She burst into happy laughter at the thought.

Turning at the meat-cleansing workshop door, we spotted a crowd in front of the kitchen at the same time as the crowd spotted us: 'Here they are . . .'

Jiaojiao gripped my hand tightly.

'Don't be scared,' I said.

'I'm not.'

The crowd parted to let us to walk up to the contest site. Four tables had been set up, each backed by a stool. My rivals were waiting. Liu Shengli bellowed at the kitchen door: 'Ready, Huang Biao? I can't wait any longer—I'm starved!'

Wan Xiaojiang went in and came right back out. 'What an aroma!' he rhapsodized. 'Meat, ah, meat, how I pine for you! Even my mother pales beside a plate of braised beef.'

Feng Tiehan was perched on his stool, smoking a cigarette, the picture of calm, as if the contest had nothing to do with him.

I nodded a greeting to the people who were staring at my sister and me, their looks either curious or reverential. Then I went over and sat on the stool next to Feng Tiehan. Jiaojiao stood beside me. 'I'm a little scared,' she whispered.

'Don't be,' I said.

'Want some tea?'

'No.'

'I have to pee.'

'Go on. Behind the kitchen.'

The crowd was whispering back and forth, too softly for me to hear, but I could guess what they were saying.

Feng Tiehan offered me a cigarette.

'No,' I said. 'Smoking affects the taste buds. Even the best meat loses its taste.'

'I shouldn't be doing this with you,' he said. 'You're just a boy. I'd hate it if something happened to you.'

I just smiled.

Jiaojiao returned and said softly: 'Lao Lan's here, but not Dieh or Niang.'

'I know.'

Liu Shengli and Wan Xiaojiang took their places behind their tables, Liu next to me and Wan next to him.

'We're all here,' Lao Lan announced. 'So we can start. Where's Huang Biao? Ready, Huang Biao?'

Huang Biao rushed out of the kitchen wiping his hands on a filthy towel. 'Ready! Shall I bring it out?'

'Bring it out,' ordered Lao Lan. 'Ladies and gentlemen, we are here today for the plant's first meat-eating contest. The contestants are Luo Xiaotong, Liu Shengli, Feng Tiehan and Wan Xiaojiang. This is a preview contest. The winner may well go on to represent the plant at one of the larger public contests to be held later. Since today holds great significance for the future, I want the contestants to pull out all the stops.' Lao Lan's comments excited the crowd, which began to chatter, the sound like birds careening into the sky. Lao Lan raised his hand and gestured for silence. 'That said, I must make something perfectly clear—each contestant takes full responsibility for himself. If there's an accident, the plant cannot be held liable. In other words, you're on your own.' He then pointed to a man elbowing his way through the crowd. 'Make room for the doctor.'

People turned to see the doctor, medical bag over his back, making his sweaty way to the front, where he then stood smiling, revealing two rows of yellowed teeth. 'Am I late?'

'No,' Lao Lan replied. 'We're just about to begin.'

'I was worried I'd be late. The minute the hospital director told me what he wanted me to do, I picked up my bag and came as fast as I could.'

'You're not late,' Lao Lan reassured him. 'You didn't have to rush.' Then he turned to us. 'Are the contestants ready?'

I glanced at my eager competitors and saw that they were all looking at me. I smiled and nodded, they nodded in return. Feng Tiehan smirked. Liu Shengli looked stern, his anger simmering just below the surface, like a man ready for a bitter fight and not one participating in a meat-eating contest. A silly smile was draped across the face of Wan Xiaojiang, replete with twitches and crinkles that drew laughter from the spectators. Liu and Wan's expressions enhanced my confidence—their loss was assured, inevitable. But I had trouble reading Feng's smirk. A barking dog never bites, and I had a hunch that this sallow-faced, smirking, composed rival was the one to look out for.

'All right, then. The doctor is here, you've all heard what I had to say, you know the rules and the meat has been prepared. We're ready to begin,' Lao Lan announced. 'I hereby declare the start of the inaugural Huachang United Meatpacking Plant meat-eating contest. Huang Biao, bring out the meat!'

'On its wa-a-a-y—' Like a server in a pre-revolution restaurant, Huang Biao drew out the call as he floated out of the kitchen holding a red plastic tub full of cooked meat. He was followed by three young women hired for the occasion. Clad in white uniforms, they moved swiftly, like a well-trained unit, smiling broadly and carrying a red tub each. Huang Biao placed his tub on the table in front of me, and the three young women did the same for my rivals.

Beef from our plant.

Chunks of fist-sized meat, cooked without recourse to condiments, not even salt.

All flank steaks.

'How many pounds?' Lao Lan asked.

'Five in each tub,' Huang Biao answered.

'I have a question,' Feng Tiehan said, raising his hand like a schoolboy.

'Go ahead,' Lao Lan said with a glare.

'Does each tub hold exactly the same amount? And all the same quality?'

Lao Lan looked to Huang Biao.

'All from the same cow!' Huang Biao confirmed. 'Cooked in the same pot, and exactly five pounds on a scale.'

Feng Tiehan shook his head.

'Someone must have defrauded you in the past,' Huang Biao said.

'Bring out the scale,' Lao Lan said.

Huang Biao grumbled as he went into the kitchen; then he came out with a small scale and banged it down on the table.

Lao Lan scowled at him. 'Put each tub on the scale.'

'You three act like you were tricked in some previous life,' Huang groused as he weighed the four tubs, one at a time. 'See—all the same, not an ounce of difference.'

'Any more questions?' Lao Lan asked. 'If not, we can begin.'

'I have one more,' Feng said.

'Where do all these questions come from?' Lao Lan asked with a little laugh. 'Well, let's hear it. I want everything on the up and up. And if the rest of you have questions, now's the time to raise them. I don't want any complaints later.'

'I can see that all four tubs weigh the same, but what about the quality? I suggest we tag them and draw lots to see who gets which one.'

'Good idea,' Lao Lan said. 'Do you have pen and paper in your kit, Doctor? You can be the referee.'

The doctor eagerly took a pen from his kit, removed his prescription book, tore off four sheets, gave each a number—one, two, three, four—and then placed one under each tub. After that he made four lots and laid them upside down on the table.

'OK, meat warriors,' Lao Lan said, 'draw your lots.'

Although I viewed all this with cool detachment, I was beginning to get annoyed with Feng Tiehan. Why fuss so? Why be so picky over a tub of meat? As I seethed silently, Huang Biao and his helpers moved the tubs according to the number of their draws.

'Any more problems?' Lao Lan asked. 'Think hard, Feng Tiehan, anything more you'd like? No? Good. Then I declare the start of the inaugural Huachang United Meatpacking Plant meat-eating contest!'

I made myself comfortable and then, wiping my hands on a paper napkin, took a quick look round me. Feng Tiehan, to my left, had stabbed a piece of meat with a skewer and taken an unhurried bite. I was secretly surprised at his civilized eating habits. That was not the case with Liu Shengli or Wan Xiaojiang, both to my right. Wan tried using chopsticks but had so much trouble with them that he quickly switched to a skewer. Grumbling, he stabbed a square of meat, took a savage bite and then began to chomp like a monkey. Liu Shengli stabbed his meat with the tips of both chopsticks, opened wide and bit off half, stuffing his mouth so full he could hardly chew. This barbaric lack of etiquette revealed them to be men who hadn't tasted meat in ages. That was all I needed to confirm that they'd be out of the fight in no time. They were eating like novices, like autumn locusts that can barely manage a few hops. Now I could focus my attention on the man with the sallow complexion, Feng Tiehan, who looked like he had the weight of the world on his shoulders. Definitely the man to beat.

Folding the paper napkin and laying it beside my tub, I rolled up my sleeves, sat up straight and cast a kindly glance at the crowd, like a boxer just before a fight. I was repaid with admiring looks, and I could tell by the appreciative sighs that the people approved of my bearing and youthful maturity. My legendary eating achievements were not forgotten. I saw the warm smile of Lao Lan and the enigmatic smile of Yao Qi, who kept himself largely hidden in the crowd. In fact, there were smiles on lots of familiar faces, looks of admiration too, as well as a few drooling mouths on those who would have loved to take my place. The chomp chomp sound of chewing filled my ears and disgusted me. And I heard the plaintive moans of the meat, its angry complaints, emerge from all three mouths, mouths it did not want to be in. I was like a marathon runner standing confidently at the starting line, sizing up the competition before streaking down the course. It was time to begin. The chunks of beef in my tub had nearly run out of patience. None of the spectators could hear them, but I could. And perhaps my sister too. Lightly patting me on the back, she said: 'You should start, Elder Brother.'

'All right,' I replied gently, 'I will.' I then spoke to the darling meat: 'I'm going to eat you now.' 'Me first! No, me!' they squealed as they fought for my attention. Their soft pleas merged with their wonderful aroma and sprinkled over my face like pollen. It was intoxicating. 'Dear meat, all you pieces of meat, slow down, there's no rush. You'll get your turn, all of you. Though I haven't eaten any of you yet, we share an emotional bond. Love at first sight.

You belong to me, you're my meat, all you pieces of beef. How could I bear to abandon you?'

I used neither chopsticks nor a skewer, but my hands—I knew the meat preferred the feel of my skin. When I gently picked up the first piece, it gave out a joyful moan and trembled in my hand. I knew that wasn't fear but rapture. Only a tiny fraction of all the meat in the world would ever have the good fortune of being consumed by Luo Xiaotong, the boy who understood and loved meat. The excitement of this tubful came as no surprise. As I brought the piece to my mouth, glistening tears gushed from a pair of bright eyes staring passionately at me. I knew that it loved me because I loved it. Love all round the world was a matter of cause and effect. I am deeply moved, meat. My heart is all a-flutter. I honestly wish I didn't have to eat you, but I do.

I delivered the first piece of the darling meat into my mouth, though I could just as easily have said that the darling meat inserted itself into my mouth. Whichever it was, at that moment both of us experienced a flood of mixed emotions, like reunited lovers. 'I hate the thought of biting into you, but I must. I wish I didn't have to swallow you, but I must. There are so many more pieces waiting to be eaten, and today is not just another day for me. Until today, our union and mutual appreciation has been something I've enjoyed, heart and soul. But now I feel a combination of performance pressure and anxiety, and my mind has begun wander. I must concentrate on the task ahead, and I can only ask your indulgence. I will eat as never before, so that you and I—we—will demonstrate the acutely serious aspect of eating meat.' The first piece of meat slid with some regret into my stomach, where it swam like a fish in water. 'Go on, enjoy yourself. I'm sure you're lonely, but not for long—your friends will join you soon.' The second piece felt the same emotions towards me as I did towards it, and it followed an identical course down to my stomach until it was reunited with the first. Then the third piece, the fourth, the fifth . . . forming a tidy queue. They sang the same song, shed the same tears, trod the same course and wound up in the same place. It was a sweet but also sad process, illustrious and filled with glory.

I was so focused on my intimate interaction with the meat that I was oblivious of the passage of time and of my stomach's growing burden. But when I looked down, I saw that only a third of my portion remained. A bit of tiredness had crept in by then, and my mouth was producing less saliva. So I slowed down, raised my head and continued to eat gracefully while I surveyed my surroundings, beginning, of course, with my closest neighbours, my competitors. It was their participation that lent this extended meal its quality of entertainment, and for that I owed them a debt of gratitude. If they hadn't thrown down the gauntlet, I'd have been denied the opportunity of displaying my special skill before such a large audience—not just my skill but also my artistry. The number of people in the world who eat is as great as the sands of the Ganges, but only one has elevated this base activity into the realm of art, into a thing of beauty—and that is me, Luo Xiaotong. If all the meat in the world that has been or will be eaten were formed into a pile, it would rise higher than the Himalayas, but only the meat being eaten by Luo Xiaotong is capable of assuming a critical role in this artistic presentation . . . But I've gotten carried away, resulting from the overly creative imagination of a carnivorous child. So, back to the contest, and another look at my rivals' eating styles. Now, it's not my intention to mount a smear campaign— although I've always favoured calling a spade a spade—so I invite you to take a look for yourselves. First, to my left, Liu Shengli. Somewhere along the line, the hulking, tough fellow has tossed away his chopsticks and begun to dig in with his coarse paws. He snatches a piece of meat like he is clutching a sparrow struggling to get free, as though it will fly away to the tree beyond the wall or float into the far reaches of the atmosphere. His hand is filthy with grease, his cheeks like slimy hillocks. But enough about him. Let's take a look at his neighbour, Wan Xiaojiang, the Water Rat. He has abandoned the skewer for his hands, clearly following my lead or trying to. But you can't copy genius, and in the matter of eating meat I am a genius. They are wasting their time. Look at my hand, for instance—only the tips of three fingers are lightly coated with grease. Look at their hands—so much grease they may as well be webbed, like the feet of ducks or frogs. Even Wan's forehead is coated with grease. How that helps him eat meat is beyond me. Are they burying their faces in the meat? But the really disgusting part of it all is the growls and gurgles they emit, no less than insults to the meat they are eating. Like beautiful maidens, this meat is fated to suffer; it is a cruel but inexorable reality. Lamentations rise from the meat in their hands and mouths, while those pieces waiting to be eaten bury their heads like ostriches in an attempt to hide in the tubs. I can only watch in sympathetic solidarity. Things would have been different if they were on my plate but that is not to be. The ways of the world are immutable. I, Luo Xiaotong, have a stomach that can never be stretched to accommodate all the world's meat any more than all the women can ever wind up in the arms of the world's greatest lover. I watch, helpless. 'All you pieces of beef lying in the tubs of my rivals have no choice in the matter. You must go where you are sent.' By now, both the men on my right have slowed considerably, and the faces earlier marked by savage impatience now sag with a stupid lethargy. They haven't stopped eating but their chewing is now in slow motion. Their cheeks are sore, their saliva has dried up, their bellies bulge dangerously. I can see it in their eyes—they are simply stuffing the meat into their mouths, only to have it turn and tumble in their stomachs, like chunks of coal bumping against a throttle gate. They have, I know, reached the point where the pleasure of eating meat has been usurped by sheer agony. Meat has become so disgusting, so loathsome, that they want nothing more than to spit out what is in their mouths and vomit what is in their stomachs. But that would mean defeat. A look at their tubs reveals that the remaining meat has been sapped of its beauty and its redolence. Shame and humiliation has turned it ugly. Hostility for its eater makes it emit a putrid smell. About a pound of meat remains in each of the two tubs but there is no room in either stomach to accommodate it. Lacking emotional ties with its eaters, the consumed meat has lost its mental equilibrium and is now involved in a paroxysm of thrashing and biting. Hard times are upon the men, and it is obvious that they can not possibly eat what remains. My two truculent competitors are on the verge of elimination.

With that in mind, I looked to see how my true rival, Feng Tiehan, was doing.

I turned in time to see him spear a chunk of meat and take a bite. Although there was a change in his sallow complexion, he lowered his eyes and his dead-pan expression gave nothing away. His hands were spotless, thanks to his exclusive use of the metal skewer. His cheeks were dry, and the only grease I could see was on his lips. He ate at a steady, unhurried pace, a study in calm-ness, more like a diner enjoying a solitary restaurant meal than a competitor in a public eating contest. It was disheartening, a reminder that I had a formidable opponent. The other two, with their exaggerated gestures, were all show and no substance. Like the flame-out from a chicken-feather fire. A slow, pig-head simmering flame, like that of my third rival, on the other hand, presented a challenge. He maintained his composure even under my scrutiny, so I studied him some more. He speared a new piece of meat but hesitated, then returned it to the tub and chose a smaller one. As he carried it to his mouth, his hand stopped in mid-air. His body lurched upward and he stifled a low murmur deep in his throat. I breathed a sigh of relief, now that I'd spotted my enigmatic rival's weak spot. His choice of the smaller piece of meat was evidence that his stomach had reached its limit, while the lurch upward forced back a belch that would have brought out the ingested meat. There was also about a pound of uneaten meat in his tub. He obviously possessed sufficient resolve and was determined to stay with me to the end. All along I'd hoped for a worthy opponent so as not to disappoint our audience. A mismatch would have bled the competition of its significance. Now I knew that my fears were unfounded. Thanks to Feng Tiehan's obstinacy, a brilliant victory was assured.

Sensing my sidelong examination, Feng cast me a challenging glance. I responded with a friendly smile, picked up a piece of meat and carried it to my mouth as if to give it an affectionate kiss. I then brushed it with my lips and teeth to gauge its streaks and ridges before tearing off a piece and allowing it to enter my mouth on its own. Then I looked down at the dark red portion of meat waiting to be eaten, kissed it and told it to be patient as I began to chew its companion with passion and sensitivity so as to fully experience its flavour and fragrance, its pliant, moist texture—in other words, its entirety. I sat up straight and let my spirited eyes sweep over the faces in the crowd. I saw excitement there and I saw anxiety. It was clear who was rooting for me to win and who was not. Most, of course, were just there to enjoy the show—for them, a good fight was enough. But what was common across all those faces was the hunger for meat. They could not comprehend why Liu and Wan were having so much trouble eating. That was perfectly understandable—no bystander could relate to the anguish of someone who's eaten until the meat is backed up into his throat and who yet has to eat some more. I communicated with Lao Lan by letting my gaze linger on his face for a few seconds. His faith in me was unmistakable. Don't worry, Lao Lan, I said with my eyes. I won't let you down. I may not boast any other skills, but eating meat is my stock-in-trade. I also spotted my parents, standing on the outer edge of the crowd, staying as inconspicuous as possible, as if they wanted to avoid affecting my mood. Like parents everywhere, they were on tenterhooks, wanting me to win but worried that something might go wrong. My father, especially. This survivor of multiple eating contests, this veteran competitor, who had emerged victorious from every challenge, knew as well as anyone the risks involved and the misery that usually followed. His face was a study in concern, for he knew that the hardest part of a contest was reached when only a quarter of the food remained. It was the equivalent of a sprint to the finish line in a long-distance race. Not only a test of strength or stomach capacity, it was also a test of will. Only the contestant with the strongest will could win. When he can't swallow another bite, that's when a competitor has reached his bursting point. One more sliver of food will be the straw that breaks the proverbial camel's back. The cruel nature of this contest had finally become evident. An old hand at such contests, my father watched with mounting apprehension as the piles of meat slowly diminished. In the end, a patina of worry, like a coat of paint, seemed to blur his features. The look on my mother's face was easier to read. As I chewed one mouthful after another, her mouth moved along with mine, an unconscious attempt to help me along.

'Do you want some tea?' Jiaojiao asked softly with a poke in my back.

I declined the offer with a wave of my hand. That was against the rules.

Four pieces of meat remained in my tub, roughly half a pound. I made quick work of one piece, then followed it with a second. Two left, each the size of a hen's egg. Resting on the bottom of the tub, they were like friends hailing one another across a pond. I shifted my body slightly to feel the weight of my abdomen and decided that there was still room down there for the last two pieces. Even if I lost the contest I'd go out in style.

I ate one of the pieces, leaving its dear friend alone at the bottom of the tub. It waved its little tentacle-like hands, opened the mouths in the palms of that digital forest and called to me. Again I shifted my body to free up a bit of space in my stomach. As I sized up the final piece, I felt relaxed as never before. There was more than enough room in my stomach for that piece, and I watched it tremble in anticipation. It had to be thinking—if only it could sprout wings and fly straight into my mouth, then slide down my throat and be reunited with its siblings. In a language only we understood, I urged it to calm down and wait its turn. I wanted it to realize how fortunate it was to be the last piece of meat I ate in the contest. Why? Because every eye in the crowd would be on it. There was a difference between it and all the nameless pieces that had gone before it. As the last, it effectively determined the outcome and thus was the centre of attention. It was time to take a deep breath, concentrate my energy and build up enough saliva to spiritedly, energetically, elegantly and gracefully bring an end to the contest. As I breathed in deeply, I took one last look at my rivals.

First, Liu Shengli, the one with a face like a mobster. Bruised and battered, he was failing ignominiously. His fingers and lips were stuck together with grease. He tried shaking his hands to get them unstuck, but that grease remained unmoved. It too was meat, and it was now exacting revenge for his maltreatment. It stuck like glue to his fingers and made it impossible for him to pick up the remaining pieces. It had the same effect on his mouth—it sealed his lips, froze his tongue and palate and forced him to strain to open his mouth, as if it were filled with gooey malt sugar. From Liu Shengli we move to Wan Xiaojiang, a little man whom meat had turned into a sad sack. The best way to describe him would be as a disgusting, pathetic rat that's been dipped in a bucket of oil. He was looking shiftily at what remained in his tub. His greasy paws shook as he held them in front of his chest, and he needed only to start gnawing on them to truly live up to his nickname. He was a big rat stuffed so full he couldn't walk, and his belly bulged alarmingly. Only an overstuffed dying rat could make the *kip kip* noises that emerged from his mouth. There was no more fight in either competitor. All that remained was surrender.

That brings us to Feng Tiehan, my true rival. He maintained his poise even at this late stage. His hands were clean, his mouth lively and his posture erect. But his eyes lacked focus. No longer was he able to stare me down with a ruthless gaze. I thought he looked like a clay statue whose base is steeping in water but which somehow preserves its dignity in the face of imminent collapse. I knew that his eyes had glazed over because his stomach was failing him, that it had fallen victim to pounds of uncooperative meat and now swelled painfully. The meat in his stomach was acting like a nest of irritable frogs anxiously searching to be free. The slightest hint of capitulation from him and he'd be helpless to prevent their escape. The bitter struggle to maintain control over his body was reflected in the alarming look of distress on his face. It may not have been distress, but that's what it looked like to me. Three pieces of meat remained in his tub.

Liu Shengli's tub held five pieces, Wang Xiaogang's held six.

A huge black fly with white spots flew up from some distant place, circled the air above us and attacked Wan's tub of meat like a hawk swooping down on its prey. Wan tried to shoo it away with a few weak waves of his hand, but then gave up. A swarm of much smaller flies converged from all sides and set up a loud buzz as they circled above us. The spectators began to panic and turned their eyes to the sky in fear—in the slanting rays of the sun, the flies looked like golden specks of starlight. But this was terrible news. The flies had come from one of the world's filthiest places, and their wings and feet carried all sorts of germs and bacteria. Even if we were able to resist the noxious effects, the mere thought of where the carriers had been would make us sick. I knew that only seconds remained before they'd land like divebombers on our meat, and that we'd be defenceless to stop them. I grabbed the last piece in my tub and crammed it into my mouth just as the attack commenced.

In the proverbial blink of an eye, the meat in the other tubs, even the rims of the tubs themselves, were covered with flies, with their skittering feet and shimmering wings, and they began to eat their fill. Lao Lan, the doctor and some of the spectators rushed up to shoo them away but all they did was send the angry insects up in the air and then down into the people's faces to kill or be killed. Many in the swarm did die in the melee but others quickly filled their ranks. The defenders soon tired, physically and emotionally, and gave up the fight.

Following my example, Feng Tiehan snatched up one of his three pieces and crammed it into his mouth, then grabbed a second before the flies overwhelmed the last.

A great many flies settled on Liu and Wan's tubs, all but turning them invisible. 'The contest doesn't count,' shouted Wan, jumping to his feet, 'it doesn't count . . .'

He had barely opened his mouth when a bite-sized chunk of meat came flying out with a loud retch, but whether the sound came from the meat or from Wan was unclear. It fell to the ground, quivered like a newborn rabbit and was swiftly covered by flies. Defeated, Wan covered his mouth and ran to the wall; then leaned against it, lowered his head, and, like an inchworm, rocked up and down as he vomited out his guts.

Liu Shengli straightened up with difficulty. 'I could have finished mine,' he said to Lao Lan, trying to look nonchalant. 'My stomach was only half full. But those damned flies fouled my meat. I'm telling you, Xiaotong, you won nothing. I didn't lose—'

The words were barely out of his mouth when he catapulted to his feet as if on springs. I knew it was the meat in his stomach, not springs, that propelled him upward. In its attempt to escape from his stomach, it was exerting an explosive force beyond his control. The moment he got to his feet, the skin on his face yellowed, his eyes froze and his face grew stiff. Panicked, he ran to join Wan, knocking over his chair and bumping smack into Huang Biao, who was running out of the kitchen with a flyswatter. Only the first word of what must have been a curse managed to leave Huang Biao's mouth before Liu Shengli opened his and, with a yelp, spewed out a mouthful of sticky, half-eaten meat all over Huang Biao. Huang Biao screeched, as if bitten by a wild animal, and then the curses really began to fly. He threw down his flyswatter, wiped his face and ran after the fleeing Liu, trying but failing to kick him before turning and heading back to the kitchen to wash his face.

It was great fun watching Liu stagger away on his weak, spindly legs, slightly bowed at the knees, feet turned out, his heavy buttocks swinging from side to side like a duck running at full speed. He lined up beside Wan, hands and head against the wall, and erupted in a frenzy of vomiting, bending over and straightening up, bending over and straightening up . . .

Feng Tiehan had a piece of meat in his mouth and another in his hand. His eyes were dull, as if he were in deep, meditative thought. Now the centre of attention, it was left to him to wage a solitary struggle. But he had suffered defeat as well. Even if he swallowed the piece in his mouth and ate the one in his hand, followed by the fly-encrusted piece in his tub, time alone made him a loser. But the spectators waited, wanting to see what he'd do. As in a marathon, after the winner has crossed the finish line, the spectators spur on the other racers, encouraging them to give it their all. I was hoping he'd dig in and finish his meat, because I had enough space for one more. Then I would gain the unalloyed admiration of the crowd. But Feng sounded the retreat. He stretched his neck, stared wide-eyed and managed to swallow the piece in his mouth to applause from the crowd. But when he brought the second piece up to his mouth, he wavered briefly and then tossed it back into his tub, startling the flies into the air with a noisy buzz, like sparks from a blazing fire. 'I lose,' Feng announced, his head down. Then, after a moment, he raised his head, turned to me and said: 'You win.'

I was moved by his words. 'You may have lost,' I said to him, 'but you did so with style.'

'The contest is over,' Lao Lan announced. 'Luo Xiaotong is the winner. Compliments also to Feng Tiehan, who performed well. As for Liu Shengli and Wan Xiaojiang,' he cast a contemptuous look at their backs, 'their spirit was willing but their flesh was weak. Today's was the plant's first such contest. United Meatpacking Plant workers must be accomplished consumers of meat. And as for you, Luo Xiaotong, don't get cocky. You beat your opponents this time but that doesn't mean you won't meet your match some day. Participation in the next contest will not be limited to plant workers. We want to make this a broad-based social activity that furthers the plant's good name. We will provide trophies and monetary rewards for the winners. If one chooses, he can take his winnings out in meat—for a year!'

'I want to compete,' shouted Jiaojiao.

The crowd heard her words, and all eyes swung in her direction. You couldn't have asked for a more delightful sight at that moment than my pig-tailed, limpid-eyed, plump little sister.

'That's the spirit,' Lao Lan called out. 'There we have a case of "Heroes come from the ranks of youth, and every trade has its master practitioner." What has the country's reform and opening-up policy achieved? I'll tell you: individual talent can no longer be suppressed. Even eating meat can bring fame and glory to an individual. All right, then, that ends the contest. If your shift is over, go on home. For the rest, it's time to go to work.'

The crowd broke up amid scattered comments. 'Dr Fang,' Lao Lan said, pointing to Liu Shengli and Wan Xiaojiang, who were still throwing up near the wall, 'do they need an injection of something?'

'For what? They'll be fine once they've emptied their stomachs.' He turned and pointed to me with his chin. 'He's the one I'm worried about,' he said. 'He ate the most.'

Lao Lan patted the doctor on the shoulder. 'My friend,' he said with a laugh, 'your concerns are wasted on that youngster. He's special, a sort of meat god. He's been sent down to earth for the sole purpose of eating meat. His stomach is built differently from ours. Isn't that right, Luo Xiaotong? Do you feel stuffed? Want the doctor to have a look?'

'I'm fine, thank you,' I said to the doctor. 'In fact I've never felt better.'

*A nightlong torrential downpour has washed away the vomit of the poison vic-
tims. The street looks newly scrubbed and the leaves on the trees oily green.
Thanks to the rain, a hole in the temple roof is now as big as a millstone, and
through it sunlight pours in. Dozens of rats, flushed out by the water, crouch
atop the crumbling remains of clay idols. The woman from last night, the
spitting image of Aunty Wild Mule, hasn't shown up and, since I'm hungry, I
go ahead and eat the mushrooms growing round the Wise Monk's straw mat.
That energizes me, puts a sparkle in my eyes and clears my head. Scenes from
my past float up from the recesses of my brain: at a gravesite backed against
the mountains and facing the sea—the ideal feng shui—a woman in black sits
in front of a marble tombstone. The headstone likeness shows that it is the
grave of Lan Daguan's son, and the mole near the woman's mouth tells me
that she is the Buddhist nun Shen Yaoyao. There are no tears on her face and
no signs of mourning. A subtle fragrance emanates from the bouquet of calla
lilies in front of the headstone. A woman walks up lightly behind Lan Daguan,
whose eyes are shut and who seems deep in thought. 'Mr Lan,' she says softly,
'Master Huiming passed away last night.' Lan sighs as if shedding a great burden. 'Now,' he says to himself, 'I am truly worry-free.' He gulps down a glassful
of liquor and then says: 'Have Xiao Qin send for a couple of women.' 'Mr—'
the woman exclaims. 'Mr what? I'm going to commemorate his passing with
frenzied, unbridled sex!' As he cavorts with wild abandon with two long-legged,
slope-shouldered women, the four craftsmen who had built the idol stagger
into the yard in front of the Wutong Temple and cry out in alarm when they
see the marred face of the rain-ravaged Meat God. The master craftsman
rebukes the three younger men for not covering its face with plastic or dressing
it in rain cloak and bamboo hat. They hang their heads and accept the tongue-
lashing without a word of protest. The two long-legged women kneel on the
carpet and plead coquettishly: 'Be good to us, Patron. Our breasts are Yaoyao's
breasts, our legs are Yaoyao's legs, we are Yaoyao's stand-ins, so treat us with*

tenderness.' 'Do you know who Yaoyao was?' Lan asks unemotionally. 'No,' they reply. 'All we know is that we can please Patron by pretending to be her. And when Patron is happy, he treats us fondly.' Lan Daguan reacts with a belly laugh as tears spill from his eyes. Two of the young craftsmen walk up with buckets of clean water while the third has discovered a wire brush. With the foreman in charge, they scrub the paint off the idol. It howls a complaint, and my skin turns itchy and painful. Once the paint has been cleaned off, I see the original colour and grain of the willow tree. 'We'll paint it again after it dries,' the foreman tells them. 'Xiaobao, go see Director Yan for the funds. Tell him we'll take the Meat God back and chop it up for kindling if he doesn't come up with the money.' 'Be careful you don't wind up with a toothache,' warns Shifu, the worker who suffered the night before. 'The Meat God knows what I'm doing,' the foreman says unemotionally. The young man takes off running, hips churning. The foreman walks into the temple to inspect the crumbling Wutong Spirit. His bookish apprentice follows him in as the foreman pats the Horse Spirit on the rump—a piece of clay falls off. 'This is our meal ticket,' he says. 'These five spirits will keep us busy for quite some time.' 'What worries me, Shifu,' his disciple says, 'is that things will change.' 'Change how?' the foreman asks with a glare. 'After what happened last night, Shifu, with more than a hundred poisoned, what are the chances that the Carnivore Festival will continue? If they cancel the festival, there'll be no Meat God Temple and they won't want to refurbish this Wutong Temple. Didn't you hear the lieutenant governor last night when he talked about the Meat God and the Wutong Temples in the same breath?' 'You've got a point,' the foreman says, 'but, young fellow, there are things in this world you don't understand. If nothing had happened last night, the festival might well have been cancelled next year. But, because it did, there's no chance it won't be held next year. And bigger than ever.' The apprentice can only shake his head. 'You're right, I don't understand.' 'That won't kill you, boy,' the foreman says. 'There are things you young people don't need to understand. Just keep doing your job and you'll understand when you reach a certain age.' 'That I understand, Shifu,' the youngster answers. With his chin the foreman points to the two men out in the yard with the Meat God. 'Those two are fine with manual labour, but I'm going to count on you for what needs to be done with the Wutong Spirit.' 'I'll do my best, Shifu, but what if my best isn't good enough and I don't live up to your expectations?' 'Don't sell yourself short. I'm an excellent judge of people. *Four of the five spirits are pretty much ruined, and it's not going to be easy putting them back the way they were. But I've got an old edition of* Strange Stories from a Chinese Studio, *which describes what the five spirits are supposed to look like, though we'll have to make some improvements to keep up with the times. We can't just imitate the old style. Take this Horse Spirit. It looks more equine than human, the foreman says as his hands move around the idol. We need to make it look more human so it won't scare all the women away. But won't other teams also want the job, Shifu? the concerned young worker asks. Only Nie Liu and Lao Han's gangs, and they're lucky if they can throw together a local earth god. These five spirits are way above their ability.' 'Don't underestimate them, Shifu,' the youngster says. 'I hear that Nie Liu sent his son to a fine-arts school to study sculpting. When he comes back to take over from his father, we won't be in his league.' 'Are you talking about his blockhead son? A fine-arts school, you say? He'd be no good even if he'd gone to an art academy. The first requirement for working on religious idols is to have the spirit in you. Without it, no matter how talented you are, you'll never create anything but lumps of clay. But you're right, we must be careful and alert. The world is full of talented people, and who's to say that a master sculptor won't show up some day? Keep that in mind.' 'Thanks, Shifu,' the youngster says. 'Now,' the foreman says, 'find a way to strike up a friendship with Lao Lan, the Slaughterhouse Village head, since it was his ancestors who built the Wutong Temple. He'll put up most of the money for the refurbishment, especially since word has it that he's recently received something like ten million from overseas. Whoever he wants to repair the idols has the best chance of getting the job.' 'Don't you worry, Shifu,' the youngster says confidently. 'My sister-in-law is the cousin of his wife, Fan Zhaoxia. I checked—people say that Lao Lan does what his wife tells him.' The foreman nods appreciatively. Lan Daguan flings his glass to the floor and gets up unsteadily. The two servants rush up and catch him under his arms. 'You've had too much to drink, sir,' one of them says. 'Me? Too much to drink? Maybe. You—' he shrugs his arms to free them from the women's grip and glares at them, 'go get two women to come sober me up.' Shall I keep talking, Wise Monk?*

Three months before Lao Lan's wife died, he and I dealt with two clandestine visits by reporters and were each proud to have managed so successfully.

The first came disguised as a peasant sheep-seller. With a scrawny old sheep in tow, he mixed in with the crowd of people who had brought animals to sell—cows and sheep on the hoof, pigs in handcarts, dogs on shoulder poles. Why shoulder poles? Try putting a halter on the dogs! The sellers dull the animals' senses with liquor-laced buns, tie their rear legs together, slip their poles under the ropes and then hoist them onto their shoulders. Since it was market day, the sellers formed a large crowd. Once I'd planned the day's production schedule, I took a walk round the plant with Jiaojiao.

Our prestige soared in the wake of the contest. Nearly all of the workers we encountered looked at us with respect. As for my defeated combatants, Liu Shengli and Wan Xiaojiang, they nodded and bowed and greeted me as Young Master. Despite their sarcasm, their admiration was genuine. Though Feng Tiehan maintained the restraint he'd displayed during the competition, there was no hiding his admiration either. Father observed everything and then took me aside for a heart-to-heart talk, urging me to act humbly and to avoid any signs of arrogance: 'People shun fame, pigs fear bulk,' he said. 'A dead pig doesn't fear boiling water,' I countered with a giggle. 'Xiaotong, my son,' Father sighed, 'you're too young to take my words seriously. It's in one ear and out the other. You won't know how hard a brick wall is till you smash your nose against it.' 'Dieh,' I said, 'I know how hard a brick wall is. Not only that, I know that a pickaxe is even harder.' 'You must do as you see fit, son,' he said resignedly. 'This isn't how I wanted my children to turn out, but there's nothing I can do about that now. I've not been a good father, so I guess I'm to blame for how you've turned out.' 'Dieh,' I said, 'I know what you wanted of us. You wanted us to go to school, to go to college. Then abroad, to complete our education. But Jiaojiao and I aren't student material, Dieh, any more than you're official material. But we have our unique talents, so why should we follow in everyone else's footsteps on the path to success? As they say, if you have something fresh to offer, you'll never go hungry. We can do things the way we want.' Father hung his head. 'What unique talents do any of us have?' he wondered aloud, dispirited. 'Dieh,' I said, 'other people can look down on us, but we can't look down on ourselves. Of course we have unique talents. Yours is evaluating livestock, ours is eating meat.' He sighed again: 'Son, how can you call that a unique talent?' 'Dieh,' I replied, 'as you very well know, it's not everyone who can consume five pounds of meat at one sitting without adverse effects. And it takes a unique talent to determine the gross weight of a cow just by looking at it. Don't you call those unique talents? If you don't, then the whole concept of unique talent is meaningless.' He shook his head: 'Son, the way I see it, your unique talent isn't eating meat, but twisting false logic until it seems true. You should be somewhere where you can show off your eloquence, somewhere like the United Nations. That's where you belong, a place where you can debate to your heart's content.' 'Would you look closely at that place where you think I belong, Dieh? The UN? What would I do in a place like that? Despite their Western suits and leather shoes, those people are all phonies. The one thing I can't stand is to be tied down. I need to be free. But even worse, there'd be no meat for me there and I won't go anywhere where there's no meat, not even Heaven.' 'I'm not going to argue with you,' Father said, exasperated. 'It's the same thing all over. Since you say you're no longer a child, then you have to answer to your-self for whatever happens. Don't come crying to me in the future if things don't work out.' 'Take it easy, Dieh,' I said. 'Future? What does that mean? Why waste time thinking about the future? There's a saying: "When the cart reaches the mountain, there'll be a road, and a boat can sail even upwind." And another one that goes: "Favoured people are free of hustle and bustle, others blindly rush about." Lao Lan says that Jiaojiao and I were sent down to earth to eat meat and that we'll go back after we've consumed our allotted amount. The future? Not for us, thank you!' I could see he didn't know whether to laugh or cry, which delighted me. I now knew that I had put Father behind me as a result of the meat-eating contest. A man I'd once revered was no longer worthy of that feeling. Nor, for that matter, was Lao Lan. I was struck by the realization that while they seem complicated, the affairs of the world are in fact quite simple. There's only one issue that deserves worldwide attention—meat. The world's vast population can be divided into meat categories. In simplest terms, those who eat meat and those who don't, and those who are true meat-eaters and those who aren't. Then there are those who would eat meat if they had access to it and those who have access but don't eat it. Finally, there are those who thrive by eating meat and those who suffer over it. Amid those vast numbers of people, I am among the very few who desire meat, who have a capacity for meat and love it, who have constant access to meat and who thrive by eating it. That is the primary source of my abundant self-confidence. *See how long-winded I get, Wise Monk, when the talk turns to meat? People find that annoying, I know, so I'll change the subject and talk about the reporter who dressed up like a peasant.*

He was wearing a tattered blue jacket over grey cotton trousers. He had yellow rubber sandals on his feet and a bulging old khaki bag over his shoulder as he joined the crowd with his scrawny, tethered sheep. His jacket was too big for him and his trousers too long, which made him look sort of lost in his clothes. His hair was a mess, his face ghostly pale and his eyes constantly darted here and there. He didn't fool me for a minute, but I didn't take him for a reporter, at least not at first. When Jiaojiao and I approached him, he looked away. Something in his eyes bothered me, so I scrutinized him more closely. Refusing to look me in the eye, he covered up his discomfort by whistling, which made me even more suspicious. But I still didn't think he was a reporter in disguise. I thought he might be a delinquent from town who'd stolen a sheep and brought it here to sell. I nearly went up to tell him he didn't have to worry, since we never asked where our animals came from. None of the cows the West County peddlers brought came with a pedigree. I took a look at his sheep—a castrated old ram with curled horns. It had been recently sheared, but not professionally, evident from the unevenly scissored patches and a few spots where the skin had been nicked. A sad, scrawny old ram with a terrible haircut that might have been remotely presentable had it been favoured with a full coat. Attracted by the short fleece, Jiaojiao reached out to touch the animal and startled it into a leap. The unexpected movement caused the fellow to stumble and jerked the lead out of his hand, freeing the animal to meander up to the queue of sellers and their animals, the rope dragging on the ground behind it. The fellow ran after it, taking big strides and swinging his arms wildly as he tried to step on the moving rope, but missed every time. It almost looked as if he was putting on an act for the crowd. Every time he bent over to grab the rope, it slipped out of range. By now, his clumsy, comical performance had everyone in stitches. Including me.

'Elder Brother,' Jiaojiao said with a laugh, 'who is that man?'

'A fool, but a funny one,' I said.

'You think he's a fool?' said an old fellow with four dogs on his pole. He seemed to know us, but we didn't know him. His jacket draped over his shoulders, his arms crossed, he held a pipe between his teeth. 'He's no fool,' he said as he launched a mouthful of phlegm. 'Look at those shifty eyes, how they take in everything. He's not an honest man,' he continued under his breath, 'not with those eyes.'

I knew what he was getting at. 'We know,' I said softly, 'he's a thief.'

'So call the police.'

I called the old fellow's attention to the queue of animals and their sellers. 'We've got plenty on our hands already, Uncle.'

'Thunder always rumbles after a temple festival. There are thieves everywhere you look these days,' he said. 'I was going to feed these four dogs another month before taking them out of their pens, but I couldn't take the chance. The thieves toss knockout drugs into dog pens—ones that are effective for days—then steal the dogs and sell them outside the area.'

'What can you tell me about those drugs?' I asked, trying to sound nonchalant. Now that the days were turning cold, men in the city were looking for tonics to increase their vitality, which meant that dog meat pots were getting fired up. We supplied the city with dog meat, and had to attend to the issue of canine water-cleansing. The animals could inflict serious damage if they were spooked, and a knockout drug could solve that problem. Once the dogs were doped, we could hang them up and start the treatment. That done, it wouldn't matter if they came to, since they'd be more like pigs than dogs and no longer a threat. All that remained then was to drag them over to the killing room, not dead but barely alive.

'I'm told it's a red powder bomb that makes a muffled noise when it hits the ground and releases a pink mist and a strange smell somewhere between fragrant and noxious. Even an attack dog will keel over after one whiff.' In a tone that was equal parts anger and dread, he added, 'Those thieves are no different than women who drug and kidnap children. They all belong to secret societies, and ordinary peasants have no way of laying hands on their formulas. It's probably some strange concoction we could never track down.'

My eyes travelled down to the old fellow's bleary-eyed dogs. 'Did you get that bunch drunk?'

'Two *jin* of liquor and four steamed buns,' he replied. 'Liquor these days has lost its punch.'

Jiaojiao was squatting in front of the dogs, prodding their oily lips with a reed stem, occasionally revealing a white fang. Their breath reeked of alcohol. From time to time one would roll its eyes and make dreamy sounds.

A man pushed a scale on squeaky wheels over to the dog pens from the warehouse, the hook swaying back and forth. For the sake of convenience, we'd built a pen exclusively for dogs near the one that held sheep and pigs. What made that necessary was an incident involving a worker who'd entered the pen holding all the animals together to pick out one of the pigs, and had been badly bitten by dogs turned half mad from being penned up too long. He was still in the hospital receiving daily shots of anti-rabies vaccine—vaccine that had already expired, according to someone from the hospital who spoke in confidence. Whether or not he'd begin to show symptoms was an open question. Naturally, the fact that a worker had been bitten wasn't the only reason we'd invested in the construction of a separate dog pen. Another was that dogs that had been plied with liquor were capable of wreaking havoc once they sobered up, attacking the sheep and pig penmates. Peace was rare in the pen, day or night. One day, after planning the production schedule, I took Jiaojiao over to see what was going on in the pen. Nothing, as it turned out, one of those rare peaceful moments. We saw dozens of dogs, some standing, others sprawled on the ground, forcibly occupying most of the space in the pen and forcing the pigs to huddle in one corner—some white, some black, some spotted—and sheep—along with a few billy goats and a couple of milch goats—in another. There was hardly any space between the pigs, who faced the railing, thus leaving their rumps vulnerable. The sheep too were clustered together, with some long-horned billy goats standing protectively. Almost none of the animals were injury-free, thanks, of course, to the dogs. Despite the peaceful moment—a rest for the dogs—the pigs and the sheep were preparing for the worst. Even when the dogs were relaxed, internal flare-ups were inevitable, including semi-serious fights between the males and the occasional cluster-fuck. At those times the pigs and sheep were so quiet that they hardly seemed to exist. But then a sort of gang fight broke out among several dozen dogs, which sent fur flying and blood spraying and resulted in some serious injuries, including a few broken legs. This was no longer a game. Jiaojiao and I wondered what the pigs and sheep must have been thinking as battles raged among the dogs. She said they weren't thinking about anything, that they were taking advantage of the dogfights to catch up on lost sleep. I would have challenged her on that, but I looked into the pen and, just as she'd said, the animals were sprawled on the ground, their eyes shut as they dozed. But dogfights were a rarity. Most of the time, the dogs, sporting sinister grins, launched attacks on the sheep and pigs. At first, the larger boars and billy goats bravely fought them off. The goats reared up on their hind legs, heads high, and charged, but the dogs nimbly sidestepped the attacks. 'I thought you said that meat dogs are stupid animals,' some might ask. 'Then how could they be as alert as wolves in a forest?' Yes, they entered the pens as stupid animals but, after being starved for a week, their wild nature returned accompanied by a surge in intelligence. They reverted to being predators, and, not surprisingly, the sheep and pigs penned up with them became their prey. After the first assault failed, the billy goats prepared for a second, rearing up as before, raising their heads and aiming their horns at the prowling dogs. But their movements were stiff, their tactics predictable and once again they were easily sidestepped by the dogs. They then steeled themselves for a third attempt, but it was a weak one, so weak that the dogs barely had to move to get out of the way. By now, all the fight had left the goats. The dogs, grinning hideously, charged their ovine prey and sank their fangs into sheep tails, sheep ears and sheep throats. The victims bleated piteously while a few somewhat more fortunate ones stampeded like headless flies. Many of them rammed their heads into the pen railings and crumpled to the ground, unconscious. The dogs made short work of the dead sheep, eating everything but the feet—unappetizing—the horns and any skin with too much fleece attached. The pigs quaked as they watched the sheep being slaughtered, for they knew they were next. Some of the larger boars tried to ward off the attack by emitting low grunts and charging like black bombs. The dogs leapt out of the way and set their sights on the pigs' rumps or ears, which they bit savagely. With yelps of pain, the boars tried to turn the tables but were immediately set upon by other opportunistic dogs that knocked them to the ground. Their screeches filled the air, but only for a few moments. Blood soaked the ground as their bellies were ripped open and their intestines torn out and dragged round the pen.

Anyone could see why the animals had to be separated, even if a dog had not bitten our worker. We'd have lost much high-quality lamb and pork, and would have raised savage dogs that we'd then have had to poison or shoot. Viewed from the perspective of entertainment, I'd have preferred not to separate them. But I was not your typical youngster—no, I was the head of one of the plant's workshops, laden with heavy responsibilities, and the last thing I wanted to do was cause financial setbacks just so I could be entertained by scenes of carnage. So we packed thirty pounds of beef with two hundred sleeping pills, and, once the killer dogs were under, dragged them over to a pen built exclusively for them. They woke up groggy after three days and their eyes glazed over as they took in their new surroundings. They then circled the outer limits of the pen, howling their displeasure. An animal's temperament and demeanour are ruled by its stomach. Before being brought to us, these dogs had been raised on a prescribed feed. Now they had to subsist on leftovers from the killing rooms and the blood of cows and sheep, reason enough for even the dumbest and tamest among them to revert to their wolfish ways only days after entering the dog pen. Part of the logic behind our decision was related to the disposal of the offal on the killing rooms floors. But we also wanted to improve the quality of the meat, and knew that these dogs would produce better meat than those animals that had been raised on a meatless diet. Winter was on its way, Lao Lan said, the season when the consumption of dog meat spikes, and it was up to us to supply a product that enhanced consumers' vitality. Added to that was a plan to present meat from these dogs as gifts to expand the plant's customer base. On many starlit nights, my sister and I watched as some of these dogs crouched alongside the pen railings, looked up at the stars in the sky and howled, a chilling wolfish cry. A single animal baying at the moon would have had little effect on us. But joined by dozens of fellow creatures, the din turned the plant into a hell on earth. One such night, Jiaojiao and I bravely stole up to the pen to peer through the gaps in the railing. The dogs' green eyes flashed like a panorama of bright little lanterns. Some of them howled into the night sky, others lifted their legs to urinate against the railing, still others ran and leapt, their hardened bodies leaving visible streaks in the air and their moonlit fur gleaming like fine silks and satins. This was no collection of dogs, but a wolf pack, plain and simple. That got me thinking that there must be a huge difference between carnivores and herbivores—one look at those dogs told us that. As tame as sheep and as stupid as pigs when they were on a prescribed diet, but as fierce as wolves once they began eating meat. Jiaojiao seemed to read my mind. 'Did you and I come from wolves?' she whispered. 'I made a face and said, 'Yes, that's exactly what we came from. You and I are wolf children.'

The dogs were not running and leaping for the sake of exercise—they were intent on leaping over the railing to freedom. Eating fresh meat and drinking warm blood had made them smart enough to realize what was in store for them. The onset of winter meant that they would be taken into the water-treatment building, where an infusion of water would bloat them out of shape, disrupt their ability to walk and make their eyes sink. Then it would be off to the kill rooms, where they'd be bludgeoned, skinned alive, disembowelled and packaged to be sent into town as a tonic for men who longed for hard-as-steel erections. Not the sort of future any self-respecting dog looked forward to. As I watched the dogs executing extraordinary leaps, I was thankful that we had built the fences tall enough. Constructed of iron posts, they were five metres high and, thanks to the thick steel wire, virtually indestructible. Lao Lan and I had been opposed to the use of iron posts at first, but my father had insisted upon it and we went along with him. He was, after all, the plant manager. And he was right. Back when he was living in the northeast, he'd developed an understanding of the link between dogs and wolves. Now, as I thought back, I cringed at the thought of what would have happened if those now wolfish animals had made it out of the pen. The entire area could have wound up under siege.

The man wheeled the scale over to the dog pen, where my father appeared, seemingly out of nowhere.

'Hey, dog-peddlers,' he shouted to the men waiting in the queue. 'Line up over there.'

The old fellow squatted down, picked up his shoulder pole and straightened up, lifting the four dogs off the ground. Oh, there's one thing I forgot. People who raised dogs believed in marking their animals, including clipping their ears and inserting nose rings. This old fellow, shunning such half-baked strategies, actually removed his dogs' tails; it gave them a dopey look but increased their agility. I wondered if his tailless dogs would turn wolfish in the pen and, if so, if they too would leap about in the moonlight. Let's say they would. Then would they be more graceful than the others or would they bounce about like billy goats? We fell in behind him, feeling sorry for the dogs yet knowing what hypocrites that made us. Showing sympathy to a dog was asking to be eaten by it. And what a waste, albeit insignificant, that would be. In ancient times, human flesh had probably—no, definitely—been a delicacy for beasts of prey, but in present times a human being eaten by beasts of prey would be turning the world upside down, confusing the roles of eater and eaten. Their purpose in life was to be eaten by humans, which makes sympathy for them both hypocritical and laughable. And yet, I couldn't help feeling sorry for those pitiful creatures hanging from the man's shoulders—or perhaps I should say that I found the sight hard to endure. Wanting to clear my head of these weak, shameful thoughts, I took Jiaojiao by the hand and headed towards the meat-cleansing workshop, where we watched as the dog-peddlers laid their animals, one on top of the other, onto the scale. The only signs of life were their low moans, a bit like an old woman with a toothache; it was hard to imagine them as living creatures. The scale operator skilfully moved the slide across the arm and announced the weight in a low voice. Father, who was standing to the side, said unemotionally: 'Deduct twenty pounds!'

'Why?' the seller protested loudly. 'Why are you deducting twenty pounds?'

'Because you stuffed each of them with at least five pounds of food before you left home,' Father said coolly. 'I'm deducting only twenty to save you a bit of dignity.'

'No one can put anything over on you, Manager Luo,' the man confessed with a wry smile. 'But these animals are here to be slaughtered and we had to let them eat, didn't we? I raised them myself. They're like family. Besides, don't you fill them full of water before you kill them?'

'You'd better be ready to prove that,' Father said with a steely look.

'Seriously, Lao Luo,' the dog-seller sneered, 'if you don't want people to know something, don't do it in the first place. Everyone knows about your meat-cleansing technique. Who do you think you're fooling?' The man glanced at me out of the corner of his eye and, in a voice dripping with sarcasm, said, 'Am I right or am I not? You're the head of the meat-cleansing workshop, aren't you?'

'We don't infuse our animals with water,' I responded. 'We cleanse the meat. Is that something you can understand?'

'Cleanse the meat?' the man sputtered. 'You fill those animals almost to the bursting point. Cleansing the meat! Well, I have to give you credit for coming up with such a fine term.'

'I'm not going to argue with you,' said Father angrily. 'Sell your dogs for twenty pounds less or take them back home with you.'

'Lao Luo,' the man said, squinting, 'you're a different man now that things are going your way. I guess you've forgotten the time you went round picking cigarette butts up off the ground.'

'That's enough,' Father said.

'All right,' the man conceded, 'you win. You can tell when a man's luck is up by the state of his horse, and a bird of prey is always round when a rabbit's luck runs out.' He reached down and arranged his dogs on the scale and then, with a forced smile, he said, 'Not wearing your green cuckold's hat today?'

Father turned red all the way to his ears. Words failed him.

I was about to shred the man with my razor-sharp wit when I heard shouts coming from the 'meat-cleansing' station. When I turned to look, I saw the so-called goat-seller racing down the path to the main gate, followed by a posse of plant workers. He kept shooting them glances over his shoulder and they kept shouting: 'Grab him—don't let him get away!'

Something clicked in my head, and I blurted 'Reporter!'

When I looked at Father, I saw he'd turned ashen white. I grabbed Jiao-jiao's hand and took off running to the gate. I was excited, pumped up, as if I'd spotted a dog running down a jackrabbit on a humdrum winter day. Jiao-jiao was slowing me down, so I let go of her and ran as if my life depended on it. The wind whooshed past my ears. There were chaotic shouts behind me— barking dogs, bleating sheep, grunting pigs, lowing cows. The man stumbled on a rock and thudded to the ground, his momentum carrying him a good three feet on his belly. His bulging canvas bag flew off and an inhuman 'oof!' burst from his mouth, like a toad getting squashed. He'd taken such a fall that I couldn't help but feel sorry for him. We'd built the path with a mixture of old bricks, gravel and cinders, all unforgivingly hard. At the very least, he had to have a bloody nose and cut lips, maybe even a lost tooth or two. Broken bones weren't out of the question. But he scrambled to his feet, staggered over to his canvas bag and picked it up. Ready for another run, he froze when he saw—as did I—Lao Lan and my mother, two formidable opponents, standing like sentries and blocking his way. By then his pursuers had caught up with him.

Lao Lan and Mother were in front of him, Father and I were behind him and the plant workers all round him. With a wave of his hand, Lao Lan dismissed the workers. The hapless fellow turned round and round, looking for a way out of our human cage. I think he assumed that I was the weak link in the chain but then he noticed Jiaojiao and the knife she clutched in her hand. His next avenue of escape was past my mother but her expression changed his mind. Her face was red, her gaze unfocused, the quintessential look of distraction. But it made him lower his head in defeat. Father, on the other hand, suddenly looked the picture of dejection. Turning his back on the reporter and ignoring the queue of animal-sellers, he headed to the northeast corner of the plant, to a rebirth platform made of pine. That had been Mother's idea. She said that a platform was needed to perform regular Buddhist rites in order to help the sad ghosts of all those creatures that had served mankind move ahead on the wheel of life after we killed them. I didn't think that Lao Lan, a lifelong butcher, believed in ghosts and spirits, and so I was surprised when he accepted Mother's idea. We'd already performed rites on the platform— we'd invited a senior Buddhist monk to recite sutras while several lesser monks burnt incense and spirit paper and set off firecrackers at the base of the platform. The senior monk was a ruddy-faced man with a booming voice and high moral airs. Listening to him chant the sutras was a deeply spiritual experience. Mother compared him to the Tang monk in the *Travels to the West* TV series. When Lao Lan jokingly asked if she wanted to feast on the Tang monk's flesh to achieve immortality, she kicked him in the calf. 'What do you think I am, some kind of demon?' she'd grumbled.

My father was a regular visitor to the platform, which stood ten metres tall and gave off a pleasant pine smell; he sometimes stayed up there for hours, not coming down even at mealtimes. 'Dieh,' I once asked, 'what do you do up there?' 'Nothing,' he said woodenly. 'I know,' Jiaoajiao said. He rubbed her head, looked glum and said nothing. She and I climbed up there a few times to look round and breathe in the scent of pinewood. We saw distant villages, the river, a misty line of riverbank scrub brush, uncultivated land and all sorts of vapours snaking skyward on the horizon. The vista emptied us of our emotions. 'I know what he does up there,' she said. 'What?' I asked. Sighing like an exasperated crone, she explained: 'He thinks about the forests up north.' As I looked into her moist eyes, I could tell there was more she wanted to say. I'd heard Father and Mother argue over this very thing. 'I'm like a carpenter wearing a cangue she made,' Mother said. Father replied, 'Don't use your narrow-minded view to judge a broad-minded person,' replied Father. 'I'm going to ask Lao Lan to take that down tomorrow,' Mother declared. Father pointed his finger at her: 'Don't talk to me about him!' he said through clenched teeth. 'Why not?' she responded, just as angrily. 'What's he ever done to you?' 'Plenty,' Father said. 'Let's hear it, all of it.' 'Are you saying you don't know what I'm talking about?' Mother's face reddened and venom seemed to shoot from her eyes. 'Dry filth doesn't stick to a person,' she said. 'You can't have waves without wind,' he said. 'I've done nothing to be ashamed of,' she said. 'He's better off than me,' he said. 'His family's always been better off than ours. If you'd rather be with him, I won't stand in your way, but you'll have to settle with me first.' He turned and stalked off. Mother flung her bowl to the floor and smashed it. 'Luo Tong,' she snarled at his back, 'the next time you browbeat me like that I'll do what you think I already did!'

I'll stop here, Wise Monk. Talking about that upsets me. I'll wrap up my story about the reporter instead.

Father climbed the platform to smoke; Mother went back to her office. Lao Lan, Jiaojiao and I escorted the reporter to my room, a walled-off corner of the meat-cleansing workshop. I could see activity on the work floor through gaps in the plywood walls. After describing our water treatment process, we offered to cleanse his insides, if he was willing, and then deliver him to one of the kill rooms, mix his flesh with camel and dog meat and sell it in town. Bean-sized drops of sweat broke out on his forehead and we saw that his pants were wet. 'Whoever heard of a grown man peeing in his pants?' Jiaojiao remarked. 'Disgusting!' If, on the other hand, he was unwilling to be cleansed and slaughtered, we'd be happy to hire him as head of our PR department, pay him a salary of a thousand yuan a month and a two-thousand-yuan bonus each time a story about the plant made the papers, no matter the length. Well, he signed on and wrote a long feature about the plant, one that nearly filled a page. True to our word and committed to seeing things through to the end, we gave him two thousand yuan, treated him to a lavish meal and saw him off with a hundred pounds of dog meat.

The next reporters—two of them—at the plant worked for a TV station. Pan Sun and his assistant came disguised as meat-sellers. Equipped with a hidden camera, they toured the facilities. We offered them the same hospitality and then invited them to serve as consultants too.

All the while Lao Lan and I were dealing with the reporter, Father was on his platform smoking. Every fifteen or twenty minutes, another cigarette butt sailed to the ground. He was in the depths of depression. Dieh, you poor man.

'If Shen Yaoyao doesn't die, I will. If she does, I'll live.' So sobbed the film star Huang Feiyun last night as she sat on a sofa in front of Lan Laoda. 'I can't help myself. I love you. I'll pretend I'm dead if she lives but I'll choose life if she dies. The child is your flesh and blood, so you have to marry me.' 'How much do you want?' Lan asked callously. 'Is that what you think I came to you for— money, you bastard?' she fumed. 'Why else would you try to palm off someone else's child on me? You of all people should remember that I haven't so much as touched you since you got married. Unless I'm mistaken, your esteemed daughter was born three years after that, and I've never heard of a gestation period that long.' 'I knew you'd say that,' said Huang Feiyun, 'but you've forgotten that your sperm samples were deposited in the Celebrity Sperm Bank.' Lan Laoda lit a cigar with his pistol-shaped cigarette lighter and looked up at the ceiling. 'You're right,' he said. 'I was tricked into making that deposit because they said I had extraordinary genes. Did you put them up to that? You've gone to great lengths, haven't you? But if that's how things stand, you can send the boy over. I'll hire the best tutor and the best nanny to educate him and take care of him and make him into a statesman, and you can concentrate on being the virtuous wife of a businessman.' Huang Feiyun was unyielding: 'No,' she said. 'Why not? Why is it so important for you to marry me?' Tears in her eyes, she said, 'I know it makes no sense. I know you're a big-time gangster, a monster who works both sides of the road, criminal and law-abiding, and that marrying you is like signing my death warrant. But that's what I want. I think of it every minute of every day, I'm under your spell.' Lan Laoda laughed: 'I was married once and she suffered because of it. Why would you want to suffer too? Listen to me when I say I'm not a man—I'm a horse, a stud horse, and stud horses belong to all the mares in a herd. After a stud horse has serviced a mare, he's done with her and she must go away. As I say, I'm not a man, and you shouldn't consider yourself a woman. And if

you're a mare, then you wouldn't entertain the absurd idea of marrying me.'
Huang Feiyun pounded her chest and said in a voice choked with anguish: 'I'm
a mare, I am, a mare who dreams night after night of coupling with a stud
horse that empties her out.' Crying, she ripped open her bodice and her now
ruined, expensive dress fell to the floor. She then tore off her bra and her
panties. Completely naked, she began running round the living room shouting:
'I'm a mare . . . I'm a mare . . .' I am startled awake by an uproar outside the
temple gate, though Huang Feiyun's hysterical shouts continue to echo in my
ears. When I sneak a peek at the Wise Monk, the look of agony in his face has
been replaced by one of serenity. Before I can continue with my tale, there is
a racket outside. When I look up I see a large truck parked by the side of the
road, piled high with sawed planks and thick logs. A gang of men begin heaving
the lumber on which they were sitting to the ground, where a boy is nearly
crushed by one of the cascading logs. 'Hey,' he shouts, 'what are you doing?'
'Get out of the way, boy,' a squat worker in a wicker hard hat shouts back, 'or
there'll be no one to weep over your corpse.' 'I want to know what you're doing,'
the boy demands. 'Run home and tell your mother that there'll be an opera
here tonight,' the man says. 'Oh, so you're going to build a stage! Which
opera?' he asks, barely able to control his delight. A long plank cuts loose and
slides off the truck. 'Get out of the way, boy!' a man on the truck shrieks. 'I
can't, not till you tell me which opera.' 'OK, all righty, it's From Meat Boy to
Meat God. *Now, will you get out of the way!' 'Sure,' he says, 'now that you've*
told me.' 'What a strange little prick, one of them says as a log rolls to the
ground. The boy hops out of the way but the log rolls after him, as if it has
him in its sights and then finally comes to a stop at the little temple gate. The
fresh, clean smell of tree sap brings news of the virgin forest and, as I breathe
in the clean fragrance of pine, I am reminded of the rebirth platform at United
Meatpacking Plant all those years ago. As usual it stirs up painful memories.
That was where my poor father went to smoke, to meditate and to be lonely.
It's where he began spending most of every day, effectively putting affairs of
the plant out of his mind.

One night a month before Lao Lan's wife died, my father and mother
had a conversation, one up high, the other down low.

'Come down from there,' Mother said.

Father tossed down a glowing cigarette butt. 'Sorry, no.'

'Then stay up there till you breathe your last if you dare to.'

'I will.'

'You're a chicken-shit bastard if you don't come down.'

'I won't.'

Even though Lao Lan put a lid on the situation, news of Father's vow to never come off the platform leaked out and spread through the plant. Mother walked about in a daze, snapping out of it only to smash the odd dinner plate and then sit at her mirror and weep. Jiaojiao and I weren't particularly upset by this turn of events; truth be known—*I must shamefully confess, Wise Monk*—we even found it all terribly funny, even something to be proud about because my old man was once again displaying his unique temperament.

He swore he wouldn't come off the platform but he said nothing about fasting. Three times a day Jiaojiao and I took him food. It was a special treat the first time we climbed up but soon it became just another chore. Father would greet our arrival without any display of emotion. We'd have liked nothing more than to sit and eat with him but he always courteously insisted that we go back down. Reluctantly, we did as he asked so his food wouldn't get cold; on our way down we made sure we took back the utensils from his previous meal. The plate and bowl would be clean enough not to need a wash. He must have licked them clean, and I often imagined that sight. He had so much time on his hands up there that licking a bowl clean was sort of a job for him.

He had to relieve himself, of course, so Jiaojiao and I took up two plastic pails, which meant that, in addition to delivering his food, we also had to dispose of his waste. After watching us apprehensively as we carried the waste pails down, he suggested that we haul up his food basket and lower the pails with a rope to spare us the trouble of climbing up and down.

Lao Lan just laughed when I told him about this conversation. 'This is your family business,' he said when he'd finished laughing. 'Go talk it over with your mother.'

Mother would have none of it, and it seemed that by then she was resigned to her husband living on the platform. She went to work every day. She stopped smashing plates and frequently engaged in friendly chats with Lao Lan.

'Xiaotong,' she'd say, 'don't forget his cigarettes when you take his food.'

The truth is, despite Mother's opposition, a rope would have been the easiest thing in the world. We didn't do it because we didn't want to. Climbing the platform three times a day to visit our exceptional father was a special treat for Jiaojiao and me.

When we delivered his breakfast one morning three weeks before Lao Lan's wife died, he sighed and said: 'Children, your dieh's wasted his life.'

'No, you haven't, Dieh,' I replied. 'You've stuck it out here seven days already, and that's quite a feat. People are starting to call you a sage in the making, waiting to be immortalized up here on the platform.'

He shook his head and managed a bitter smile. We brought him good food every day, and the fact that his bowl was always licked clean was proof that there was nothing wrong with his appetite. But in seven days he'd lost weight. His beard had grown, long and as prickly as a hedgehog, his eyes were bloodshot, sleep filling their the corners, and he smelt foul, really foul. Just the sight of him reduced me to tears, and I blamed myself for not taking better care of him.

'Dieh,' I said, 'we'll bring you a razor and a basin to wash in.'

'Dieh,' Jiaojiao added, 'we'll bring you a blanket and a pillow.'

He sat there, leaning up against a pole and staring into the wilderness. 'Xiaotong,' he said full of sorrow, 'Jiaojiao, you two go down there, light a fire and immolate your dieh.'

'Dieh,' we cried out together, 'stop that! What would life be like for us if you weren't around? You have to stick it out, Dieh. Not giving up will be your victory.'

We laid down the food basket and picked up the plastic pails, ready to climb down, when Father stood up, rubbed his face with those big hands of his, and said, 'I'll do it.'

He took one of the pails, swung it back and forth a couple of times and then chucked it over the wall.

He then picked up the second pail and did the same thing.

Shocked by his outburst, I had a sudden feeling of impending disaster. I rushed over wrapped my arms round his leg. 'Don't do it, Dieh, don't jump,' I pleaded tearfully, 'you'll die!'

Jiaojiao rushed up and, crying, wrapped her arms round his other leg. 'Don't do it, Dieh, you'll die!' she echoed.

Father stroked our heads and looked at the sky. When he finally looked down again, there were tears in his eyes.

'Why would you think such a thing, children? Why would I want to jump? Your dieh doesn't have the guts.'

So he followed us down the platform and headed for the office. Strange looks followed us as we made our way through the plant.

'What are you looking at?' I demanded. 'I dare any of you to try climbing that platform. My father spent seven days up there, so keep those stinking mouths shut till you've spent eight.'

They slunk away under my withering attack.

'You're the best, Dieh,' I said proudly.

Not a word from my ashen-faced father. He followed us into his office, where Lao Lan and Mother met his arrival with seeming indifference. It was as if we'd just come from one of the workshops or the toilet and not off the rebirth platform.

'Good news, Lao Luo,' Lao Lan said. 'The Riches for All supermarket finally paid up what they owed us. We'll keep our distance from unscrupulous concerns like that from now on.'

'Lao Lan,' Father said glumly, 'I quit. I don't want to be plant manager any longer.'

'Why?' Lao Lan was surprised. 'Why do you want to quit?'

Father sat on the stool, his head hung low. 'I've failed,' he said after a long moment.

'You're too old to be pouting like a child,' Lao Lan said. 'Was it something I said or did?'

'Don't pay any attention to him, Lao Lan,' Mother said contemptuously. 'He's his own worst enemy.'

On the verge of losing his temper, Father merely shook his head and kept quiet.

Lao Lan flipped open a colour edition of a newspaper. 'Take a look at that, Lao Luo,' he said softly. 'My third uncle has given up his wealth, left all those women who've been in love with him, shaved his head and become a monk at the Yunmen Temple.'

Father merely glanced at the newspaper.

'My third uncle is a man of great, if strange, substance,' Lao Lan continued emotionally. 'I used to think I understood him, but now I realize I'm too vulgar to comprehend a man of his calibre. I tell you, Lao Luo, life's too short to be caught up with things like women and wealth, fame and status. You're born without them and you'll leave them behind when you die. My third uncle has seen the light.'

'You will, too, very soon,' Mother said sarcastically.

'My father was up on the platform for seven days,' Jiaojiao said, 'and he saw the light.'

Lao Lan and Mother turned to her in surprise. 'Xiaotong,' Mother said after a moment, 'take your sister outside and let the grown-ups talk. You don't know what this is about.'

'I do,' insisted Jiaojiao.

'Go outside!' Father barked angrily, banging the table with his fist.

His hair was a tangled mess, his face coated with grime, he stank, and he was in a foul mood. Seven days of meditating on a tall platform will do that to a man. I took Jiaojiao's hand and fled outside.

Are you still listening, Wise Monk?

Lao Lan's wife's bier was placed in the family living room. A heavy-looking purple cinerary urn rested on a black square table and a framed black-and-white photograph of the deceased hung on the wall behind it. The head in the photograph was larger than it had been in life but what caught my attention was the trace of a wry smile at the corners of the mouth, reminding me of how nice she'd been to Jiaojiao and me when we ate at their house. How had they made it so large? I wondered. The small-town newspaper reporter who'd hired on with us was taking pictures inside and outside the house with a snap-on lens. He bent for some shots and knelt for some others. I could tell how hard he was working by the sweat stains on his white T-shirt, with the newspaper's name across the chest; it was actually sticking to his back. He'd gained so much weight since he'd joined the team that the skin on his face was taut, thanks to the added flesh underneath. His cheeks had taken on the appearance of rubber balls. I went up to him while he was putting in a new roll of film. 'Hey, Skinny Horse,' I said under my breath, 'how did they make that photo on the wall so big?'

'It's called an enlargement,' he explained patiently. 'If you like, I could make a picture of you as big as a camel.'

'But I don't have a picture.'

He raised his camera, pointed it at my face, and—*click*. 'Now you do. You'll have an enlargement in a couple of days, Director Luo.'

Jiaojiao ran up.

'I want one too,' she bawled.

He aimed his camera at her. *Click.*

'Got it.'

'I want one of the two of us,' she said.

He aimed his camera. *Click.* 'Got it.'

This made me so happy I wanted to keep chatting with him, but he was off taking more pictures. A man walked in through Lao Lan's open front door, wearing a wrinkled grey suit, a white shirt with a filthy collar, and a pink bolo tie made of fake pearls. One trouser leg was rolled up, revealing a purple sock and an orange, mud-coated leather shoe. We called him 'Big Four'—big mouth, big eyes, big nose and big teeth. Actually, his ears were big enough for him to have been called 'Big Five'. On his belt he wore a beeper, something we called an electric cricket at the time. Lao Lan was one of the few people within a hundred square li who owned a cellphone—the size of a brick, it was carried by Huang Biao and, although seldom used, it was quite a status symbol. While not in the same category as a cellphone, a beeper conferred status too. Big Four, the township head's brother-in-law, was also the best-known contractor of construction labour in the area. He won contracts for virtually every township project, whether a public road or a public toilet. Given to swaggering round most people, he didn't dare try that with Lao Lan or with Mother. Tucking his briefcase under his arm, he went up to my mother, nodded and bowed.

'Director Yang . . .'

My mother had been promoted to serve as Huachang Corporation's office manager and assistant to the general manager, as well as chief accountant for United Meatpacking. She had on a full-length black dress with a white paper flower pinned to the breast and a pearl necklace. Shunning make-up, she wore a solemn expression and a piercing glare, like the sharp edges of a Chinese written character, like a sober eulogy, like a stately pine tree.

'What are you doing here?' Mother demanded. 'Why aren't you out supervising the tomb construction?'

'I've got gravediggers there now.'

'You should be supervising them.'

'I have been,' Big Four said. 'I wouldn't dare be careless on a job for Boss Lan. But . . .'

'But what?'

He took out a notepad from his pocket: 'Director, the gravediggers are almost finished and next comes the coffin chamber. For that we'll need three tonnes of lime, five thousand bricks, two tonnes of cement, five of sand, two cubic metres of lumber, and other odds and ends . . . can you advance some money for that?'

'Don't you think you've bled us enough?' Mother was not happy. 'Building a tomb can't cost that much, yet you come asking for money. Use your own and get reimbursed when the job is finished.'

'Where am I supposed to get the money?' Big Four whined. 'I get paid for the project in my left hand and then pass it on to the workers with my right. I'm a middleman, with nothing left over for me. Without some money now, we're looking at work delays.'

'I can't believe I'm even talking to you,' Mother said as she headed over to the eastern wing, with Big Four hard on her heels.

Father was sitting stony-faced behind a table on which lay a rice-paper accounts book. A brass ink box with a writing brush on top of it sat to the side. He accepted memorial gifts from a steady stream of people—cash or packets of yellow worship paper, a hundred sheets for some, two hundred for others—and entered them into his account book, while the Inspection Station's assistant head, Xiao Han, manning a squat table behind him, stamped the paper with the mark of an ancient copper coin, thus turning the paper into spirit money that could then be burnt for the deceased. Some people brought packets of actual spirit money issued by the 'Bank of the Underworld' and displaying the imagined likeness of King Yama, in denominations no smaller than a hundred million RMB. Picking up a billion-yuan note, Xiao Han said with a sigh: 'Won't bills this big cause inflation down there?'

An old man named Ma Kui, who'd brought a hundred RMB in cash and two packets of worship paper, shook his head. 'That stuff's almost useless. Only imprinted worship paper counts as money in the underworld.'

'How do you know that?' asked Xiao Han. 'Have you been down there to check it out?'

'My wife came to me in a dream and said that's considered fake money down there.' He kicked piles of it on the floor. 'You need to tell Lao Lan to throw it away. If she takes fake money with her, she'll be arrested as a counterfeiter.'

'There are police down there?' Xiao Han asked.

'Of course there are. They've got everything we've got up here,' Ma Kui replied confidently.

'We've got a United Meatpacking Plant and we've got you—how about those?'

'Don't get smart with me, young fellow. Go see for yourself if you don't believe me.'

'Going down is the easy part. How do I get back? You'd like to see me dead, you old fart!'

Mother walked in and nodded to Ma Kui. 'Where are you going, Inspector Han? Are you looking for a promotion?' Mother picked up the phone before he could respond and dialled a number. 'Is this the Finance Department? Xiao Qi, This is Yang Yuzhen. Big Four's on his way to see you. Give him five thousand RMB, and don't forget to get a receipt with his thumbprint.'

'Make it ten thousand, Director Yang,' Big Four said brazenly. 'Five won't do it.'

'Don't get greedy, Big Four,' Mother said sharply.

'That's not it.' He took out his notebook. 'Five thousand isn't nearly enough. See here. Three thousand for bricks, two thousand for lime, five thousand for lumber . . .'

'Five thousand, and that's it,' Mother cut him off.

Big Four sat down in the doorway. 'In that case, we'll have to stop work . . .'

'King Yama would tremble if he ran into the likes of you,' Mother said as she picked up the phone again. 'Give him eight thousand,' she said.

'You're an iron abacus, Director Yang. Make it an even number. After all, it's not your money.'

'I can't authorize ten thousand precisely because it isn't my money.'

'Lao Lan knew what he was doing when he hired you.'

'Get out!' Mother spat at him. 'Just the sight of you gives me a headache!'

Big Four stood up and bowed to Mother. 'There's no one better than Director Yang, not my mother and not my father.'

'You can substitute the word "money" for Director Yang! You're an expert at cutting corners on roads and buildings. If you do that on this tomb, Big Four, you'll live to regret it.'

'Don't give it another thought, Director,' Big Four said snidely. 'I'll spend less and work harder, even if the money runs out. I'll build you a tomb that's impervious to an atom bomb.'

'You can't find ivory in a dog's mouth.' Mother said, losing her temper. 'You don't have the money in hand yet,' she added as she reached for the phone. 'Let's see which is faster, your legs or my fingers on the dial.'

'Damn this stinking mouth of mine!' Big Four said as he made a show of slapping himself. 'Director Yang, Elder Sister Lan, oh, no, I mean Elder Sister Luo, my dear Elder Sister. I was just trying to soft-soap you. I'm too coarse to say the right thing . . .'

'Get out!' Mother grabbed a handful of spirit money and threw it at him.

The paper fluttered in the air.

Big Four made a face at the others in the room, turned and scooted for the doorway, where, in his rush, he collided with the wife of Huang Biao. 'You're not fighting to wear the parental mourning cap, are you, Big Four?'

she blurted out, her face red with anger. 'Don't worry, there's one waiting for you.'

'I'm sorry, Elder Sister Lan, no, I mean Elder Sister Huang. I can't control this mouth of mine,' he said, rubbing his head. Then he stuck his face up next to her and said softly, 'I haven't bruised your breasts, have I?'

'You can go to hell, Big Four!' she said as she kicked him in the shin and fanned the air in front of her face. 'Have you been eating shit—is that why you stink so bad?'

'For someone like me,' Big Four replied, feigning humility, 'the only shit I could find would turn out to be cold.'

She tried to kick him again, but he moved away in time and slunk out through the doorway.

Everyone in the room was still speechless at Big Four's antics and could now only stare blankly at the new arrival. She was wearing a short blue cotton jacket with a floral pattern, a high collar and buttons down the side over cotton warm-ups that scraped the floor. Black embroidered shoes popped in and out of view. Though she had the look of a rich family's nanny, there was also a bit of the modern schoolgirl about her. She wore her oiled hair in a loose bun; dark eyebrows rested atop a pair of limpid eyes over a button nose and fleshy lips. A dimple formed in her left cheek when she smiled. Her breasts jiggled like a couple of little rabbits. I've spoken of her before—she worked for Lao Lan, taking care of his wife and daughter. After I signed on as a workshop director at United, I stopped taking my meals there, so it had been quite a while since I'd seen her, and my impression this time was that she'd somehow become a loose woman. Why? Because just looking at her made my pecker stand up, no matter how hard I wished it back down. To be honest, loose women have always disgusted me, but that had no effect on my desire to keep looking at her, which in turn led to feelings of guilt. I should have looked away. But she was like a magnet for my eyeballs; and when she saw me staring at her she flashed me a smile that reeked of sex.

'Director Yang,' she said, 'Boss Lan is asking for you.'

Mother glanced at Father with the strangest expression.

Father kept his head down and continued making entries in the book.

So Mother followed the shifting buttocks of Huang Biao's wife out the door. Damn her, she made my face itch. She ought to be shot.

Xiao Han, whose eyes had been glued on those buttocks, said emotionally: 'A man of substance can't find a decent mate, a warty toad winds up with a flower of a woman.'

'Huang Biao is just a front man,' said Ma Kui, who was chain-smoking free cigarettes. 'Who knows who's the real husband!'

'Who are you talking about?' Jiaojiao asked.

Father banged his writing brush on the table, spilling ink in the box.

'What's wrong, Dieh?' Jiaojiao said.

'Shut up!' he barked.

'Luo Tong,' Ma Kui said with a shake of his head, 'why erupt like that?'

'Fuck off,' Xiao Han retorted. 'Do you plan to smoke those free cigarettes till you've got your hundred-RMB's worth?'

Ma Kui plucked two more cigarettes out of the tin, lit one with the smouldering butt of another and tucked the other behind his ear. Then he stood up and walked to the door. 'If you want to know,' he said on his way out, 'Boss Lan and I are related, since his third uncle's daughter-in-law is the niece of my son-in-law's third uncle.'

'Xiaotong,' Father said, 'go home, and take Jiaojiao with you. I don't want you getting mixed up in all this.'

'No,' Jiaojiao said. 'It's too much fun here.'

'I said take her home, Xiaotong!' he insisted.

The look on his face, the sternest I'd seen since his return, scared me enough to make me grab my sister's hand and take her home. But she dug in her heels and grumbled, her body swaying as she resisted my efforts. Father was about to slap her when Mother walked in. He dropped his hand.

'Lao Luo,' Mother said gravely, 'Boss Lan wants us to let Xiaotong take the role of the dutiful son. He can join Tiangua to keep a vigil at the bier and smash the clay pot used to burn the spirit money.'

A look of desolation spread across Father's face. He lit a cigarette and puffed on it so intensely that a smoky cloud blurred his features and increased the look of desolation. 'Did you agree?' he said at last.

'I don't see any problem,' Mother said, slightly embarrassed. 'Huang Biao's wife says that when he and Jiaojiao were taking their meals there, her mistress said she'd like him as a surrogate son. Lao Lan says that having a son had been her lifelong wish and this would fulfil that wish.' Mother looked my way. 'Xiaotong, do you know if that's something Aunty said?'

'I'm not sure . . .'

'How about you, Jiaojiao? Did Aunty ever say she'd like your brother to be her surrogate son?'

'Yes, she did,' Jiaojiao confirmed.

Father reached over and rapped Jiaojiao on the head. 'You can't stop sticking your nose into things! You've been spoilt rotten.'

Jiaojiao burst into tears, and those tears made up my mind.

'Yes, she did say that, and I told her I'd be happy to. And not just Aunty but Uncle Lan said the same thing, in the presence of Bureau Chief Qin, no less.'

'It's no big deal,' Mother said indignantly, 'certainly not worth blowing up over. It could give the deceased a bit of consolation.'

'Does the deceased know that?' Father said icily.

'What do you think?' Mother said, looking glum. 'A person's heart lives on after death.'

'Please stop spouting nonsense!' Father railed.

'What do you mean, nonsense?'

'I'm not going to argue with you.' Father lowered his voice. 'He's your son, have him do what you want.'

Xiao Han, who had been crouching nearby, stood up.

'Don't be so stubborn, Manager Luo. Since Director Yang's already told Boss Lan it's all right, and Director Xiaotong has no objections, why not let them have their way? Besides, it's just play-acting. Xiaotong could play the role of dutiful son ten thousand times, but he'd still be your son and no one could take that away from you. In fact, most people would fight for an opportunity like this.'

Father kept his head down and said nothing.

'That's just what he's like—bullheaded,' Mother said. 'He'll pick a fight with me over just about anything, and I'm stuck. That's the story of my life.'

'You'll leave one of these days,' Father said unemotionally.

'That's ridiculous,' Mother said unkindly and then turned to me. 'Xiaotong, go see Huang Biao's wife and get her to help you change. I don't want you goofing off when the reporters show up. Aunty Lan treated you like a son, so repay her by acting like one.'

'I want to go change too,' Jiaojiao whined.

'Jiaojiao!' Father growled as he glared at her.

Jiaojiao's mouth trembled as though she were about to burst out crying. The unyielding look on Father's face put a stop to that, although a few tears seeped from her eyes.

Dusk has just settled in and work on the opera stage is done; the four workmen are carrying the freshly painted Meat God to one side of the tall stage. Its face comes alive in the moist rays of the setting July sun; its feet are nailed to a wooden base to keep it from tipping over. My heart tightens with every thud as they pound in those long, thick nails and my feet twitch in pain. I didn't realize I'd fainted till I came to. The wet stains on the front of my pants are proof, as is the taste of blood from a bitten tongue and the pain in the pinched spot between my nose and mouth. A young woman, a medical-school badge pinned to her blouse, straightens up and says to a male student with dyed blond hair: 'Probably an epileptic seizure.' He leans over and asks: 'Is there a family history of epilepsy?' Confused, I shake my head, which is pretty much empty. 'How is he supposed to understand that kind of question?' she says as she glares at him. 'Has anyone in your family ever had a seizure?' I think really hard but I'm so weak I can hardly lift my arms. A seizure? Well, Fan Zhaoxia's father frequently passed out on the street, foaming at the mouth and suffering from violent spasms, and I heard people say those were seizures. But no one in my family had them, not even when my mother was furious with my father or me. I shake my head and struggle to prop myself into a seated position with arms as weak as limp noodles. 'It could have been a symptomatic seizure caused by emotional trauma,' the woman says to the man. 'What kind of traumatic experience can someone with a simple intellectual life have?' He is not convinced. Fuck you! I fume inwardly. What do you know about my so-called simple intellectual life? My life is complex as hell. The woman raises her voice. 'Avoid heights, don't go in the water, do not drive a car or a motorbike and no riding horses.' I understand every word but I doubt that the look on my face shows it. 'Let's go, Tiangua,' the man says. 'The opera is about to begin.' Tiangua? My heart lurches as an avalanche of memories thuds into my head. Is it even remotely possible that the slim-waisted, long-legged university student with shoulder-length hair, finely formed features and kind heart is Lao Lan's daughter, the girl with the dull, colourless hair, Tiangua? She has developed into quite a young woman. There's really no telling what a girl will look like when she grows up. Tiangua! It could have been me calling out or it could have been the crumbling Horse God. I hope it was me, because they say that if the Horse God calls out to a pretty girl and she makes the mistake of responding— she'll have a hard time escaping from a debilitating fate. This time she turns to see who called her name. I mean absolutely nothing to her, so she can't possibly have expected to see the swaggering Luo Xiaotong of her childhood, not in the current state, a barely conscious beggar—I'm not a beggar but I'm sure that's what she and her boyfriend think—lying on the floor of a broken-down temple recovering from some kind of seizure. She stands there, her belly up against the face of the Wise Monk, who doesn't flinch. She doesn't seem to think any-thing of it as she leans forward, reaches out and strokes the Horse Spirit's neck. 'Have you read the Wutong story in Strange Tales from a Chinese Studio*?' she asks her friend without turning to look at him. 'No,' he says with evident embarrassment. 'We only studied our textbooks so we could get into college. The competition was brutal, since the required test scores were so incredibly high.' 'What do you know about the Wutong?' she turns to asks him, a mis-chievous grin on her face. 'Nothing.' 'That's what I thought.' 'So what is it?' he asks. 'No wonder the writer Pu Songling said "After Wan's success with weapons, the area of Wu had no trouble with the remnants of the Wutong spirit,"' she teases. 'Huh?' is all he can manage. She smiles. 'Forget it. But look here. She holds out her mud-stained hand. See? The Horse Sprit is sweating.' He takes her hand and leads her out of the temple. She turns to look back, reluctant to leave, and though she is looking at the idol, she's talking to me when she says: 'You should go to a hospital. You're not about to die but you do need some medical attention.' My nose begins to ache, in part out of gratitude and in part over the vicissitudes of life. More and more people have joined the crowd outside, including the very old and the very young, bringing with them stools to sit on, assembling from both sides of the road and the cultivated fields behind the temple. What I find strange is that there isn't a single vehicle on the usually busy road, a departure that can only be explained if the police have cor-doned it off. I wonder why they haven't erected the stage in the open field across the way instead of on the cramped temple grounds. Nothing is the way it should* be, nothing makes sense. I look up and there's Lao Lan, his arm in a sling and a gauze bandage covering his left eye, looking like a defeated soldier, walking up to the temple from the cornfield behind us, escorted by Huang Biao. The girl they'd named Jiaojiao runs happily ahead of them, holding a fresh ear of corn she's just picked. Her mother, Fan Zhaoxia, cautions her: 'Slow down, honey, you could trip and fall.' A middle-aged man in an undershirt, holding a folding fan and smiling broadly, runs up to greet the new arrivals: 'Boss Lan, how good of you to come.' A man next to Lao Lan makes the introductions: 'This is Troupe Leader Jiang of the Qingdao Opera Troupe. He's a true artist.' 'You can see why I can't shake your hand, Lao Lan says. My apologies.' 'There's no need for you to apologize, General Manager. The troupe survives on your support.' 'We help each other,' Lao Lan replies. 'Tell your actors to put on a good show to thank the Meat God and the Wutong Spirit. I offended the gods by firing a gun in front of the temple and got what I deserved.' 'Don't you worry, General Manager, we'll sing our hearts out.' Electricians with tool bags over their shoulders climb ladders to instal stage lighting, and watching them go up and down reminds me of the brothers who did electrical work back in Slaughterhouse Village years before. How things have changed. The surroundings are the same but not the people. I, Luo Xiaotong, have sunk to the lowest tier of society and am pretty well assured of never being able to turn my life round. My abilities do not extend beyond sitting in this dilapidated temple, propping up a body exhausted by the occurrence of what might have been an epileptic seizure and relating dusty old stories to a Wise Monk whose body is like rotting wood—

A large, gleaming purplish red coffin rested in Lao Lan's living room. In it lay a fancy urn full of bones. Why go to all that trouble? I wondered. But then Lao Lan knelt by the coffin and smacked it with his hand as he keened, and I got my answer. A hand on an empty coffin was the only way to create such a soul-stirring sound; only a grand coffin suited the sight of the imposing Lao Lan kneeling alongside; and only a coffin of that grandeur was capable of encapsulating the appropriately sombre atmosphere. I had no way of knowing if my conjectures were correct, because what happened later made me lose all interest in this train of thought.

I sat at the head of the coffin, draped in hempen mourning attire. Tiangua sat at the opposite end, similarly clad. A clay pot for burning spirit money had been placed in the space between us. She and I lit sheets of yellow paper embossed like money from the flame of the bean-oil lamp resting atop the coffin and fed them into the clay pot, where they quickly turned to white ash and swirls of smoke. The stifling heat of that lunar July day, coupled with the rope-belted hempen cloth I was swathed in and the fire in the pot made the sweat spill from my pores. I looked at Tiangua—she was in a similar state. We took turns removing sheets of paper from the stack in front of us and burning them. Her sober expression was short on grief and there were no signs of tears on her cheeks; perhaps she had no more tears to shed. I was faintly aware of talk that the woman in the casket wasn't her birth mother and that she'd been bought from a human trafficker. Another rumour had it that she was born of an affair between Lao Lan and a young woman in another village, then brought back to be raised by his wife. I kept looking at her and at the face of the woman in the framed photograph behind the coffin but saw no resemblance. Then I compared her with Lao Lan and saw no resemblance there either, so perhaps she had been bought from a human trafficker after all.

Mother walked up with a cool wet towel and wiped my sweaty face. 'Don't burn it too fast,' she whispered. 'Just enough to keep the fire going.'

She folded the towel, walked over to Tiangua and wiped her face as well. Tiangua looked up at Mother and rolled her eyes. She should have thanked her but she didn't.

Intrigued by our burning of the spirit money, Jiaojiao tiptoed over and crouched down next to me. Picking up a sheet, she tossed it into the clay pot and whispered: 'Could we barbecue meat in that?'

'No,' I said.

The two newspaper photographers we'd hired walked in from the yard, one carrying a video camera, the other a light, to film the activity round the bier. Mother rushed up to take Jiaojiao outside; she balked and Mother had to grab her under her arms and drag her away.

Since I was being filmed, I affected a sombre expression as I placed a sheet of paper into the bowl. Tiangua did the same. After turning his lens to the fire, nearly touching the flames, the cameraman moved first to my face and then to Tiangua's. Next my hands, then her hands and from there to the coffin. Finally, to the framed picture of the deceased, which drew my attention back to the pale, oversized face on the wall. There was sadness in Aunty

Lan's eyes, belying the trace of a smile on her lips, and as I stared at her I became aware that she was staring at me. I was awestruck by how much was hidden in her gaze; I looked away, first to the reporters in the doorway and then to Tiangua, who sat head-down, looking stranger to me by the minute. She grew less like a person and more like some sort of sprite, while the real Tiangua died along with her mother (birth mother or not, it didn't matter). What filled my eyes next was a funeral cart pulled by four horses along a broad dirt road heading southwest from their yard, carrying Aunty Lan and Tiangua, their baggy white attire billowing like butterfly wings.

At noontime, Huang Biao's wife called Tiangua and me into the kitchen; there, she laid out a platter of meatballs, a winter melon soup with ham and a basket of steamed buns for the two of us and Jiaojiao. I didn't have much of an appetite—the day was hot and I'd spent most of the morning breathing in smoke from the burning paper. But Tiangua and my sister wolfed down their food—a meatball washed down with a spoonful of soup, followed by a bite from a steamed bun. They ate without looking at each other, as if engaged in an eating contest. Lao Lan walked in before we'd finished. He hadn't combed his hair or shaved, his clothes were rumpled, his eyes were bloodshot and he looked utterly dejected.

Huang Biao's wife went up and gazed at him with her limpid eyes. 'General Manager,' she said, her voice heavy with concern, 'I know how painful this is for you. One night between a man and a woman produces a lifetime of affection. And you were together for so many years. Your wife was a virtuous woman, so saintly that we are as saddened by her departure as you. But she has left us, and there is nothing we can do about that, while you have your family to look after. And the company cannot operate without you. You are the village backbone. So, my dear elder brother, you must eat something, not for yourself but for all us villagers . . .'

His eyes red and puffy from crying, Lao Lan said: 'I appreciate your kind thoughts but I can't eat. Make sure the young ones are fed. I have many things to do.' He rubbed my head, then Jiaojiao's and Tiangua's, before walking out of the kitchen with tears in his eyes.

Huang Biao's wife followed him with her eyes. 'He's a fine man with a good heart,' she said emotionally.

When we finished eating, we went back to burning spirit paper at the bier.

A steady stream of people walked in and out of the yard, undisturbed by the family's dogs, which had been struck dumb after the death of Lao Lan's wife. They lay sprawled on the ground, resting their heads on their paws, teary-eyed and sad; only their eyes moved as they followed the people in the yard. The saying 'Dogs share human qualities' could not be truer. A group of men carrying papier-mâché human and horse figures entered the yard and made a big show of looking for a spot to place them. The artisan was a fit old man whose eyes darted this way and that. His head was as smooth and shiny as a light bulb, and he sported a few mousey whiskers on his chin. Mother signalled to him to have his men stand the figures in a row in front of the house's western wing. There were four altogether, each the size of a real horse, white with black hooves and eyes made of dyed eggshells. Horse-sized though they were, they had the mischievous look of ponies. The camera focused first on the horses, then moved to the craftsman and then finally to the human figures, of which there were two, a boy and a girl. Their names were pinned to their chests. His was Laifu—Good Fortune—hers Abao—Treasure. People said that the whiskered old man was illiterate, and yet at the end of every year he set up a stall in the marketplace and he sold New Year's scrolls. He didn't write what was on his scrolls—he simply drew what had been written by others. He was a true artist, a master of plastic arts. There were many stories about the man but none that I can go into here. He also brought along a money tree, its branches made of paper and from which hung leaves, each a shiny coin whose sparkle dazzled the eye.

But before Mother had seen off the first paper artisans, a second group showed up, this one with a Western flavour. The leader, we were told, was an art-institute student, a girl with short hair and glittering hoops in her ears. She was wearing a short fishnet blouse and what looked like rags over a pair of jeans. Her midriff was bare and her trouser legs shredded, like mops, with holes at the knees. Imagine a girl like that taking up a trade like that. Her men carried in a paper Audi A6, a large-screen TV, a stereo system—all modern things. None of those seemed especially out of place—what did were her human figures, also a boy and a girl. The face of the boy, dressed in a suit and leather shoes, was powdered, his lips painted red; the girl wore a white dress that showed her breasts. Everything about them said bride and groom—and not funeral figures. The cameramen were captivated by these new arrivals—they followed their subjects and knelt for close-ups. (The one from the small-town paper would one day gain fame as a portrait photographer.) Yao Qi wove his way through the paper figures crowding the small yard ahead of a band of funeral musicians, led by a man with a suona hanging at his waist and a cassocked monk working his prayer beads. They went straight to Mother.

'Lao Luo,' she shouted towards the eastern wing as she wiped the sweat from her brow, 'come out here and give me a hand.'

Even as the afternoon sun blazed down I remained at the head of the coffin, mechanically tossing paper money into the clay pot, gazing out at the excitement in the yard and casting an occasional glance at Tiangua; she was yawning, barely able to stay awake. Jiaojiao had run off somewhere. Huang Biao's wife, full of energy and reeking of meat, busied herself like a whirlwind, shuttling back and forth in the hall. Lao Lan was in the next room, holding forth loudly—I couldn't say who he was speaking to, given the dizzying number of people who had come and gone. The house was like a command centre, replete with staff officers, clerks, assistants, local officials, society bigwigs, enlightened gentry and more. Father emerged from the eastern wing, bent over at the waist, with a dark look on his face. Mother had shed her coat and was now wearing only a white shirt tucked into a black skirt. Her face was as red as a laying hen. As she surveyed the two teams of paper artisans, she pointed to Father, who was as wooden as she was efficient and passionate, and said: 'He'll pay you.' Without a word, Father turned and re-entered the eastern wing; the two craftsmen exchanged a brief disdainful look before following him in. By then Mother was talking to Yao Qi, the musicians and the monks. Her voice, loud and shrill, pounded against my eardrums. I felt my eyelids grow heavy.

I must have dozed off; the next time I looked into the yard, all the paper figures had been squeezed together to make room for a pair of tables and a dozen or more folding chairs. The blistering sun was now hidden behind clouds. A July day, like the face of a woman, is always apt to change, or so they say. Huang Biao's wife went out into the yard. 'Please, please,' I heard her say when she returned, 'please don't rain!'

'You can't stop the rain from falling or your mother from marrying,' said a woman in a white robe. Her hair newly permed, her lips painted black, her face covered with pimples, she had materialized in the doorway. 'Where's General Manager Lan?' she asked.

Huang Biao's wife looked the new arrival up and down.

'So, it's you, Fan Zhaoxia,' she remarked disdainfully. 'What are you doing here?'

'Are you inferring that you're welcome but I'm not,' Fan replied with the same disdain. 'Boss Lan called and asked for a shave.'

'That's a lie, and you know it, Fan Zhaoxia,' hissed Huang Biao's wife. 'He hasn't eaten in two days, hasn't even touched water. Shaving is the last thing on his mind.'

'Really?' Fan said icily. 'It was him on the phone. I recognized his voice.'

'You're sure you're not hallucinating?' asked Huang Biao's wife. 'That would explain everything.'

'Why don't you cool off?' Fan Zhaoxia spit in contempt. 'Her body's still warm and you're already acting like you're in charge.' She tried to walk into the room with her barber's kit, only to be stopped by Huang Biao's wife who spread her arms and legs to block the way. 'Move!' Fan demanded.

Huang Biao's wife looked at her feet and pointed with her chin. 'There's a tunnel for you.'

'You bitch!' Fan cursed angrily as she aimed a kick at the woman's crotch.

'How dare you!' shrieked Huang Biao's wife. She lunged at Fan and grabbed a handful of her hair; Fan retaliated by grabbing Huang Biao's breast.

Huang Biao took notice of the frenetic activity in the yard when he walked in through the gate with his basket of cooking utensils. But when he spotted the catfight between two women—one of them his wife—he shouted, threw down his basket, sending the pots and pans crashing loudly to the ground, and joined the fray, fists and feet. But his blows were seriously off target, and he wound up kicking his wife in the buttocks and punching her in the shoulder.

A relative of Fan Zhaoxia's ran up to even the odds, quickly driving his shoulder into Huang Biao. One of the strongest porters at the train station, the man had muscles like steel and shoulders that could carry five hundred pounds. His shove sent Huang Biao stumbling backward, until he sat down hard next to his basket. Infuriated, he began hurling plates and bowls, filling the air with flying porcelain, some thudding into the wall, some landing amid the crowds of people, some shattering and some rolling across the ground. My kind of fun!

Lao Lan appeared at that moment. 'Stop it,' he said, 'all of you!'

Like a hawk flying into the forest and quieting the birds or a tiger leaving its den and sending animals into hiding, one shout from him was all it took. 'Are you people here to help me,' he asked hoarsely, 'or to take advantage of a bad situation? Do you really think you've seen the last of Lao Lan?'

With that, he turned and left. The two scuffling women stopped fighting and merely glared at each with loathing. They both needed to catch their breath and nurse their wounds. Fan Zhaoxia was missing a handful of hair and a piece of her scalp. Huang Biao's wife's robe was missing its buttons; it lay open like a torn flag, exposing the tops of her scratched breasts.

Mother entered. 'All right,' she said to the women in icy tones, 'you can leave now.'

Out in the yard, the monks—seven altogether—and the musicians—also seven—took their places, like competing teams, under the direction of their leaders. The monks took seats at the table to the west, on which they laid their wooden fish, their chimes and their cymbals. The musicians took seats at the other table, on which they laid their horns, their suonas and their eighteen-holed flutes. The leading monk wore a saffron cassock, the others grey. The musicians' clothes were so tattered that we could see the abdomens of at least three of them. When the large wooden bell in Lao Lan's house was struck three times, Mother turned to Yao Qi. 'Begin,' she said.

From his position between the two tables, Yao Qi raised his arms like a conductor. 'Begin, Shifu!' he announced as he dropped his arms flamboyantly, thoroughly enjoying his moment as the centre of attention. It should have been me out there, but I was stuck inside, acting the dutiful son at the head of the coffin. Shit!

At Yao Qi's signal, two kinds of music erupted across the yard. On this side, the clap-clap of wooden fish and the clang of chimes and cymbals and the drone of chanted sutras. Along with that, a dirge with horns and wood-winds and flutes. A mournful sound indeed. As a murky dusk settled outside, the room grew dark, the only light a green sparkle from the bean-oil. I saw a woman's face in that light, and after staring at it for a few moments, I recognized it as Lao Lan's wife. Ghostly pale and bleeding from every orifice. 'Look, Tiangua!' I whispered, scared witless.

But she had dozed off, her head slumped onto her chest, like a chick resting against a wall. A chill ran down my spine, my hairs stood on end and my bladder threatened to burst, all good reasons to leave my post at the bier. Wetting my pants would surely be disrespectful towards the deceased! So I grabbed a handful of paper, threw it into the pot, jumped to my feet and ran out into the yard where I breathed in the fresh air before heading to the latrine next to the kennel and opening the floodgates with a shudder. The leaves on the plane tree quivered in the wind, but I could hear neither the wind nor the leaves, for both were drowned by the music and the chants. I watched the reporter taking shot after shot of the musicians and the monks.

'Put some oomph into it, gentlemen!' Yao Qi shouted. 'Your host will show his gratitude later.'

Yao Qi's loathsome face glowed, a petty man intoxicated by his perceived glory. The same man who had once approached my father with a plan to bring Lao Lan to his knees was now his chief lackey. But I knew how unreliable he was, that he had the bones of a backstabber and that Lao Lan would be wise to keep him at arm's length. Now that I was out, I had no desire to return to the head of the coffin so, together with Jiaojiao, who had shown up from somewhere, I ran round the yard taking in all the excitement. She had gouged out the eyes of a paper horse and was clutching them like treasured objects.

As the music from the monks and musicians came to an end, Huang Biao's wife, who had changed into an off-white dress, pranced into the yard like an operatic coquette and placed tea services on both tables. Biting her lower lip, she poured the tea. After a drink of tea and some cigarettes, it was time to perform. The monks began by intoning loud, rhythmic chants, liquid sounds filled with devotion, like pond bullfrogs croaking on a summer night. The crisp, melodic clangs of cymbals and the hollow thumps of the wooden fish highlighted the clear voices. After a while the minor monks ended their chorus, leaving only the strains of the old monk's full voice, with its uncanny modulation, to mesmerize the listeners. Everyone held their breath as they drank in each sacred note emerging from deep in the old monk's chest; it seemed to send their spirits floating idly, lazily, into the clouds. The old monk chanted on for several moments, then picked up his cymbals and beat them with changing rhythms. Faster and faster, now throwing his arms open wide and bringing them back, now barely moving. The sounds changed with the movements of his hands and arms, heavy clangs giving way to thin chattering clicks. At the moment of crescendo, one of the cymbals flew into the air and twirled like a magic talisman. The old monk uttered a Buddhist incantation, spun round and held the remaining cymbal behind his back, waiting for its mate to drop from the sky atop it; as it landed it produced a metallic tremble that lingered in the air. A cry of delight rose from the crowd and the monk flung both cymbals skyward—they chased each other like inseparable twins and, on meeting, sent a loud clang earthward. As they descended they seemed to seek out the old monk's hands. The performance that day by the wise old monk, a Buddhist devotee of high attainments, left a lasting impression on every one of us.

Their performance ended, the monks sat down and returned to their tea. The crowd now turned its attention to the musicians in anticipation of something new. The monks' performance would be a hard act to follow, but we would have been disappointed with the musicians for not surpassing it.

Without a moment's hesitation, the musicians stood up and began as an ensemble, opening with the tune 'Boldly Move Forward, Little Sister', followed by 'When Will You Return' and then the brisk 'The Little Shepherd'. When they laid down their instruments, they turned their eyes to their shifu, who peeled off his jacket, revealing a frame so slight you could count his ribs. He shut his eyes, raised his head and then began to play a funereal tune on his suona, his Adam's apple sliding up and down rhythmically. I didn't know the tune but its sad effect on me was unmistakable. As he played, the suona moved from his mouth up into one of his nostrils, which muted the notes while retaining the instrument's mournfully melodic tone. His eyes still shut, he reached out his hand and into it a disciple placed a second suona. The reed of this one too he inserted into a nostril, and now two suonas created a tune of surpassing sorrow. His face grew bright red, his temples throbbed and his audience was so moved it forget to cheer. Yao Qi had not exaggerated when he said he'd engaged a suona master of great renown. When the tune ended, he extracted the instruments from his nostrils, handed them to his disciples and fell into a chair. Disciples rushed up to pour him tea and hand him a cigarette, which he lit and immediately blew two streams of thick smoke from his nose, like dragons' whiskers. And then blood slithered, worm-like, out of both nostrils.

'Your reward for wonderful performances—' Yao Qi bellowed.

Xiao Han, the meat inspector, ran out from the eastern wing with a pair of identical red envelopes and laid one on each table. The old monk and head musician immediately began a man-to-man competition, and it was hard to tell who won. *But I doubt that you're interested in hearing about such things, Wise Monk, so I'll skip this part and move on to what unfolded next.*

Back in the eastern wing Yao Qi was boasting of the great service he'd rendered my father, Xiao Han and several of the men who had helped out, telling them how he had travelled five hundred *li* to engage the services of the two troupes, 'wearing out the soles of my shoes in the process'. He lifted his foot as proof. Xiao Han, known for his caustic tongue, couldn't resist a barb: 'I hear you used to think of Lao Lan as your mortal enemy. You must have changed your mind when you decided to be his chief lackey.'

Father's lip curled and, though he held his tongue, his face spoke volumes.

'We're all lackeys,' Yao Qi remarked nonchalantly. 'But at least I sell myself. Some people sell their wives and children.'

Father's face darkened. 'Who are you talking about?' he demanded, gnashing his teeth.

'Only myself, Lao Luo, why so angry?' Yao Qi replied slyly. 'I hear you're going to be married soon.'

Father picked up his ink box and flung it at Yao Qi and then stood up.

A brief look of anger on Yao Qi's face was supplanted by a sinister grin. 'What a temper, Old Brother, you have to "out with the old" before you can "in with the new". For a big-time plant manager like you, nothing could be easier than getting your paws on a young maiden. Just leave it to me. I may not have what it takes to be an official, but as a matchmaker I'm peerless. How about your young sister, Xiao Han?'

'Fuck you, Yao Qi!' I cursed.

'Director Luo, no, it should be Director Lan,' Yao Qi said, 'you're the crown prince of the village!'

Xiao Han rushed at the man before Father could, grabbed him by the arms and spun him so hard that his head drooped. Then he pushed him towards the door, jammed his knee into his buttocks and gave him a shove that sent him out the door as if he'd been shot from a cannon. He lay sprawled on the ground for a long while after.

At five that evening, it was time for the formal funeral ceremony to begin. Mother grabbed me by the scruff of my neck and dragged me back to the coffin, where she pushed me down into the dutiful son's spot. A pair of white candles as thick as turnips burnt on the table behind the coffin, their flickering light heavy with the rancid odour of sheep's tallow. Light from the bean-oil lantern showed up about as bright as a glowworm's tail alongside the burning candle, and that in a room in which hung a twenty-eight-bulb crystal chandelier encircled by twenty-four spotlights. If they had all been turned on, you would have been able to count the ants crawling across the floorboards. But electric lights lacked the mystique of candles. Tiangua looked even stranger and less human as she sat across from me in the flickering light, but the more I tried to avoid looking at her the harder it was and the less human her image became. Her face underwent constant changes, like ripples on water. She was a bird one moment, a cat the next and then a wolf. And then I realized that her eyes were locked onto me, refusing to let go. Yet what really made my heart race was her posture—she was sitting on the edge of her stool, legs bent and taut, leaning forward like a predatory animal poised to attack. At any moment, I imagined, she'd spring from her stool, bound across the clay pot with its burning paper and pounce, then wrap her hands round my neck and gnaw on my face—*crunch crunch*, like a turnip—until she'd eaten my head. Then she'd howl and take on her true form, with a long, bushy tail, and flee without a trace. I knew that the real Tiangua had died long before, and that the figure seated across me was actually an evil spirit that had assumed her form and was waiting for the right moment to partake of the flesh of Luo Xiaotong, a meat-eater and thus tastier than other children. I'd once heard an alms-begging monk talk about retribution on the wheel of life; he'd said that individuals who ate meat would themselves be eaten by other meat-eaters. That monk had achieved a high degree of Buddhist attainments, one of many such monks in that place of ours. Take that alms-begging monk, for instance. He once sat in the snow in the middle of the winter, naked to the waist, lotus position, without eating or drinking for three days and nights. Many kindhearted women, afraid he would freeze to death, brought him blankets to keep warm, only to discover that his face was nice and ruddy and that steam rose from his scalp, almost as if his head were a stove. Blankets were the last thing he needed. Admittedly, there were people who said he had taken a 'fire dragon' pill, that he had no special gift. But who has ever seen one of those pills? The stuff of legend. But the monk in the snow? I saw him with my own eyes.

The face of Cheng Tianle, who had just lost a tooth, was mapped with more than eighty creases. Chosen as the master of ceremonies for the memorial service, he had a white ribbon draped over his shoulders and wore a white, heavily pleated hat like a rooster's coxcomb. He made a late appearance, though, causing people to wonder where he'd hidden himself for so long. He smelt heavily of alcohol, salted fish and damp earth, which made me surmise that he'd spent the time in Lao Lan's cellar. Well on his way to being drunk, he had trouble focusing his bleary eyes, almost gummed together with sticky residue. His assistant was Shen Gang, the man who'd once borrowed money from my mother. Smelling the same as Cheng Tianle—his cellar mate, obviously—he was dressed in black, with a pair of white oversleeves. In one hand he carried a hatchet and in the other a rooster—white with a black cockscomb. An important individual who walked into the room with them cannot go unmentioned—Su Zhou, younger brother of Lao Lan's wife, a close relative of some note who ought to have made an early appearance. His late arrival was either planned or was the result of his being delayed on the road.

Father, Yao Qi, Xiao Han and a clutch of brawny fellows followed the trio into the main room. A pair of low benches had been set up in the yard, where men with poles waited under the veranda eaves.

'Homage to the coffin—'

As Cheng Tianle's shout echoed in the air, Lao Lan rushed out of his room and fell to his knees in front of the coffin. 'Oh, dear mother of our daughter—ah huh huh huh—' he wailed, pounding the lid, 'you have cruelly left Tiangua and me behind—'

He thumped the coffin lid loudly with his hand and tears streaked his face, revealing the depth of his overwhelming grief (and immediately squelching a good many rumours).

Out in the yard the musicians played a dirge as the monks chanted, loudly and with enthusiasm. Inside and out, sound triumphantly created an aura of unbearable grief. For the moment I had no thoughts for the evil spirit across from me, as tears cascaded down my face.

Even the heavens lent a hand, first with rolling thunder, then with rain-drops the size of old coins that beat a tattoo on the ground. The rain pounded the monks' shaved heads and battered the faces of the musicians. Soon the drops grew smaller and the curtain of rain grew denser. But the monks and musicians persisted. The water splashing on the monks' heads had a relaxing effect on the people, though the brassy sound of horns and funereal strains of the suona became increasingly sorrowful. But nothing suffered more than the paper figures. Pounded by the relentless rain, they softened, then began to fall apart, with gaping holes in the front and at the back revealing the sorghum stalk frames on which they were fashioned.

With a silent signal from Cheng Tianle, Yao Qi led the grief-stricken Lao Lan to one side. Mother had me stand at the head of the coffin; Huang Biao's wife had Tiangua stand at the foot. Our eyes met across its length. Like a con-jurer, Cheng Tianle whisked out a brass gong and brought an abrupt end to the chants and the music outside. Now the only sound was the patter of raindrops. Shen Gang walked up stiffly to the coffin and laid his rooster, legs tightly bound, on top. He raised his hatchet over his head. The gong rang out. The rooster's head rolled to the ground.

'Lift the coffin—' shouted Cheng Tianle.

The pallbearers stepped up, prepared to pick up the coffin and carry it out into the yard, then place it atop the benches, fit it with ropes and shoulder it out the gate onto the street all the way to the cemetery. It would be interred in the waiting tomb, which would then be sealed; once a headstone was in place, everything would be brought to an orderly end. But it was not to be.

Lao Lan's young brother-in-law, Su Zhou, abruptly rushed up and threw himself across the coffin. 'Elder Sister—my beloved elder sister ' he wailed, 'how tragically you died—how unjustly—how suspiciously—'

As he pounded the coffin lid, staining his hand with chicken blood, the congregation fell into an awkward silence. We could only look on, wide-eyed and helpless.

Finally Cheng Tianle regained his senses; he walked up and tugged at the man's clothing. 'That's enough, Su Zhou. Now that you've poured out your grief, it's time to bury your sister and let her rest in peace.'

'Rest in peace?' Su Zhou demanded, his wailing abruptly ended. He jerked up straight, turned away from the coffin and then leapt backward to sit on it. Rays of green light emerged from his eyes and shone over the crowd. 'Rest in peace? You will not destroy the evidence of a heinous crime. I won't let you!'

Lao Lan kept his head down and held his tongue but Su Zhou's outburst made it impossible for others to intervene. So it was up to Lao Lan to reply, however dispiritedly: 'Go ahead, Su Zhou, say what you have to say.'

'What I have to say?' the man was boiling over with rage. 'I have to say that you murdered your wife, you evil man!'

Lao Lan shook his head, his anguish obvious: 'You're not a child, Su Zhou, who can get away with saying anything. You have to weigh your words. The law does not permit that sort of libel.'

'Libel?' Su Zhou sneered. 'Ha-ha, ha-ha, libel, he says. What does the law say about the murder of one's wife?'

'Where's your proof?' asked Lao Lan calmly.

Su Zhou banged the coffin with his bloodied hand. 'Here's my proof!'

'You're going to have to be clearer than that.'

'If you weren't hiding something, why were you in such a hurry to cre-mate her? Why didn't you wait for me to come and seal the coffin?'

'I sent people for you more than once—they told me you were off in the northeast replenishing your stock or having a good time on Hainan Island.

It's so hot that even the rolling pins are sprouting, but still we waited two full days for you.'

'Don't assume you've destroyed the evidence by cremating her body,' Su Zhou said with an icy laugh. 'Years after Napoleon's death they were able to determine that he'd died of arsenic poisoning by examining his bones. Pan Jinlian burnt up Wu Dalang, but Wu Song discovered scars on his bones. You won't get away with this.'

'What a monumental joke,' Lao Lan said to the crowd as tears gushed from his eyes. 'If my marriage had been an unhappy one, I could easily have demanded a divorce. Why in the world would I do what he's saying? My fellow villagers are not easily fooled. I ask you, is Lao Lan capable of anything so stupid?'

'Then tell me: how did my sister die?' Su Zhou demanded fiercely.

'You give me no choice, Su Zhou,' Lao Lan said as he crouched down and wrapped his arms round his head. 'You're forcing me to reveal a family disgrace. For some idiotic reason, your sister took the easy way out—she hanged herself . . .'

'Why?' Su Zhou insisted tearfully. 'Tell me, why did she hang herself?'

'Mother of my children, how could you be so foolish . . .' Lao Lan wept as he pounded his head with his fist.

'You bastard, Lao Lan,' Su Zhou said through clenched teeth, 'you and your secret mistress killed my sister, then made it look like suicide. Now I'm going to avenge her death!' He grabbed the hatchet, jumped off the coffin and rushed at Lao Lan.

'Stop him!' Mother shrieked.

People leapt to their feet and grabbed Su Zhou round his waist. But not before he flung the hatchet at Lao Lan's head. It glinted in the light as it sliced through the air, trailing a bloody path above our heads. Mother quickly pushed Lao Lan out of the way. The hatchet dropped harmlessly to the floor and she kicked it across the room. 'Su Zhou,' she cried out in alarm, 'what savage impulse drove you to try to kill him in broad daylight?'

'Ha-ha, ha-ha,' Su Zhou laughed wildly. 'Yang Yuzhen, you wanton woman, it was you, you conspired with Lao Lan to kill my sister . . .'

Mother's face turned from red to white and her lips quivered as she pointed to Su Zhou with a shaky finger. 'You . . . slinging unfounded . . . slander . . .'

'Luo Tong,' Su Zhou shouted as he pointed to Father, 'you worthless excuse of a man, you green-hatted cuckold! Are you a man or are you not? They made you factory manager and your son a director so she could sleep with your boss. How can you still have the nerve to show your face in the village? If I were you, I'd have hanged myself long ago.'

'Fuck you, Su Zhou!' I rushed up and buried my fist in his gut.

Some men ran up and pulled me away.

Yao Qi tried to calm things down. 'Young brother,' he said to Su Zhou, 'you don't hit a man in the face and you don't try to humiliate him, especially in the presence of his son and daughter. Now that you've brought this out in the open, how is Luo Tong supposed to hide his shame?'

'Fuck your old lady, Yao Qi!' I screamed.

Jiaojiao threaded her way up front and joined me: 'Fuck your old lady, Yao Qi!'

'A couple of brave children,' Yao Qi said with a smile. 'Always ready to fuck someone's old lady. But do you know how do that?'

'Mind your language, everyone,' said Chen Tianle. 'We've heard enough. I'm the master of ceremonies and what I say goes. Lift the coffin!'

No one paid him any attention—they couldn't take their eyes off Father, who had backed into a corner, his head raised, as if studying the patterns in the ceiling. Neither Su Zhou's curses nor Yao Qi's sarcasm seemed to have had any effect on him.

Outside, the sleeting rain splashed loudly. The monks and the musicians stood like wooden statues, unmoved by the downpour. A yellow-bellied swallow swooped into the room and darted round in a panic, the gusts of wind from its flapping wings making the candle flames flicker.

Father breathed a sigh and walked away from the wall, taking slow steps—one, two, three, four . . . blank stares followed him—five, six, seven, eight. He stopped in front of the hatchet, looked at it, then bent over and picked it up, holding the wooden handle with the thumb and index finger of his right hand. He wiped the chicken blood off the blade on the front of his jacket with the meticulous care of a carpenter cleaning his tools. He then took hold of the hatchet with his left hand. My father was the village's most famous lefty—I was one too and so was my sister. Lefties are known for being smart; but when we were at the table eating, our chopsticks invariably clashed with Mother's, since she was right-handed. Father walked up to Yao Qi, who hid behind Su Zhou. He then walked up to Su Zhou, who hid behind his sister's coffin, followed at once by Yao Qi in an effort to keep Su Zhou between him and Father. The truth is, they meant nothing to Father. He walked up to Lao Lan, who got to his feet and nodded calmly. 'Luo Tong, I once thought highly of you but the truth is that you were no match for Wild Mule and you're no match for Yang Yuzhen.'

Father raised the hatchet over his head.

'Father!' I shrieked as I ran to him.

'Father!' Jiaojiao shrieked as she ran to him.

The local reporter raised his camera.

The cameraman turned his lens to Father and Lao Lan.

The hatchet circled the air above Father then swung down and split open Mother's head.

She stood as still as a post for a few seconds and then slumped into Father's arms.

Two nimble-footed electricians pound a nail into the temple's interior wall, attach a wire and hang a floodlight from it. When it's switched on its blinding light turns the dusky hall as pale as an epileptic. I squint to protect my eyes as spasms wrack my arms and legs, and the loud buzz of a cicada rings in my ears. I fear a relapse and desperately want to urge the Wise Monk to let us into his room behind the idol to escape from that light. But he sits there calmly, looking quite comfortable. That's when I discover a pair of fancy sunglasses on the floor beside me, possibly forgotten by the medical student— I can't be sure if she is in fact Lao Lan's daughter, since the world is full of people with the same name. I owe her for saving my life, and returning the glasses would be the right thing to do. But she's gone without a trace, so I put them on to keep the bright light out of my eyes. If she comes back I'll give them to her. If not I'll keep wearing them. I know a young woman like her would not want her glasses worn by someone like me. Everything has changed colour, taken on a soft, creamy hue, and I feel comfortable again. Lao Lan strides through the door, brings his uninjured arm up to his chest in a salute, then bows deeply and says almost in jest: 'Revered Horse Spirit, to atone for my ignorance and for offending you, I will put on an opera especially for you. I ask you to help me in my goal of becoming rich. When I do I will donate what- ever it takes to refurbish your temple and give you a new coat of gold paint. I will even supply you with a bevy of young women to enjoy at leisure, so you will no longer have to enter people's homes in the dead of night.' His vow draws titters from his entourage; they cover their mouths with their hands. Fan Zhaoxia curls her lip. 'Are you asking for something from the Spirit or trying to make it angry?' she asks. 'What do you know? The Spirit understands me. Revered Horse Spirit, what do you think of this wife of mine? I'll be glad to offer you her services if you like.' Fan Zhaoxia gives him a swift kick. 'You really do have a dog's mouth that can't spit out ivory,' she says. 'The Horse Spirit will show itself and use its hooves to put you out of your misery.' 'Papa, Mamma,' their daughter calls from the yard, 'I want some cotton candy.' Lao Lan pats the Horse Spirit's neck and says: 'Goodbye, Horse Spirit. Let me know in a dream if you spot the woman you like, and I'll see that you get her. Women these days go for big guys.' Lao Lan exits the temple with his large retinue. A bunch of children holding sticks of cotton candy dart this way and that. A peddler of roasted corn on the cob fans his charcoal brazier with a moth-eaten fan. 'Ro-o-oasted cor-r-r-n,' he shouts, drawing out each word. 'One RMB an ear, free if it's not sweet.' The crowd has swollen in front of the opera stage, and the musicians fill the air with the clang of cymbals, the pound of drums and the twang of stringed instruments. A boy with tufts of hair standing up on either side of his head, wearing a red stomacher, his face heavily rouged; a Qingyi in a side-buttoned robe and baggy trousers, her hair gathered in a bun; an old man in a bamboo hat and straw sandals, sporting a white goatee; a blue-faced comic actor; and his female counterpart with a medicinal patch at her temple. They all clamour their way into the temple. 'You call this an actor's lounge?' the Qingyi is angry. 'There isn't even a chair!' 'Try to make the best of it, can't you?' pleads the old man with the goatee. 'No,' she says. 'I'm going to talk to Troupe Leader Jiang. This is no way to treat people.' Jiang walks in as he hears his name: 'What's the problem?' 'We're not famous actors, Troupe Leader,' the Qingyi says, and we don't make unreasonable demands. But we are human beings, aren't we? When there's no hot water we drink it cold, when we have to do without rice and vegetables we eat bread and when we don't have a dressing room we get ready in a car or truck. But a simple stool isn't asking too much, is it? We're not mules that can sleep standing.' 'Put up with it as best you can, Comrade,' he says. 'I dream of getting you to Changan Municipal Theatre or the Paris Opera House, where you'd want for nothing. But what are the chances, I ask you? Let's be frank. We are high-class beggars, or not even that. Beggars can smash a pot just because it's cracked, but we— we can't stop thinking that we're better than that.' 'Then why don't we go out and start begging?' the woman snaps. 'I guarantee we'd make more than we do now. Look at all the beggars who live in Western-style houses.' 'You can say that if you want,' reasons the troupe leader. 'But you'd never make it as beggars even if you had to. Comrades, try to make do. I damn near had to kiss Lao Lan's arse for the extra five hundred. I'm a drama-school graduate, I'm sup-

posed to be an intellectual. Back in the 1970s, a play I wrote even won second prize in a provincial contest. But if you'd seen how I degraded myself in front of Lao Lan's lackeys, well, I'm ashamed of the sickening talk that came out of my mouth. Afterwards, when I was alone, I actually slapped myself. And so, assuming we are all reluctant to give up this bit of income and still cling to this poor, pedantic art of ours, we must all endure a bit of humiliation to do what we've come to do and, as you said, when there's no hot water drink it cold, when you have to do without rice and vegetables eat bread. And if there are no stools please stand. Actually, standing is better, for you can see farther.' The young boy, the one made up to look like the legendary celestial Prince Naza, scoots between me and the Wise Monk and leaps onto the back of the Horse Spirit. 'Aunty Dong,' he cries out brightly, 'come up here, it's great!' 'You're a silly little meat boy,' the Qingyi says. 'I'm not a meat boy, I'm a meat god, a meat immortal,' he says as he bounces up and down atop the horse. Its water-soaked, crumbling back soon gives way and the frightened boy quickly slides off. 'The Horse Spirit's back is broken,' he shouts. 'That's not the only thing that's broken,' the Qingyi says as she surveys the temple. 'The whole place looks like it's about to collapse. I hope it doesn't tonight and make meat patties out of all of us.' 'Don't worry, miss,' says the man with the goatee, 'the Meat God will protect you, for you are his mother!' The troupe leader runs in with a rickety chair. 'Get ready to go on stage, meat boy,' he says and places the chair behind the Qingyi. 'Sorry, Xiao Dong,' he says, 'but this is the best I've got.' The meat boy dusts himself off, rubs his hands to clean off the mud, bounds out of the temple and mounts the wooden steps to the stage. The drums and the cymbals fall silent and give way to the two-stringed huqin and flute. 'I've come to rescue my mother,' the meat boy says in his high voice, 'travelling day and night,' and then runs to the centre of the stage as he fin- ishes his line. Peeking through the gap between old blue curtains behind the stage, I see him turn a couple of somersaults. The drums and the cymbals set up a raucous din that merge with the crowd's ardent shouts of approval for the boy. 'I cross mountains, ford rivers and pass through a sleepy town—to see a physician of great renown—he prescribes a concoction for mother mine—what a mix of ingredients—croton oil, raw ginger, even bezoar, a strange design—at the pharmacy I hand up the slip—the clerk demands two silver dollars for this trip—from a family with no money to enjoy—causing agonizing distress for this dutiful meat boy.' He rolls about the stage to display his agonizing distress. With the beat of drums and clang of cymbals all round me, I feel like he and I have fused into one. What's the relationship between the story of the meat-eating Luo Xiaotong and the me who's sitting across from the Wise Monk? It's like some other boy's story, while my story is being acted out up on the stage. In order to get the concoction for his mother, the boy goes looking for the woman who buys and sells children to offer himself up for sale. The child merchant mounts the stage, bringing with her a happy, humorous air. Her lines all rhyme: 'A child-seller, that's me, my name is Wang. My clever mouth takes me far and long. A chicken, you know, can be a duck, a donkey's mouth on a horse's arse is stuck. You'll believe me when I say the dead can run, the living in the underworld a sad song have begun . . .' As she speaks, a naked woman, her hair in disarray, climbs up a post and then tumbles onto the stage. An uproar at the foot of the stage ends in excited shouts of Bravo! that split the clouds. 'Wise Monk!' I cry out in alarm. I can see the face of the crazed nude and—my God!—it's the actress Huang Feiyun. The meat boy and the child-seller move out of her way; she circles the stage as she were all alone until her attention is caught by the Meat God at the stage's edge. She walks up and pokes it in the chest with a tentative finger. Then—smack smack—she slaps it across the face. Men rush up to her, perhaps to drag her off stage, but she slips out of their grasp as if she were greased. Several leering men rush up, link their arms, form a wall round her and close in. She smirks and backs up slowly. 'Back, back . . . Leave her alone, you bastards!' That's my heart shouting. But the unfolding tragedy is inescapable. Huang Feiyun falls off the stage, drawing cries of alarm from below. A moment later I hear a woman's shout—it's the medical student Tiangua—'She's dead, you sons of bitches!' Why did you have to do that? That breaks my heart, Wise Monk, I can't hold back my tears. I feel a hand on my head—it's ice cold. Bleary-eyed, I can see it's the Wise Monk's hand. This time he doesn't try to mask the sadness he feels. A soft sigh escapes from his mouth. 'Go on with your tale, son,' I hear him say. 'I'm listening—'

Mother was dead, Father was under arrest. Lao Han, who supposedly knew the law, said that Father was guilty of a capital crime and that the best he could expect was a death sentence with a two-year reprieve. A death sentence without a reprieve was a distinct possibility.

Jiaojiao and I were now orphans.

I'll never forget the day they arrested Father. It was ten years ago today. It had rained heavily the night before, and the morning was as hot and humid as it is today, with the same blistering sun. A municipal police car drove into the village a little after nine in the morning, siren blaring. People poured out of their homes to stare. The car stopped in front of the village office, where Lao Wang and Wu Jinhu of the local militia brought Father out of the Township Station house. Wu removed the handcuffs and a municipal policeman came up and cuffed Father with a new pair.

Jiaojiao and I stood by the side of the road staring at Father's puffy face; his hair had turned white overnight. My tears flowed (although I must confess that I didn't feel all that bad). Father nodded to us, a signal for us to go over, which we did, hesitantly. We stopped a few steps before we reached him, and he raised his hands as if he was going to touch us. But he didn't. His handcuffs sparkled in the sunlight, temporarily blinding us. 'Xiaotong, Jiaojiao,' he said softly, 'I lost my head out there . . . If you need anything, go see Lao Lan, he'll take care of you.'

I thought my ears were deceiving me. I looked to where he was pointing, and there was Lao Lan, his arms hanging loose, bleary-eyed from drink. His freshly shaved scalp was a mass of bumps and dents. He'd also just shaved, revealing a big, strong chin. His deformed ear was uglier than ever, actually quite pitiful looking.

After the police car drove off, the staring crowd slowly dispersed. Lao Lan wove his way up to us on unsteady legs, a look of abject sadness on his face. 'Children,' he said, 'from now on you'll stay with me. You'll never go hungry as long as I've got food, and I'll make sure you always have clothes to wear.'

I shook my head to drive out all the emotional turmoil and concentrate my energy on thinking clearly. 'Lao Lan,' I said, 'we can't stay with you. We haven't got everything figured out yet, but that's not going to happen.'

I took my sister's hand and walked back to our house.

Huang Biao's wife, in black, with white shoes and a yellow hair clasp shaped like a dragonfly, was waiting at the gate with a basket of food. She couldn't look us in the eye. I wanted to send her away because I knew she was there on Lao Lan's order. But I didn't have to; she laid the basket on the ground and left before I could speak to her, walking off quickly, wiggling her bottom and without another glance in our direction. I felt like kicking the basket away but the meaty fragrance stopped me. With a dead mother and a departed father, we were filled with sorrow, but we hadn't eaten for two days and hunger gnawed at our insides. I could go without, but Jiaojiao was just a child; every missed meal cost her tens of thousands of brain cells. Losing a little weight was all right but, as her older brother, how could I do justice to Father and Aunty Wild Mule if I let hunger turn her mad? I recalled some films and illustrated storybooks where revolutionaries capture an enemy field cauldron filled with fragrant meat and steaming white buns. In high spirits, the commander says, 'Dig in, Comrades!' So I picked up the basket and took it inside; I removed the food, laid it out on the table and, like the commander, said to my sister, 'Dig in, Jiaojiao!'

We gobbled up the food like starving beasts and didn't stop till our bellies bulged. I rested briefly, and then it was time to think about life. Everything seemed like a bad dream. Our fate had changed almost before we knew it. Who'd caused this tragedy? Father? Mother? Lao Lan? Su Zhou? Yao Qi? Who were our enemies? Who were our friends? I was confused, I was unde-cided; my intelligence was being put to its greatest test. The face of Lao Lan flickered in front of me. Was he our enemy? Yes, he was. We were not about to take Father's advice. How could we possibly live at his house? I was still young but I'd led the meat-cleansing workshop and I'd participated in a meat-eating contest and, in the process, seen all those grown men bow their heads before me in defeat. I had been pretty tough to begin with; I was even tougher now. 'When mother-in-law dies, daughter-in-law is matriarch. When father dies, eldest son is king of the roost.' My father hadn't died but he might as well have. My time as king of the roost had arrived, and I had revenge on my mind.

'Jiaojiao,' I said to her, 'Lao Lan is our mortal enemy and we're going to kill him.'

She shook her head: 'He's a good man!'

'Jiaojiao,' I said earnestly, 'you're young and inexperienced, and you can't tell what a man is like by his appearance alone. Lao Lan is a wolf in sheep's clothing. Do you understand what that means?'

'Yes, I do,' Jiaojiao said. 'Let's kill him then. Shall we take him to the workshop first and give him the water treatment?'

'"For a gentleman to see revenge, even ten years is not too long," as they say. It is for me but we can't be in too big a hurry. Not today but not in ten years either. First, we need to get our hands on a good, sharp knife. Then, we wait for the right moment. We need to pretend that we're a couple of pitiful children, make everyone feel sorry for us, lull them to sleep. Then strike! He's a powerful man—if we fight him on his terms we'll lose, especially because he has the protection of the martial-arts master Huang Biao.' I had to consider our situation from every angle. 'As for the water treatment, let's wait and see.'

'Whatever you say, Elder Brother.'

One morning, not much later, we were invited to share a pot of bone soup at the home of Cheng Tianle. Nutritious and loaded with calcium, the soup was just the sort of thing Jiaojiao, who was still growing, needed. It was a big pot, with lots of bones. If anyone knew his bones it was me—horse, cattle, sheep, donkey, dog, pig, camel and fox. Mix a donkey bone in with a pile of cow bones and I could pick it out every time. But the bones in this pot were new to me. The well-developed leg bones, the thick vertebra and the rock-solid tailbone put the thought of a fierce feline in my mind. Cheng Tianle was a good man, that I knew, and he liked me. He'd never do anything to hurt me, so there would be nothing wrong with what he fed us. Jiaojiao and I sat at a square little table next to the pot and began to eat, one bowlful followed by another and another, until we'd each had four. Cheng's wife stood by with a ladle, filling our bowls as soon as they were empty while Cheng urged us to eat our fill.

At Cheng's house we managed to get our hands on a rusty dagger with a blade shaped like a cow's ear. We didn't want a big knife but one we could hide on us, and this one fit the bill. We carried a whetstone into our house, turned up the volume on the TV, shut the door, blocked out the windows and then began to sharpen the knife with which we were going to kill Lao Lan.

My sister and I seemed to have become honoured guests at homes throughout the village during that time and were fed nothing but the best food. We ate camel's hump (a lump of fat), sheep's tail (pure lard), fox brain (a plate full of cunning). I can't list every item we ate, but I have to tell you that at Cheng Tianle's, besides bone soup, we were treated to a bowl of a green, bitter liquor. He didn't tell us what it was but I guessed its origin—liquor in which had been steeped the gallbladder of a leopard. I assumed that the bones in the pot were those of that same leopard. So Jiaojiao and I ate leopard gallbladder—the so-called seat of courage—which converted us from timid, mouse-like creatures into youngsters whose courage knew no bounds.

By plying us with the best food they had, my fellow villagers instilled us with enviable strength and courage. And though no one breathed a word about it, we had no doubts about what lay behind all this nurturing. Usually, after we'd been treated to a fine meal, we'd thank our hosts with vague expressions of appreciation: 'Elder Master and Mistress, Elder Uncle and Aunt, Elder Brother and Sister, please be patient. My sister and I are people who know their history and are committed to the cause of righteousness. We will avenge every slight and repay every kindness.'

Every time I uttered this little monologue, a sense of solemnity flooded my mind and hot blood raced through my veins. Those who heard our little piece were invariably moved; their eyes would light up and heartfelt sighs escape their mouths.

The day of reckoning drew nearer.

And then it arrived.

A meeting was held that day in the plant's conference room to discuss a major structural change—the shift from a collective ownership to a stockholder system. Jiaojiao and I were stockholders, with twenty shares each. I won't waste time talking about that foolish meeting; the only reason it became the talk of the town, so to speak, was because of our attempt to wreak vengeance. I drew the dagger from my belt. 'Lao Lan,' I shouted, 'give me back my parents!'

My sister pulled a pair of rusty scissors from her sleeve—before we set out I'd asked her to sharpen them but she'd said that rusted scissors would give him tetanus. 'Lao Lan,' she shouted, 'give me back my parents!'

We raised our weapons and ran at Lao Lan behind the podium.

Jiaojiao tripped on the stairs, fell flat on her face and began to bawl.

Lao Lan stopped talking, walked over and picked her up.

He turned up her lip with a finger, and I saw a cut—there was blood on her teeth.

My plans too fell flat. Like a punctured tyre, I felt my anger dissipate. But then how would I face my fellow villagers or fulfil my debt to my parents if I just gave up? So, holding my breath, I raised my dagger once more and, as I moved towards Lao Lan, I had a vision of my father moving towards the same man with his hatchet held high.

Lao Lan dried Jiaojiao's tears with his hand. 'That's a good girl,' he said, 'don't cry, don't cry . . .' There were tears in his eyes as he handed my sister to the barber Fan Zhaoxia in the front row. 'Take her to the clinic and have something put on this,' he said.

Fan took her in her arms. Lao Lan bent to pick up the scissors and tossed them onto the podium. Then he picked up a chair, carried it up to me, set it down and sat in it.

'Right here, worthy Nephew,' he said as he patted his chest.

Then he closed his eyes.

I looked first at his pitted, freshly shaved scalp, then at his newly shaved chin and the ear my father had taken a bite out of and finally at the trails of tears on his twitching face. Sorrow washed over me along with the shameful desire to throw myself into the son of a bitch's arms. At that moment I realized why Father had buried the hatchet in Mother's skull. But there was no one close to Lao Lan, and I had no argument with anyone in the seats before us—so who was I supposed to stab? I was stuck. But, as they say, heaven doesn't shut all the doors at once. Lao Lan's bodyguard, Huang Biao, burst into the room. That tiger-feeding bastard—killing him would be like cutting off Lao Lan's right arm. So I raised my dagger and charged at him, a war cry on my lips, my mind a blank. I've already told you about Huang Biao. Who was I, a young weakling, to take on a man with his uncommon martial skills? I thrust the dagger at his midsection but he merely reached out, grabbed me by the wrist and jerked my arm upward.

I heard a *pop* as my shoulder dislocated.

My act of vengeance came to a whimpering end.

For a long time after that, Luo Xiaotong's 'act of vengeance' was the most popular joke in the village. My sister and I suffered both from considerable humiliation but also from a spot of fame. Some people even came to our defence and said that we were not to be taken lightly, that Lao Lan's day of judgement would come once we grew up. Be that as it may, people stopped inviting us to their homes for a meal. Lao Lan had Huang Biao's wife send food over a few times, but not for long. Huang Biao put aside any grudges he might have had to deliver a message from Lao Lan: I was invited to return to United Meatpacking as director of the meat-cleansing workshop. I turned him down. I may have been small and insignificant but I had my pride. Did he really expect me to go back to work at the plant, now that neither my father nor my mother was there? But that decision had no effect on my memories of the good times in the plant, and Jiaojiao and I often found ourselves walking past it without intending to. Our legs just carried us over on their own, and there we were confronted by an imposing gateway of black granite that sported a new sign—the company's name in a large bold script—and an automated double gate, all modern improvements. The plant had been transformed from the modest United Meatpacking Plant into the imposing Rare Animals Slaughterhouse Corporation. The grounds were landscaped with exotic plants and trees and the workers streaming in and out all wore white smocks. People familiar with the place knew it was a slaughterhouse, but everyone else would have thought it was a hospital. There was one thing, however, that hadn't changed—the pine rebirth platform, which still stood in a corner of the yard, a symbolic link to the past. One night, both Jiaojiao and I dreamt that we climbed the platform and saw Father and Mother moving rapidly along a newly paved road in a wagon pulled by a camel. She saw both our mothers seated at a table groaning under plates of good food, repeatedly clinking their glasses for a toast. The liquor in their glasses was green, she said, and she wondered if it was infused with leopard gallbladder.

What I suffered from most during those days was neither hunger nor loneliness but embarrassment, a result of my failed attempt to wreak vengeance. It simply could not continue; I had to break the hold of this emotion and find a way to make Lao Lan suffer. Killing him was no longer possible, nor was it absolutely necessary. If I managed to stick a knife in him and end his life, we'd wind up suffering a similar fate. There must be better way. But what? Then it came to me—the perfect plan.

At noon on one fine autumn day Jiaojiao and I strode into the plant with our dagger and scissors. No one tried to stop us. We were met by Huang Biao. When we asked him about Lao Lan, he nodded in the direction of the banquet hall. 'Hey, brave boy,' he called out as we walked towards the hall.

Lao Lan and the new plant manager, Yao Qi, were entertaining clients and feasting on delicacies such as donkey lips, cow anuses, camel tongues and horse testicles—everything that sounded terrible but tasted divine. We were greeted by the pungent odours of their meal. Neither Jiaojiao nor I had tasted meat in a long time, and the sight of that loaded table made us drool. But we were on a mission and would not be distracted. Lao Lan spotted us when we stepped into the room. The infectious smile on his face was immediately replaced by a frown. At his discreet signal, Yao Qi stood up to greet us: 'Ah, it's you, Xiaotong, Jiaojiao. The food is in another room. Come with me.'

'They are the orphaned children of two former workers,' Lao Lan explained to his guests softly. 'The plant is responsible for their welfare.'

'Out of my way!' I pushed Yao Qi aside and approached Lao Lan. 'Don't be afraid, Lao Lan,' I said. 'You don't have to break into a sweat or get tied up in knots. We're not here to kill you—we're here to let you do the killing.' I turned the dagger round in my hand, Jiaojiao did the same with her scissors, and we offered them, handles first, to Lao Lan. 'Go ahead, Lao Lan,' I said. 'We've lived long enough, more than long enough, so come on, kill us!'

'If you don't,' Jiaojiao added, 'you're a cowardly son of a bitch!'

The blood rushed to his face. 'What kind of a joke is this?'

'It's no joke. We're here to ask you to kill us.'

'Children,' he said with an unhappy smile, 'You are the victims of a huge misunderstanding. You're too young to truly understand what happens with adults. I'll bet some evil person has put you up to this. You'll understand some day, so I won't try to explain things to you now. If you hate me so much, you can kill me any time you please. I'll be waiting.'

'Kill you? Why would we want to do that? And we don't hate you. We just have no desire to go on living and would like to die at your hands. Please, do it for us.'

'I'm a son of a bitch, a real son of a bitch. How's that?'

'Not good enough,' Jiaojiao insisted. 'You have to kill us.'

'Xiaotong, Jiaojiao, be good children and give up this charade. I feel terrible about what happened to your parents, just terrible. I have no peace of mind. And I've been thinking about your future. Listen to me. If it's a job you want, I'll take care of it, and if you'd rather go to school, I'll take care of that too. What do you say?'

'Dying is the only thing we want. You have to do it today.'

'Where'd you get these two?' one of the clients, a fat man, laughed. 'I'm impressed.'

'They're a couple of whiz kids,' asnwered Lao Lan with a smile. Then he turned back to us. 'Xiaotong, Jiaojiao, go get something to eat—have Huang Biao give you the best meat we've got. I'm busy right now but I'll make sure we find a way to deal with this problem.'

'No,' I said. 'I don't care how busy you are, this'll only take a minute. Two quick stabs is all you'll need. Once we're dead, you can go on with what you're doing. We won't take much of your time. If you don't finish us off now, we'll keep pestering you for as long as it takes.'

'You really are a pain, you foolish children!' Lao Lan said gruffly, clearly upset. 'Huang Biao, take them out of here!'

Huang Biao came up and grabbed me by the neck with one hand and Jiaojiao with the other. We did not put up a fight as he dragged us out of the room. But the second he let go, back we'd run, weapons in hand, begging for Lao Lan to kill us.

Our prestige soared, like fireworks lighting up the sky, and we took advantage of that by seeking out Lao Lan every day. And when we found him we begged him to kill us. When he stationed guards at the gate, we sat outside, waiting for a glimpse of his car. Then we'd run over to it, kneel before it, raise our weapons over our heads and beg him to kill us. Eventually, he stopped leaving the compound, so we stood outside the gate and shouted: 'Lao Lan, oh, Lao Lan, come out and kill us—Lao Lan, oh, Lao Lan, do us a favour and kill us—'

When we were alone we sat there quietly, but when there were people about we stood up and began to shout. Passers-by came up to ask what we were doing. 'Lao Lan, oh, Lao Lan,' we'd respond, shouting even louder, 'come kill us—we beg you—'

We knew it wouldn't take long for news to reach half way round the county, and it didn't. Actually, it was more like half way round the province, or even the country, because Huachang's customers came from far and wide.

One day Lao Lan disguised himself as an old man and tried to leave the plant in an old Jeep. Jiaojiao and I detected his peculiar odour long before he reached the gate. We blocked the Jeep, then dragged him out and crammed our dagger and scissors into his hand. 'An unlanced boil,' he said, scowling at us, 'will cause trouble sooner or later.'

He placed his right foot on the Jeep's running board, rolled up his trouser leg, took aim with the dagger and embedded it in his calf. Then he placed his left foot on the running board, rolled up his trouser leg, took aim with the rusty scissors and embedded them in his other calf. Then he stepped down, held up both trouser legs above the wounds and their embedded weapons and circled the gate area twice, leaving a trail of blood on the ground. Then he stepped onto the running board with his right foot, plucked out the dagger—releasing a spurt of dark-red blood—and threw it at my feet. Next he stepped up with his left foot, plucked out the scissors—releasing a spurt of blue blood—and threw it at Jiaojiao's feet. 'Let's see what you're made of, you little punk,' he said with a look of contempt in my direction. 'Do what I just did if you've got the guts.'

I knew at once that we'd suffered another crushing defeat. The bastard had backed us into a corner once again. I understood that all Jiaojiao and I had to do was stab ourselves in the same way to defeat Lao Lan so resoundingly he'd have to kill himself to salvage his shredded dignity. But stabbing myself in the calf would have hurt like hell! Confucius said: 'Your body is a gift from your parents, and keeping it from harm is the first rule of filiality.' Stabbing ourselves would be an affront to Confucius and an admission that we were unfilial. All I could think to say was: 'What the hell was that for, Lao Lan? Do you think you can scare us off with some hooligan trick? We're not afraid of dying. But we're not going to stab ourselves—that's what we're asking you to do. You can pare off all the meat on your calf but it won't change a thing. If it's peace of mind you're looking for, the only way to get that is to kill us.'

We picked up the bloodstained dagger and scissors and handed them back to him. He snatched the dagger out of my hand and flung it as far as he could. It flew across the street and landed who knows where. Then he snatched the scissors out of Jiaojiao's hand and did the same.

'Luo Xiaotong, Luo Jiaojiao,' he howled, almost in tears, 'Enough of this preposterous nonsense. What do you want of me?'

'That's simple,' Jiaojiao and I said together. 'We've lived long enough and we want you to kill us.'

He climbed into the Jeep, bloody legs and all, and drove off.

There's a well-known phrase that goes: Give the man a taste of his own medicine. *Do you know who said that, Wise Monk*? Neither do I. But Lao Lan knew, because he drew on that wisdom to find a way out of his dilemma. After he drove off, we scoured the area with a horseshoe-shaped magnet borrowed from Li Guangtong at the township TV repair shop and managed to retrieve the knife and scissors, so we could continue trying to get him to kill us. At noon, three days after that incdent, we were sitting outside the plant gate shouting at a wedding procession when a short fellow with a bulbous nose and a prominent beer belly hobbled up to us with a butcher knife. A mean-looking bully of a man.

'Recognize me?' he asked grinning deviously.

'You're . . .'

'Wan Xiaojiang, the guy you beat in the meat-eating contest.'

'You've gotten fat!'

'Luo Xiaotong, Luo Jiaojiao, like you, I've lived long enough, more than enough. Another minute will be too long, so I'm asking the two of you to kill me. You can do it with your dagger or that pair of scissors, or you can use this butcher knife. I don't care one way or the other, it's up to you. Just do it.'

'Get lost,' I said. 'We've got no beef with you, why would we want to kill you?'

'That's right,' he said, 'you've got no beef with me but I still want you to kill me.' When he tried to force his knife into my hand, both Jiaojiao and I backed away. But he was relentless—he kept coming at us, moving a lot quicker than we'd have guessed, given his bulk. He was like the offspring of a cat and a mouse. We had no idea what you'd call something like that but we couldn't shake him no matter how hard we tried.

'Are you going to kill me or aren't you?'

'No.'

'All right, then, if you won't do it, I'll do it myself—slowly.' He turned the butcher knife on himself and sliced a deep gash in his belly, which immediately began to ooze yellow fat and then blood.

Jiaojiao threw up at the sight.

'Are you going to kill me or aren't you?'

'No.'

He stabbed himself a second time.

We turned and ran but he followed us relentlessly. Knife raised high and blood streaming from his belly, he came after us, shouting over and over: 'Kill me—kill me—Luo Xiaotong, Luo Jiaojiao, do a good deed by killing me—'

The next morning, we'd barely shown up at the Huachang gate when he ran up on his stubby legs, knife in hand, and opened his shirt to show us his wounds. 'Kill me—kill me—Luo Xiaotong, Luo Jiaojiao, kill me—'

We ran off, but even from far away we could hear his cries.

Back home, before we even caught our breath, a man in dark glasses rode up on a motorcycle with a green sidecar and stopped at our gate. Wan Xiaojiang climbed out of the sidecar and staggered into our yard, still holding his knife, still showing us his wounds, still shouting: 'Kill me—kill me—'

We slammed the door shut; shouting, he attacked it with his substantial buttocks. His voice, which cut like a knife, sounded like it could slice through glass. We covered our ears with our hands but to no avail. The door was starting to give way, the hinges pulling free. A moment later it fell apart with a crash and the splintering of glass. Wan burst into the room: 'Kill me—kill me—'

Jiaojiao and I slipped under his armpits and ran as fast as we could. But when we reached the street the motorcycle was following us, as were Wan Xiaojiang's shouts.

We ran out of the village and into the overgrown fields, but the rider—the man must have been a motorcross racer—rode straight into the waist-high grass and across the water-filled ditches, startling clusters of strange-looking hybrid animals out of their dens. As for Wan Xiaojiang, his unnerving shouts never stopped swirling round us.

That's what did it, Wise Monk. We left home and began living a rootless life, all to get away from that rotten Wan Xiaojiang. Three months later, we returned, and the minute we walked in the door of our home we discovered that we'd been cleaned out by thieves. No TV, no VCR, the cabinets thrown open, the drawers pulled out, even the pot was gone. All that was left were two stovetop frames, like a pair of ugly, toothless, gaping mouths. Fortunately, my mortar still rested in a side room under its dusty cover.

We sat in the doorway and watched the people on the street, both of us sobbing, high one moment, low the next. The neighbours brought jars, baskets, even plastic bags, all filled with meat, fragrant, lovely meat, and laid them at our feet. No one said a word. They just watched us, and we knew they wanted us to eat the meat they'd brought. All right, kind people, we'll eat it, we will.

We ate it.

Ate it.

Ate.

We ate so much we couldn't stand; we looked down at our bulging bellies and then crawled inside on our hands and knees. Jiaojiao said she was thirsty. So was I. But there was no water in the house. We looked round till we found a bucket under the eaves, half filled with foul water, perhaps rainwater from that autumn. Dead insects floated on the surface but we drank it anyway.

Yes, that's how it was, Wise Monk.

When the sun came up, my sister was dead.

At first I didn't realize it. I heard the meat screaming in her stomach and saw that her face had turned blue. Then I saw the lice crawling out of her hair and I knew she was dead. 'Baby sister,' I cried out, but I'd barely got the words out when chunks of undigested meat spilt from my mouth.

I vomited, my stomach feeling like a filthy toilet and the putrid smell of rotting food filling in my mouth. It was the meat, hurling filthy curses at me. Chunks of meat thrown up from my stomach began to crawl like toads . . . I was disgusted and filled with loathing. *At that moment, Wise Monk, I vowed to never eat meat.* I'd rather eat dirt from the road than a single bite of meat,

I'd rather eat horse manure in a stable than a single bit of meat, I'd rather starve to death than a single bite of meat . . .

It took me several days to clear my stomach of meat. I crawled down to the river and drank mouthfuls of clean water with bits of ice in it; I ate a sweet potato someone had thrown onto the riverbank. Slowly my strength returned.

One day child came running up to me. 'Luo Xiaotong. You're Luo Xiaotong, aren't you?'

'Yes, but how did you know?'

'I just know,' he said. 'Come with me. Someone is looking for you.'

I followed him into a two-room hut in a peach grove, where I saw the old couple who had sold us the beat-up mortar years earlier. The mule, now aged a great deal, was there too, standing alone beneath a peach tree eating dry leaves.

'Grandpa, Grandma . . .' I threw myself into the old woman's arms as if she really were my grandmother and wet her clothes with my tears. 'I've lost everything,' I sobbed. 'I've got nothing. Mother's dead, Father's arrested, my sister's dead and I can't bear to eat meat any more . . .'

The old man pulled me out of her arms and smiled. 'Look over there, son.'

There in the corner of the hut stood seven wooden cases. On them were printed words that were as unfamiliar to me as I was to them.

The old man opened one of the cases with a crowbar and peeled back a sheet of oiled paper to reveal six long, tenpin-shaped objects with wing-like fins. My god—mortar shells—I'd dreamt of possessing them—mortar shells!

He carefully removed one. 'Each case holds six of these, except this last one, which is missing a shell. A total of forty-one. I tested one before you arrived. I tied a rope to one of the wings and threw it over a cliff. It blew up just the way it was supposed to. The explosion echoed through the mountains, frightening the wolves out of their dens.'

I gazed down at the shells and at their strange lustre in the moonlight. Then I looked into the old man's eyes, glowing like burning coal. I felt my weakness vanish and the rise of a magnificent heroic spirit.

'Lao Lan,' I said, clenching my jaw, 'your day of reckoning has arrived!'

The production of the opera From Meat Boy to Meat God *nears its finale. The dutiful meat boy is kneeling on the stage, slicing flesh from his arm to brew for his ailing mother. She recovers but, owing to a prolonged state of exhaustion, starvation and loss of blood, he dies. In the last scene, a surreal dreamlike sequence, the mother reveals through her tears how she misses her son and grieves over his death. Then the meat boy, splendidly attired and wearing a golden headdress, appears, as if descended from a cloud of mist. His mother holds her head and sobs when they meet, but the meat boy consoles her with the news that the Celestial Ruler, moved by his dutiful act, has anointed him a Meat God whose domain is the world of meat-eaters. The opera appears to have ended happily but it has done nothing to dispel my feelings of desolation. The mother, still weeping, sings an aria: 'Better to feed my son weak tea and simple food on earth than see him as a Meat God in a heavenly berth . . .' The mist fades and the opera is over. The performers return for their curtain call (there is, of course, no curtain), and are greeted by sporadic applause. Troupe Leader Jiang rushes onstage to announce: 'Ladies and Gentlemen, tomorrow's performance will be* Slaying the Wutong Spirit. *Don't miss it.' The crowd chatters noisily as it disperses. Now the food-vendors make their final attempts at a sale. 'My daughter,' Lao Lan says to Tiangua, 'you can spend the night with us. Your aunt and I have made up the best room for you.' An uncomfortable Fan Zhaoxia says: 'Yes, come home.' Tiangua looks at Fan with loathing but says nothing. She walks up to a lamb-vendor. 'Give me ten kebabs and add plenty of cumin.' Happy to oblige, the vendor takes out a handful of kebabs from a filthy plastic bag and lays them atop a charcoal brazier. He squints to keep the smoke from his eyes and makes a puffing sound with his mouth, as if to clear it of dust. Now that the crowd and the actors have dispersed, Lan Daguan mounts the stage, followed by a foreigner in gold-rimmed glasses. He strips naked to show off his erect penis. 'Tell me if I was boasting!' he says angrily to the foreigner. 'Take a good look and tell me.' The foreigner claps his hands and six blonde, blue-eyed naked women go up on the stage and lie in a row. Lan Daguan takes them one at a time, drawing yelps of pleasure all the way down the line. Six more women go up on stage. Then six more. And six more. And six more. And six more. And five more. Forty-one women in all. I keep my eyes on the tireless Lan Daguan as the combat rages on and watch as he, as if on cue, transforms into a horse. He whinnies loudly, showing off his powerful muscles and his strong limbs. Truly a noble stallion radiating vitality. A magnificent head, its perfect, pointed ears like cut bamboo. Bright, shining eyes. A small mouth below a large snout. A graceful neck lifted high between broad shoulders. A smooth rump, a tail raised captivatingly. A rounded torso encasing resilient ribs. Four slender, graceful legs with bright hooves that shine with a light-blue glow. He gives a rousing performance on the stage, moving from a trot to a gallop, dancing one moment and leaping the next, displaying every dazzling movement possible, demanding acclaim as the acme of perfection. Then comes the finale: Lan Daguan rises from atop the forty-first woman, seemingly coated with a layer of greasepaint, points at the foreigner with a single finger and says: 'You lose.' The man draws a fancy revolver and aims it at the horse's genitals. 'I don't,' he says and pulls the trigger. Lan Daguan thuds to the ground, like a toppled wall. At that same moment, I hear a loud crash and look to see the Horse Spirit crumble to the floor, now a mere pile of clay. And then the lights go out. It's the middle of the night and I can't see a soul. I remove my dark glasses and am treated to a resplendent night sky, with strange white figures a-dance on the stage. Bats fly in and out, birds in the trees flap their wings, the temple grounds are alive with the chirp of insects. Let me hurry and finish my tale, Wise Monk—*

The moon was out in all its glory that night, the air was fresh and clean and the peach trees sparkled as if varnished. Even the mule's hide seemed to glow. We fixed an old wooden frame to its back, tied three cases of mortar shells to each side and then set the seventh case on top. The old couple took care of the cases as if they had been doing this every day. The mule bore its burden stoically, its fate tied to the couple, almost as if it were their son.

We left the peach grove and headed down the road towards the village. Winter had begun to settle in, and though there was no wind the moonlight brought a chill to the air; a layer of frost painted the roadside plants a pale white. Off in the distance, someone was burning dead grass, creating an arc of fire like a red flood engulfing a sandy beach. The boy they'd sent to fetch me, who looked to be seven or eight years old, walked in front of us and led the mule along. He had on a tattered coat that nearly covered his knees, secured at the waist by a white electric wire. Barelegged and barefoot, his head a mass of wild hair, he had the spirit of a raging prairie fire. What was I compared to him? A corrupt youngster, a shameful degenerate. Time to pull myself together. This was too good an opportunity to let pass. I had to fire these forty-one mortar shells on this lovely moonlit night, rock the air with a series of explosions and cement my status as a hero of my age.

The old couple walked beside the mule, one on each side to steady the cases. He was wearing a shearling coat and a dog-skin cap, with a pipe behind his neck, a quintessential old-style peasant. She'd once had bound feet—now freed—and each raspy breath that broke through the surrounding silence let us know how painful every step was for her. I walked behind the mule, vowing to model myself on the boy up front, the old man and the woman and the me of my childhood. On this night, walking amid the icy moonbeams, I would fire my forty-one mortar shells, explosions that would shake heaven and earth and bring life to a village as dead as a stagnant pool. And I would keep the memory of this night alive. One day Luo Xiaotong would become a mythical figure, his tale passed down through the ages.

And so we walked through the wilderness, followed by a variety of inquisitive wild creatures. They shadowed us warily, their bright eyes like little green lanterns, as curious as a pack of children.

The pleasant, melodic tattoo of the mule's hooves told us that we'd entered the village on its concrete roadway. There were a few gleams of light. The village was quiet, the streets deserted. A village dog cozied up to the strange animals following us but was sent yelping into a nearby lane with a bite. Moonlight made the streetlights superfluous. An iron bell on the tall scholar tree at the village entrance, a relic from the commune days, looked dark green in the light. Once upon a time its every peal had been a command.

Our entry into the village went unnoticed but we would not have been deterred even if it hadn't. No one would have imagined that our mule carried forty-one mortar shells; if we'd tried to explain, they'd just have been even more convinced that Luo Xiaotong was a 'powboy'. In my village 'pow' also meant to brag and to lie. Children who boasted and who shot off their mouths were called powboys. That nickname didn't cause me any shame, though. It actually made me proud. Our revolutionary leader Sun Yat-sen bore the resounding nickname of Big Pow Sun, though he'd himself never fired a gun. Luo Xiaotong was about to surpass Sun Yat-sen in that regard. The weapon was ready for action, carefully hidden at home where I'd babied it by restoring every part to its original condition. The shells seemed to have dropped from the skies, each smeared with grease, awaiting only a careful cleaning to shine. The mortar tube called out for the shells; the shells longed for the tube, just as the Wutong Spirit called out for beautiful women, who in turn longed for it. Once I'd fired my forty-one shells, I'd be a powboy of legend, a part of history.

An unlocked gate allowed us entry into our yard, where we were welcomed by dancing weasels. I knew that my yard was a weasel playground now, a place where they fell in love, married and multiplied in numbers sufficient to keep out scavengers. Weasels have a charm that women find irresistible; they make them take leave of their senses and provoke them into singing and dancing and, in some cases, even running naked down the street. But they didn't scare us. 'Thanks, guys,' I said to them, for guarding the mortar for me. 'You're welcome,' they replied. Some wore red vests, like runners on the stock-exchange floor. Others had on white shorts, like children at a public swimming pool.

First we took apart the mortar in the side room and carried the parts into the yard. Then, after leaning a ladder against the eaves of the westside room, I climbed onto the roof. The roof tiles on the neighbourhood houses glinted in the moonlight. I could see the river flowing behind the village, the open fields in front and the fires burning in the wild. I couldn't have asked for a more opportune moment. Why wait? I asked my companions to tie each part with a rope, and tie it well, so that I could then haul it up onto the roof. I removed a pair of white gloves from the tube, put them on and then swiftly reassembled the weapon; before long, my very own mortar crouched on the roof, gleaming in the moonlight, like a bride emerged from her bath and waiting for her new husband. Pointed into the sky at a forty-five-degree angle, the tube seemed to suck up the moonbeams. Several playful weasels climbed up beside me, scurried across to the mortar and began to scratch at it. They were so cute that I didn't stop them. Had it been anyone else I'd have thrown them off without a second thought. Then the boy led the mule up to the foot of the ladder and the old couple unloaded the cases, moving with precision and confidence. Even one shell dropped to the floor would have meant disaster. Each case was tied with rope; I hauled them up, one at a time, and then laid them out on the roof. That done, the old couple and the little boy climbed up to join me. The woman was gasping for breath by then. She suffered from an inflamed windpipe, and I knew she needed to eat a turnip to feel better. If only we had one. 'We'll take care of that,' one of the weasels said. Before long, eight little creatures scrambled up the ladder, chanting a rhythmic hi-ho, carrying a turnip two feet long and with a high water content. The old man rushed up to lift it from the weasels' shoulders and hand it to his wife. Then he thanked them profusely, a manifestation of the common man's simple manners. The old woman broke the turnip in half over her knee, laid the bottom half beside her, took a crisp bite out of the top and then began to chew, suffusing the moonbeams with the smell of turnip.

'Fire a round!' she said. 'Eating a turnip dipped in gunpowder smoke will cure me. Sixty years ago, when my son was born, five Japanese soldiers shot a mortar in our yard, sending gunpowder smoke in through the window and into my throat, damaging my windpipe. I've had asthma ever since, and my son was so badly shaken by the explosions and choked by the smoke that it weakened his constitution and killed him.'

'The five men who did that got the death they deserved,' continued the old man. 'They killed our little cow, then chopped up and burnt our furniture to make a fire to roast it in. But it was only partially cooked, and they all died of salmonella poisoning. So we hid the mortar in the woodpile and the seven cases in a hollow between the walls. Then we escaped up Southern Mountain with our son's body. Later, people came looking for us, calling us heroes for poisoning the meat of our cow and killing five of those devils. We weren't heroes—those devils had had us shaking in our boots. And we certainly hadn't poisoned the meat. The sight of them writhing on the ground had brought us no pleasure at all. In fact, my wife, who was still ill, had boiled a pot of mung-bean soup for them. Usually that's a good cure for poison but theirs ran too deep in their bodies and they could not be saved. Years later, another man showed up and insisted we admit to killing them. A militiaman, he'd stabbed an enemy officer in the back with a muck rake while he took a shit. He'd then taken the man's pistol, twenty bullets, a leather belt, a wool uniform, a pocket watch, a pair of gold-rimmed glasses and a gold Parker pen, and turned it all over to his unit. For that he'd received a second-class merit award plus a medal he wore pinned to his chest and refused to take off. He told us to turn over the mortar and the shells but we refused. We knew that one day we'd meet up with a boy who'd fall in love with it and who'd continue the work we'd begun at the cost of our son's life. A few years back we sold the mortar to you as scrap because we knew you'd treasure it. Dealing in scrap was only a pretext for us. Our greatest desire has been to help you fire these forty-one shells, avenging what you lost and establishing your honoured name. Don't ask what brought us here. We'll tell you what you need to know, nothing more. And now, son, it's time.'

The little boy handed the old man a shell that had been polished to a high gloss. I began to cry, and waves of heat washed over my heart. Bitter hatred and loving kindness sent hot blood racing through my veins, and only by firing the mortar could I release what bubbled inside me. So I dried my eyes and composed myself, then straddled the mortar and, instinctively estimating the distance, took aim at the western wing of Lao Lan's house, about five hundred yards ahead of us. Lao Lan and three township officials were playing mah-jongg on a Ming Dynasty table worth at least two hundred thousand RMB. One was a woman with a large, doughy face, thread-thin eyebrows and blood-red lips—an altogether disgusting sight. Let Lao Lan take her with him. Where? The Western Heaven! I took the shell from the old man, placed it into the tube and gently let go. The tube swallowed the shell, the shell slid into the tube. The first sound was soft, muted—the sound of the ignited shell touching the base of the tube. Then a detonation that nearly shattered my eardrums drove the weasels scurrying in fright. The shell tore like a siren across the sky, blazing a tail through the moonbeams, and then landed exactly where it wanted. First, a bright blue light, then a deafening *POW!*

Lao Lan emerged from the cloud of gunpowder smoke, shook off the dust and sneered. He'd survived unscathed.

I adjusted the tube until it was aimed at Yao Qi's living room, where he and Lao Lan were sitting on a leather sofa, engaged in a whispered conversation about something shameful. Good—Yao Qi, you and Lao Lan can go meet the King of the Underworld together. I took a shell from the old man and let go. It screamed out of the tube, flew across the sky, tore through the moonbeams and then hit the roof of its target with a *POW!* Shrapnel flew in all directions, some into the walls and some up into the ceiling. One pea-sized sliver hit Yao Qi in the gums and he screamed in pain.

'You'll never get me with one of those,' sneered Lao Lan.

I took aim at Fan Zhaoxia's beauty salon and accepted another shell from the old man. That the first two had missed their target was a bit disheartening but I had thirty-nine to go. Sooner or later one of them would rip him to pieces. I dropped the shell down the tube. It flew out like an imp with a song on its lips. Lao Lan was sitting back in the barber's chair, his eyes closed, and Fan Zhaoxia was giving him a shave. His skin was so smooth you could wipe it with a silk rag and not produce a sound. But Fan kept shaving. Shaving. People talk about the pleasure of a good shave. This was obviously a very good shave, for Lao Lan was snoring. Over the years, he'd got into the habit of napping in the barber's chair. He suffered from insomnia; and when he did finally sleep he was visited by dreams that kept him from a deep sleep; the buzz of a mosquito was all it took to startle him awake. Sleep never comes easily to people with a guilty conscience—it's a sort of divine retribution. The mortar shell tore through the shop's ceiling and landed giddily on the terrazzo floor in the middle of a pile of prickly hair before disintegrating with an angry *POW!* A piece the size of a horse's tooth struck the mirror in front of the barber's chair; another, the size of a soybean, hit Fan Zhaoxia in the wrist. She dropped her razor and fell to her knees with a cry of alarm. The razor lay, cracked, beside her.

Lao Lan's eyes snapped open. 'Don't be afraid,' he consoled her, 'it's only Luo Xiaotong up to his old tricks.'

The fourth shell was aimed at Huachang's banquet room, a place with which I was very familiar. Lao Lan was hosting a banquet for every villager over the age of eighty. It was a generous act and possessed of immense pub-licity potential. The three reporters I'd met were busy with their cameras, filming the five old men and three old women. In the middle of the table sat an enormous cake with a line of red candles. A young woman lit them with a lighter and asked one of the old women to blow them out. Possessed of only two teeth, she tried her best to do so as the air whistled through the gaps in her gums. I held onto the fourth shell a bit longer, worried about hurting the old villagers, but this was no time to stop. I said a silent prayer for them and spoke to the shell, asking it to hit Lao Lan on the head! To kill him and no one else. The shell screamed out of the tube, streaked across the river, hov-ered briefly above the banquet room and then plummeted. You can probably guess what happened next, right? Right. It landed smack in the middle of the cake. Most of the candles were extinguished, all but two. Rich, buttery frosting flew into the old people's faces and covered the lenses of the cameras.

The fifth shell I aimed at the meat-cleansing workshop, the site of my greatest pride and deepest sorrow. The night shift was injecting water into some camels, each with a hose up its nose, making them look as strange as a clutch of witches. Lao Lan was giving the man who had usurped my posi-tion—Wan Xiaojiang—instructions; he was loud but not loud enough for me to hear what he was saying. The screech of the departing shell drowned out his words. Wan Xiaojiang, you little bastard, it was because of you that my sister and I had to leave our village. If anything, I hate you more than I hate Lao Lan, and if Heaven has eyes, then this shell has your name on it. I waited till I had calmed down a bit, then took several deep breaths and let the shell slip gently down the tube. It slipped out like a fat little boy who'd grown wings, flew towards its designated target, burst through the ceiling, landed in front of Wan Xiaojiang, smashed his right foot and then—*POW!* His bulging belly was carried away in the explosion but the rest of him was intact, like the quasi-magical handiwork of a master butcher.

Lao Lan was blown away by the blast and I blanked out. When I came to, the wretch had crawled out of the fouled water he'd landed in. Except for a muddy bottom, he was unmarked.

The desk of Township Head Hou was the target of the sixth shell. An envelope stuffed with RMB was shredded. It had been lying atop a sheet of reinforced glass under which the township head had placed photographs of him and several seductive transvestites—memories of his Thailand vacation. The glass was so hard it should have caused an explosion but didn't. Which meant that that particular shell was a peace projectile. What, you wonder, is that? I'll tell you. Some of the men who worked on this ammunition were anti-war. When their supervisors were not looking, they pissed into the shells. Though they gleamed on the outside, the powder inside was hopelessly wet, turning them mute on the day they left the armoury. There were many varieties of peace projectiles; this was but one. Another variety was stuffed with a dove instead of explosives, while yet another was filled with paper on which was written: Long live friendship between the peoples of China and Japan. This particular one was flattened like a pancake; the reinforced glass was shattered and the photographs of the township head were sucked into the flattened shell, as clear as ever, except in reverse.

Firing the seventh shell was agonizing for me because Lao Lan was standing in front of my mother's grave. I couldn't see his face in the moonlight, only the back of his head, like a glossy watermelon, and the long shadow he cast. The words on the headstone I'd personally placed at her tomb recognized me, and her image floated up in front of my eyes, as if she were standing in front of me, blocking my mortar with her body. 'Move away, Mother,' I said. She wouldn't. Her silent miserable stare felt like a dull knife sawing away on my heart. The old man, who was right beside me, said, 'Go ahead, fire!' Sure, why not? Mother was dead, after all, and the dead have nothing to fear from a mortar shell. I shut my eyes and dropped the shell into the tube. *POW!* It passed through her image and flew off weeping. When it landed, it blew her tomb into pieces so small they could be used as road paving.

Lao Lan sighed. 'Luo Xiaotong, are you finished yet?'

Of course not! I slammed the eighth shell angrily into the tube, which was turned in the direction of the plant kitchen. The shells were beginning to fidget after the failure of seven of their brethren. This one turned a couple of somersaults in the air, which took it slightly off course. I'd intended for it to enter the kitchen through a skylight, because Lao Lan was sitting directly beneath it enjoying a bowl of bone soup, very popular at the time as a tonic for vitality, plus a good source of calcium. Nutritionists, who blew hot and cold over such things, had written newspaper articles and appeared on TV, urging people to eat plenty of calcium-rich bone soup. Truth is, Lao Lan was in no need of calcium, since his bones were harder than sandalwood. Huang Biao had cooked a pot of soup with horse-leg bones for him, spicing it up with coriander and muttony pepper to mask the gamey smell, even adding some essence of chicken. He stood there with his ladle while Lao Lan dug in, sweating so much that he had to remove his sweater and drape his loosened tie over his shoulder. I tried to wish the shell right into his bowl of soup or at least into the pot. Even if it didn't kill him, the hot soup would scald him raw. But that frisky shell went right into the brick chimney behind the kitchen and *POW!*—the chimney collapsed on top of the roof.

For the ninth shell, I took aim on Lao Lan's secret bedroom at the plant. A small room attached to his office, it was equipped with a king-sized bed whose new and prohibitively expensive linen was redolent with jasmine fragrance. The room lay behind a hidden door. Lao Lan had only to lightly press a button under his desk for a full-length mirror on the wall to slide open and reveal a door the same colour as the wall round it. After turning the key in the lock and opening the door, another button was pressed and the mirror slid back into place. Since I knew the location of the bedroom, I made my calculations, figuring in the resistance of moonlight and the shell's temperament to bring the probability of error down to zero and ensure that the projectile landed smack in the middle of the bed; if Lao Lan had company, then the woman had no one but herself to blame for becoming a love ghost. I held my breath, hefted the shell, which felt heavier than its eight predecessors, and then let it descend at its own pace. It slid out of the tube in a bright burst of light, soared to the very heights, then plummeted smoothly earthward. Nothing marked Lao Lan's secret room more clearly than the satellite dish he'd illegally installed. Silver-coloured and about the size of a large pot, it was highly reflective. And it was those reflections that temporarily blinded the shell's navigational system and sent it careening into the plant's dog pen, killing or maiming a dozen or more killer wolfhounds and blowing a hole in the barricade. The uninjured dogs froze for a moment before leaping through the opening as if waking from a dream, and I knew that a new threat to public safety had just been introduced in the area.

I took the tenth shell from the old man, but my plan changed before I could send it on its way. I'd been aiming at Lao Lan's imported Lexus. The car was parked in front of a modest building; Lao Lan was sleeping in the back seat, his driver in the front. I planned for the shell to crash through the windshield and blow up in Lao Lan's lap. Even if it turned out to be a peace projectile, its inertia alone would make a nasty mess of Lao Lan's belly, and his only hope for survival would be a complete stomach transplant. But just before I fired, the car started up, drove onto the highway and sped towards town. My first last-second plan change momentarily confused me but my desperation spawned a new one. With one hand I adjusted the direction of the mortar and with the other I dropped in the shell. The subsequent blast blew waves of heat into my face and, given all the powder inside, turned the tube red hot. It would have burnt the skin right off my hands if I hadn't been wearing gloves. The shell locked on to the speeding car and, I'll be damned, landed inches behind it as a sort of send-off for Lao Lan.

The eleventh shell was slated for a longer journey. A peasant-turned-entrepreneur had opened a hot-spring mountain resort in a wooded area between the county seat and township village, a get-away spot for the rich and powerful. They called it a mountain resort but there was no mountain nearby, not even a bump on the ground. Even the original grave mounds had been levelled. A few dozen black pines stood like so many columns of smoke, obscuring the white buildings. I detected a heavy sulphur smell on my rooftop perch. Beautiful girls in revealing miniskirts greeted visitors as they stepped into the lobby. With the slightest touch on the loosely girded cloth belts the girls were naked. They had an affected way of speaking, like parrot-talk. Lao Lan frolicked in the pool with its Venus de Milo centrepiece. Then into the sauna to sweat; after that, dressed in a pair of baggy shorts and a short-sleeved yellow robe, it was into the massage parlour for a Thai massage. A muscular girl put her arms round him, and what ensued between them looked more like a wrestling match. Lao Lan, your day of reckoning has arrived. Freshly bathed, you'll make a very clean ghost. I dropped in the shell, and thirty seconds later it carried my compliments to Lao Lan like a white dove. This shell is for you, Lao Lan. Holding on to an overhead bar, the girl stood on his back as she shifted her hips back and forth. I couldn't tell if what he uttered were yelps of pain or cries of pleasure. But once again the shell went off course and landed in the pool, sending a geyser of water into the air. The head of the plaster Venus snapped off at the neck, bringing men and women running out of the dimly lit rooms, some wearing just enough to cover their embarrassment, others not even that.

Lao Lan, unmarked and unmoved, lay on the massage table, head turned to drink tea while the girl hid under the bed, her derriere sticking up like an ostrich with its head in the sand.

Lao Lan and the sex-starved wife of his bodyguard were playing the beast with two backs on Huang Biao's brick bed. In the name of good manners, this was not the time or place to fire a shell. But what a way to die. To leave this world at an orgiastic moment is the height of good fortune, and that was definitely too good for Lao Lan. Yet there was that thing about manners. Not firing was not an option, so I raised the tube's elevation slightly and fired the twelfth shell. It landed in Huang Biao's yard and made a crater big enough to bury a buffalo. With a cry of alarm, Huang's wife flattened herself against Lao Lan.

'Don't be scared, little darling,' he said with a pat on her behind. 'It's only that little creep Luo Xiaotong playing games. You needn't worry. He'll never manage to kill me. With me dead, his life loses all meaning.'

Thirteen is supposed to be an unlucky number, making it the perfect shell to send Lao Lan up to the Western Heaven. He was on his knees praying in the Wutong Temple, our temple. There's a legend that says praying to the Wutong Spirit can double the size of a man's penis. Not only that, it can make you a man of untold riches. Lao Lan carried a joss stick and a candle into the temple by the light of the moon. The place was rumoured to be haunted by the ghost of the hanged, which kept devotees from entering with their wishes, despite knowledge of its efficacious powers. But Lao Lan had more courage than most. Never imagining that ten years later I'd be sitting in this very temple, I went ahead and took aim at it. Lao Lan knelt before the idol and lit his joss stick and candle, the flames turning his face red as a sinister 'heh-heh' came to him from behind the idol. That sound would have sent shivers up the spine of most people and had them rushing headlong out the door. But not Lao Lan. He responded with a 'heh-heh' of his own and shone his candle on a spot behind the idol. Even I could see the five spirits lined up behind Wutong. The one with a horse's body and a human head was the best-looking, a colt, of course. To its left were a pig and a goat, each with a human head. To its right a donkey and the remains of an indeterminate creature. Then a hideous, frightful face appeared, and my heart lurched and my hands went slack as the shell slid into the tube. Off it went, straight for the temple, landing with a *POW!* Three of the idols were destroyed, leaving only the colt with the boy's head, a lascivious or a sentimental smile frozen on its face for all eternity.

Lao Lan emerged from the temple, his face coated with mud.

The Xie Family Restaurant in town was justifiably famous, near and far, for its meatballs. It was run by an old woman with her son and daughter-in-law; they prepared exactly five hundred of the beefy delicacies every day. Customers signed up a week in advance. What was so special about the Xie-family meatballs? Their unique flavour. And what made the flavour unique? The choice cuts of beef. But, even more importantly, the Xie family's meat-balls never came in contact with metal. The meat was sliced by sharpened bamboo strips, then laid out on cloth-washing rocks and beaten with a date-wood club into a meaty pulp. Special millet crumbs were kneaded into the meat before it was rolled into balls and put, along with kumquats, in earthen jars to be steamed on trays. Then the kumquats were thrown out and only the meatballs remained, a true taste sensation . . . I hated the thought of destroying a restaurant which produced such delicacies, especially since old Mrs Xie was such a kind woman and her son a friend of mine. Sorry, Mrs Xie and my old buddy, but killing Lao Lan is more important to me. I dropped in the fourteenth shell. It sped off into the air only to run smack into a wild goose headed in the opposite direction. Nothing but bones and feathers were left of the bird while the shell was knocked off course and landed in a pond behind the Xie house, raising a column of water and turning at least ten big crucian carp into fish paste.

The township's most notorious female free spirit, whose name was Jiena but whom everyone called Little Black Girl, had a remarkable voice. Her songs had been broadcast daily over the loudspeakers in the days of the Cultural Revolution. A bad family background stood in the way of a splendid future, and she had been forced to marry a dyer from a working-class family. He went out every day on his bicycle to pick up clothes to be dyed. High-quality fabric was in short supply in those days, so young people tore up old white cloth and had it dyed green to resemble faddish army gear. Even caustic soda was ineffective in cleaning the green stains from the dyer's hands, and what that would have meant for Jiena's milky white breasts is not hard to contemplate. And so Jiena strayed from her marriage vows. Her relationship with Lao Lan went back a long time, so when he made his fortune she looked him up. I'd always liked this charming woman. She had a captivating voice, thanks to her musical past. But I could not let that stop me from aiming the fifteenth shell at her house, where she and Lao Lan were reminiscing, teary-eyed, over a shared bottle and indulging in pillow talk. The missile landed in an old dye vat, sending green dye flying everywhere. The dyer would not only wear the green hat of a cuckold but also live in the green house of one.

The sixteenth shell was supposed to hit the meatpacking plant's conference room but it was missing one of its wings and began to wobble in midair. It landed in Yao Qi's pigsty, killing the sow they had spoilt so badly.

The meat-inspection office was the recipient of the seventeenth shell. Chief Inspector Han and his deputy were lightly wounded. One piece of shrapnel, big enough to end Lao Lan's life, hit the model-worker brass medal, presented by the city officials and pinned to the left breast of his jacket. The impact sent him reeling into the wall. His face paled and he all but spat blood. It was the most damage any of my shells had inflicted on him so far; and even though he survived the blow it scared the hell out of him.

If any of the shells was assured of taking Lao Lan out it was the eighteenth—because he was standing in an open-air public toilet relieving himself, totally exposed. The projectile could easily slip through the gaps of the parasol-tree branches overhead. But then I was reminded of the hero from the old couple's village who had killed an enemy soldier while he was taking a shit—what a shameful way to kill a man. Killing Lao Lan while he was taking a leak would not bring me glory, and so I had no choice but to alter the course slightly and have the shell land in the nearby privy. *POW!* He was covered in shit. A lot of fun but a low blow.

After firing the nineteenth shell, I realized that I had just violated an international treaty. It landed in the township treatment room and sent glass flying everywhere. The nurse on duty, the lazy sister-in-law of the deputy township head, normally sat in a chair behind a patient spread-eagled over a table, arse in the air, ready to receive to an injection. When the mortar shell hit she was so frightened that she squatted on the floor and cried like a baby. Lao Lan lay in bed hooked up to an IV drip filled with artery-cleaning serum. The blood of people like him who feast on rich, fatty food sticks to the artery walls like glue.

Along with the municipalization of agricultural populations came the rise of rampant consumerism. A bowling alley had been built near the township headquarters. Lao Lan was a champion bowler, a master of strikes, despite his terrible form. He used a twelve-pound purple ball. Spurning an approach, he walked to the line, swung his arm and the ball, like a shell from a mortar, shot straight into the pins; they toppled over with cries of anguish. My twentieth shell landed on the bowling-alley lane. Smoke rose and shrapnel flew.

Lao Lan emerged unscathed. Was the son of a bitch wearing a protective talisman?

The twenty-first shell landed in the meatpacking plant's fresh-water well. Lao Lan was standing beside it gazing at the reflection of the moon, and I assumed he was musing over the story of the monkey that tried to scoop the moon out the water. I can't think of anything else he might have come out to see in the middle of the night. *That well played a prominent role in my life, as you know, Wise Monk, so I won't go into that here.* The moon was bright and pristine. When it fell into the well, the shell failed to explode but it did shatter the moon's pristine reflection and muddy the water.

Despite the twenty-first shell's failure to kill Lao Lan, his poise and aplomb had deserted him. Sooner or later an earthen well jar will break—it's inevitable. One of these exploding shells has your name on it and the Western Heaven awaits your arrival. Resorting to trickery, Lao Lan put on a worker's clothes and tried to pass himself off as one of the night-shift men in the kill room. What looked like an attempt to become one with the masses was in fact a ploy to save his skin. He greeted the workers, even slapped some of them familiarly on the shoulder, producing smiles from those favoured by such an unexpected but welcome gesture. At the moment they were slaughtering camels, those ships of the desert, dispatched in great numbers because their hooves were sought after at formal banquets on the tables of Han and

Manchu diners. Camel was the 'in' meat of the day, as a result of Lao Lan's success in buying off several nutrition experts and local reporters who then published a series of articles extolling the virtues of camel meat. There was a plentiful supply of the animals from Gansu and Inner Mongolia, although the finest were imported from the Middle East. By this time the kill rooms were semi-automated. The animals were transported by hoists from the meat-cleansing workshop into Kill Room No. 1, where they were first washed with cold water and then subjected to a steam bath. Their legs flailed wildly as they hung from the hoists. Lao Lan was standing under one of the suspended camels, listening to the workshop foreman Feng Tiehan, when I seized the moment and dropped the twenty-second shell into the tube. Trailing a live wire, it flew to its target, exploding on the roof and severing the steel cable supporting the unfortunate camel. It plunged to its death.

The twenty-third shell entered the workshop through the hole opened by its predecessor and rolled on the killing floor like a giant spinning top. With no thought for his safety, Feng Tiehan threw himself at Lao Lan, knocking him to the floor and covering him with his body. *POW!* Blast waves and billowing gunpowder smoke swept through the workshop. Four hooves flew for a distance and then fell onto Feng's back, where they looked like frogs engaged in a serious discussion.

Lao Lan crawled out from under Feng's body, wiped the steel splinters and camel blood off his face and sneezed. His clothes lay in tatters at his feet; all that remained on him was a leather belt. 'Luo Xiaotong,' he screamed, picking up a rag to cover his privates, 'you little prick, what did I ever do to you?'

You've never done anything to or for me. I took the twenty-fourth shell from the old man and dropped it down the tube. This would be my answer. Taking the same course as its two predecessors, it landed in the new crater. Lao Lan hit the ground and rolled over to take cover behind the camel carcass. The edge of the crater blocked splinters of shrapnel and saved him from injury. Some of the other men lay flat on the workshop floor but a few stood stock still. One especially brave man crawled up to Lao Lan. 'Are you hurt, General Manager?' he asked. 'Get me some clothes,' Lao Lan said. Hiding behind a dead camel with his bare arse sticking up in the air put him in a very sorry state.

The courageous worker ran into the foreman's office to fetch a set of clothes, but as he handed them to Lao Lan the twenty-fifth shell streaked towards him. With a burst of inspiration, he caught the flying missile in the heavy canvas clothing and flung it out the window. That action not only displayed how cool-headed and decisive he could be, but was also testimony to his superior strength. If he'd been a soldier during wartime, he'd have been a hero extraordinaire. The shell exploded outside the window—*POW!*

Before it was time to fire the twenty-sixth shell, the old woman hobbled up to me, took a piece of turnip from her mouth and stuffed it into mine. That was revolting, I don't deny it. But thoughts of how pigeons exchange food and crows feed their aged parents turned my revulsion into a feeling of intimacy. I was also reminded of an incident with my mother. It was back when my father had gone off to the northeast and Mother and I were dealing in scrap. We were taking a break at a roadside stall—she'd spent twenty *fen* that day for two bowls of beef-entrail soup for us to soak our hard biscuits in. A blind couple with a chubby, fair-skinned baby were eating at the stall. The baby, obviously hungry, was crying. The woman, hearing my mother's voice, asked if she would feed the baby. So Mother took the baby from her and a hard biscuit from the man, which she chewed into pulp before feeding him mouth-to-mouth. Afterwards she said: 'That's what's called pigeons feeding each other.' I swallowed the turnip the old woman put in my mouth and felt suddenly sharp-eyed and clear-headed. I aimed the twenty-sixth shell at Lao Lan's bare arse, but it was still in the air when the workshop collapsed with a roar. It was an amazing sight, like those demolitions you see on TV. The shell landed amid the rubble and knocked aside a steel beam that had pinned Lao Lan underneath, creating an opening through which he crawled free and once again escaped death.

I was beginning to get flustered, if you want to know the truth. The twenty-seventh shell had Lao Lan's bare arse in its sights once more. When it exploded, the blast sheared the roadside trees in half. But Lao Lan survived yet again. Goddamn it, what's going on?

I began to wonder if the destructive power of the shells had deteriorated because of their age. So I left the mortar and walked over to the ammunition cases to examine the contents. The boy was conscientiously cleaning the grease off each shell, which then sparkled like fine jewels. Anything that looked that good had to be powerful. So the fault lay not in the shells but in Lao Lan's cunning. 'How am I doing, Big Brother?' the boy asked. I was moved by his slightly fawning attitude and struck by how much he resembled my sister, even though one was a boy, the other a girl. I patted him on the head. 'You're doing a terrific job. You're my number three artilleryman.'

'Do you think I could fire one?' he asked me shyly, after he'd finished cleaning the shells. 'No problem,' I said. 'Maybe you'll be the one to blow Lao Lan to bits. I led him over to the mortar, handed him a shell and said, 'The twenty-eighth shell. The target—Lao Lan. Distance—eight hundred. Ready—fire!' 'I hit him, I hit him!' the boy shouted, clapping joyfully. Lao Lan had in fact been knocked to the ground. But he jumped to his feet, panther-quick, and took cover in the packaging workshop. Tasting blood, the boy asked if he could fire another. I agreed.

I left him on his own for the twenty-ninth shell, which veered off course and landed in a pile of coal at the little train station's abandoned freight yard. Coal dust and gunpowder smoke blotted out great swaths of moonlight.

Embarrassed by this mistake, he scratched his head and went back to his cleaning station.

This gave Lao Lan time to change into blue work clothes, then stand on a pile of cardboard boxes and shout: 'Give it up, Luo Xiaotong. Save the remaining shells for hunting rabbits.' That really pissed me off, so I took aim at his head and fired the thirtieth shell. He sprinted into the workshop and shut the door behind him, thereby saving himself from injury once again.

The thirty-first shell tore a hole in the workshop roof and landed in a pile of cardboard boxes, shredding at least a dozen of them and turning camel steaks into a meaty pulp, then searing it in the superheated air. The smell of burnt flesh merged with that of gunpowder.

Lao Lan's arrogance made me lose my bearings, and I forgot to conserve my ammunition. In rapid succession I fired off shells thirty-two, thirty-three and thirty-four to form a tight triangular pattern, as taught in artillery courses. They did not succeed in killing Lao Lan, but they did blow up the packaging workshop just as an earlier shell had blown up the kill room.

The old man, like a child, asked to fire off a few rounds. I wanted to say no but he was my elder and the one who had supplied the mortar shells; I had no excuse to refuse his request. He took a position alongside the tube, raised his thumb and shut his eye to gauge the distance. This thirty-fifth shell would take out the guardhouse beside the main gate. *POW!* No more guard-house. With shell thirty-six, the newly erected water tower. *POW!* An enormous hole opened up halfway down the tower, releasing a powerful jet of water. The world-renowned Huachang United Meatpacking Ltd lay in ruins. But then I realized that six of the cases now stood empty, leaving only the last one with its five shells.

Night-shift workers were running pell-mell amid the ruins, stepping in bloodied water. Some of the workers may even have been trapped in the rubble. A red fire truck, siren blaring, was on its way from the county seat, followed by a white ambulance and a yellow motor crane. Orange tongues of flame licked the air here and there, probably from torn electric wires. Amid the chaos, Lao Lan climbed up the rebirth platform in the northeast corner of the yard. Once the highest structure in the compound, now that the workshop and water tower had been levelled, it looked taller and more impressive than ever, seemingly able to reach the stars and touch the moon. You're encroaching on my father's domain, Lao Lan. What are you doing up there? Without a second thought, I fired shell thirty-seven at the platform, some eight hundred and fifty yards away.

The shell passed through the gaps in the trees and struck an enclosing wall made of bricks taken from gravesites. A fireball blew a hole in the wall. I'd once heard a story about something that had occurred during a tomb-opening campaign; I had not been born and was thus denied the opportunity to witness the madness. A crowd had gathered in front of an old tomb with statues of men and horses—Lao Lan's ancestral tombs—holding handkerchiefs over their noses as they watched men carry out a rusted piece of artillery. A specialist from the urban Institute for Archaeological Studies commented that he'd never seen anyone buried with a cannon. Which posed the question: Why here? No credible explanation had been offered so far. When Lao Lan mentioned the desecration of his family tombs, he was both aggrieved and bitter. 'You bastards have destroyed the Lan family feng shui and made impossible the birth of a future president of the country!'

Lao Lan was supporting himself by a wooden post at the top of the platform as he gazed off to the northeast. That was where my father used to gaze too. I knew why—it was where he and Aunty Wild Mule had spent days of sadness and moments of joy. What right have you to copy him, Lan Lan? I set my sights on his back. *POW!* Shell thirty-eight took the top off the spire. He remained unmoved.

The unhappy boy did such a sloppy job in cleaning the thirty-ninth shell that, as he was handing it to the old man, slipped out of his hands and hit the ground. I yelled, taking cover behind the mortar. The shell spun round and round on the rooftop, then we heard a clank. The old man, the old woman and the young boy stood there transfixed, mouths agape. Damn! If the thing explodes here and sets off a chain reaction with the last two shells, all four of us are dead. 'Hit the ground!' I shouted but got no reaction from the frozen figures. The shell careened up to my feet as if it wanted to have a heart-to-heart talk. I grabbed it round the neck and flung it as far as I could. *POW!* It blew up down the lane, wasted. What a shame.

The old man handed me the fortieth shell as if it were a precious object. I did not need a reminder that, after this one left the tube, the end game of the battle against Lao Lan was upon us. I took the shell with care, as though I were carrying the sole infant heir of a hereditary line. My heart was pounding. Briefly reflecting on the first thirty-nine firings, I had to admit that failing to kill Lao Lan was mandated by the heavens; it had nothing to do with a lack of skill on my part. Apparently, even the King of Hell wanted none of Lao Lan. I double-checked the sight, recalculated the distance and reviewed the procedures. Everything was as it should be. Unless a force-three gale erupted while the missile was in flight or it was struck by falling debris from a dying satellite, unless something beyond my ability to predict occurred, this shell ought to land on Lao Lan's head. It would kill him even if it failed to explode. Just before letting the shell slide down the tube, I whispered: 'Don't fail me, mortar shell!' It flew into the air. No wind and no satellite debris. It landed on the tip of the platform and—nothing happened.

The old woman threw away what remained of her turnip, took shell forty-one from the old man and shouldered me out of the way. 'Idiot!' she muttered. Standing beside the mortar and huffing loudly, she dropped it in the tube. Shell forty-one fluttered out like a kite cut loose from its string. It flew and it flew, a lazy, distracted arc, on and on aimlessly, this way and that, like a young goat running amok. In the end it fell reluctantly to the ground about twenty yards from the rebirth platform. One second and counting, two seconds, three—and nothing. Damn! 'Another dud.' The words were barely out of my mouth, when *POW!* The air shuddered, like ripped cotton. A single piece of shrapnel, a little bigger than the palm of my hand, whistled through the air and sliced Lao Lan in half . . .

An immature crowing floats on the air from a distant village, the sound of one of this year's young roosters learning how to announce the dawn. I've welcomed the dawn with a narrative replete with artillery fire that has criss-crossed the earth with scars. During the course of my tale, most of the Wutong Temple has crumbled, leaving only a single column perilously holding up part of the dilapidated tile roof, now more like a mat screen against the morning dew. Dear Wise Monk, it no longer matters whether or not I renounce the world. What I want to know is: Has my tale moved you? What I hope you can tell me is: Is what Lao Lan said about his third uncle true or is it all a lie? Can you tell me, or not? The Wise Monk sighs, raises his hand and points to the road in front of the temple. I am surprised to see two processions. The one from the west comprises beef cattle in fancy dress, each with a big character written on its raiments, together spelling out slogans that oppose the con-struction of the Meat God Temple. There are exactly forty-one heads of cattle. They trot down the road and form a circle at our temple, with the Wise Monk and me in the middle. Daggers have been tied to their horns. Lowering their heads, they seem ready to charge, slobber snorting from their noses, flames of anger shooting from their eyes. The one from the east comprises naked women with big characters written on their bodies, together spelling out slo-gans that support the rebuilding of the Wutong Temple. There are exactly forty-one naked women. They run down the road, then mount the forty-one bulls like equestriennes and surround the Wise Monk and me. Scared witless, I take refuge behind the Wise Monk but even that is no guarantee of safety. Niang, help me . . .

Here she comes, followed by Dieh, carrying my sister on his shoulders. She's waving to me. Behind her come the lame and blind Lao Lan and his wife, Fan Zhaoxia, carrying the pretty little Jiaojiao in her arms. Then come the kindly Huang Biao and valiant Huang Bao. Huang Biao's pretty young wife is behind them, smiling enigmatically. They are followed by the swarthy Yao Qi,

the corpulent Shen Gang and the hateful Su Zhou. My three meat-eating com-
petitors—Liu Shengli (Victory Liu), Feng Tiehan (Ironman Feng) and Wan
Xiaojiang (Water Rat Wan)—are next, followed by Lao Han, director of the
United Meat Inspection Station, and his assistant Xiao Han. They are followed
by the now toothless Cheng Tianle and Ma Kui, almost too old to walk. Behind
them come the four skilled artisans from Sculpture Village and, in their wake,
the old-school paper craftsman and his apprentice, who are right in front of
the silver-lipped, golden-haired new-school paper craftswoman and her assis-
tant. The foreman, Big Four, wearing a suit with the trouser legs rolled up,
and his assistants follow them and are in turn followed by the old, nearly
toothless master musician and members of his troupe. They come just ahead
of the old monk from Tianqi Temple, with his wooden fish and his flock of
semi-authentic little acolytes. They are followed by Teacher Cai of the Hanlin
School and a group of her students. Behind them come medical-school
students Tiangua and her sissy boyfriend. They are followed by the boy who
polished my mortar shells and the chivalrous old husband and wife, then the
crowds who showed up in the Meat God compound, on the highway and at
the open square. Next come the photographer, Skinny Horse, and the video-
cameraman, Pan Sun, and his assistant. They climb a tree with their equip-
ment to record everything below. But there is also a large contingent of women,
led by Miss Shen Yaoyao, followed by Miss Huang Feiyun and the singer Tian
Mimi—I can't make out the rest, but in their finery they are like a gorgeous
sunset. The entire scene is a painting fixed in time, as a woman who looks like
she has just emerged from her bath, exuding feminine charms, her appearance
five parts Aunty Wild Mule and five parts a woman I've never seen, splits the
people and the bulls and walks towards me . . .

Narration Is Everything

A good many people will, consciously or unconsciously, often wish they never had to grow up. This sort of evocative literary theme was explored in a work by German novelist Günter Grass decades ago. But here's the problem. When you read something someone else has written and try to make it your own, yours becomes derivative, a form of copying. Oskar, the protagonist of Grass' *The Tin Drum* (1959), who had witnessed so much ugliness in the world, falls into a wine cellar at the age of three and stops growing. Only his physical growth is stunted; mentally he keeps maturing, but in almost evil ways, out-growing everyone in this regard, gaining a greater complexity. Nothing like that is likely to happen in real life, and for that very reason its appearance in fiction is not only deeply meaningful but also thought-provoking.

With *POW!* my only option was to do things in opposite fashion. When my protagonist, Luo Xiaotong, is in the Wutong Temple narrating his child-hood to Wise Monk Lan, he has matured physically but not mentally—he is now an adult but his mental growth stopped when he was a boy. Someone like that would usually be considered an idiot. But Luo Xiaotong is no idiot. If he were, there would be no need for this novel to exist.

The desire to stop growing is rooted in a fear of the adult world, of grow-ing old and feeble, of dying and of the passage of time. Luo Xiaotong tries to recapture his youth by prattling away with his tale; writing this novel was my attempt to stop the wheel of time from turning. Like a drowning man grasp-ing at straws, I was desperate to keep from sinking. While I knew that my attempt must end in failure, it had a comforting effect.

While it may seem that the protagonist is narrating the tale of his child-hood, in reality, I have employed this 'narration' to create my own childhood, as a way to hold on to it. Making use of the protagonist's mouth to recreate the days of my youth and to contend with the blandness of life, to counter the futile struggle and the passage of time may well be the sole source of pride for me as a writer. Narration can bring satisfaction to all the unsatisfying aspects of real life, and that fact has provided me with considerable solace. Relying upon the splendour and fullness of a narrative to enrich one's bland life and overcome character flaws is a time-honoured tradition among writers.

Seen in that light, the story line of *POW!* isn't all that meaningful. Throughout the novel, narration is the goal, narration is the theme and narration is its construct of ideas. The goal of narration is narration. But if I were forced to make a story out of this novel, I'd settle for the story of a boy prattling on and on about a story.

A writer's existence is found in narration, which is also the process in which he finds satisfaction and absolution. Like everything else, a writer is by nature a process. Many writers are children who have never grown up or who are afraid to. Not all of them, of course. The conflict between a fear of growing up and its inevitability is the yeast that gives rise to a novel, and from that can sprout many more novels.

Luo Xiaotong is a boy who endlessly spouts lies, a boy whose utterances tend to be irresponsible, a boy who gains satisfaction through the act of narration. Narration is his ultimate goal in life. In that muddy stream of language, the story is the conveyor of language and a byproduct of it. What about ideology? About that I have nothing to say. I've always taken pride in my lack of ideology, especially when I'm writing.

At first there is an element of truth in the story Luo Xiaotong is telling, but that gives way to an improvisation that swings between reality and illusion. Once the narration begins, it establishes its inertia, propelling itself forward, and, in the process, the narrator slowly evolves into a tool of narration. It is not so much him narrating a story as it is a story narrating him.

The affected tone of the narrator's prattling makes it possible for the 'unreal' to become 'real'. Finding the means to exhibit that 'affected tone' is the key to unlocking the sacred door of fiction. To be sure, this is only something I've recently come to realize, and I'm willing to state that candidly even if it is thought of as shallow or biased. Actually, I cannot claim it as my discovery. Many writers have thought the same but have stated it in their own way.

During the course of writing this novel, Luo Xiaotong was me. He no longer is.

Mo Yan